"Dramatic, colorful, sure to please . . . Rofheart's Cleopatra is a fully delineated, fascinating, and wholly sympathetic figure: charming, intelligent, sensuous, politically acute, and consummately ambitious. . . . An absorbing story from start to finish."

—*Publishers Weekly*

"I followed your Cleopatra with passionate interest. Your book is totally absorbing and the tragic suspense as the story unfolds is almost more than one can bear."

—Lynn Fontanne

"The exciting story of a richly endowed human being . . . Mrs. Rofheart moves her story along at a lively pace."—Granville Hicks, *American Way*

"Pleasurable tension . . . Martha Rofheart is a very good writer of historical fiction."—*Bookletter*

THE ALEXANDRIAN

A Novel by

Martha Rofheart

HBJ

A JOVE/HBJ BOOK

Published by arrangement with Thomas Y. Crowell Company

First Jove/HBJ edition published October 1977

Library of Congress Catalog Card Number: 76-3659

Printed in the United States of America

Jove/HBJ books are published by Jove Publications, Inc.
(Harcourt Brace Jovanovich)
757 Third Avenue, New York, N.Y. 10017

To my son, Evan

BOOK I
Alexandria

1

TODAY I WENT AGAIN to the tomb of Alexander. I have done this several times a year, since I first found the place, whenever I have been angry, or confused, or when it has been my birthday. Today it is for all three reasons. I am fourteen, a woman now, heir to the double throne of Egypt, and as forgotten as if I were dead already, like Alexander. His blood flows in my veins, and when I look upon his face, still beautiful after three centuries, I feel that blood in my wrists, tingling, and at my throat, and pounding in my chest, shaking me.

When I say I share Alexander's blood, unfortunately I share it will all my brothers and sisters, and all the old ruling Ptolemies of our line. One has only to look at our murderous and foolish history to smile at how thin that blood has run! And my poor, weak, Rome-fawning father! His only virtue is his music, the one thing a great Pharaoh has no need of. I put him—Auletes, the Piper, they call him—out of my mind, and think of my true fathers; my teachers, the best in the world, and the great writers of our Greek past . . . and Alexander. For though he left no descendants, the first Ptolemy of Egypt was his half-brother; both were sired by Philip of Macedon. The whole world knew it, then as now, though of course Ptolemy was illegitimate. He did well enough, for a bastard; he took Alexander's city and raised it to greatness, and founded our dynasty. In spite of its flaws, our royal house here in Alexandria has kept alive all that was Hellene; the Roman barbarians howl and slaver at the very gates, like wolves, but they do not rule as yet. My simile is sadly apt, for the Romans pride themselves on ancestors suckled by wolves!

One of the Roman wolf cubs is here today, in the Palace; name of Marcus Antonius, a soldier and an aristocrat—or what passes for one in that upstart city. Which is why I am neglected on my birthday; Father is as flustered as a bride, as he is always when a Roman comes near. I shall have to be present at the official banquet for this Antonius tonight, but as yet I have not laid eyes on the man, though he rode in yesterday. I was at my lessons and did not even peep from my window; what crass Roman brute compares with Socrates and Plato? The rest of the household made up for me, though; the windows were black with them, from kitchen slave all the way up to my sister, Arsinoëe, next in succession! She swore, Arsinoëe, rolling her stupid black eyes, that he was the handsomest Roman she had ever seen; I shrugged. "That is not saying a great deal," I said. The poor fool cried, great tears like pearls, as she does always when I speak slightingly to her. Try as I may, I cannot help doing it over and over again; she *asks* to be scorned, like father.

Of course, I was curious about the Roman, much as I pretended not to be; when we were alone, I questioned my other un-royal sister, Iras, "How does he look, the barbarian?"

She looked stern for a moment, as people do when they think; then her eyes crinkled. "Like a face on a coin," she said. We both began to giggle then, and could hardly stop. I knew exactly what she meant; there are old coins, rubbed thin, from Greece in its days of glory, delicate and beautiful, but nowadays we have no such coin artists, and every feature is grossly exaggerated, with thick lips, bulging eyes, and huge noses. "And he is very hairy," she said, going off again, and burying her face in a cushion.

"You seem to have got a good look," I said.

"Well, his tunic was all rucked up," she said. "I could almost see—"

"Stop," I cried, beating my fists on the couch and nearly choking. "Stop—or I shall die of laughing!"

"But he is very big," she finished, trying to straighten her face.

"Truly?" I asked wickedly, with round eyes, setting her off again.

"I mean tall—and broad . . . like a god," she said.

"A goat-god," I answered, thinking of the hairy legs. "He and Father should do well together. Father can play the pipes . . ."

She looked at me reproachfully, no longer laughing. I think she is really fond of him, our Pharaoh-father. Well, he has been good to her, after his fashion; her mother was only a slave.

We were born on the same day, Iras and I, and both our mothers died of it, mine in the royal bedchamber and hers belowstairs. She is fairer even than I, her hair yellow as corn, for that slave-mother was of a northern race, Gaulish or German. Father had spotted her as she walked at the heels of her husband, a Roman mercenary, and had taken her for his own bed. They say she died cursing him, but no one knows for sure, for no one could understand her heathen tongue. These northern women are very constant; I have seen them in the legion camp, cooking and mending, nursing their babies. For of course we have had a Roman legion here, "protecting" us, for a generation or so. My father was not the first Rome-lover in Alexandria.

Iras is my dearest friend, who shares all my secrets, and so I have told her about my visits to the tomb. Otherwise, no other person knows, not even Apollodorus, who first showed me the entrance to it, here beneath the Palace. Alexander used to lie, or so all the old books say, in a building called The Soma, and all my ancestors with him. A century ago it was bricked over, and is now just an empty mound, like a great hill, with a path one can walk to the top, and a view of the sea. It had been struck by lightning and split open, so the robbers came and took away the gold of his casket. Whatever Ptolemy was the Pharaoh then replaced it with an alabaster one and moved it to the mausoleum here. One must go down several sets of stone steps and through dark low halls that wind interminably in and out, and carry a lantern. It is not lit, the mausoleum, or even guarded; I will change all that, when I am queen; it is not fitting that our divine dead should lie in such neglect; I think the place is swept once yearly, if that!

Today, thinking to honor her, I took Iras with me to those cellar chambers, but she walked in horror all the way. Some people have a great fear of closed places; I feel it myself, but not so cruelly. Iras' breath came short and the light cast shaking shadows, like shades of the dead, where she carried her torch. She is a brave girl though and set her chin high and took the torch in both hands to steady it; it is a pity she is not the royal one instead of Arsinoëe!

After the tortuous path that winds underground for more than a thousand paces (I have counted them), one comes to a great carven door; it is not bolted and a mere touch will swing it inward, for the architect was a master. This is the mausoleum proper, where the dead of our royal Macedonian house lie, row upon row in their vast ornate marble beds. They are enclosed, in the Egyptian manner, within cunningly painted, hinged shells, shaped to the bodies they hold. One can lift the lids and look, but Iras, beside me, hid her eyes. What is inside is not so very awesome, just a body, wrapped all about with narrow bands of linen, not even yellow with time. The first Ptolemy, Alexander's brother, lies at the farthest end of the hall; I looked again, though each time it makes my flesh creep, for the linen swathings have rotted at one side of the head and one can see the skin beneath, brown and smooth, stretched tight over the bone of the cheek. It is exposure to the air that has turned it brown, Apollodorus said; under its coverings the body is exactly as it was in life. I cannot see how he would know for sure, since, once the wrappings were unwound, the air would work its damage. However, one does not say such things to one's nutritius, here in Egypt; such men are nearly as high as priests. Besides, I love Apollodorus dearly, far more than Father, and would not wish to show any disrespect.

One whispers in such places, though of course the dead cannot hear. Iras whispered in my ear, a question; I answered, low. "Alexander lies elsewhere, alone. Come."

We are both tall, for girls, taller than the Egyptians who built the place, and had to scrunch our heads down into our shoulders to pass through the low doorway that led to the secret chamber. Cobwebs hung thick as vines; we had to clear our way with our hands, choking. The place is hidden well; I had to play the light for minutes along the wall before I found the spot to press, the spot that swings open the door. It is just above the first letter of Alexander's name; it is written in the Egyptian picture script, and I am one of the very few Greeks who has learned it, so it is very secret indeed.

Inside, the air smells like the grave; I fought back a bubble of laughter, for of course it *is* the grave, and a very solemn place and sacred. The chamber is small, but high enough for us to straighten up; the alabaster casket glows like a lamp, drawing one to it.

We drew close; at the core of the alabaster was a soft density, a darkness, barely perceptible, the body of Alexander. I took Iras' wrist and drew her closer still, pressing her hand for silence. There was no need; I knew she felt it too, as I had felt it each time before, the beauty and the wonder of that face, lambent across the centuries.

For the space that held the head was all of glass, faintly

smoky and miraculously curved and sealed, seeming to have no jointure. We stared, not drawing breath; Alexander stared, too, upward, for the eyes had been left open, ice-blue like gems. One felt they might turn, at any moment, and see us where we stood, outside the glass. Like a fallen statue he lay, but colored as no artist could color him, the tints of nature, delicately flawed, even to the faint sprinkle of freckles across the bridge of the nose and the blue unpulsing vein at the temple. He was young still, at his death, and the look of youth was on him forever. Here was proof of the arts, old as times and secret from the world, of our Egyptian subjects: they sought to keep the body perfect, for the soul to use another time; it was the old religion and still practiced among the fellahim up the Nile; there are kings three thousand years old and more that sleep beneath the Pyramids, in flesh as perfect as this we looked upon now.

Beside me Iras' breath came noisily, as though she had been running; she had been holding it too long. "It might be you," she whispered. "It might be you—lying there . . . do you see it—how like he is to you?"

I had thought it before, but privately, not daring to voice it, even to myself. I took from my girdle a little polished silver mirror; it was dented in places where my youngest brother had used it for a teething toy when he was an infant; still one could see an almost clear image in it.

It was true, the likeness, except that my eyes were green; the nose, a little long, but with the true Hellene straightness, the low, broad forehead and the thick, arching brows; narrow, rounded chin, and full lips precisely chiseled and indented at the corners. It is a better face for a man than a woman; there is boldness there, and too much strength. Alexander's hair is hidden, for he wears the Persian mitered crown; from his fairness, though, one might fancy it light brown, like my own.

I looked long into the little silver mirror, and put it away, satisfied. There is a good omen there, for my first birthday as a woman grown. Here, in the Egypt of my adoption, have lived great women that have ruled along with men for many thousands of years, and before that, even, alone upon the throne of the Pharaohs. And he whom I resemble is called, even now, Alexander the Great. I am the seventh Cleopatra of my name, but I mean the world to forget all the others and remember me alone.

2

HOW TO DESCRIBE my father—or, more aptly, to explain him—truly it is not an easy task. There is a game the legion soldiers play, with their round small shields and a stitched leather ball; we children of the Palace have watched them at it on many a rainly afternoon, and taken bets among ourselves. There are two groups, or teams, of players, all armed with shields; the idea is to keep the ball in the air as long as possible; when a team member lets it hit the ground it counts against the team. Such a ball is my father, the rightful Pharaoh of Egypt. The difference is that when he hits the ground, it is he who must pay. He is mostly up in the air, however. Which describes him and explains him all at once.

As to how he looks . . . shall I say unprepossessing? That means so many things. His features are good, really, straight and neat and clean of line, except when he has been drinking, which is most of the time. He has the look of a scribe or a clerk, one who spends his time closeted with figures and papyrus rolls; this is deceptive, for he has no head for learning at all. He is at his best when he plays the flute or strums his lyre; his thin mouth softens then and his eyes grow large and lustrous. He coaxes wonderful sounds from these instruments, too, the complicated Greek pieces and also the sad, wailing songs of the native Egyptians; one could weep to listen. Iras has inherited this talent; she can play any song, having heard it once. I am very accomplished myself, but my skill comes from long hours of practice; I am not god-gifted. My accomplishments are many; this is no idle boast. One can learn anything, if one has the hunger, the will, and the pride for it.

The High Kings of Egypt were always called Pharaoh, a title that has nowadays lost its meaning; the kings of our line are called Ptolemy, after the founder, though sometimes they have other, private names as well. My grandfather, for instance, was called Alexander, and my uncle, too. I truly do not know Father's other name; he is known as Auletes. It translates freely as "the Piper," and of course it must have been derisive in the beginning, for the pipers at the Saturnalia and the other feast days are always slaves; Father takes it for a compliment, however, and tells his intimates to call him Aulie! Even his meanest subjects snigger behind his back, and there is always a hint of scorn below the courtiers' smiles. When I was younger I used to blush for him, painfully, my fair skin blotching with it; now I turn on the offender and stare like the basilisk; no one turns to stone, but the smiles fade. I am practicing a haughty face; the Roman dines with us tonight. Apollodorus, just now, caught me at it, and reprimanded me. "You will make a line between your eyebrows," he said, frowning himself; I could not help but smile. He darted a glance at me, but said nothing. He is right, of course; a queen, here in Egypt at any rate, must keep a goddess look.

I must explain about Apollodorus, who he is and so on; I have known him all my life, or so it seems to me. He is my "nutritius," a title that is hard to explain, because it is only here, in Egypt, that his position exists. From time before memory the royal children of this Nile-land have been given to the care of special servants, from their earliest days; often a child has one such all to himself. "Nutritius" translates literally as "male nurse," but of course they are not nurses in any true sense; I would say they are advisers or mentors, not precisely tutors, though they do teach manners and courtesies and many other things. The relationship at its finest is almost that of a foster father; certainly Apollodorus is that to me.

I have often puzzled over this relationship and its origin; the nutritius is always a servant and sometimes even a slave, yet he wields a great deal of authority and is treated as a blood kinsman. I think, though I have never voiced it, that once, long ago, the royal child's nutritius was the true father. It is not so strange as it sounds; here in Egypt the double throne is occupied, always, by brother and sister, in imitation of the god Osiris and his sister Isis, from whom all Pharaohs are descended. Now this is incest, to a Greek, and the rulers of our dynasty have only pretended, marrying third or fourth cousins, or even outsiders, and calling them "sisters." Indeed, our great doctors say that marriage between brother and sister, after a few generations, would breed idiots. Egypt has always had great doctors, from the dawn of the world; I am sure the Pharaohs of old got around this custom, too, somehow, for I have heard of no idiots among them. I think the sister sat beside her brother on the throne, but took another "brother" into her bed; this true father brought up the child, as its "nutritius." Of course, that was centuries ago—but it must have begun in some such way.

It is, in any case, a position of much familiarity and trust, though it can be abused. My two young brothers share an evil creature named Pothinus, a eunuch, but power-hungry. Arsinoëe's Ganymede is no eunuch (I have seen him pawing her, and worse!), but he, also, is ambitious and must be watched. I am the fortunate one, for Apollodorus is a man of integrity and intellect.

Apollodorus is a Sicilian Greek; he was given as a child to serve Apollo in his temple, hence his name. The priests of Apollo are famous teachers; Apollodorus is a very learned man, and in his turn became a teacher, at the temple here in Alexandria. How he came to be chosen to serve me I do not know; he has been in the Palace ever since I can remember. His is probably not so very old, but his hair is pure white, like the foam on the sea, or like a cloud; he says he saw the first white hairs when he was my age, or thereabouts. As to his looks, he is like Socrates, an ugly man, thick-bodied and coarse-faced; look again, though, and the beauty that is trapped within looks out of his eyes, clear gray and shining; so might a thought look, if it had shape.

Apollodorus is not a eunuch, for I asked him once, when I was too young to know the question was unseemly. He answered, with a smile that creased his heavy face, "No—there was no need to geld me, for no woman would lust after me. Besides—I have taken the celibate's vows." There are many sects within our Greek religion which demand this, and more spring up every year, some living secluded lives and some dedicated to medicine or the arts. Even Rome has its Vestal Virgins; one might be certain such vows would not be asked of the Roman men! Most of them have had several wives and the gods know how many concubines; they are quite common men, too—not kings like Father. This Marcus that is being feasted tonight has had two already, and he is quite young yet, they say, only twenty-seven.

The banquet tonight might be called a celebration; in a way this Marcus has given Father back his throne. Father could have taken it back himself, if he had acted quickly enough; as far as that goes he would never have lost it, if he had not gone Rome-trotting.

It is a long and involved story. Briefly, Rome has been eyeing the kingdom of Egypt for many years; the Romans would like nothing better than to add us to their conquests. My father, instead of using his head and planning how to hold on to our country, has flown into a panic whenever the Romans make a move, bribing them to the extent of putting himself in fearful debt over the years. His subjects have to pay dreadfully high taxes to make up for it; naturally they do not love him, and will welcome any ruler who promises better things. The last time Father carried bribe-gold to Rome, his oldest daughter Berenice, my half-sister, seized the throne. This was three years ago, and the kingdom has been in turmoil ever since. Now, poor lady, her day is done, and she is held prisoner somewhere here in the Palace.

I never have known Berenice; she is more than twice my age, sired when Father was a boy, along with a twin sister who was called Cleopatra, like me. Cleopatra is a royal name; she was the sixth to bear it. That sister died two years ago, quietly, in her sleep, or so it was given out. Iras, who is allowed to go belowstairs, even into the kitchens, says the gossip is that Berenice murdered her, either by poison or smothering with a cushion, for that sixth Cleopatra had raised a small army of followers and was plotting for the throne herself. I can believe it, for the thread of murder runs through our history like the flaw in a woven linen. Father is said to have murdered his first wife, Berenice's mother; this I do not credit, not that he is softhearted, but that he is far too weak. However, he probably paid to have it done, while he was absent from the kingdom.

The blood-filled intrigues of our house are as nothing to what the Romans practice, however; one cannot keep track of them, truly! Rome is a republic, so-called; there is not even a throne for prize! It was never the Greek way; the Greeks held life precious. When I am queen and must rid myself of an enemy, I shall do it openly by execution; what is power for? Of course, I hope that I shall have no enemies.

The events that led to Berenice's fall are as complicated as those which brought her to power; it is enough to say that Father's craven heart and devious mind were the cause of those events. Unrest and rioting have marked all the years of his reign; he is not a good king. Rome is mixed up in it too, of course, for the Romans wish to master the whole world.

Father, after many enormous bribes that did not work, finally was able to buy a Roman named Gabinius, the governor of Syria; the payment was vast, two and a half million pounds of silver. Gabinius agreed to invade our country and get back Father's throne by war. Berenice was married to a man named Archelaus, the High Priest of Komana in Cappadocia. Archelaus was the friend of the Roman, Pompey, who had great power and influence; I guess he and Berenice expected Pompey's help, but he failed them. Gabinius declared war on Archelaus, saying at Rome that Archelaus was a pirate endangering Roman possessions on the African coast, and that his fleet was a menace to Roman sea power, thus obtaining official aid. Soon a Roman army was marching across the desert from Gaza to Pelusium. The cavalry in advance of the army was commanded by Marcus Antonius. Pelusium fell to him, and he marched on into our Alexandria. The legions went over to him (they were Roman, after all) and Archelaus lost his life along with his power. Berenice was locked up somewhere and Father regained his throne. This is the situation, put simply. And Father is feasting this Marcus, and I am commanded to attend, along with my royal brothers and sister, Arsinoëe.

I will take Iras with me to the banquet hall as my lady in waiting, and Apollodorus will go as well, to see that I mind my manners; as if I did not know how to behave royally! I am troubled about my clothes, for I have outgrown everything this last year and I have been given no money to buy new clothes. That is what comes of having no women about; Apollodorus will always be more concerned about my mind's adornment than my body's. Both are important, for a queen.

I must share with Iras, too, or she would go naked; there are no seamstresses, even in the Palace. All the slaves are worse than useless; they bow and walk backwards from my presence, but dust lies in every corner. The turmoil in our house is so longstanding that it has put a stop to all order; sometimes I must send Iras to the kitchens to fetch the midday meal, or go without it. Though I am first heir and the oldest, after Berenice, I have no authority; Father never thinks about any of his children, I am sure, except on occasions of state, or if, as in the case of Berenice, they become a menace.

If Arsinoëe were a different girl, we might put our heads together against this Roman, but we are as unlike as can be imagined; we might belong to different races! Of course, she had another mother, a distant kinswoman with a claim to royal blood. I remember the lady, for she died only a few years ago. Thin and dark and ailing she was; I never saw her out of bed. There are two other children of that union, my young half-brothers; strange to think she could manage it, sick as she was. She did not die of childbirth, either, but simply wasted away; the doctors never could put a name to her malady. Her home was far away, in Spain; perhaps she sickened for it. At any rate she is gone now; Father has not taken another wife, only concubines, quite low-born. There are no ladies in the Palace to consult about proper dress, and no one to borrow from; I have had to make do with odds and ends that I can find. The gods know where my mother's jewels are; perhaps Father has pawned them! This is no jest; there are pawnshops throughout the Phoenician quarter, all with the royal scarab sign above their doorways.

The only jewels I possess are two tiny pearls for my ears; I wear them always, even when I sleep. They are too small for Father to covet, but I treasure them. They were given to me on a happier birthday, when I was five, by my uncle Alexander, who petted and spoiled me as Father had never done. This uncle, Ptolemy XII, was Father's twin brother, the ruler of Cyprus. When the Romans invaded his country and it was about to fall to them, he took his own life rather than be a Roman subject. And so I remember him with admiration and respect, as well as fondness. He had a daughter that I remember, a girl a bit older than I was, named Charmion, but no trace of her has been found; the Romans probably killed her.

Of necessity, I have dressed simply, copying a statue from Athens for the drape of my dalmatica, and wearing my hair unbound, for it is beautiful and straight as rain. I have a chaplet of yellow roses for a crown; only the fairest skin can wear yellow. My robe is a pale tint of saffron, too, and I have painted my eyelids green to bring out my eyes. I passed inspection, except for this eye paint; Apollodorus said, frowning, "Take it off . . . royal maidens should not look like dancing girls." Behind me, Iras giggled; it served her right, for he heard and made her wash off her own blue. It took some rubbing and made our eyelids red; never mind, I thought, he is only a Roman. I held my head higher.

The feast was set for sundown, and I had thought we were early, for red still streaked the sky framed by the western windows where we walked along the corridor. They must have started on the wine, though, for we could hear Father's flute above the drummers long before we got to the doorway of the great hall; he does not play in company unless he is a little flown.

The hall blazed with light; I have never seen so many candles; with the braziers at every couch, the heat was stifling, for it was still summer. Egyptian nard hung heavy in the air, with the sweet-sour smell of grapes; trust Father to pick up the worst customs! Each guest had a cone of perfumed wax, a fashion from Old Egypt, meant to be placed on the head and so melt gradually, perfuming the whole body. Of course, the old Egyptians went nearly naked, so it did not soil their clothes; nowadays it is rather disgusting, for it darkens the robes like sweat. I saw that none of our Greek aristocrats were using the cones and had merely placed them on the tables to melt among the candles, beside the huge bowls of dark Italian wine. The Romans did not wait for slave service, but served themselves from the bowl with dippers, staining the tablecloths. One could pick out the Romans at a glance; they all wore purple somewhere—a sash or a border on their robes—for they thought it a royal color; kings, of course, have given it up long ago, when the dye became plentiful.

No one noticed us as we entered, much less our red eyelids; smoke from the braziers made a blue haze, and besides, the Romans were already drunker than Father. He will like that, I thought. He once threatened an eminent courtier with execution because he would not drink with him; I never heard how it turned out in the end, it was before my time.

We were not announced, for Father was still piping away; a slave led us to our table. The Romans sat in the couches of honor, where Father should have been; he had taken a place a little to the right, and we were opposite, to the left. The little Ptolemies, my brothers, were seated already, with their nutritius, the eunuch Pothinus; so also was Arsinoëe, sharing a couch with her Ganymede. Iras and I both gasped when we saw her; talk about dancing girls! I have never seen so much paint, even in the circus. Her dress was transparent, the flesh showing rosy beneath it, and gold gleamed on her arms and at her throat. She had dressed her hair high, in the true Greek manner, though it could not make her look Greek and was too old a style for her. She wore a slim gold diadem, too, with the royal scarab set in; I felt my cheeks go hot red; where had she got it? For that matter, where had she found the gold armlets and the rest! Probably stolen by her nutritius, Ganymede, for he was got up like an eastern idol himself and winked with gems. He always looked more like a woman than a man, with his long black lovelocks and his bright garments, though his reputation is otherwise; I saw that his hand rested on the thin stuff that covered her knee. In any other court he would be put to death for such a liberty; she is a royal princess, under his care, after all.

I looked at the Roman table; there were some dozen of them, looking, to me, all alike. I leaned toward Iras, whispering. "Which one is Marcus?"

"The one picking his nose," she said. I held back a smile; he was not, really, only scratching; I think he was being courteous, listening to Father, and had got a little bored; as I watched, he rose a small way from his couch, hitching his robe away from his thighs in back; it was probably sticking to him and no wonder, in this heat! As I looked, I could not understand why I had not picked him out; he was easily the biggest, by far, among them. And he did look like a face on a coin, the features all larger than they should be and the hair in close curls, as though drawn with an unwieldy stylus. He also looked like a bull, thick in the neck and shoulders and with popping eyes. Still, there was a noble look about him, difficult to define; one saw why the Cretans had worshiped the animal. Close to, when Father had finished and led me to this bull-god, I saw a thinking brain behind the bulging eyes; it was not luck alone that had put him in high place.

He greeted me in a halting, careful Greek; I answered in perfect Latin, surprising him. "Your Roman speech is very good," he said, switching to the Latin himself. "There is almost no accent."

"My teacher was a Roman slave," I said, coolly. He laughed.

"Your youngest daughter has a stringent wit, Auletes."

"I am Cleopatra, the oldest, and heir to the throne," I said.

"And will not forgive a Roman mistake either, I can see!" His full lips curved and a dimple, womanish, appeared in his cheek.

"A thousand pardons, Cleopatra," he said, smiling now. "I did not mean to offend. But the maiden who sat with you yonder—she of the diadem—she looks a full two years older."

It was the diadem, of course. I shot Father a baleful glance.

"Where did she get it?" I hissed, in swift Alexandrian Greek.

He spread his hands and shrugged. "I will make her take it off," he said. "You will have it, I promise."

"I do not want that one, Father. I want a bigger one. I want the serpent crown . . ."

I had not thought the Roman could understand, but it seemed he did. "Why should she not have it, Auletes? The head that wore it can have no more use for it . . ." I froze. He meant Berenice!

Father went white to the lips, staring at Marcus. "Is it . . . is it—"

"Yes," said the Roman, flatly. "It is done. She is in Hades."

Father began to sob. The Roman did not look his way, but spoke to me. "I will send you the serpent crown tomorrow, little princess. See that you wear it with more grace than she who has lost it." His words were bland, but there was a threat under them; I knew he spoke for Rome.

I took a deep breath to steady my voice and answered. "Thank you, Roman, for the crown. And for the warning." And I turned away, taking my time about it.

As I went I heard him let out a breath, laughing, and speak to the man who sat beside him. It was a Gaulish dialect, barracks-talk, and he could not know I took his meaning. But there have been Gaulish mercenaries about the Palace since I can remember; I learned my swearwords at their knees. "Whew!" he gasped. "Good riddance to the skinny bitch! Bring on Miss Big Tits!"

I knew he meant Arsinoëe, even before I saw my father lead her forward, her mouth in a simper and the big globes of her breasts poking out before her through her dress. She will be a cow, I thought, before she is twenty. Then I smiled to myself, a little sourly. Well, he is a bull after all.

I hated him.

3

ALEXANDRIA IS A BEAUTIFUL CITY, the second city of the world, after Athens. Of course I have not seen many, I have scarcely traveled at all, but I have been to Athens once. Even then, when I was still a child, I saw it through a mist of tears and a cloud of longing; all our glorious Greek past is there; it is more shrine than city. It is old, so old; one feels the gods walk there still.

Apollodorus took me to Athens; Father has never taken us anywhere. Father's trips to Rome have been all begging missions, and he always said that the old Egyptian cities were nothing but ruins and that Egypt's interior was unhealthy and riddled with disease. I do not believe that Father has ever been up the Nile either; he takes no thought of his subjects except to tax them. What he says may be discounted; some day I shall see for myself. After all, Egypt's past is glorious, too. For centuries it was the most powerful of kingdoms; Thebes and Cairo and the rest must hold sights of wonder still.

The island and coastal cities of Greece are merely ports, bustling and busy with trade, but tiny compared to our own city. To the east, the towns are no more than a sprawl of tents or a cluster of mud huts. At least, that is all I have seen.

But even those who have traveled far and seen every foreign place—even they call Alexandria beautiful. In Alexandria there is always a blaze of flowers; one walks over ground scarlet and gold with them, wherever there is not a street laid down; flowering bushes crowd the walkways, towering above one's head; in the rainy months wet, fragile petals fall with the raindrops and cling, a shower of brilliance against the gray. Even the newest walls have their creepers, heavy with blossom; our Palace shows little stone; it is covered with climbing vines. Every week workmen must cut back the growing things; otherwise we should have no windows and no doors! It is something in the climate that encourages this growth; Apollodorus says, smiling himself, that the gods smile on us here.

Alexander chose his city-site well; it was meant mainly for a Greek trading-post, where Greek goods could be landed easily and produce from the Nile shipped north and west. It stands on the Delta, erected on a strip of land between the Mediterranean and the Marcotic Lake, and completely separate from Egypt proper; Alexandria is thus free from the rest of the land, and in dominion over it, all at the same time. The harbor is perfect; the island of Pharos lies between the city and the sea, and two long arms of land encircle the space between, a haven for shipping. Much of the city was laid out by Alexander himself; I have read his brother Ptolemy's account of how the great hero marked off the streets with rope and wooden stakes driven into the ground by his own hand; he died before he saw it finished, though many of the streets still bear the names he gave them.

It is odd how one sees a place more clearly when one approaches it from another place; I knew my city better after I came back from Athens. From shipside, I remember, as we sailed in to harbor, the first thing I saw was the lighthouse on Pharos. It is called one of the wonders of the world, but I had not realized its majesty till then. It is built entirely of white marble; the sun, striking it, makes shining rainbow stains upon its smooth walls. They rise, unbroken, for five hundred feet; from a distance it is like a finger pointing to the sky. We sailed in by day, but they say the beacon light at the top is the most powerful in the world; it faces sea-ward, of course, otherwise I suppose there would be no night in Alexandria! It was designed by the famous architect Sostratus two hundred years ago, but it looks as though it had been built yesterday; even close up the marble is perfect, each block rounded and fitting to the next without a sign of a join; it is like the work of a master-sculptor.

Our ship came around the great lighthouse and into harbor; I remember the marble base, white as bone against the wild dark water that boiled and foamed angrily against it. The sailors said there were treacherous rocks there, but we came in safely; now that I think of it, no ship was ever wrecked there; perhaps they were just talking it up to impress a girl. At any rate, in the harbor itself there are no rocks, for the water is almost transparent and one can see right down to the bottom. There is seaweed there of all colors, though I had always thought it was green; under the water it looks like the hair of drowned maidens. Where the waters are deeper there are dolphins, wonderful fish as big as humans, that jump up into view and play like children. I had seen them before, of course, for they will come right in to shore and take bread from your hand. But I had never seen so many, in the hundreds, as I saw from shipside. They are the nicest of animals, I think; their mouths are formed in a smile, not like a cat's, which is smug, but a joyful smile.

Once in harbor, the whole of Alexandria lies before the eye, the great buildings crowding the shore like a forest of trees, with others behind them, disappearing into a misty distance. I caught my breath at the sight of it, in full sunlight; there can be no other sight like it in the world! First there is our Palace, spread over the Lochias Promontory and covering the whole western shore; at the shore's end another royal pavilion on the little island of Antirrhodos, and the Royal Harbor, where stairs come right down into the water. I live there and walk all about, but it does not look nearly so splendid when one is in it; from sea, one sees what the architect had in mind. Of course, all visitors come this way, so they are as stunned by the view as I was. The Museum is right behind, with all its courtyards and walks, tree-lined, where the philosophers hold converse with their pupils, in imitation of those great Athenians, long ago. Beyond stands the Theater, vastly curving, open to the sky, and beyond that the temples of the gods, each on its own small hill. Then come the courts, the gymnasiums, the Forum, the parks and public gardens, and so on into the foreign quarters, which have their own buildings; the city is huge.

Huge as it is, I have explored most of it; what else have I had to do? Especially in the years after Father got back his throne and we lived in a kind of uneasy peace. Marcus Antonius went back to Rome, but he left, by Gabinius' orders, more of the Roman mercenaries; we were prisoners of Rome, really, though no one ever said so. I never went anywhere in the city, walking or by chariot, without an armed escort of Gauls or Germans. It was partly for my protection, and partly so that I would not attract followers and seize the throne before my time. Rome was not sure of anything Alexandrian; we were all watched and guarded.

They were right, of course; even in peacetime there were plots and counterplots. The boys, my brothers, were too young to know what their nutritius was about, but Pothinus had spies everywhere, and Arsinoëe's Ganymede fomented several small riots, though they came to nothing. Arsinoëe, though, was in it with him, you may be sure; she was not so young, nearly my age, and she was always greedy for power. She was greedy in other ways, too, but stupid as well, for she bore a child to him. It did not live; she had wound tight canvas bands around her body, under her clothes, to hide it, and it suffocated in the womb. In the end, everyone knew, for she howled all through a night. Father, belatedly, took heed of his daughter's good name, and Ganymede was sentenced to death. What could he do? He denied it, saying the child was Marcus Antonius'. Arsinoëe bore him out; she was not so stupid as not to see that she needed Ganymede. It was believed and Father swallowed his ire; what could he do against a Roman? Besides, the child was dead; the whole thing was soon forgotten, and Ganymede was back at his plotting. Privately, I do not think the child was Marcus', in spite of his dallying with her; I can count, after all.

I went everywhere; it was no hardship to me to have my soldier-guards with me, for these northern races have an easy, open friendliness that is not found in other peoples. Besides, I like to learn where I can, language and customs; it is a form of travel, after all.

We went even to the foreign quarters, Iras, Apollodorus, and I, accompanied by our guards. I have always felt a queen should know her people, even the poorest of them; most rulers do not, and therefore do not rule wisely. I did not go among them with the intention of ingratiating myself and winning followers, but somehow it turned out that way. Wherever I went, I was recognized by someone, and the word was spread; I was pretty, and they thought me good; I smiled, and they thought me kind. I was never good or kind in my life, except when it suited me to be; in that I am like most people. I have been fortunate in that so often it *has* suited me.

Alexandria is a Greek city; except for a few Egyptians, all the high court places are filled by Macedonian Greeks, many of them kinsmen of our royal house. The population, though, is made up of many other nationalities—Assyrians and Phoenicians, Italians, Cretans, Cypriots, Persians,

Jews, and Egyptians; the city swarms with these, for they make up the merchant and the craftsman class, with wares and services to sell. For the most part they are a dark people, and small of stature; when I came among them, slight and fair, with golden Iras and white-haired Apollodorus, and our troop of big-boned, harsh-tongued warriors, we must have looked as though we had dropped from the sky. These peoples each have their own languages, plus a kind of street speech common to all; I took pride that I could speak with any, and be understood. It was one of the reasons why the lowest of my subjects loved me, and hailed me, in time, as a goddess; there was nothing superhuman about it; I had studied hard, and had the gift of tongues, as well.

For the most part, these many races lived peaceably enough together, if one excepts the Jews. These are a strange people, proud and isolated; they never intermarry, as the others do, for their god forbids it. Unlike all other religions, they worship one god, and do not make images of him, but worship him through books and laws. I was curious, and read their holy writing in a book called the Torah, the works of many prophets and demigods. But when I approached one of their priests to discuss it, as I would with all others, he backed away as though I carried a plague upon my breath. Even their great-eyed children would not come near, but stared from behind their mothers' skirts, unsmiling; at me, who will be their queen! These experiences put me off them a little; I never persecuted my Jews, as some rulers do, but I never raised them to high places, either.

We sometimes went on picnics outside the city gates, followed by a swarm of children, begging for scraps. There was the little settlement of Eleusis, on the outskirts, which had a sacred spring and a little grove of laurel trees, with a shrine. The god or goddess of the place had vanished long ago, the stone of its image lying in broken splinters on the ground beneath its altar; it was a lovely, dusty, sunny spot, though, with bees humming lazily in the little wild roses that climbed up the altar-stone, and a carpet of grass to sit on. Or we would eat in one of the parks; they are beautiful places, with well-tended gardens, and enormous shade trees; there, we could never be alone, for a crowd would gather, watching every bite as it was eaten. I could not eat, either, for I knew them to be hungry, and there was not enough to go around. I made a vow then, that, when I came to power, no one would starve in my city; I was little more than a child then, and did not know that such vows are easier made than kept.

The best picnic-place, and my favorite, was on the Marcotic Lake. There was a Phoenician settlement there, at the edge of the water, a market, really. They are merchants and traders, the Phoenicians, and a well-off people; one could feast among them without feeling guilty, and sample their strange, wonderful-smelling foods as well. We used to go in little boats, hired by the hour (Phoenician-owned, of course) and row right out to the middle of the lake. In the shallow water reeds grew and broad palms; we spread our food upon the palm-leaves that we picked and laid upon our laps; it tasted delicious, always a little wet from the palm-leaves, and with the lovely, woody fragrance of growing things all about us, and the Phoenician women and children pushing up in their own little boats, laughing and talking at once, and reaching out their hands to touch me, suddenly shy.

I loved those noisy, bright-eyed people, so warm and friendly. I loved those long days, innocent and dreaming; I knew they could not last.

4

IN THE SPRING of the year when I was eighteen, Father died. It was not sudden; he had been coughing through the winter—still one never expects death. It leaves a gap, even when someone like Father has been filling it.

Father left a will, written in two copies. One was kept at the Palace, sealed and guarded, and the other had been sent to Pompey at Rome.

This man Pompey was the most powerful of all the Romans, after Julius Caesar, who was away conquering some more helpless savages in northern Gaul, or perhaps it was Britain; I get them mixed up. At any rate, this Julius was out of the picture for a while. Father's move was wise, for him; he asked, in writing, for the protection of Rome for his kingdom and his heirs, and Pompey was a man of honor, as Romans go.

In this will Father decreed that his oldest surviving daughter and his oldest surviving son should rule jointly after him, and he called upon the Roman people in the name of all their gods and in view of the treaties he had made with them, to see that the terms of his testament were carried out. It was the best he could do, poor man.

I was that oldest daughter, and the oldest son was a boy of ten, my brother, Ptolemy XIV, whom we always called "Mouse," because he was afraid of them, like a girl, and because he looked like one, too, a little. He was undersized, even for ten, with pale skin so thin that the veins showed through, a pointed nose, and soft, silky, colorless hair.

As I have mentioned before, the Pharaohs of Egypt had ruled jointly, in this way, brother and sister marrying to secure the throne as the representatives of the brother-sister gods Osiris and Isis. In our case that was out of the question, because of the difference in age; though the eunuch Pothinus suggested it, none of the other court officials would agree. I suppose, being a eunuch, he saw nothing wrong in a grown woman wed to a child!

Pothinus, as I have said, had much influence over both the young boys, having, in a way, reared them from boyhood. Now most eunuchs are easy fellows, content to bask in those bodily comforts that have been left to them, eating and drinking and lying upon soft beds; Pothinus, however, was different, grasping and power-hungry. He had little of the eunuch-look, being slim rather than fat, though there was an unhealthy soft look about him; he was bald and wore turbans, in the eastern fashion. I do not know his origins, but I think they were perhaps Persian, mixed with some other dark race. His face was nearly expressionless, flat-featured, with hooded eyes, like some predatory bird; one could never tell what he was thinking. His age, too, was a mystery, unlined as he was; he had been Berenice's tutor once, so he must have been nearly as old as Father.

Pothinus had formed an alliance with two other court officials, men as unsavory as he himself. Theodotus, a Greek, was one. He bore the title of Royal Tutor, but he had not taught for years, since Father was a boy. He fancied himself as an orator, and took every opportunity to make speeches, full of rhetoric and bombast and sprinkled with quotations from the more dubious ancients. He was long-winded and dull, and his Greek was poor; Iras and I had laughed at him, thinking him a fool; this was a mistake, for his foolishness hid great evil. He looked the part of rhetorician, haughty-featured, with weak, watery eyes; most of the court revered him, being fools themselves. The third man about my young brother-king was the commander of the Royal Guard, an Egyptian with a Greek name, Achillas. He, a soldier, had the eunuch-looks that were missing in Pothinus. He was fat, dark, and oily, a loathsome creature. These three together used poor little Mouse like a boy-doll; it was horrid to hear their words recited in his piping child's voice.

Apollodorus was my friend and a wise and learned teacher, but he was not a worldly man, and there was only one of him; he was no match for those three vultures. I had to fight them alone. In the years of their power I did not draw an easy breath. I never spoke an uncalculated word or took an unguarded step. My escort of Gaulish legionnaires I kept by me always, even posting them before my chamber door when I slept.

Because the king was a child still, the bulk of the formal business of ruling fell to me; I knew it as an empty privilege, however, though I dressed up in fine ceremonial clothes and sat upon an inlaid ivory throne once every week to hear the complaints of my subjects and pass judgments. Those judgments, though I took them seriously and tried hard, were usually countermanded by the three who truly ruled Egypt—Pothinus, Theodotus, and Achillas. I had no real power, and I knew it, for I was intelligent. The best that can be said of those early years was that they taught me patience. My position with my people were strengthened, also; there was nothing that evil trio could do to diminish my popularity, short of putting me to death. Egypt had to have a ruling figure, one who rode in processions and officiated in temple ceremonies, or the people would revolt. Little Mouse was no good at all; besides being a child, he was shy and retiring, with a bad stammer and a weak voice; he never liked to show himself in public, either, and trembled like a leaf that is about to fall. When I went about Alexandria, cheers deafened the ears, and the crowds in the temples prostrated themselves before me as their goddess. They loved me, even as I was, powerless; it was not enough, but it was something. I waited.

This is not to say that I was idle, growing up as queen; I will always turn my hand to something, it is my nature. As I have said, I loved learning, and the great learned men of my court loved me for it. Like Apollodorus, these scholars were unworldly men who presented no threat to Pothinus and the rest; I was able to allocate part of the royal treasury for libraries and schools, and for study; under me, even then, Alexandria led the world in the knowledge of art and science. Dioscorides, the physician, was my dear friend and teacher; Sosigenes the astronomer and Photinus the mathematician came to full flower at my court; young scholars came to them in flocks, even from Rome, to study. I gave my own small private banquets for these folk, teachers and students; often we talked the night through, excited, disputing, drunk on old and new knowledge, headier than any wine.

The young Romans were all in love with me, though Iras is prettier; I am queen, after all. Every day there were poems written, dozens of them, to my lips, my hair, my soft skin; I might have become insufferably vain, had I owned less wit, or fewer mirrors. My mouth, though nicely formed, was too big for my face, my hair too fine to handle, and my skin too freckled. At least I did not come out in spots, like Arsinoëe!

Certain things, being queen, I was able to change. I had my own apartments now, in the Palace, the chambers which had been Father's; Arsinoëe and both my brothers had theirs; sometimes we four of the royal house did not see one another from one state occasion to the next; we were all happier for it. The Ptolemies led children's lives, of course, no matter that they were Egypt's heirs, and Arsinoëe and I had never agreed on anything. The entire household ran more smoothly now; I had replaced all the useless slaves with skilled workers, and brought in women to tire hair, draw baths, and sew. It was considered quite an innovation, and the girls had to be taught everything; they had been used for rough work in the kitchen and the courtyard, before my time. For my personal retinue I picked a few girls of good family and some education; they did light tasks of a ceremonial nature, but were in fact my companions. I enjoyed having them about me; except for Iras, I had had no intimates in all the years of my growing up. I chose the most personable, all Greeks, as befits our Greek house; they were well dressed and had beautiful manners, doing me credit. Now, when I showed myself to my subjects, it was as a flower among flowers.

These noble girls fought among themselves for this privilege; Court was an adventure to them, after their confining lives. Though they enjoyed much liberty in my household, there was no license; if a maiden abused her freedom, she was dismissed, for I wanted no backstairs brats. In this way, I kept the respect of all our noble Greek families; we had not had it before, since the early days of our dynasty. For generations now the court of the Ptolemies had been worse than a brothel, avoided by the better aristocrats; there was order now, and regular hours and decent habits. I was not prim, really, or I do not think so, but Arsinoëe's plight had made me very wary; my ladies in waiting were watched with hawk eyes; whatever I might miss, Apollodorus saw, for his duties were light at the Palace, now that I was grown.

There was a maiden, daughter of one of the Court scribes, of an old family that could trace its lineage back to Philip of Macedon. Her name was Cleito and she was gentle and biddable as a tame fawn, or so I thought. One morning, as we sat at an early meal, I happened to glance her way; she was pale as a peeled almond and her face was beaded with sweat, though it was an early hour and still cool. I feared a fever, for we are plagued with them in Egypt always, and asked her what ailed her; she answered that she thought the fish had gone bad. I was a little annoyed, since I had eaten mine all up and noticed nothing.

"But you have not touched your fish, Cleito," said Iras. The girl said nothing, but her face was green. Suddenly she bent over and threw up, red pomegranate juice and seeds, a disgusting sight.

She was pregnant, of course, but early days, for it did not show on her yet. I was furious; her family was almost as powerful as my own in Alexandria, with a long history of dissension and intrigue against the throne. I could not send her back to her father in this state, as I might another girl, and she would not tell the name of her seducer.

I put her on bread and water for a week; she was delicately nurtured and weak; she named the man, whispering low, one of the Roman students. "Well, he is of the equestrian class, I said, "Not good enough for you . . . but no matter—you will have to marry him."

"He has a Roman wife," she said, looking sick again.

"Gods!" I cried softly. "You might have thought what you were doing—was there no unwed Roman to throw yourself away on?" It was cruel, but I could not help myself; I despise a fool. And of course it was the man's fault, surely; she was as shy as a bird.

"Was it rape?" I asked. "Even a Roman can be put to death for that . . ."

"Oh, no—" she cried softly. "I love him!"

"Then he must put his wife away and marry you," I said. "They do it all the time in Rome."

I sent my Gauls to seize him and put him in chains. He did my bidding, after a bit. But it was a touchy business, and he had to be paid off, and the Roman wife as well. After the child was born he was called back to Rome and Cleito went with him. I never knew how it turned out, and if she was happy with her lot; I thought it unlikely, with a Roman.

5

AFTER CLEITO'S DISASTER, I should have liked to send all the other students packing, but it was impossible. Father had involved us with Rome for good and all; one had to accept it. I could not forget, either, that the throne itself was under Roman protectorate; I could no longer defy Romans, as I had done as a girl, with Marcus Antonius. I needed Rome, and must learn to use her.

The troops of Gabinius that Marcus had left here after he had restored Father's throne was still in Alexandria, a standing army, augmenting our own. There had been little use for them; we had been at peace for several years now. Soldiers that are idle will always grow lax; they never drilled or trained and did not even keep strict hours, but lay abed long after cock-crow and diced and drank the night through. I knew it well, for we had a contingent of them in the Palace; I had often lain awake, hearing their distant clatter and their rough voices, loud with wine. I had no power to enforce discipline, they outnumbered our Alexandrians two to one. I had complained of this, writing letter after letter to Gabinius at Rome; there was never an answer, not even from a secretary.

When two Romans, in full armor and wearing the purple, stepped ashore from a Syrian war-vessel, I thought they were come to see to this matter personally. It turned out they had nothing at all to do with Gabinius, and had come to take the troops away; they were welcome to them.

The governor of Syria was a Roman named Bibulus, who had been consul the same year as the famous Julius Caesar; these two were his sons, Calpurnius and Titus, come to press Roman legions into service in their father's campaign against the Parthians. I had spies in Syria, but I thought to myself they had better be replaced, for I had had no word of a campaign against Parthia. Still, I was not really surprised; Romans are always planning war somewhere.

I received them courteously but without any great ceremony; they were coming to take, not to give, after all. Still, one never knows when Syrian friendship might come in handy; I wore the serpent diadem, served them roast kid stuffed with mussels, an Alexandrian specialty, and put myself out to be charming. It was not difficult; they were very provincial, with the table manners of a Syrian outpost; the younger, Titus, was only a year or two older than I myself. They goggled at me, two raw-boned lads with thin identical faces who did not know what knife to use.

Calpurnius cleared his throat and swallowed, a lump of kid large enough to bring tears to his eyes went down; one could see it working past his throat, a distasteful sight. He said, "That must be the latest style from Rome, eh, Miss?"

I supposed he meant my dalmatica; it was draped in the Greek style, of Egyptian cotton, blue. I smiled, making dimples to mask my scorn.

"I have never been to Rome," I said.

"Like us," he said, shaking his head sadly. "Father promises, but . . ." his voice trailed off, disconsolate. They were a sorry pair; I was hard put to it to keep a decent conversation going. We got through the meal somehow, all three of us stifling yawns as the last sweet was brought in; it had been a long day.

"Well," I said, smiling, "I will bid you farewell, as your business is finished here. You sail tomorrow, along with the troops you asked for . . ."

"At first light, yes," said Titus. They bowed, and took their leave of me, saying they would stop in at the Gabinian barracks before retiring. "A gesture of goodwill," said Calpurnius. "Father says a commander should get to know his men . . ."

I wished them joy of each other, the two raw commanders and their noisy men, but silently, and went to my bed.

I was not to get much rest, or they the joy I had willed them, for they were killed before midnight in a drunken brawl—stabbed, both, in the back, with short Roman swords. My Gauls, those who share the quarters, had seen the deed, and brought the murderers before me, their wrists bound with strong rope.

There were three of them, hairy hulks with stupid faces, smelling of sour wine and vomit. I asked them to speak up, to save themselves, but I could not follow their coarse tongues, and must hear them through an interpreter; I know most of the dialects, but it was the first street-Roman I had heard. It seems they resented this demand and did not want to fight in a war they knew nothing about; they said they spoke for the whole Gabinian army. I sympathized with them; they had a soft life here in the Palace, but still, they were murderers, no matter how provoked, or how drunken. I pondered what to do with them.

After some thought, I decided to send them to Bibulus in Syria, with word that they were his sons' murderers, apprehended by my efficiency and promptitude.

The bodies, too, I sent on the Syrian galley; I had turned them over to our Egyptian doctors and they were decently laid out, in new togas, and their flesh embalmed for the journey.

Bibulus kept the bodies, but sent back the prisoners unharmed, with a letter that the right of inflicting punishment in such cases belonged only to the Roman Senate. Poor stiff-necked Roman patriot, I thought—once consul, now shunted off to an obscure command, still adhering to some incomprehensible, outmoded code. Well, the Senate could have them! I packed the three murderers off again, in chains, to the Senate house at Rome, with a written order for the gold of their passage, to be paid on arrival. I never got it, of course; I do not know what happened to the prisoners; for all I know, they may still be in their chains, waiting for the Senate to meet!

For the Senate had greater business than to decide the fate of three common felons; for all I know, the clash between the two greatest Romans of all was not Senate business either, but it was certainly on the lips and the minds of the rest of the world. Rome was divided into two factions, that of Pompey and that of Caesar. These men had grown so large that one city, even Rome, could not hold them. It would come, and quickly, to civil war. And it could not help but affect the whole world. I was grown now to womanhood and a measure of wisdom. Like it or not, the world *was* Roman.

These two, Pompey and Caesar, had once been part of a powerful triumvirate, with another man, Crassus; upon the death of Crassus, the two former friends discovered irreconcilable differences, and began to vie with one another for the love of the Roman people. This is putting it all far too simply, but Roman politics are intricate to the point of bewilderment. Rome is not a monarchy, you see, but a so-called republic; every war of policy and power must look as though the people willed it, and the outcome must have the people's sanction. What it boils down to, of course, is that each wishes to have supreme power, though there is no throne for symbol. Every Roman politician longs for this, but these two have a fighting chance, for they have great deeds, good and bad, to their credit.

They are both of them quite elderly men; Caesar must be fifty at least, and Pompey is six years older, yet both are supreme military commanders in the field; Caesar, they say, marches a hundred miles a day, when on campaign. Each of them has incredible victories behind him, and equally incredible brutalities. Pompey, for instance, put down the great slave rebellion that was led by Spartacus; it was a tremendous loss of property, for no slave was given back to his master; all were crucified, a savage death dear to the Romans. It is said they numbered in the thousands. On the other hand, Caesar has massacred a million Gauls and Germans, mostly women and children, to insure his conquests in the Gaulish territories. Though one might say that Pompey saved the civilized world from the threat of rule by slaves, one cannot say much for Caesar; the Gauls were not trying to overrun Rome, it was the other way around.

The lives of these two are entwined, as all high-placed Romans' are, by marriage. Caesar's second wife (he is now on his fourth) was a cousin of Pompey's, and Pompey's last and youngest wife was Julia, Caesar's only child. He was fifty-seven and she was seventeen; she died a year ago in childbirth before she was as old as I am now. Both men were inconsolable, or so it was said, but it did not keep them long from their trade of war; they had been at it ever since.

I cannot help but feel that, of the two, Caesar will prevail; Pompey has given great sums of money to the state, but Caesar has given more lives. The Romans are a young race and love the smell of blood.

6

In the very next year, I fell in love. I was late coming to it; one might have thought me a Vestal Virgin, bound by some vow, or a Moon maid of the Artemis cult, sworn to maidenhood.

The truth is, I had no dreams of love, as other girls had; I dreamed only, when I was solitary and picturing things as they would be some day, of myself seated upon a throne here in Alexandria, but a throne, a city, and a kingdom far vaster than it was, encompassing the world. The throne of Egypt is a double throne, from long ago, but the figure seated beside me was misty always; if it had a face, it was Alexander's. Which is to say, the twin of my own.

The young men of our Greek court were all conscripted into the standing army of Alexandria, under Achillas; they imitated Romans and spoke bad Latin; I thought them boors. The Roman students imitated Greeks; I thought them effeminate (of course, they were not; look at poor Cleito's plight!). I was fond of my Gaulish guards, but in those early days I thought them less than human. Of Romans, I had met only three, the unprepossessing sons of Bibulus, murdered now, and that Marcus Antonius who had preferred Arsinoëe. I was not prepared for Neo, the son of Pompey. Neo, the aristocrat, Neo the athlete, scholar, poet. . . . Neo, the image of a god.

For that is how he seemed to me when I first saw him, standing at the rail of the trireme with two others, laughing, the sun full on him, for it was almost noon. He could not see me, though the ship was right in to shore; I was hidden behind a tent of striped canvas, and looked through a chink in its wall. Perhaps that is how it happened; I have always been looked at before. I took a good long look before I let Iras put her eye to the chink after me.

We had been bathing behind the tent; now it had been drawn up onto the sands and we were wrapped well against the sunlight, drying our hair. We wore great-brimmed hats, crownless, and had drawn our hair through the hats' opening and spread it out to dry quickly and bleach a little in the sun. Iras did not need it, and no sun would ever make mine his golden shade.

I had thought all Romans dark, and his two companions had hair like crows' wings, but he who leaned lightly at the rail of the Roman ship was as fair as a Greek. It was hot, and the tunic he wore left his arms and legs bare. It was dyed a color like amber and a bright dagger hung from his belt; even from our little distance I could see a thin gold circlet on his head, darker than his hair, a sign of some nobility, though he wore no jewels. He looked dipped in gold; a trick of the light I thought it, but he looked so always.

He was presented to me officially that evening in the great hall; by then I had heard his name. Gneus Pompey, and his rank, Commander of the Twelfth Legion of the Adriatic. He bowed over my hand; when he looked up, his eyes met mine and widened. They were a light color, like the misty sky in the rainy season, more gray than blue.

He leaned closer, speaking low. "I had heard the people of Egypt worshiped cats," he said, his lips curving ever so little, "but I had not heard their queen had cat eyes."

It was a presumptuous remark, for anyone but a Roman. I kept my eyes upon him, but withdrew my hand, for it trembled. "The cats of Egypt are not worshiped for their eyes," I said coolly. "Nor is their queen."

The curve of his lips spread into a smile, showing very white teeth; truly, there was no end to his beauty! "Worshiped?" he asked. He had a runaway eyebrow, which flared high; it was the only oddness in his face.

"The queen of Egypt is goddess-on-earth," I said.

"But you are Greek," he answered, still speaking softly, and to me alone, another presumption. "You are Greek, of the blood of Alexander. We are kin, you and I. Am I then a god?"

My heart gave a small leap, but I said, in level tones, and shrugging, "Philip of Macedon had many bastards . . ."

"I am descended from the distaff side . . . my mother was in the direct line of Olympias of Epiros."

"Alexander's mother," I said. No wonder that he had the Greek look!

"So you see, I can claim a little godhead, too . . . Olympias counted Achilles her forefather."

I was dismayed, though I think I did not show it. I had not thought before how Alexander came by *his* god-claim. Of course, it was all quite silly, in our day and age; we know now that the god-tales were only tales. Still, one would like to be in the proper line, just in case.

I shrugged again, and spoke, raising my voice a little. "And your mother?"

"She had a Roman name—Mucia. But the family was pure Greek. Father married her for her bloodline." He laughed. "It only shows in me. . . . My brothers and sisters are all proper little Latins."

I had heard the gossip about his mother; his home life, like all Romans', was as vicious as my own. I did not continue the conversation, from decency; besides, we had been talking too long; there was an uncomfortable silence around us. I motioned him to sit, on my left. My brother, Ptolemy, was on my right, for this counted as a state occasion; Pothinus sat next to him, and Theodotus the rhetorician beyond. I sighed, remembering all the speeches to come, and signaled for the meal to begin. At least, I thought, we can have the first course and a little wine to fortify us, before Theodotus begins!

A dish of lampreys was set before us, with the wine. I took up the glass and sipped, so that the others could follow; besides, I needed it, for my mouth was dry. I saw he did not touch the nasty lampreys either. I said in a whisper, "Mussels are next."

"I rather hoped as much," he whispered back. I glanced sideways at him, and smiled.

"I warn you," I whispered, "Egyptian banquets go on forever."

"So do Roman," he said. "For all I know it is the same the world over . . ."

Theodotus rose; he cleared his throat, and began, a long, rambling speech about Pompey's career; it was far from dull, but he made it seem so. He had not yet gotten to the point, which was of course, to welcome Pompey's son, when the mussels were brought in. Gneus Pompey leaned toward me. "Is it permitted to eat during . . . ?"

"The queen does," I said, digging out a mussel from its shell.

I had not spent, ever, a more pleasant banquet time; I had never really dared, queen that I was, to be openly rude to that bore, Theodotus. Now I wondered why, for it came so easily, like breathing. When his windy speech finally ended, it was to scattered applause, and I heard Gneus Pompey's name. He rose.

We had gotten to the lamb, always a little greasy; he made the company wait while he dipped his fingers into the bowl of water which sat before him. Then he straightened up, smiling and easy, and made some offhand compliment to the rhetorician, bringing his hands together in a signal for more applause. When it was finished, he addressed each dignitary in turn, ending up with a flourish and a low bow to my brother-Pharaoh and a hand laid over his heart as he turned to me. His words were few; he did not state his business, saying that it was with the legions of Gabinius, Roman business. Something turned over in my chest; I remembered that other Roman business, with those very same legions. My voice was hoarse as I gave orders for the company to be at ease.

No one else seemed to have taken notice; there was a general movement as the diners rose to stretch their legs and gather in groups about the room, while the slaves took away the chairs of state and brought in couches before the last course and the dessert wines.

Gneus walked beside me to the great window that looked out upon the gardens; it was open to the evening and a little breeze stirred the hangings. "Will you walk with me, Lady," he said. "The gardens look cool . . ." I turned to glance once over my shoulder. Between the scurrying slaves I caught a climpse of Pothinus, staring, his heavy eyes fixed on Gneus.

When we were out of earshot I spoke, a little breathlessly. "I beg you—do not place yourself at the mercy of those legions—you do not know—"

"I do," he said, smiling grimly. "I know the fate of the sons of Bibulus. I know how lax soldiers become without discipline—especially mercenaries. My errand, though, is more to their liking . . . I come to conscript them for my father—against Julius Caesar."

"I think," I said, slowly, "I think they will not like it at all . . . they are well off here in Alexandria. Why should they fight for one Roman against another? Is this Julius then so hated?"

"Far from it!" he said. "He is the darling of all the soldiers—everywhere . . . the gods know why! Still, they will come with me. Some of them will come. Father has authorized me to promise citizenship for every man who follows his banner."

I stared at him. "Why should they care?"

The smile died on his lips. "There is no soldier who would not give his sword arm for Roman citizenship!" I bit my lip; truly, Greek mother or not, these Romans are all alike!

I said, mildly, "What if he does not win—your father?"

"Well, life is a hazard, after all. . . . They are dice players, all of them. Besides, he *will* win."

I said nothing, not wishing to offend. We walked in silence toward the hall; I did not want brows raised at our absence.

"Well," I said, before we reached the window, "it will probably fall out as you say. As long as you surround yourself with plenty of guards . . ."

"Oh, no!" he said. "They will hate a show of force—"

I took his hand, heedless of the eyes in the hall. "Look," I whispered. "You do not know Pothinus. He is perfectly capable of placing his own soldiers among them—to do you harm . . . he is greedy for power. I think he may have had something to do with the other time, the murders, though I have no proof . . ."

His eyes narrowed. "Yes," he said slowly. "So my father thinks. The little Ptolemy—your brother—can he be got alone?"

"Well," I said, frowning a little. "He likes to go fishing . . ."

"Good," he said. "Arrange it for tomorrow."

"I will have to come too," I said, "and my escort of Gauls . . ."

"I was counting on it," he said, flashing a smile. I felt myself flush, and nodded. Then I went inside, taking my leave of him and joining Iras on a low couch. Her eyes were very bright, with a question in each one. For once I told her nothing, and talked of other things.

7

THE BEST TIME TO FISH is early morning, and the best place, the Marcotic Lake. Our little Mouse was excited to the point of running a fever, for, like his sister-queen, he was dazzled by the golden Roman. He woke me while it was still dark; I was cross, for it was an hour when even the gods do not stir; besides I had tossed long in the night before sleep finally came.

"Well, since you are here," I said, rubbing my eyes, "let us at least have some breakfast." And I sent Iras, yawning, too, to fetch something from the kitchens. She brought back a melon and some bread from last night's baking, with honey and wine. He shook his head. "I am not hungry."

"That's nothing new," I said, biting into a slice of melon. "The gods know how you have grown even this far—" I glanced at him, seeing that indeed he *had* grown in this last year. He was of a height with Iras now, though he was still skinny as a worm. Poor Mouse, I thought, you do not make much of a Pharaoh, even for our worn-out house. His nose was more pointed than ever, and he had an irritating habit of blinking his eyes each second. Perhaps there was something wrong with them; I should have to speak to the doctors. With all of Pothinus' watching and guiding, he did little for the boy in the way of common care. I finished the melon and took a piece of bread.

"Oh, Clee-clee," he wailed, calling me by my baby-name. I drew back my hand as if to smack him, and scowled; I meant it for a joke, but he cringed like a cur-dog that has been kicked. My hand itched to clout him in earnest, but I only said, "What is the matter with you? When did I ever hit you?"

"Lots of times," he said, nodding sagely. "Before you were queen."

I stopped chewing and thought. "Never," I said. "You are thinking of Arsinoëe."

"Oh, her," he said. "She doesn't count."

Well, that was true anyway. I looked at him again; I

thought he had a funny look, like a cat full of goat curds. "Did Pothinus say anything about Arsinoëe?"

He wiped the look off, and just looked stupid, as usual. "No . . . just that I ought to act like a king, because I *am* one now."

"Well," I said. "Even a king has to eat. And we go nowhere until you do." I pushed the plate toward him. "I'm going to dress," I said. I went through into the little dressingroom, beckoning for Iras to come and help me. As I slipped out of my nightrobe, I called to him, "And don't dump the plate out the window—I will know if you do!"

"You have eyes that can see through walls, I suppose," he said, in a fretful voice.

"Yes." There was silence after that, and when I came out I saw the plate was lighter and there were crumbs on his chin.

"Can I have my wine now?" His voice was sulky.

"I'll pour it," I said, taking up a small glass. He was rationed, because of Father. He scowled at the glass when I handed it to him, and drank it down in one gulp.

"You're greedy enough when it comes to that," I said. "All right, let's go." It was light enough now to snuff out the candles; the dawn had come and gone while we bickered; I thought it a pity to miss it, and was cross all over again. "Get moving, silly," I said, pushing him.

"You're not going like that?" he said, staring at me.

My legs were bare under a short boy's tunic, and I had tied my hair at my neck against the wind. "Should I wear court dress to dip a fishing rod?"

He grinned. "He won't think much of you, the Roman."

I shrugged. Nonetheless, I felt a little pang of doubt. I had thought the look became me, being slim.

I need not have worried. Gneus Pompey, shining from his morning shave, straightened up from the gear he was stowing into a little pack, "How wonderful you look—like Diana! All that is missing are the bow and arrows . . ."

We had met in the place I assigned, a little courtyard that faced away from the sea, toward the town. "It is not very far, our fishing place," I said. "Chariots will rouse the whole town . . . do you mind if we walk? Xeno will carry our things . . ."

Xeno was a Nubian slave, a powerful man with glistening blue-black skin, gentle eyes, and the bearing of an emperor; his soft tread had been part of the royal nursery's life since I could remember. He, with my Gauls, and Ptolemy's own escort, made up our party; still, it was a small one, for royalty. Apollodorus was not with us, nor Iras, though I knew she had wanted to come; we should have to hire a sizable boat as it was. Besides, she was too pretty.

It was an odd feeling to be abroad at this young hour; our sandals made soft, lonely sounds in the empty streets; doorways and corners seemed to wait for us and watch us as we passed. It was not until we came to the Street of the Weavers that we found folk up and about; I knew that the looms clacked all night, for when I was wakeful I had heard them, under the slosh of the waves. A new shift of workers was just taking its place, settling to the job, tying the linen threads, some of them had brought their breakfasts in oiled parchment wrappings; there was a smell, strong, of dried fish and sharp, bitter wine.

Gneus turned back to me, from where he walked beside my brother. "I love your city," he said. I knew he meant it, for liveliness danced in his eyes.

"You have seen less than nothing," I answered. "It is sleeping still, and we have taken a shortcut. Wait."

I tried to see it with his stranger's eyes, the bright-colored woven goods spread out, the low wordless buzz of voices not quite heard, a glimpse of the Street of the Potters, round shapes and the whir of the first wheel beginning, and the Market beyond, smelling wonderfully of roasting meat and hot bread.

The Market Street was in the Phoenician quarter; here the city was wide awake; these people are always the first up, to catch the breakfast trade. Small, dark, and lively, with clever eyes and talking hands, one would think they never slept at all!

At the fruit stall, I shook my head slightly at the round-armed merchant wife, indicating that I did not want attention brought to me; she gave a great slow wink after she ran her eyes over Gneus. I flushed; it was just that I did not want to be bowed to, but how to explain? I yanked Mouse forward, bidding him choose from her wares. "It is your Pharaoh," I hissed, "but keep it under your apron." I hoped that would make matters clear; at least there would not be street gossip to come to the ears of the court vultures!

I saw that Gneus looked about him with a lively interest. There were runners from the ships in harbor, bargaining for their breakfasts and going back to their fellows, laden with the hot breads and smoked fish and steaming meats. One fellow lost the tray he bore on top of his head, colliding with one of the swarming children that ran in and out at knee level, the hot food spilling over the street and the children snatching it and running. Of course, an argument ensued; I threw a Roman denarius onto a counter, saying, "Work it out among yourselves—call it a gift of the state, but be quiet about it. . . ." I turned on my brother, who was dawdling, as usual. "Hurry, Mouse . . . make up your mind . . ." He got flustered, and ended up buying all the fruit on the stall; I clucked my tongue impatiently. Gneus smiled. "I will take care of the rest," he said. "We must have some of everything. All these strange foods smell wonderful." After a bit, poor Xeno was laden with foodstuffs; we would never eat it all. Gneus threw down another denarius; the whole market could close for the day on our largesse!

It was only a step or so from Market Street to the lake's edge. I was glad now that we had had an early start, for the city was beginning to stir in earnest. Freedmen emerged from their tenement dwellings, carrying their bedrolls, stopping at the stalls to sip wine and make a quick meal before beginning their day's business.

Gneus stopped in his tracks to stare after one of these, rubbing his chin and looking puzzled. "So many rug sellers," he said. "Is this the main occupation of Alexandria?"

I laughed. "They are not rug sellers," I said. "This is not the quarter for it. But most Alexandrians carry their belongings so—inside a rug . . . the rug is their sleeping mat, you see."

"But why do they carry them about? I should have thought they would leave them home."

"Well," I said, patiently, "most of these people have no fixed dwellings, but bed down where they find themselves, sometimes in a different house each night. They rent space from a tenement family . . . that way they have no worries . . . and the families profit. And those who have paid their rent a week or a month ahead—well, it is not safe to leave valuables, for the doors are not guarded, you see . . ."

"Ah," he said. "It is not so different, then, from Rome. We have magistrates, of course, to deal with robbery and disputes . . ."

"Here, I am the magistrate," I said, with as haughty a

look as I could command. I thought his lip twitched, but he said no more; truly, it *was* a sorry duty for a queen!

A big fellow crossed our path, carrying over one shoulder a huge rolled-up carpet, tied tightly with rope. Gneus laughed, saying, "That one might be carrying the bed of a large family—or perhaps he is smuggling a spy! There is plenty of room for a good-sized person inside his roll . . ." It was true, but of course there was no one inside; one could see the linen and the blankets through the open end; I looked, just in case. I saw Gneus had noticed and was smiling at me.

"Well," I said. "You never know . . . Pothinus just might. . . ."

"Which reminds me," he said. "I must neglect the lovely queen of Egypt for her not-so-lovely brother. A matter of policy . . . forgive me in advance."

It was true; after we hired our boat and pushed out into the lake's center, I was left alone, while he sat beside Mouse, his head close, his hands busy with their fishing rods and lines. Over and over I heard Mouse laugh, a pleased sound; I had seldom heard it before from this peevish boy. It was rank flattery, of course, and I was surprised that Mouse did not see through it, but he did not; he was not the cleverest of children, Pharaoh or not.

In the end, we had decided to take only Xeno in the boat, leaving the escort of soldiers on shore; after all, we were in full sight, and the only boat, for it was not a holiday. While the oddly matched pair, golden and drab, sat together on one side, whispering gruff man-talk, or what passed for it, I lolled upon the cushions under the canopy, idly trailing my hand in the cool water; Xeno, with my line, caught a bucketful of red and yellow fish to their three, for of course they were far too noisy. After a bit, I regretted not bringing Iras; at least I might have had some company and conversation!

The sun rose, beating straight down; finally they were forced to give over, creeping under the canopy into the cool. I saw with a little malice that the Roman's snow-white tunic was dark with sweat where it touched against his flesh. Ptolemy, of course, was sunburned, and would peel later, for he had left off his wide straw hat, in imitation of Gneus.

"Oh, you have caught so many!" cried the Roman.

"Mine are bigger," said Ptolemy. It was not even true,

but we kept silent. "Even though we were talking secrets," Mouse finished, smugly. Gneus winked at me; I cast down my eyes, trying not to smile.

I had set Xeno to laying out our foodstuffs, and pouring wine and native beer; he stood above the table and fanned with a huge palm leaf to keep off the buzzing bluebottle flies. These were the curse of lake waters, rising in a cloud and clinging, to madden one.

Suddenly Gneus bent down and grabbed a fish, still squirming, from the bucket; his smooth face was tight with a small fury, and the knife from his belt flashed as he slit the fish's belly and threw it overside. It landed some yards away, the guts showing like a nest of silver worms for a moment, then covered, black, with flies. "That's what we do on campaign," he said, showing his white teeth.

"It is a Roman trick," I said, for the sight had disgusted me.

"No matter," he said, shrugging. "It works."

And so it did; our flies had left us. I signed to Xeno that he might put down his fan and take some food. Ptolemy ate without urging, a thing I had never seen before; however, he drank to wash it down, mixing wine and beer, unwatered, and fell asleep. I was glad, for I took his place at the rail and had a fishing lesson of my own, Roman-style. I caught few fish, it is true, but I learned the proper way to handle the line, hand against hand, firm and guiding, and skin brushing skin with fire.

He told me he would take Ptolemy with him to the Gabinian barracks, as hostage, and keep him close. I answered that it was a good move; the eunuch Pothinus would not dare anything that might harm Ptolemy, for he needed him as tool. We spoke low, in Latin; it is a cold tongue, suited to law and intrigue; beneath our words, eyes and hands spoke the wilder language of love.

8

PTOLEMY, CHARMED, ACCOMPANIED Pompey's son on his Gabinian errand; it was successful, and perhaps little Mouse was not even needed. From the account I heard, those rough troops treated my little brother as a kind of mascot, that is to say, with a mixture of scorn and indulgence. He did not know this, of course, but thought of himself as a sort of honorary captain, and put on airs, afterwards. He also prided himself on his manly friendship with the beautiful Roman; it was difficult to get rid of him, for he never took a hint. Gneus and I were forced to complicated plottings, just to be alone for a bit.

I say Gneus, but no one ever called him that; I thought that Neo was an intimate nickname, for me alone, but no—one heard it from the lowest soldier. He was the sort of person whose name would be inevitably shortened; there was a kind of easy open quality about him which I, for instance, do not have. Except for that baby Clee-clee of my brother's, I have always been given my full name, though it is long. It is no good regretting this; one can only be oneself.

The Gabinian troops were roused to follow him; there were five hundred volunteers, nearly half the garrison, and he was promised, as well, fifty warships. He spent a great deal of time with these legions, waiting for these ships to be fitted out and watching the work in progress there in the harbor. Often I went with him; it was fascinating to see the great battering rams and catapults being fitted to the decks, and the tiers of oars go up. For the most part, there were three galley levels, one above the other, where the rowers sat, but the larger of the ships had a layer or two more, for speed. These places were manned nowadays by slaves, for sailors refused the job; if a ship hit, he explained, it was death for the rowers, packed closely as they were. "Slaves are expendable," he said. A typically Roman thought, for surely slaves are a country's wealth, and should be cared for.

I said as much, with a certain scorn and sense of superiority. One expects brutality from Rome, of course, though I did not say so. But, "Surely it is not sensible to so endanger property . . ." I finished.

"Oh, well," he answered, "these are condemned criminals . . . property of the state, yes, I suppose. But still, they must be fed and clothed . . ."

I said nothing; the poor wretches that I had seen wore a filthy strip of rag at their loins and their ribs stood out in bony arches above. "It is another sign of progress," he said. "Another country, less humane, would put its felons to death without mercy—"

"But Rome puts them to work," I said, thoughtfully. "Yes, progress. I see."

He glanced at me sharply, but said nothing. I did not pursue the thought; he would never see things my way, no Roman could. Besides, I did not want to quarrel with him; far from it!

It was difficult to be alone, though we managed, with the help of Iras; she was thrilled at my love-adventure, and I knew her faithful even to death. Late at night, when all the household slept, she opened my chamber door to him, and stayed awake on guard, like a true love soldier. Though we kissed and caressed till dawn—all manner of love tokens exchanged from body to body—still I kept my maidenhead. Even in a slave it puts up the price; for a highborn damsel it is an invaluable asset of bargaining power; for a queen it is more. It is a weapon. He understood this as well as I; his political shrewdness almost matched my own. We spoke of marriage, between us—coldly, after the nights' enchantments. I thought we might agree well, and make a good match; his lineage, though not royal, was as noble, truly, as my own. He said, looking wiser than his youth allowed, that all depended upon the outcome of the civil strife in Rome. If his father won, and I saw he was not nearly so certain as he had said at first, it might be arranged; Pompey would not be averse to have a son upon the double throne of Egypt—who would? And the alliance would strengthen me against my brothers and my sister and their minions. Nor would Rome frown upon it; that city is aching to worship something. A republic is a hard line to stick to; people in the mass love to bow before an image; now the poor Romans have nothing but the golden eagles of the legions!

We plotted nothing, Neo and I, though later we were accused of it; we dreamed, that is all. And we were in love. Or at least I was. He was the first man whose hands and lips I knew; the first man's body, lean and hard, that I had felt, meltingly, against my own. He was never out of my thoughts, Neo, in those days. Somewhere, deep inside, he was present always, like a grace put on me by some god, so that I knew I truly lived. Sometimes, now and again, I feel it still—after so long.

It was over soon, so soon. There was haste, for the war was brewing, and the troops and ships were needed. We said our good-byes secretly, the night before, a kiss between each broken word.

He gave me to understand that the legions of Gabinius were mine. "They have given their Roman word," he said, and I did not smile, for love of him. "If you have need, show this—and they will follow you." He pressed a small medallion into my hand, a poor thing, of some old dented metal, iron perhaps; graven on it was an eagle, crude as the scratching of a child, and words in a language I did not know. "It is one of the earliest symbols of the Roman state," he said. "They cannot read the Etruscan either—but they will all know it. You will have an army when I am gone. Malbius—he is your man—the captain over a hundred. See that it gets to him—promise me." I nodded, but I did not know that I would ever really need it, or so soon.

I watched him go in the morning, by sea, as he had come. I stood beside my little brothers, and my ripe sister, and sweet Iras, and I stood straight and tall like a statue. I have been taught. He was in full armor, brazen, and the sun loved him as it had before.

I watched while all the fifty ships pulled anchor, each with its own salute, deafening. His was the last, and it was high noon, as it had been that first day when I looked through the chink of a tent. He blazed golden, even after the sails of the ship had disappeared, a pinpoint of light, like a daytime star. I held my eyes wide open and kept them dry. I never saw him again.

9

THE NEXT YEAR I WAS TWENTY-ONE, and made into a goddess in truth. It is not a joyous thought; purest necessity forced the hands of the Alexandrian vulture-nobles. For the crops of fertile Egypt failed, disastrously. They blamed me, as I had given Neo all our spare corn for his troopships. But of course this had nothing at all to do with it.

Egypt is rich for one reason and one only: the Nile. This river, each year, in some mysterious manner, rises and inundates the land about it. What would have been a desert becomes a paradise, and all things grow in abundance, unbounded. Some years the river rises as much as thirty feet—never in living memory less than twenty. I had marked a slight decrease each of the past few years, when the priests of the Nile temples reported to me. This year the rise was recorded at eight feet only; it might as well not have risen at all! The land was bone dry; the people starved and died; famine reigned along its banks; the skeletons of oxen, antelope, and men were found, picked clean by the hundred buzzards, in the shallow mud that lined the river.

I sat in council; the Nile priests came to me, bowing low. Their spokesman, a venerable ancient, thin as one of this year's Nile bones but with black eyes burning in his brown holy face, said the sacred bull of the Nile had died, and that the river mourned and would not rise till another god was ordained. They had chosen the successor, a white bull, born at Hermonthis in Upper Egypt. In this animal lived the soul of the sun-god, Amon-Ra; until I, as the living Isis, the Mother-god, escorted my new son (the bull) by barge to his holy temple, the Nile would not rise.

I did not smile; I am not a fool. I bowed my head for a moment; then I spoke, in the Old Egyptian which none of the Ptolemaic rulers except me have bothered to learn; I saw he revered me for it, the Old One. As well he might; it is a difficult language

I said I must consult my husband, Osiris. The gentle, burning eyes smiled. He took it to mean my brother-king, poor Mouse. But of course it was Alexander I meant.

I went to his tomb alone, with my Gaulish watch posted above the cellar doorway. I did not hope for a sign from the dead; as I have said before, I am not a fool. But I needed time. I needed solitude, which no ruler has without much guile. I stayed above an hour, in a silence broken only by my own breathing, and gazed at that still face behind the alabaster, so like my own. I came to my conclusion then; it was right and it was wrong, as all such mortal decisions are.

I was a Greek, with all the inbred intelligence and reason of that great race of men; the idea of impersonating a bull's mother, however white and sacred, was distasteful to me. But I was queen of these people, and I was needed by them, and in their own way, or it would not help. I decided to do this thing, to dress in the robes of Old Egypt, the goddess-garb, not unmindful of the fact that I was almost the only Greek slender enough to look well in those scant, transparent shifts of the wall paintings, virginal enough to bare my breasts, and strong-featured enough to not be lost beneath the heavy ceremonial wig. I would show myself to these of my subjects that as yet I did not know; I would be queen as none of our line had yet been ruler; all Egypt would be mine. As I looked at Alexander's face, I fancied the full lip curved, ever so little, as did my own.

My other thoughts were thoughts of policy, which no queen can be without, ever. I could not take Mouse, as Osiris; this was a thing between the bull-god and his mother. Like Neo, I knew Mouse was my best hostage for safety. I could take my Gaulish guards, for I could tell the priests they were my body slaves. I could take, as well, all my high-born Greek waiting women; surely all of them together, with their powerful family backgrounds, would serve as well as the one hostage I could not have. It was a woman rite, you see; this posed a problem for me. Apollodorus could go, for he was a proven celibate. I would take Iras, of course. I would take, and here I smiled in triumph, Arsinoëe as well; without her, Ganymede was powerless to harm me and my kingdom. Also, I knew I could count on him to keep an eye on his power rivals, the faction of Pothinus. They would cancel each other out. I decided to go.

In Old Egyptian I informed the priests. Tears rolled down their thin brown faces. "Egypt is saved!" they cried softly, "Egypt is saved for another thousand years!"

We went upriver by our own galley-powered boats; it did not take long, but each day grew hotter, and each day the heat took a little more life from our poor Alexandrian-bred bodies. I wondered, truly, how these people, my subjects, had survived. The sun was merciless, the dark brown Nile waters reflecting it with fierce intensity; at times I thought I might die, though we lay beneath canvas tents and fans moved above us all day long. At night the cold leapt like a wild beast and we wrapped ourselves in the skins of lions and leopards; it is a land of contrasts, my Egypt.

At Hermonthis I was formally introduced to my son, the white bull; his name was Buchis, a ritual name handed down from generation to generation of his kind. He was young, and his legs were spindly, but his horns were beginning to sprout already, and he had a wicked eye, red-rimmed and rolling. I had been instructed to give him my hand to kiss, smeared with a little honey. Perhaps honey is an aphrodisiac to the bull kind, or maybe he liked my smell, for he tried to rape me. He only got at my leg, before the attendants pulled him away, bellowing sadly. But the temple priests and worshipers raised soft cooing voices all around; they considered it a good omen.

We traveled by barge down the Nile to Thebes, where my holy son would live out his days. It was slow, so slow; we were forty barges in all, filled with all the Hermonthian and Theban dignitaries, and a few from Cairo as well. Mine was the royal barge, over a thousand years old, and looking it, under the gold paint. I had to stand the whole of the way; it is the ancient custom, and no awning either. I was covered thick with paint, so I did not burn in the sun, and my black wig was heavy enough to protect the brain beneath. They had built a contraption, like a slightly slanting board, against which I leaned, or I could never have done it at all; that too was ritual, so I was not the only mortal among the dead immortals who had made this trip before me. The bull was tethered firmly by each thin leg, and perhaps a little drugged as well, for he never turned his head or his lewd thoughts toward me. Maybe the drug loosened his bowels, or he had worms, as young animals sometimes do; he defecated constantly. Though I heard Iras, somewhere behind me, giggle, no one else seemed to notice, and the slaves silently shoveled it over the side into the Nile. My Gauls and Germans knelt behind me, and they were quietly merry, repeating one word over and over, low. It was a short word, and no one understood it anyway except me; I do not know how to write it, but it sounds something like "shet." I knew what it meant all right, but I kept a straight face, for I had to. The smell, though, was awful, in the heat.

I looked beautiful, truly; nearly naked I was, and the Alexandrians would have been horrified, but here it was expected and I felt no shame. Iras was just as beautiful, of course, and some of my other damsels as well, but they were all kneeling with heads bowed and no one looked at them. Arsinoëe fared worse, for she is overfat, to the Roman taste or the Oriental; I thought of her once or twice with malice, for the boat was a bore, no question.

My subjects, the fellahim and their women and little ones, lined the river, thick as the black plague-flies of our land. I was forbidden to turn my head, but under the green antimony of my lids I stole glances from side to side, observing them. Zeus, they were thin, so thin! Each bone showed clear and the heads looked over-large, like babies' heads; my heart wept for them, for I thought of them as my own. I made a vow that they should never again suffer so in my time as queen; I have even kept it, or nearly.

They are a delicate and lovely people, never mind their starved looks. I had thought the paintings on the old walls idealizations, but they were not. I saw, there on the banks of the Nile, those wide serene brows, taut cheekbones, and lips like firm small cushions; the color a golden brown like polished wood. They are small of stature, like ten-year-olds among Greeks, and grace moves in them as it moves in flowers.

I grew to love these people, for their beauty and their ancient wisdom; they loved me, too, because I wore their goddess guise and could speak their tongue and read and write their picture language. Before I went from them, the ceremony being over and the bull-god enthroned, the old priest came to me with a token not unlike the one that Neo had given me; it was a scarab, gilded but tarnished now with age. He said in his thin old voice that when I showed it to any of my Egyptian subjects, no matter where or when, they would get help to me when needed. It was a true thing he said, and I have used it more than once. It has never failed me.

10

I WAS NOT IN UPPER EGYPT more than a month, but, in some strange and subtle way I sensed a change in Alexandria. I put it down at first to the climate, so perfect and flowering, after the dry reaches of the dead Nile valley, or to the people, so varied, so richly attired, so sleek with oil and honey and grain. But it was not that; there was a charged feeling, a kind of shimmer within the Palace walls, as one sometimes feels before a storm breaks.

Iras did not notice it, though she bemoaned the lack of slaves about the house. "Oh, well," I said, "when the cats are away, the mice will play . . ." It was an old saying of some dullard, Hesiod, maybe, and I knew it was not answer enough. For what she said was true; there were barely enough servants to wait upon us, almost as it had been in my father's time. The only worrisome thing, to my mind, was that Xeno, the faithful black presence of my nursery days, could not be found.

"Slaves do sometimes run away," said Apollodorus, that gentle soul.

"Not Xeno," I said, shaking my head. "He loved me." I questioned everyone, and sent runners throughout the city, into all the foreign quarters, but they found no trace. Arsinoëe shrugged. "It is only a black slave," she said.

But she turned her great dark eyes on me with hate. "It is your fault," she said. "Something is wrong, I feel it . . . it is your fault for going—to be worshiped. Your fault for taking me away . . . O Zeus—what shall I do? Pothinus' eyes . . ." And she shivered, and fell to weeping and wringing her hands.

I had not noticed Pothinus' eyes, and began to shake her.

"What of Pothinus' eyes? What is it you know?"

"Nothing . . ." she wailed. "It is just a feeling . . ." Well, I had it too, the feeling, so I stopped shaking her and said, cruelly, "Go ask your lover. Ask Ganymede."

I guess she did, but events shaped so quickly I never heard the answer, nor thought of her or her minion; for all I know, the two of them disappeared that very day.

To me, Pothinus' eyes looked much as usual, hooded and evil; Mouse, though, had a cat-look, smug, and a honey-sweet way, unlike him, kissing my cheek and calling me pretty names.

I got hold of Theodotus, for though I did not trust him, he was always polite. "Where are all the servants?" I asked.

"Oh, Lady, dear," he answered, his rheumy eyes looking grave, "we have had to dispatch them to fetch and carry for the army . . ."

"The army?"

"Achillas' troops are posted all along the seacoast, and guarding the gates as well."

"What—has the war worsened? Are we in it? Why was I not informed?" I grew angry.

"Caesar is on the march, dear lady."

"But he will not come here, you dolt!" I cried. "He is on the march toward Pompey. All the world knows that! They will probably do battle at Pharsalia—half a world away!"

He shrugged. "Well, dear lady, one never knows. We must be prepared for anything . . ."

Anything, I thought. My head was whirring, clicking, counting up, adding. I saw I frightened him with the look of my face, and smiled within, silently. I stared at him a moment, then I pounced. "And Xeno? Have they given Xeno to the army as well? He is a Palace man, my own, and nothing to do with the State."

His jowls shook and he turned his head from side to side, quickly. "I know nothing of Xeno . . . nothing!" I stared again, seeing that truly he *did* know something. I measured him, cold, while the beads of sweat formed slowly and slowly ran down his face.

I spoke, finally. "I could put you to death. I am queen, and there are enough here still to do my bidding." It was not really true, of course, but he was not man enough to answer me, and fear stood in his weak old face. "Well, I will spare you for your ancient days. But keep out of my sight from this day on." He backed out of my presence. It was a good feeling. But underneath, I knew myself in deadly peril—from something.

On an early morning, two of my Gauls found Xeno, outside a little-used gate of one of the small Palace gardens; he had been dumped there to live or die; it was just above one of the old army dungeons. In truth, when they brought him to me, I could not see how he could survive, he had been used so evilly. I knew it for Pothinus' work, or Achillas', and cursed myself that I had not taken him with me. By old law the testimony of a slave may be obtained by torture; he was an intimate of the Palace and all those close to me, and I should have thought of it.

I am not familiar with instruments of torture; with all our faults the House of the Ptolemies has been free of such cruelties. He had deep burn marks all over his body, raw and bleeding, and his joints were swollen to twice their size and discolored; one foot was mangled to a pulpy mass. I sent for the doctors; after they felt him over gently they said the bones were still unbroken, but that much muscle and tissue had been ruined; he might be lamed. They put a draught of something strong to his lips to rouse him; his tongue had been cut out! I had been calm up to then, though my insides were crawling; now I burst into a storm of weeping.

Poor Xeno! He must have the strength of Hercules, for

he roused and, distressed at my weeping, made feeble passes in the air with his hand. I stared; of course! He wanted a stylus or a pen; he had been taught to write, long ago, when it was seen that he had intelligence above the ordinary sort. And so they had ruined a human being for nothing, those beastly men; he could tell us everything, after all.

The first words he wrote, poor hen-scratchings they looked, he was so weak, were "Eat nothing untasted . . ." The flesh on my scalp crept cold under my hair; they meant to poison me!

"He must rest now," said Dioscorides, the doctor, "or he may not come through at all . . . a few hours, and he will be strong enough to write it all."

Xeno slept heavily, but breathing well; it was juice of poppy, unwatered, that they gave him. They bathed his many wounds and put healing balms upon them, and packed snow from the mountains, worth its weight in gold, about his swollen parts. The poor crushed foot Dioscorides tended himself, handling it as if it were clay, pushing it back into a foot shape, and then encasing it in a true clay and hardening it with fire; it was to form a sort of mold and hold the foot in place. "He will have to wear it a week or two," he said, as he worked. "Then, I believe, it will be a foot he can use again, with only a little limp." Truly, our Alexandrian doctors can work wonders! Of course, Xeno will never speak again; that is beyond any skill yet learned.

When he woke, he was much refreshed; they gave him broth and bits of bread softened in wine. He wrote it all out for us upon a wax tablet. He did not describe his tortures; he had a great soul. He swore, though, by his own strange gods, that he had told them nothing. ". . . not out of bravery," he wrote, "but that I knew nothing. I knew no plots . . ." But I think, truly, that most people, not just slaves, would have babbled out anything that came to mind to escape the torture. "You *are* brave, Xeno," I said. "Brave as a king . . ." A little ghost of a smile played on his swollen lips; perhaps he *had* been a king, among his own tribe, when he was taken and sold away into bondage. Or perhaps not; there are those who are natural rulers and never see a throne.

It was Achillas' men who had taken him and thrown him into the cellars, chained, and Pothinus who did the questioning, day after day. "Who did the torture?" I asked. But he shook his head and would not write it. Never mind, they were all party to it, and would die for it, all three, in time; I swore this to myself, silently.

They questioned him in barracks-Latin, but spoke among themselves in Greek, their plots and plans, how they would rid themselves of me and take the throne for Mouse, whom they could rule. They had not thought Xeno to have knowledge of Greek, but he must have shown something in his eyes, or cried out in pain, a Greek word, for they took his tongue. Naturally they would not know that he could write.

He did not know when they meant to get rid of me, or by what poisoned food, but poison it would be, a kind that would look like a natural death. "Flee, Lady . . . and quickly. And have all food and drink tasted before you touch it . . ."

It was a dreadful time, for I could not simply run away, mindlessly; I had to plan every step. The danger of the poisoning was very real; this was certain. Dioscorides suggested we test our food upon a slave, but I was horrified and would not hear of it. "There are certain felons condemned to death and awaiting it, in the prisons," said Apollodorus. "For them it would be a mercy killing, compared to what they can expect from Court justice." But there was no access to them, for the prisons were guarded by Achillas' men.

"Can we not use an animal," I said. "A dog, perhaps?"

Dioscorides rubbed his chin and thought. "The dosage is different . . . but if the dog died—yes, surely we could count it poison. Yes . . . it will do."

One of the Gauls, Longinus by name, brought his own pet hound, a spotted creature with a narrow head and sad, intelligent eyes. I knew it grieved him; with tears I thanked him for his loyalty. As for the rest of us, we tried to take no notice of the hound or even learn his name, for we did not want to grow fond of him.

Meantime, we racked our brains. I decided to make for Syria, for I felt that Bibulus owed me refuge, seeing that I had brought his sons' murderers to justice. I wrote and sealed a letter to him and sent one of our fastest runners, secretly; one man can always slip through a guard. We knew he got out and on his way; a Phoenician merchant brought us word, under cover of presenting his wares. He told me, as well, that in all the foreign quarters the people were with me, and conscripts were even now being gathered from the young men to follow me into Syria.

It gave me a thought, heartening me. I would rally an army to my side and fight; I would not give up my kingdom. I sent Longinus the Gaul to the Gabinian barracks, bearing the ancient Roman keepsake that Neo had given me, for now, if anytime, was the time to use it. The word came back that they, too would follow, five hundred trained legion men.

The poor dog died in convulsions; I had given him one mussel from my dish; it was a favorite of mine, that mussel dish, and clever of the enemy, for I almost never passed it by. It was time; we must get out of the Palace.

Apollodorus knew a way; it led through the tomb of Alexander, and he promised that no one knew it except him and one other priest, who had died the year before. It led underground, clear through the city, and came out upon the bank of the Marcotic Lake. He showed the place to Neo's man; I prayed that we could trust him. He said they would give us a day and follow after, the whole five hundred; we would meet just over the Syrian border. With luck, none of us would be missed till we had gotten clear away.

My waiting women wept to see me go; I could not take all those high-born, delicate maidens into an army camp. Besides, they were instructed to give it out that I was very sick; Pothinus would think it was the poison working, and wait for my end, unsuspecting. Iras I took along; I could not be companionless among all those soldiers; besides, when it was discovered that we had disappeared, they would very likely kill her if she were left behind. I did not love my sister Arsinoëe, but I did not wish her death, and sent folk looking for her; she could not be found, nor her paramour.

As to the rest of our little band, it was Apollodorus, Dioscorides, Longinus, and my Gauls and Germans, about twelve in all; two of the guard carried Xeno on a litter, for he was still weak, and the heavy clay still held his foot. He would slow us up, but I never would have left him behind.

Iras and I wore boys' tunics, and wore dark-hooded army cloaks and carried short swords; neither of us had any idea how to use them.

I lingered for a moment at the alabaster casket that held great Alexander. I tried to read his face, but it told me nothing. I leaned down swiftly and placed a kiss upon the cool glass that covered his head. My breath misted it over for a fleeting second, and then was gone. I stooped and went through the small secret door and pulled it shut behind me. The passage where we went was thickly black; a pinpoint of light in Apollodorus' hand led us, and we held hands to keep together. All through that dark and winding way, crouching and creeping, I held the face of Alexander in my mind for luck. I had always counted him my talisman, my fate. I prayed to him, for, truly, I had no other god.

11

I CANNOT DWELL UPON THE FLIGHT to Syria; it was a nightmare I would rather forget. Except for the great loyalty of my subjects. At the Marcotic Lake a little band of Phoenicians awaited us; they had been posted there each night since they had known of my peril. They had swift horses for us, and provisions, too; twenty-two young men, mounted and armed, joined us on our way, their eyes bright with the expectation of fighting.

At Eleusis, that holy place, there were more, twice the number, and some Egyptians among them. I sent one of them up the Nile where I had gone in state not very many days ago; he was reluctant, for he did not want to miss anything. I told him his mission was the most important of all, for he carried that scarab token that would bring me more followers. "We all depend on you, my friend," I said. "Be careful . . . take no chances. You must get through. It is for Egypt."

"For Egypt," he said, looking awed; he knelt and kissed my hand.

I went with fear always; fear that my runner had not gotten to Bibulus; fear that Bibulus would not heed him, and would refuse us entrance into Syria. And then we were weary, so weary. I had never gone long stretches on horseback; none of us had, in truth. When we halted to rest and eat a bite, we had to lie upon our stomachs, groaning. Iras and I both had raw saddle sores upon the insides of our thighs, where the flesh is most tender, and we were sunburnt as red as boiled crayfish, our lips cracked and dry. At every night stop, though, there was a change of horses waiting for us; I never knew how the word had spread. And the last few days some peasants brought us wide-brimmed hats, woven close of some reed-plant; they were almost like sunshades.

The Syrian border is marked by a range of low hills; we saw them from far off, and a long line of horsemen coming toward us. Close to, we saw they were elegantly caparisoned, even to the horses, and the leader bore a Roman seal, and a letter from Bibulus, to welcome us and escort us over the border. I could have wept for relief and joy. The Roman barbarians, some of them at least, have their own stern virtue; Bibulus was repaying my decency in kind.

He had even ordered a camp set up, with good tents, horses, food, and wine; it was almost comfortable, as such places go, and placed beside a running stream. In the large tent I shared with Iras, there were unguents and soap, fresh linen and sandals; he had even sent some slave girls to wait upon us!

These girls had no Greek or Latin, and spoke a dialect of the East that even I could not follow; it did not matter much, for they mostly giggled. They looked half-witted to us, but I learned later those giggles are much admired as feminine traits among the Syrian peoples, and they had been trained to it. They all looked like my sister Arsinoëe, rounded of body, with tightly curling black hair and swarthy skin. They wore very little, just gilded strips across their breasts and hips, but they were hung with beads and bangles; thin veils covered the lower part of their faces, their huge cow eyes rolling above, thickly painted on the lids and a black line drawn round to make them even larger.

They drew baths for us from the stream; cool water in big painted jars, and poured wine and laid out food. We never saw them again, though, after that first day, except from a distance. They went the rounds of the camp like a fever, sleeping with all the soldiers; I guess it was more fun.

We did not really miss them; it was no great chore to draw our own bath water and comb our own hair, and the soldiers brought us roasted kid and fowl baked in clay. We did not eat with the men; in Syria it is not done, Apollodorus explained. We were grateful for Syrian hospitality, and did not wish to offend. It was lonely, though, sometimes, especially at night, when the soldiers sang around their fires; the sounds of an army at rest are beautiful—short bursts of laughter and the clink of the wine jars, a horse whinnying softly, a sudden breeze whipping the tent flaps, and the far-off cry of some wild creature. And then the quiet settling down; snores, and a rustle, a thin last clank of armor as someone moved in sleep. And, looking from the tent, all the rows upon rows of soldiers, flung down upon the ground to sleep under the stars, with the soft darkness breathing all around. I shall always love it, knowing it is a thing most women never hear or see.

By day we had nothing to do; we waited. The soldiers were always busy, mending armor or polishing it, firing horseshoes, oiling their leather tunics or sharpening their swords. And new recruits came nearly every day, from all over my kingdom, to cast their lot with me; at the end we had upwards of five thousand. Many were untrained, from the Nile villages or the slums of the cities, but all of them were ardent, loving me as their queen and hating Pothinus. They knew him for their oppressor, who had taxed them to the starvation point; I was thankful they were too simple to know it was my father who had begun it! They looked to me as their goddess, who would lead them to a better life and supply their wants. I swore within myself that I would try, when I came to power.

News filtered in with the new recruits, and we had spies as well. The trio of evil counselors had set little Mouse upon the throne of Egypt and were ruling in his name; we heard dreadful tales of reprisals against those nobles who opposed them; there were executions every day. The city of Alexandria was held like a prison, all movement curtailed and a curfew imposed at sundown upon pain and death.

We heard, too, that the two Romans, Pompey and Caesar, had met at last upon the plains of Pharsalia, as I had guessed. The hardened legions of Julius Caesar demolished the aristocratic troops of Pompey, and Pompey himself fled by ship to Mitylene. And here the story grows really dreadful, for he did not stay there to lick his wounds and pick up new men, but, accompanied by his wife, Cornelia, he made his way to Cyprus, and from there took a galley ship for Egypt. I think he was hoping to get help from Ptolemy, my brother, or perhaps he had not heard of the upheaval in our court. It was rumored that his fleet still held; he probably thought to gather forces at Alexandria and do battle once more for the mastery of the Roman world.

As soon as his ship was sighted off the shores of our city, those three men who ruled my brother sent word to him that he must wait while they deliberated as to what to do. It is probable that they feared the wrath of Caesar if they succored Pompey; on the other hand, if they did not, he might join forces with me. I am guessing, of course, for I was not present. But I heard later that it was Theodotus who decided his fate, for his remark is famous, or infamous, according to how one thinks of it. "Dead men cannot bite," he said. I suppose he thought it clever; it is, however, typical of his inferior mind, for living men do not bite either. Men are not dogs.

In any case, his proposal—in effect, death for the great Roman—was approved by the others, and entrusted to Achillas. This soldier engaged the services of two renegade Romans who had once served under Pompey, Septimius and Salvius. These three, with a few attendants, set out in a small boat and headed for Pompey's galley.

When they had come alongside the galley, Septimius, supposedly loyal, stood and saluted Pompey, addressing him by his military title. Achillas invited him to step into their boat, saying that the Alexandrian harbor waters were too shallow for the galley. Pompey must have known this was not true, for there are always a great many galleys riding at anchor shoreside. They say that his wife begged him not to go. Perhaps he trusted the two Romans, or resigned himself to his fate; one cannot know. But he kissed her and took his leave, stepping down into the small boat, along with two of his centurions, a freedman and a slave.

I cannot help but imagine myself in her place, Cornelia's. It was September, and the Nile muddies the waters of the harbor; the sky is leaden in the rainy season and reflects the brown sea. It is the only time that Alexandria has a look of bleakness. The poor woman saw the whole scene of horror against a background which matched it.

The boat touched shore; Pompey took the hand of his freedman to help himself out; Septimius, his own soldier, stabbed him in the back. He fell into the boat, and Achillas and Salvius hacked him to pieces. As Achillas held aloft the severed head, Cornelia screamed a great scream that was heard on the shore. She was no fool, though, for immediately she gave orders to weigh anchor and her galley was soon too far away for pursuit.

The decapitated body was thrown into the water, and the murderers carried the head into the Palace. Pompey's freedman and slave, who had been thrown overboard alive, found Pompey's body and dragged it on to the shore. A shocked crowd collected and watched them gather wood, mostly drift from the sea, to build a makeshift pyre. The two loyal servants wrapped Pompey's remains in their own togas for a burial sheet, and lit the funeral fire. They mourned beside it all night, keeping the fire burning and singing songs of praise for the dead. No one molested them, though Achillas' soldiers were among the crowd as always; I suppose they were too lowly to be considered enemies.

The next morning, one of Pompey's generals, Lucius Lentulus, arrived by a second galley, bringing the two thousand men that were left after the defeat at Pharsalia. This man had barely set foot on shore when he, too, was murdered. His men, however, managed to retrieve his body and get it back on board the galley. They then set sail for the Adriatic, where Pompey's son, my Neo, commanded a small fleet.

So I, counting up the days, figure that Neo got the news of his father's death at about the same time I did. I had never known Pompey, but I mourned him, for the sake of his son.

12

A FEW DAYS AFTER THE TRAGIC END of Pompey, Julius Caesar arrived at Alexandria; it must have been on about the second day of October, as I reckoned it, getting the news a little late.

He had been in pursuit of Pompey; he anchored well outside the harbor, for he had only a small force with him, and sent emissaries in to shore to demand that his enemy be turned over to him. As I understand it, the three despots nearly came to blows over who should have the honor of delivering Pompey's head. What happened I do not know; perhaps they cast lots for it! At any rate it was silky old Theodotus who embarked for the galley of Caesar, bearing the head and a finger with Pompey's signet ring. I can just picture the old fool, who could hardly keep his feet on a boat, looking proud and smug all at once, holding out his grisly trophy! I can also see his jowls drop when great Caesar turned in horror from the sight, bowed his own head in his hands, and sobbed aloud. When he had done weeping, he raised his head and cried, "Out of my sight, fool and slave! And begone from Alexandria, and away from Egypt, for I shall hound you to your death if ever I lay eyes upon you!"

These words are made up by the messenger who brought the news, for they have a heroic ring, false as such words always are, but in effect that was what he said. And in truth, it was the last anyone saw of Theodotus in Egypt. I presume he stopped long enough to warn the other two, for they wasted no time in obeying Caesar's orders.

This victor, Caesar, did not leave his galley, but sent his orders by messenger; it appears they were followed to the letter. He demanded that the head of Pompey, with the finger as well, be given honorable burial, near the sea, in the grove of Nemesis; it is a lovely and peaceful spot, outside the eastern walls; I had not realized it, but this Caesar knew our city, probably from before my birth. He could not have chosen better, to do honor to a great enemy. He ordered it made into a park, and a great monument raised as well, and promptly. He then had the ashes from Pompey's pyre gathered, put into a gold casket, and sent to Cornelia, who had fled to their estate at Alba. After—and all these orders came within a matter of hours—he demanded the release of all political prisoners. "For I shall judge their cases myself," he said.

He was autocratic, but obviously prudent as well; he waited for his ships and men, some four thousand seasoned warriors. Then he calmly sailed up to the steps of the Palace, entered it, and took over all command! "I am Rome," he said, to the astonished court; at least, that is how it was reported to me.

Much of the story from here on is confusion, for each messenger had his own version of events; besides, the events were many. It seems to be true, though, that rioting broke out in all parts of the city, at the sight of the Roman legions; Caesar wisely kept them afterwards within the Palace walls. He must have seen immediately that he could hold the Palace forever with four thousand men, at least from the land side. And, from sea, there could come nothing except more of his own Romans; the remnants of Pompey's fleet were far away in another sea, too far for menace.

My last spy brought with him a Roman officer, bearing a letter with the seal of Julius Caesar, and asking that I return to take up my duties upon the double throne. ". . . for in your father's will he entrusted his children's estate to the Roman people, and I represent the Roman people." He signed it, in a bold hand that slanted upwards on the parchment, "I, Julius Caesar, Conqueror of all Gaul and Master of Rome."

I laughed aloud, showing the letter to Apollodorus and Iras. "Master of a dung heap . . . the old rooster!" I said.

My own messenger smiled, but Caesar's man narrowed his eyes; I had spoken in Greek. I said it again, to test him; he did not understand.

I tried Latin. "What is your name, soldier?"

"Cadwallader, son of Cadwalladon." Or so it sounded; the accent was strange and lilting.

In Gaulish dialect I said, "I remarked just now that your master is a proud man."

He understood, and answered, though his accent was difficult to follow; I had not heard it before. "The Julio is not my master. I am a free Belgae."

"But a Roman soldier, yes?"

He shrugged. "For pay."

"What is Belgae?" I asked. "Gaulish?"

He shrugged again. "Gaul, Celt . . . whatever you like." He grinned. "A barbarian, anyway." He grinned whitely.

"I am a Greek," I said. "To us the Romans are barbarians."

"Depends where you sit, Lady." His mouth still curved as he looked down at me. He was tall as all those northern peoples are, and very broadly built. He was much like my own Gauls and Germans, except that his hair was like a flame and worn long, tied behind with a leather thong; he had taken his helmet off and a line showed sharp where it had pressed upon his forehead. Above it the skin was white as milk, and below, burnt red by the sun, the wrong red for his hair. But for that he would have been a handsome man; his face longer than most Gauls and the cheekbones set high under fine deep sea-colored eyes. I think he was young, too; younger perhaps than I, though it is hard to tell with these big-boned races.

"Well, Cadwallader—" I began. He burst into a loud laugh; I was not saying it correctly.

"Speak it again for me—slowly," I said, for I was proud of my ear for language. I listened. The "l" and the "r" were both rolled, a musical sound. I tried again. He clapped his big hands together.

"Well done, Lady. You might be a true Brython."

"Brython . . . ? Briton? You are from the Misty Isles?"

He bowed, his hand over his heart.

"And your father?" I asked.

"The king . . . or was. The Romans killed him. He was hostage for the tribe . . . they gave out that it was an accident and punished the soldier who did it. Hung him on a cross—ugly."

I saw that the memory of that death truly sickened him, and marveled, for by all accounts he was a savage.

"You have a Greek heart," I said.

"Nearly, Lady . . . my people are descended from Trojans, though . . . I guess they may have been much like the old Greeks. Brutus it was who founded our race. Brutus, son of Priam."

"I do not know the name," I said. "There is Paris—and Hector, too—but Brutus is not in our tales."

"Well," he said, with another white grin, "there is more mist in our island than rises from the swamplands . . . who knows what is what, after all the songs are sung?"

"Well, Cadwallader, my friend," I said. "There is mist in our old songs too . . . but I, for one, must clear it from my head for the moment and set to thinking how best to obey my Roman master."

"You will go, then?"

"Of course. I want my throne."

He looked at me, a long look. "I think that you will get it, Lady."

Apollodorus whispered something in my ear, pointing out that neither of the two messengers had been given food or wine, or even a moment of rest. "I have forgotten my own Greek manners, friend," I said, smiling. "Please be at ease."

When they were rested and refreshed, we talked at more purpose. I had thought that Achillas' forces were encamped at Pelusium, on the Syrian border, but north of us, and planned in my head to take my own army back the way we had come. But it seems he had gone back to Alexandria and was manning all the walls and occupying that part of the city where there were no Roman troops.

"They say, also, Lady," said my own messenger, "that his army is twenty thousand strong."

I caught my breath, for we would never get through to Caesar with our little band. And I had thought myself to have an army! "Where have they come from, these troops of his?"

"I think he has conscripted all of Alexandria," said my man. "He has called them up in Ptolemy's name . . . on pain of death if they refuse."

"Perhaps," I thought aloud, "I could shear my hair and put on soldier's dress, and so slip through the lines, disguised."

The Briton shook his head. "It will never work, Lady. They will all be looking for you . . . every Alexandrian knows your face. Too dangerous . . ."

"I think my subjects would not betray me," I said, meaning it.

"Lady . . . among so many, there are bound to be some traitors." He shook his head again, sadly. "No . . . you must go by sea."

I stared at him. "How? We have no boats."

"You will only need one. You must leave your people here. . . . Look you—this fellow and I," and he gestured to my man, "we two will go back the same road we came, giving out that you have refused to obey Caesar and will not come to the city . . . you, meantime, will take ship—a very little one that no one will notice—go round by sea, in disguise as you said, and with only one other. Enter the Palace by night when the guard is smaller. If luck holds, I will be there before you, and on the lookout. I will manage it, for the Julio likes me . . . I have never known why."

We sat long into the evening, thinking, trying to plan. Iras began to weep. "I don't want you to cut off your beautiful hair—please don't do it!"

It was a silly thing, but I fell to weeping, too. It was nerves, really, and also I knew I would have to leave her behind. One maiden was enough to smuggle through.

Apollodorus, too, thought the plan dangerous. "The disguise is not good enough . . ."

It was not till I saw Xeno, barely limping now, spreading

out Apollodorus' bedroll, carpet first, unrolling it, that the thought came to me, as though some god gave it. I remembered Neo's remark in the marketplace, looking at the bedrolls on all the workingmen's shoulders. How he had said a spy could go anywhere that way, rolled up in the carpet, and slung over a strong shoulder. And I weighed little and was slim. The blood raced wildly through me. We would do it Neo's way. Apollodorus, and his black slave carrying his bedroll . . . what could be easier? I leaned forward and whispered my plan.

13

IT WAS ONLY THE SECOND TIME I had entered Alexandria by sea, and I saw nothing of it, for of course I was hidden in Apollodorus' bedroll. It was night; we hád waited till sunset, beached just outside the harbor. I did not even see the beacon of the Pharos lighthouse, for we thought best to roll me up well ahead of time. At my head and feet were stuffed gauzy fabrics; I could breathe easily, but Apollodorus, like a fussy old woman, insisted on cutting a small hole in his carpet; it was a shame, truly, for he had had it many years, and it was finer than any of today's kind, and not a worn spot on it. He was dressed in his priest's robes of his youth; there was a hood and he had never worn them about the Palace; it was not likely he would be recognized. As for Xeno—most people think all Nubians and Africans look alike; there was not too much danger there.

It was a strange feeling, wrapped all about in darkness, hearing the oars slip softly through the water, and the waves lapping against the sides of our little boat. Once I heard a voice call something, but I could not understand the words; probably a sentry on the walls, far away.

I felt the boat stop, rocking a little, and the small jolt as Xeno lifted me to his shoulder, and the walking up the shallow steps; I counted them: twenty-four. Then I heard whispers, and the words, softly, "The password is THE LARK." I wondered why. There were no more words or whispers, only padding footsteps, more than just the two with me, I thought. I knew when we entered the Palace, for the air got close and thick, and I smelled things, food and leather and a musk perfume that was always flung about in our halls. Odd, how strong odors become, and how loud sounds, when one cannot see.

We went up more steps; I heard the password twice, once in Apollodorus' voice and once in the Briton's. I knew when we entered my own chambers; I suppose it still had my smell about it, but all the windows must have been closed and a brazier lighted. I was suddenly hot to the point of stifling. I heard a sneeze; someone blew his nose.

Xeno lowered me gently to the floor; I heard a Roman voice, a little nasal. "Is this the treasure you promised, Cadwallader? The rug is not even antique—just old. . . ."

"Wait, Julio . . ." the Briton said, softly.

I felt myself being unrolled; although we had practiced it, still Xeno ended me up on my face. I pulled down my boy's tunic and scrambled as best I could to a sitting position, but I was turned the wrong way, and faced my dressing-room door.

I heard the nasal voice ask, with the hint of a laugh in it, "Is it a boy or a girl?"

I turned to the sound of the voice, taking off my Phrygian cap and shaking out my hair so that it fell loose about me. I smiled at Julius Caesar, for of course the voice was his. "I have heard, Roman, that you do not care one way or the other!"

He laughed loud then, and long; it must have set his nose to running again; he had to blow it. I waited, saying nothing.

He rose from where he sat beside the brazier, and came to take my hand, drawing me to my feet. We were of a height; he was not a tall man.

"Well," he said, looking into my eyes and smiling a thin smile, "I guess you are a girl . . . and perhaps the prettiest I have ever seen."

"I am Cleopatra," I said. "You sent for me."

14

It has been said of me that I used Caesar, and of him that he used me, each for our own selfish ambition. I do not know; I know only that we had great love, each for each, from the first moment when I rose from my carpet in disarray to face an aging barbarian with a reddened nose.

We stood a long moment, a moment out of time; the smell of strong herbal medicines hung heavy in the air, chokingly. I saw a thin man, hard as wood, bald, with a clever mouth and eyes like live black coals. I do not know what he saw, but something ran between us, from hand to hand, like a small secret fire, and it did not matter.

I think I spoke first. "You have taken my chamber, Roman."

"It was the best."

I laughed. "But you should open a window," I said. "The air is foul."

"I did not notice," he said, courteously. "My nose is stuffed." His thin lips twitched. "It is just as well . . . or I should smell the army on you, little Greek."

I laughed again. "No, for I was more royally served than you, Caesar . . . Bibulus gave me a fine Eastern tent, with perfumes and oils, and fresh bath water every day."

"Bibulus . . ." he said, drawing out the name, and smiling now. "I shall reward him handsomely . . ." He raised his voice suddenly, not moving. I heard the commander over thousands. "Well, who shall see to the window?"

"I will, Julio," answered the Briton.

"He calls you 'Julio'," I said. "Is he not then your captive?"

"He is my friend," said Caesar.

The sea wind rushed in, blowing out the curtains and sending the brazier flame leaping; he shivered, letting go my hand and turning to accept the fur robe that Cadwallader hung over his shoulders.

I ran to the window, leaning out and drawing great breaths of the salty air. When I turned back into the room, I saw he had seated himself again before his brazier. I whirled myself about for joy, raising my arms and spreading them wide. "I am back in my Alexandria again! Thank you, Caesar." And I flung myself, uncaring, upon my knees before him, and buried my face in his lap.

I felt his hand under my chin, raising my face, and one finger tracing the tears beneath my eyes. "Child," he said, "I only summoned you. It was your courage and your cleverness that got you here. . . . Tell me about it," he finished, with a new gentleness.

And I did; I talked the night through. I told him everything, like a river that has burst through its dam. Our history, my childhood, my hopes, my fears. He answered little, but to nod or sigh; he had long since sent the others from the chamber, leaving us alone.

I remember little of that long night, but for my own outpourings, his still, steady face, and the rope of fire that ran between us. I know that food was brought, and medicines for him, with wine for me. Perhaps the wine talked too; I hope not, for I wished him to hear me and only me.

When dawn broke, the color of pale apricots, we went to bed; my bed. I never questioned that he should be my lover, and take my maidenhead, though I had been so careful before. I had no thought of politics or strategy; or perhaps I did; I have an instinct for such things, as a cat has a predator's heart. One must be honest, at least to one's self.

There cannot be, nor ever was, a lover like my Julio; I knew it then, though I had no standard of comparison. He knew every inch of a woman's body, and how to please, even an untried virgin. It surprised him that I was, as it surprised me that it did not hurt.

There is a bawdy song the legions sing about him; some soldier made it upon a march back to Rome, and it caught on. It goes something like, "Lock up your wives, Romans . . . here comes the bald adulterer . . ." There are a great many verses, each dirtier than the one before, but larded throughout with affection, for the soldiers love him, even as I. It ran through my head afterwards, and I taxed him with it. He laughed, and said it was an exaggeration. I asked him how many women he had had; it was quite light by then, and I saw his face clearly; a little spasm, perhaps of humor, passed over its stillness. He shrugged and said, "Counting war prizes, and brothels, and a hospitable night in some friend's house . . . ? Oh, perhaps a thousand or so . . ."

I think now that he mocked me, laughing inside; I believed it then. It did not bother me, somehow, but some dark feeling prompted me to ask, "And what of the boys . . ."

"Oh," he said, airily, "I was not counting them . . . and they are in the dim past of my youth." He bent closer to look into my face. "You are shocked . . . why? Have you, then, never lain with a woman?"

"Oh, no!" I cried, in horror. He was amused.

"How can that be?" he asked. "You are not made of

ice—far from it. And you are not slow to learn, either . . ."

"I am quick at everything," I said. "I have to be. I am a queen . . . and a goddess, too."

He laughed hugely at that, till it set him to coughing.

We spent the whole day in bed, and not sleeping much, either. It was the first of many such wild hours.

When the dark came, like a blanket, he said to me, "That was a good day's work—better than a campaign in Gaul. I love you, little goddess. I hope that we have made, between us, a god . . ."

My thoughts raced wildly into the future, joy pumping fast in my blood. There was no doubt in my mind that—perfect lover aside—here lay beside me the greatest man in the world. And he would acknowledge our son! I knew he truly loved me.

It was a perfect night, and day, and night again, never mind all those that came after. Only two things I regretted.

I should never have told him about Neo.

And then, too, I caught his cold.

15

I TOOK BARGE AGAIN upon the Nile, but this time not as Mother of the Sacred Bull-God, but as Queen-Goddess Isis of all Egypt, with her royal consort, a god, too, Jupiter-Amon—my own Julio—and carrying within me the child of our union, who would be god of all the world!

This time I did not stand, in view of all my subjects, but reclined upon cushions; the child was close on seven months and I was large with it. I could not bend to fasten my sandal, and had to be lowered into my tub of bath water. Privately I knew that I could have done it all myself, in spite of my bulk; I have always been impatient with servants. But Julio would allow me no activity at all. "I shall get fat!" I cried.

"Not you," he said. "You are still as thin as a reed, except in one place . . ." But it was not so; in my mirror I saw my cheeks were rounded, and another chin, tiny, lay beneath my own. I held my head high, making a long neck, and waved away sweet comfits. Truth to tell, I was dismayed, unused to womanly arms and breasts as big as my poor sister Arsinoëe's; what if they stayed that way always? Julio smiled and said it would not happen. "For I have seen it many times . . . you will be like a maiden again when it is over."

I glanced at him sharply. "I thought you had only fathered one child . . ."

"One legitimate child," he said. "But there are others, all over the world, I have no doubt. I have a son in Rome . . . a fine young man, and an aristocrat. I could never acknowledge him, for his mother was wed to her advantage and could not set her husband aside." He looked at me thoughtfully. "You will like him . . . he is about your age . . . no, older. When you come to Rome, after Caesarion is born, I will point him out."

"Then we will call her Julia . . . after my dead darling . . ." And he wept, in his own strange and godlike way that I never ceased to marvel at. His face never moved, but stayed still as the face of a statue while the tears poured down it like rain.

He was a man of many strangenesses, my Julio. He could go for many hours without sleeping, and, sitting upright, eyes open, fall asleep for ten minutes and wake refreshed, suddenly. He cared nothing for wine, and less for food. He would drink quarts of heavily watered wine at once, if he was thirsty, and eat hugely when he was hungry—but again, he might go hours without food or drink, like a camel of the desert. Much can be explained away by his long campaigning life, but not all. I have seen him watch, impassive, at a dreadful execution, or dabble his arms up to the elbow in bloody entrails, for a ceremony to an old god he did not believe in. But he could not abide a grain of sand beneath his fingernail, or a dirt smudge upon his tunic. I knew, for I had talked long with the Briton, Cadwallader, that in war he had ordered the slaughter, in cold blood, of whole villages, mostly women with children clinging to their robes, or, even, like me, carrying them within. Yet he never left my side, and would not let me lift a finger to help myself, but saw to everything, that I might lie in luxury, like some great swollen bee. He loved me, of course; I knew that. But what I did not comprehend then I see now. I always forgot his age; I always forgot that this child that I bore might be the last that he would father, and he yearned for immortality, my Julio, in this way also.

This barge that floated on the Nile was as great as a palace, with colonnaded courts, banqueting salons, sitting rooms, shrines to all the gods—Roman, Greek, and Egyptian—and it was propelled by many banks of oars. Its wood was cedar and cypress, and gold leaf decorated all its fittings. The furniture was Greek, but of an ornate sort, to the Roman taste. He had had it built especially when he learned of my pregnancy, for he wanted to view our kingdom with me; how he could have done it, with all else that he had accomplished, in that niggardly seven months, I shall never know.

For in that seven months, seven years had passed in effect, or seventy. All strife in Alexandria had come to an end; all my enemies were vanquished; Egypt, all, was mine—and my lover's. There had been revolt, dissension, rebellion, and treachery; it was all laid to rest, and Egypt prospered. The evil Pothinus and the brutual Achillas were dead, by the executioner's axe; Theodotus was fled the land. Arsinoëe and her Ganymede, who had fomented a rebellion, were prisoners of the state. Poor Mouse, alas, was dead, drowned in the mud of the Nile; his heavy brazen corselet had dragged him down before he could be rescued; vain boy—in a way I loved him, and mourned his passing, though he had schemed against me all his young life.

I sat upon the throne of Egypt with my littlest brother, aged ten now; one can only call him Mouse II; I suppose he has a royal name, but no one seems to know it. There has been no formal marriage, of course, and will never be, but no one knows of this but Julio and me. This trip will make Caesar king and god in one, as I am; afterwards, when all is put to rights, we will rule jointly over Egypt. And Rome, as well. But we are quiet about it, and I lie, somnolent, among my cushions, and trail my hands in the Nile waters, cool now and pleasant in the spring, and wait for my child.

We are accompanied by a fleet of four hundred vessels; a show of strength, though I doubt that it is needed. But Caesar is a cautious man; it is a quality I must learn.

He had been made dictator in Rome for another year; word had been brought to him several months ago; he had the whole Roman fleet available to him, and as many garrisons as were near. There was no way that his enemies and mine could win against this strength. I thought that he would go back to Rome, but I had just told him of my pregnancy and he refused to leave me. I was flattered, but urged him to go, for policy. He smiled, and said, "It is more politic this way . . . though I am popular, still I have the enemies of all who sit in high places. . . . Best let it simmer down, let Pompey be forgotten a little." His face shut in upon itself in an odd sort of way, and he went on, "So we are all forgot—after we died. In time . . . so are we all . . ."

I said nothing; it is a sobering thought. And though I knew it to be true, and that he, once a close friend, had nearly forgotten Pompey, still, there were those things he did not forget. It was not for Pompey, I knew, that Julio had hunted down Pompey's son, my Neo.

Neo had been commander of the fleet in the Adriatic, the last, perhaps, to hold out against Caesar. It is understandable that it had to be subjugated, perhaps even decimated, as it was. But there was no need, really, to make sure of Neo's death; he had surrendered already, and placed himself in Caesar's hands.

Sextus Pompey, Neo's brother, was spared, and given his freedom. But Neo was executed, while Caesar watched to see the deed was done. He gave it out afterwards that Neo had committed cruel outrages upon the Julian troops; it was even written down, by his command, so that all who came after knew Neo for a cruel felon. Perhaps it was so; I do not believe it. Julio did it for me; he was jealous, to put it simply.

Strange, for often he had spoken of his other, earlier loves; always his feelings were light, and he bore no malice toward husband or lover, before or after. But with me he was different. Perhaps it was that he was old.

It did not work the other way, however. Word came to me that he dallied with the wife of the commander of the garrison from where he fought the Pompeian fleet; the commander himself was only too happy to be so honored, it appeared. The night of Neo's execution, even, Julio went to this woman's bed; her name, I think, was Euphemia. I never said a word about Neo, but I taxed him with this affair of Euphemia; I was jealous, in my turn.

He stared at me in bleak surprise. "But it meant nothing at all! It is the custom . . . a sort of hospitality, always offered . . ."

"Hospitality!" I roared, and, with all my strength, brought back my right arm, and hit him in the face. He stood quite still, astonished; the mark of my hand stood out white against his sunburned skin, and a little trickle of blood ran down his cheek, where my royal scarab ring had caught him.

He reached out and took my two wrists, firmly gentle, and looked straight into my eyes, unsmiling. "No other has ever done that," he said, quietly. "And you will not do it again."

"No," I cried, my face bright scarlet, "next time I will take a knife to you!"

"Look," he said, still holding my wrists, "let there be peace between us. If you dislike the thought of other women, however light . . . I will forego them. As I can go without food for many days . . ."

"And as you cannot tell the difference in foods!" I cried, still angry.

"The analogy was not meant to be taken literally in all ways," he answered, smiling. The smile infuriated me; I felt very young. He went on. "All women are different. One does not feel the same about each of them, naturally." He laughed, suddenly. "If I felt always as I felt for you, my dear . . . well, I should certainly be dead long ago!"

I felt my anger ebb away, and a bubble of laughter rise in my throat, but I forced the bubble down and made myself scowl.

"What was she like . . . this Euphemia?" I asked.

His eyes went vague, thinking. Then they cleared. "Black," he said, nodding.

"Black!" I cried, aghast. Blacks have been slaves, always, in Egypt, and it took a bit of getting used to.

"Yes, Nubian," said Julio. "And her husband, too. Roman citizens, of course. They had to pay through the nose for their papers, of course. It is only a small seacoast monarchy." He let go my wrists, carefully, and took me by the shoulders. "It was rather expected of me, you know . . . my reputation runs ahead of me . . ." He gave me a glance sidelong, curiously shy; I saw how he had looked as a boy. My anger was all gone away, but I pretended still.

"Well, from now on it is not expected of Caesar!" I said. "Caesar is mine!"

He smiled and put his hand to his cheek. "How not?" he

said, "seeing that you have marked me . . ." He held out his finger, smeared with his own blood. I lowered my eyes to it; nausea rose in me, but I did not vomit; I fainted.

That was how I became certain of the life I bore within; I had suspected it for days. The doctors confirmed it, and I was put to bed to insure that I would not faint again, till the child was a little larger and less vulnerable. And Caesar promised me everything I asked.

And that is how I came to be trailing my hand in the Nile, idle beside the man they called "the Conqueror of the World." Once, softly, in the night, he told me how he had, years ago, wept tears as he read of Alexander, who had conquered so much at such an early age. "I was older already than he, you see . . ."

My heart hurt for him; I had so often felt the same. I promised to show him the secret place where Alexander lay, once we returned to the city.

"But," I whispered, "you have already a bigger chunk of the world than he . . ."

"Not I," he answered. "Rome."

"But you *are* Rome," I said. "Or will be. You will be king—as you are here . . . god, as you are here . . ."

And so I injected the king-poison, the god-poison, into him day by day, a drop at a time. I did not even know, then, that I did it; I had lived on the stuff all my days, after all.

16

CAESARION WAS BORN on Midsummer Night under a full moon; the astrologers called it favorable, with charts to prove it. Julio always listened to every sort of thing from the lips of sages; I knew astrology for an ancient science, and unexact, but he crossed his fingers, just in case, and welcomed the good omens. For me, it was enough that he was a boy, and healthy; in such heat the child sometimes dwindles in the womb.

I looked down at him in my arms and laughed softly; he was Julio in little, even to the baldness; a half-century-old head on a newborn. He would not look so always, the doctors said; each day his face grew more his own, and some light brown fuzz was sprouting on his scalp, like new grass.

It was an easy birth, made easier by the poppy juice given me by Dioscorides. Caesar marveled, for he said that women in Rome, even the wealthiest and noblest, suffered greatly in childbirth. They were not usually attended by doctors, but by women called midwives, just like the Alexandrian poor of the foreign quarters. Another proof that Romans are barbarians, and I said so. Julio smiled and said I might think as I would, so long as I felt well and brought forth a fine son.

Fortune had indeed smiled upon us. There would be no hindrance to our plans.

All Egypt accepted our son as Amon, "Heir to the World." He was crowned, symbolically, in the Temple of Isis, when he was three weeks old, dressed in the long trailing robe of the Pharaohs. When the serpent scepter was held out to him, his small fingers curled around it tightly, and he brought it to his mouth, biting on it with his toothless gums. He never laughed, for this was serious business, but even the oldest of the priests chuckled at the sight. As for me, my heart felt gripped as by an iron fist; my son teething upon the royal symbol of Egypt! It now remained to cage the Roman eagle for his toy!

In the weeks after our return from the Nile adventure, I had been put to bed; Dioscorides believed in rest and even languor when the child was nearly due. It was wretchedly hot, for Alexandria, or perhaps I felt it more, in my condition. Julio said afterwards that I should thank the gods for it, as at the birthing I sweated off all my extra fat! It was true; I was thinner than before, and the face that looked out of my mirror was newly contoured, taut at the cheekbones and with subtle shadows under. I looked older, but I had grown more beautiful; I was pleased.

Julius Caesar is not a man to be idle for long; while I rested, before the birth, he worked hour after hour with Sosigenes, the astronomer; they were reforming the calendar! The gods know it needed it; each year there were days that had to be accounted for; it would never work out evenly.

They managed it between them, though, taking one month and making it shorter—a winter month. That had been done, in a way, before, but still it did not quite work. I do not know which of them had the thought, but they gave that month, in the new calendar, an extra day once every four years, making it perfect mathematically. This calendar they called the "Julian calendar." The months were named for gods, mostly, though they ran out at the end and used numbers; one month, also, when Caesarion was born, they called the month of "Julius," for Julio, too, had been born at that time of year. They finished the new calendar, working overtime, before Julio went back to Rome; it is still in use in most of the civilized world.

For the dictator of Rome could stay no longer in Alexandria, happy though we were. We had made our plans, and he must begin putting them into effect. There were campaigns, still, to be fought on the Mediterranean borders; Parthia had still to be subdued; all of India must be conquered. When this was done, and only Egypt was outside Roman dominion, he would announce his marriage to me, the queen of that country; we would incorporate Egyptian wealth with all the riches of the Roman world and establish ourselves as the sole monarchs of the earth.

This was our plan, and I was content to tend our son, and wait until Julio called me to Rome.

BOOK II
Rome

1

CAESARION WALKED EARLY; he was ten months old when we journeyed to Rome, and a handful. I had never given him over to the care of nurses, as is done with most royal children; I was always mindful of his identity as "Heir to the World," great Caesar's son, and my charm of fortune. I was terrified when he fell and skinned his knees, or knocked his head; I have often thought that truly it is a marvel that children grow up at all! They are forever missing by a hair having their brains dashed out on a marble table edge or an ironwork bench; and then they will eat anything, even dog dung, if they are not caught in time. Once Caesarion drank a whole jar of the almond milk I use for my skin; I did not know what was in it and flew to Dioscorides, trembling with fear. He said there was nothing harmful, only a little honey. But I took it out on poor Iras; she had been set to watching him while I went behind a curtain to use the deck-bucket. I was sorry afterwards, for she was seasick the whole crossing and could hardly hold up her head, much less watch a tireless baby fireball. By some god-gift, he did not come to harm on the slippery, tilting deck, or fall into the sea, or down the cargo-place. I have since learned that children seldom do, but I was a new mother then, and not all that happy riding the ocean myself.

He still bore a great resemblance to his father, though he now had a thick mane of light brown hair, like mine, and round, dimpled cheeks. Julio's eyes were there, though, deep-set and dark; hot eyes. And, even though he toddled, the walk was the same, the little chest arching, the head high, and the toes turned out, amusing to watch. He was a sunny child, and very winning of temperament; he seldom cried, and could always be consoled easily by a hug or a sweet.

He seemed to love everyone, me, Iras, Apollodorus, the doctors, the slaves, the sailors. He had no favorites, except perhaps black Xeno and red-gold Cadwallader; Xeno was his tireless steed, and the Briton sang sweet, lilting songs to him and told him little tales of his misty land. To my secret chagrin, he adored Arsinoëe, climbing into her lap and playing with the bangles she hung about her always, even now, a captive.

For Arsinoëe and her lover, Ganymede, were traveling with us too; they were to appear in Caesar's Triumph, walking in chains for the crowd to jeer at. She had asked for it, Arsinoëe, but still it made me uneasy; I could not care if Ganymede rotted in the filthy hold, but my sister I kept by me on the journey, unfettered and sharing all our dubious comforts. She did not thank me for it, but whenever I looked her way, sent me dumb glances dark with hate.

She was loving and kind with my little boy, though; you may be sure that I watched her like a hawk when he was by her. But she gave him her arm rings to play with, and jounced him on her knee till he squealed with joy. Now and then I would see her clasp him close, the easy tears flowing down her cheeks; at such times I pitied her, though she had conspired vilely against my throne, and even my life.

My co-ruler, Ptolemy XV—my eleven-year-old brother—was traveling with us, too, and more trouble than Caesarion. Twice he nearly drowned, for he always leaned out too far; I shuddered at what would be said, after his brother's death in the Nile; they could not, in fact, lay that death at my door, try as they might, for I was nowhere near Mouse. But this one was on the same boat with me! He was even more seasick than Iras, and grew pale and thin on the voyage; by the time we reached solid earth again, he looked as though he had been starved and beaten; I could have cheerfully wrung his neck! Caesar had advised that I bring him, writing that insurrection ran in my family and it was better to be on the safe side. I cannot believe that this sickly little brother could get up the nerve to lead a rebellion, or that anyone at all would follow him. Of course, he might, if left in Alexandria, die or be assassinated, and I would be accused of it; one way or another, Caesar is always right!

Caesar was not on hand to greet us, after our hot overland journey; it seemed to take forever, with all our slaves and belongings, and I was just as glad he was not there to see me in such a mess. He had sent an escort, though, headed by a young man with a thoughtful, solemn face; he introduced himself as Brutus, and said that Julio was his godfather. As he gave me an arm up to mount my horse, though, I saw his hand clearly, like a thing apart. It was lean and brown, with long fingers that tapered in a strange way, squared off at the tips. I nearly exclaimed aloud; this was the very mate of Caesar's hand! Dioscorides has said often that when there is no other resemblance, the hands will tell all. So this must be the unacknowledged son that Julio had spoken of. I looked covertly at him from time to time as he walked beside my horse, making courteous conversation. I could not see another feature like Caesar's; he must take after his mother, then. He was bigger and more solidly put together, and all the parts of his face were blunt, as Caesar's were sharp; when he smiled, I fancied I saw a ghost of Julio at the lips' corners, but I may have been looking for it. He left me after a polite few moments and took his own mount to ride along with us to Rome.

We were conducted to Caesar's transpontine villa, a house on the right bank of the Tiber, set apart from Rome proper, and wonderfully pretty, like a small jewel, among its flowering gardens. When we entered, I saw it was not small at all, except when compared to my Alexandrian palace, and it was completely staffed, with a meal and wine set out, and all the chambers aired and ready.

The prisoners, Arsinoëe and Ganymede, were accommodated in the stables; this was not at all like it sounds, for there was another building, quite large, apart from the horse-quarters, and a number of slaves were put in with them to serve them; guards, of course, were posted all around, for Caesar took no chances with this pair.

It was getting on for evening; the sun was low, making a ruddy sky. The meal was served upon a terrace in a spacious courtyard, overlooking the river; on the other bank one could see Rome, as if it were laid out for us alone. It is not beautiful as Alexandria is, but it has its own magic. It is a very new city, Rome; its outlines are all sharp, not softened by the formal dark green cypress trees that are planted everywhere. From where we watched, it looked, somewhat, as though a child had built it for a toy city; it is spread upon seven hills, and very evenly; a child's order prevails. There is much marble, pinkish now on the western side, and the buildings are set in long rows, and some of them very high—four stories or more. I saw at this first look many imitations of Greek temples and forums; thin columns of smoke go up in several places. It is too hot for anything but small cooking fires; they must be sacrificing in the temples, evening services. There is no color except the sun's reflection, and the blackish green of the cypresses; the city is all blinding white. The river Tiber is greenish black, too, not blue like the sea, or brown like the Nile; from here it looks to have a strong current, the small boats speeding along with it. I wondered where they were going, and what they carried. I questioned the young man Brutus, and he replied that it was a common means of travel, in the fair weather; people liked the cool breezes rather than the narrow, stuffy street-ways.

We were not to wait for Caesar, he said; he would come at sunset, when the Senate dispersed. I answered that I was still weary, and would take only a slice of melon and a little wine. "Though I doubt that Caesarion can wait," I said, eyeing him where he yawned and rubbed his eyes. "He must be given some porridge and milk and put to bed . . . he is in no state to meet his father . . ."

Brutus looked over at the boy. "He is the image of Caesar, for sure," he said, thoughtfully. He wore a little musing smile. "It will confound the doctors and seers, for they have all said that Caesar cannot father a male child . . ."

I stared; did he, then, not know about himself? I hesitated a moment and then said, watching him, "That is odd . . . for Caesar has told me that he has bastards all over the known world—and even in Rome."

His face did not change, except that his smile broadened. "Well . . . he ought to know . . ."

I dropped the topic and we talked idly of other things, a new play that was in preparation, a play in verse by the poet Catullus; the chariot races and the vast sums that were wagered on them; and of the coming Triumph. "It will be greater even than Pompey's," he said, "though less costly. Something for the plebes to remember . . ."

"Plebes?" I queried.

"The common folk . . . the lower sort of citizen. They love a spectacle; their lives are drab. And there will be free food at every corner, and the conduits running with wine."

I said, before I thought, "How horrid! They will all get sick from the street filth!"

"Oh, no," he said, gravely, shaking his head. "It is a custom . . . and they are used to it. Besides, the streets are washed down first."

I kept my thoughts to myself; what barbarians! Well, little by little, I will change all that, when I come to power.

Night was coming down fast; the lanterns had all been lit already before we saw a flicker of light upon the river. "That will be Caesar," said Brutus.

By now we were alone upon the terrace, except for attendant slaves. One by one I had sent the others off to their rest; we waited for Julio.

It seemed to me that a great change had come over Caesar; he looked to have aged ten years, though he was sunburned and smiling. Deep folds were graven into his cheeks beside his mouth, and his neck was corded and the skin sagged. The latest coin portraits of him had this look, but I had thought it simply the work of an inferior craftsman. His movements were all brisk and his arms hard when he embraced me, but when he sank onto the bench beside me, he seemed to droop a little in all his body. He reached out to take the wine goblet from me, and I saw his hand was shaking. I said nothing; he drained the goblet and silently held it out to Brutus to be refilled.

Then Brutus spoke what I had not dared. "Was it a hard day at the Senate, Caesar?"

"Tolerably," he answered, shortly.

There was a little silence. Brutus smiled. "I am not sorry to have missed it."

"Well," said Julio, heavily, "Let us not dwell on it . . . it was a day—like any other. All days are trying in the Senate." His own smile had a bitter tinge. He turned to me. "I have not asked you of your journey . . ."

"Oh," I said. "It went well, though some of us were seasick."

"You look fresh as a flower . . . and our son?"

"He was ready to drop . . . I have put him to bed . . . but we will look in on him later . . . after we have supped."

"You waited for me? You should not have; I am not hungry."

Even as he said it, though, he picked up a rusk of bread and ate it quickly, reaching for another. I signaled to a slave to bring the first course.

I talked while he ate, picking at my own food; he did not notice and ate hugely. Gods, I thought, he has forgotten to eat anything all day! It is a thing one must watch with Caesar; the Briton has told me he has known him to march twenty miles on an empty stomach. He has probably been doing this for nine months now, on all those great campaigns. No wonder he looks as he does!

As Brutus took his leave of us, I walked with him down the steps to the waiting boat, while Caesar rested against the cushions. Brutus smiled. "I have never seen him put away so much food. You are good for him . . ."

"I have to be," I said simply.

Together we tiptoed into the chamber where I had put Caesarion to sleep; I motioned the nurse to stay seated in her corner, putting my finger to my lips. Caesar looked long at his son, saying nothing. The boy lay, as always, on his back, with his arms bent and flung down on the mattress beside his head, the fingers curled into fists.

Julio laughed softly. "He feels the scepter in his fist already."

"Both fists are tight," I said lightly. "He might be wishing for the two snakes of Hercules . . ."

"He is fat," said Caesar, wonderingly.

"How not?" I said sharply. "All babies are fat. He is healthy, that is all."

He was silent for a moment. "Perhaps I have seen too many of the other kind . . ." His voice was somber; it was the first time he had ever hinted at the sights he had seen—and caused—in his conquering road. I said nothing, though once I might have. It is his problem, I thought, to wrestle with alone; nothing of mine. But it was a thing that sobered me always—those butchered millions.

Perhaps it was that thought that stole throughout my limbs and made me languorous; or maybe it was that I had not felt the touch of a man for so long. But when we lay together that night, nothing went as it should. I was long arousing, and he too quickly spent. Afterwards, I felt an aching void inside me; when it passed, I still could not sleep, weary as I was. It was as though I had an itch somewhere, and could not find it to scratch it.

I do not know what he felt; nothing at all, perhaps. For he fell asleep immediately and snored. I reminded myself that he was old, and that the day had been long.

2

LATER THAT WEEK, CAESAR FELL into a fit, frighteningly. The doctors called it epilepsy, and said he had been born with it, but it was the first I had ever seen of it.

Immediately, on my arrival in Rome, Caesar had commissioned a very famous sculptor, Archesilaus, to do a full-sized statue of me. I thought he meant it for the Triumph, to be pulled through the streets on wheels, as a sign of the subjugation of Egypt, and I was furious, and would not pose for the poor fellow when he arrived with his marble and chisel. I made him wait all day till Caesar came and I could confront him with it. I was pacing up and down the terrace, worked up into a fine rage, by the time Caesar stepped ashore from the river.

"How dare you use me so! How dare you—barbarian! I will show you Triumph . . . you will get no more monies from me or my country . . . I will raise arms against you . . . you will see who masters the world!"

He caught my wrists, the poor tired old statesman, and forced his voice to a cool level. "Listen, Cleopatra . . . listen, my love . . . The statue was meant as a surprise to you . . . and to all the Roman people . . . listen! There is a new and magnificent temple I have built, consecrated to Venus—for we Julians are descended from her, as you know. It will be ready by the end of summer, and opened to the public in a great ceremony. The statue of you is meant to stand within, in the most sacred shrine spot. It is to show your divinity as Venus—Astarte . . . and my consort . . ."

I was overcome, and burst into tears of remorse, throwing myself at his feet and sobbing aloud. He raised me quickly, saying, "Hush, child . . . do not let the artist hear you, or the household. You are not behaving like a queen . . ."

My tears stopped instantly and sparks flew in front of my eyes, but I stopped myself in time, and did not shout; I heard the wisdom in his words, as ever. Gods, when would I ever learn!

I was docile then, so much so that I made him smile.

"Do not overdo it, my darling . . . let us simply forget the whole matter . . ."

He had taken me in his arms, and I leaned against him, my head bowed onto his shoulder, when it happened. I felt his body stiffen and his hands grip me convulsively; I looked at his face, surprised, and thinking that he had angered suddenly. I had to back away, for what I saw so terrorized me. His eyes were fixed on nothing and bulging, and his face like stone, set in a grimace. I was like stone myself, for a moment, and in that time I watched him fall slowly, slowly to the floor. I thought he had been stricken, or his heart had failed, for he went over like a tree that has been felled. Just for an instant he lay stiff and still; then his limbs began to writhe, frighteningly, like serpents; his face turned purple, and white foam appeared at the corners of his lips. I knelt beside him, but I could not hold him, nor do I think he knew me at all. His body was like a thing apart, with no will, and rocked and shuddered in convulsions, while something hoarsely rattled in his throat. I ran for help, bringing Xeno and Cadwallader to hold him, for I thought he might do himself some damage.

The Briton looked at him for a moment, calm, then nodded to the black man. "Pin down his arms, Xeno . . ." He then took up a wooden stylus from my desk and thrust it between Caesar's teeth. I had seen someone do that once, long ago, with a dog that had run mad. "Fetch the doctor, Lady!" I rushed to do his bidding, not even thinking that I was obeying a slave!

By the time I returned with Dioscorides, the Briton and the black had bound Caesar's legs and arms, so that they did not thrash about; a cushion had been thrust beneath his neck, forcing his head to arch backwards; his eyes were open still and staring, but the foam had been wiped from his face. Dioscorides gave Cadwallader a sharp look. "Where did you learn that . . . to put something under the neck, against the vein?"

"The Druids . . . the priests of my country—I had some little training from them before . . . they call it 'the Demon disease' . . ."

The doctor's mouth was wry as he mixed a powder in some wine and stirred it. "Yes," he said. "And the Israelites call it 'the Prophets' Ecstasy' . . . and we call it a god-sign . . ."

Caesar's body quieted, after the medicine had been

forced into his mouth; he was put into his bed, and now lay, eyes closed, sleeping peacefully. Dioscorides said he would most probably sleep the night through, and the next day, for the sickness drained away energy. "Then he will be as if nothing had happened—indeed I think they do not remember . . . poor souls."

I questioned him closely about that sickness; he told me a great deal, but said that not a great deal was known; it was believed to be hereditary. I thought of Caesarion, and my face must have shown it; Dioscorides said, gently, that it most often skipped a generation. "And, then, too, Lady . . . they do not die of it, except if it brings on a stroke."

I asked, a little timidly, "Is it—weariness that causes it?"

"Perhaps . . . or a great deal of stress . . . too much for the nervous system."

"Oh," I wailed, "Then it is I who have caused it!" And I flung myself onto a couch and sobbed wildly.

"If you behave like this too often—yes," he said, raising me with a firm hand and looking close into my eyes. "Why do you do these uncontrolled things? You are a sensible woman, and intelligent."

It sobered me; I thought hard, and was honest in my answer.

"It is not with intent . . . I suppose it comes of being told always—or telling myself—that I am a goddess . . ."

"And a goddess has larger emotions than others?" He smiled and shook his head. "It should be the other way around . . ."

I was not angered at his presumption, for he had known me since I was a small child. I resolved to try to follow his advice. I was learning, however, that such resolutions are not always so easy to keep; a habit of years sticks. But with Caesar, and his son, I succeeded, in the main; the disease was an ugly one, and disquieting.

I asked Dioscorides if Caesar was aware of these attacks of his; he answered that he thought not, when they happened. "But he knows that there is something that he does not recall, and he knows he has been ill . . . that is usual. But I must call in a Roman doctor—one who has attended him before . . . there is no cure, but if I can understand how often and how long he has been afflicted, there is perhaps an easement."

When he had consulted with other physicians, he told me that Caesar's attacks had all been in his childhood and early youth, until now. He had been thought to have outgrown it. Oddly, he said that Caesar had been worried, for he had been taught by his mother that it was an illness that proved he was a god; he feared that the sign had been lifted from him!

"Do you think it is a god's disease, Dioscorides?" I asked. "And tell me the truth."

He smiled and shook his head. "There are beggars who have it . . . and doctors . . . and kings. It is a sign of nothing, a weakness—that is all."

"A superstition, then . . ." I said, slowly, for I was thinking. "But it can be useful . . . I want you to tell him of this attack—when he recovers."

Dioscorides looked at me strangely, but nodded.

As for me, I knew what I was doing. Caesar was a rational man. One must have within a bit of unreason to believe in one's own godhead. And, though he might be emperor in Rome—he could never rule in Egypt without it.

3

THE STATUE OF ME WAS FINISHED before the Triumph; it seemed to me that the sculptor hurried. I still had some suspicions that he had been ordered to have it ready for Caesar to parade through the winding streets of Rome, but I never again taxed my Julio with it; I simply ordered it shrouded and the chamber where it stood locked; I myself kept the key. When Caesar came to view it, I bade him wait while I fetched the key from its hiding place. He gave me a shrewd and knowing look, and then softened it into a smile, approving. "Yes," he said, "it is well . . . let us keep it hidden until the great day when we place it in its rightful niche within the Temple." He carried it off well, but I never knew the rights of his intent. When I refused his request for a companion key, he shook his head sadly, but I ignored it; it was he who had taught me caution, after all!

I did not much admire the sculpture; it was to the Roman taste, lifeless, and ornate, with much too much attention paid to the fall of the draperies and the representation of the royal jewelry, all of which Caesar insisted that I wear. Before it was painted it had a certain austere dignity, for the marble itself has beauty; when the paints were laid on, though, it had a vulgar look. Our Hellene artists have a light touch with the coloring of marbles, using soft tints and subtle hues and blending them with delicacy, so that the marble shone through with its own character. I could forgive the garish colors of the robes and jewels, but the flesh was as pink as boiled shrimp, the lips painted like a courtesan's, and the eyes had emeralds set in! He had given me golden hair as well, though that was not so bad, for the Venus is always represented so, from custom. And then, too, I thought it did not in the least resemble me, except for the mouth; Caesar, however, admired it greatly; taste, I have found, is an acquired thing; one must be exposed to fineness over and over until it sinks in. I resolved to put my mind to it with this great man, my lover; however, this was not the time to begin. I merely said I thought the colors overbright. He answered that it was done on purpose, so that the statue would age well. I thought, by that time I will have it replaced, my dear barbarian!

I showed it to Iras and Apollodorus, privately; I could see by their faces that they thought as I did. Caesarion, though, wriggling in Iras' arms, stretched out his chubby arms to it, and cried, "Mama!" I shall have to work on him as well. Luckily, we have an early start.

I had as yet made no public appearances in Rome, though the young man Brutus had taken me across the river to see the sights of the city. I went in my plainest dalmatica and with my hair covered, without jewels, and with only one slave from the villa, so I was not even stared at. Close to, the city, except for its grand public buildings, is unprepossessing. There are no broad avenues such as we have in Alexandria, and no planting, except the sudden formal groves of cypresses, which look quite scraggy and brown. The streets are indeed so narrow that one is forbidden by law to take a carriage into them; all traffic is by foot, even produce being carried in baskets on the heads of slaves. I wondered how the Triumph could be conducted through such alleys, but Brutus said it would be mostly by barge on the river Tiber, until it reached the open forum before the Capitol.

The rows and rows of buildings, so white from a distance, were really quite dirty, though the city is so new. And the streets are really filthy, though it was explained that there is a very sophisticated sewage system, with underground pipes that carry the waste to the river. Still, there seem to be no laws against littering; one treads on refuse of all sorts, and must be very careful indeed not to slip on the squashed fruits and the spilled oil. And then there seem to be so very many poor folk, unwashed and in rags, some begging, others squatting in corners like flung-away refuse themselves. "They all seem so idle," I said. "Do their masters have no work for them then?"

"Oh, they are not slaves, Lady," answered Brutus. "They are all Roman citizens. They cannot do slaves' work . . . they are all free."

Free, I thought; free to beg, to steal. I said aloud, "If they do not work, how then do they live? What do they eat?"

"Well, there is a dole every morning . . . the Senate voted on it. Of course, it is first come, first served . . ." He shrugged. "What can be done? The poor are everywhere . . ."

I frowned. "Instead of a dole, there should be a work program. Surely there are public buildings being erected, and workmen needed, masons, carpenters . . ."

"There are slaves for that," he said, shaking his head. "Except for the skilled craftsmen . . ."

"Then these free people should be taught a trade," I said. "One cannot simply say, 'You are free, now live on your freedom . . .' " I was indignant, for truly, the meanest subject in Alexandria does not look so starved, except in a famine. "I will speak to Caesar about it . . ."

He gave an odd look at me, and said, "Caesar is not king . . . he can do nothing without the Senate."

I set my lips; change would have to come. These Romans needed a king! But I said no more, for I saw that this young man had no understanding of me at all, or what I meant.

One thing the Republic had created; whether for good or not is open to question. There is an ease of movement in public places; even the noblewomen go attended by one slave, or even none, through all the meanest streets. I saw many richly dressed aristocrats rubbing shoulders with the vulgar citizenry. I was curious, and asked about it. "Are they not in danger of being set upon and robbed?"

"Well, no, Lady," he said. "Except after dark, of course." And he pointed to a pair of soldiers, armed with swords, and carrying thick clubs. "There is the Special Legion, to keep the peace—two at every corner. Oh, the Roman streets are well patrolled . . ."

"I see." And I looked closely at one of these soldiers as we drew near. He was very young, barely into his teens, I guessed, but with an arrogant look; he gave me back stare for stare.

"And they are citizens?" I asked. "And who pays their salaries?"

"Well," he said, laughing, "there are two questions you have asked. They are citizens, yes . . . and they are paid by private parties, that own the buildings and the land . . ."

"Oh, I had thought it all state property."

"Oh, no, Lady . . . this block of tenements, for instance, belongs to the family of Calpurnius—" He cast a quick look at me, and actually blushed, cutting off his sentence. I was amused, but made no sign; the property holder must be Caesar's wife's father, or uncle; her name was Calpurnia. I had never bothered a great deal about her, though the marriage was still in effect; the union had been purely political, and the couple had lived apart for a long while.

"It is a wealthy family then?" I scanned the row of houses, all alike. They were all in need of a coat of paint, and mostly the doors hung off their hinges or were missing altogether, and the shutters broken at the windows. They looked to have been hastily built, too; some of the undertimbers had rotted and the roofs sagged; one had a gaping hole in it. "The Calpurnians do not seem to care for their property," I said. "These are in very bad repair . . ."

"Well," he said, "what can you expect? The rents are low . . . and then the tenants are a destructive sort, not used to good things . . ."

I smiled wryly, for I could see the poor tenants for myself; mostly they sat, the women and children, upon the high stoops that led to the doorway; inside was probably airless; one could smell the musty smell of poverty even in the streets. This was the sort of thing I held council for, at home; to right the wrongs done by the landlords, and listen to the tenants' complaints. Apparently there were no laws to that effect here in Rome. A small child, very dirty, caught my eye and advanced to me, holding out her little grubby paw; she was not a great deal older than Caesarion. I reached into my purse and took out a small coin.

"Ah, Lady," said Brutus. "Now you have done it! They

will all be begging . . ." And it was true; already a little silent group had gathered, children with deep, hungry eyes and sullen mouths.

I was aghast, and emptied my purse, putting coins into every small hand I could reach. Of course the coins gave out, for as if by some magic, a crowd gathered, clamoring; he hurried me away from the clutching hands. As we reached the corner, I saw the two soldiers, grasping their clubs, pass us, to go among them; their eyes were hard.

"What will they do?" I asked, frightened. "They will not beat them . . . ?"

"Oh, no . . . just frighten them away. It does not do to let a crowd collect."

"But they are only children!"

"They must be taught early."

I set my mouth, for I did not approve; I had mutinous, angry thoughts all the way home, and that evening, when Caesar came to sup with me, I spoke of it to him, angrily.

He heard me out, then said, heavily, "Yes, I have spoken over and over again to the Calpurnians . . . they have no civic sense."

"But nor do any of them!" I cried. "All the tenements are filthy . . . and dangerous to live in. They are packed like salted fish in a barrel! What if a fire broke out?"

"We have fire fighters . . . it is a law just passed . . ." He was infuriatingly calm; besides, he had drawn me off the subject, which was the injustice of the whole system. I brought him back to it, explaining carefully and not with heat, and ended up, ". . . and that is why I hold weekly council, you see. A queen must take care of her subjects."

He smiled at me, maddeningly indulgent, and said, drily, "My dear, you will find that Rome is a more difficult city to rule than your Alexandria . . . there are so many factions here, you see . . . and all of them must be satisfied . . ."

I was silent a moment, and then said, slowly, "Yes . . . that is why a head of state is needed . . . not just the title of dictator, which is good in its way. But Rome needs a wise ruler . . ." And I looked at him steadily. He gnawed a little at his lip, then said, abruptly. "Well, my dear, you may be right. And now let us talk of pleasanter things . . ." And he put his arm around my shoulders. His face, though, still wore a thoughtful look; I had sown a seed.

4

I HAD HEARD of the great Roman Triumphs; every victor in every war of Rome celebrates his victory in this way, provided, of course, that he has enough money to pay for it. The last expensive and elaborate Triumph had been Pompey's; my father saw it, and was much impressed. Of course, that means little, for he was impressed with anything Roman, poor man. They say Pompey spent more than Caesar; I cannot see how, for Caesar's Triumph lasted four days, and the streets ran, as promised, with wine; oxen were roasted at every corner, and only a small portion given to the gods. Besides, there was the cost of the interminable processions, including barges, ramps, and the demolition of several whole blocks of tenements to make room in the narrow streets. I personally paid the owners of these, and bought, as well, a block of small villas, just built, outside the city, to house those tenants that had been displaced, more than three thousand plebes. Later, I heard that many highly placed Romans wondered how I had such a firm hold on the hearts of the poor! This was just the first of my Roman charities. On the other hand, I refused Caesar a loan when he overstepped his bounds in the Triumph: I considered it was enough that I let him name my country as one of his conquests. He answered that it was a policy agreed upon. I said that policy did not include beggaring myself as well. He took it well; I think he had not had much hope of my paying anyway.

I was present throughout the four days, seated on a raised platform with all the notables of the city; it was my first public appearance. I wore the classic Ionic chiton, of finely pleated eastern silk, saffron-dyed; Caesarion, in my arms, was dressed in blue. The crowd of common people cheered me when I took my seat; the word of my bounty had spread. Indeed, whenever I rose, or was bowed to, in all the four days, I was acclaimed with shouting and the stamping of feet.

Caesarion I kept with me only till his father rode by and greeted him; such small children grow restless quickly, and besides, the point was made; I had a nurse take him home before he cried and spoiled the effect.

I saw myself, in my mind's eye, seated beside those other ladies of Rome, and smiled within. I had dressed my hair simply; low on the nape of my neck, with no jewels except my slim serpent crown, which is elegant and very becoming, and the two large British pearls, gifts from Caesar, that I wore at my ears. It was late in the summer and very hot, but my silk dress was thin and cool, and I sat under a canopy, which I had ordered. All the ladies carried sunshades or were fanned by slaves, but they looked hot and uncomfortable. It was the fashion in Rome to be slender; those who could not starve themselves down to size wore tight bindings under their robes, a miserable feeling in such weather. Elaborate wigs were in style that year as well; one could see, even from a distance, the droplets of sweat that beaded the carefully painted faces.

The young man Brutus attended me, dividing his time between my place and the section where his wife sat; I presume Caesar had ordered him to explain things to me, see to my refreshments, and make a path for me as I came and went. His wife was named Portia; I never knew how she felt about his partial desertion; she looked quite amiable when he pointed her out to me, bowing and smiling. She sat in a sort of enclosed box, with some other ladies and their attendants; Caesar's wife, Calpurnia, sat next to her. And very stiff she looked; but perhaps it was the fashionable tight bindings. There was too much distance, but she did seem older than I had believed her to be, upwards of thirty at least. She had produced no children, but was not barren; there had been a series of miscarriages. Privately I thought, no wonder, she has crushed them all with those corselets she wears. Well, I shall not voice the thought, for the poor creature's miscarrying is my good fortune. Besides, I am quite sure he has not been to her bed for some years; certainly not while I have been here! Even Caesar could hardly manage that! Also, as Iras whispered, Calpurnia looked biddable, rather than beddable; Iras has a mischievous wit.

The fellow Marcus Antonius came to my side to pay his respects; I thought he had improved in looks, and manners, too. But then Caesar thought highly of him, and perhaps my feelings were tempered by that, as they were so often by Caesar. When he had taken his leave, Iras whispered, in a voice trembling with mirth, that he had shaved his legs for the Triumph. I refused to laugh; I knew that Caesar needed all the friends he could hold on to.

The first day of the Triumph celebrated the victory in Gaul and the Gaulish lands. Caesar led it, in a chariot covered with gold leaf, and wearing the victor's wreath in gold. When he passed me, he put his hand to his heart and bowed low; I inclined my head. For some reason this delighted the crowd; I could hardly keep from smiling, for I overheard their comments. "Give it to him, lass!" . . . "Give the queen treatment!" . . . "Watch her snub the old lecher . . . good for his soul!" . . . "Watch out, Old Baldy!" I do not know if he heard, too; probably not, for the chariot wheels were just beneath him, and he was followed by forty elephants. I did not understand the significance of this, for Gaul has no elephants; I presume they were just there to dazzle the people, who were not familiar with those great beasts, as we are at home. The rest of the day was taken up with the passing of the many legions who had fought in the Gaulish wars; some of them, too, were very slow, for they were comprised of old men, maimed men, half-men; some hobbling on one leg, between two comrades, many missing an arm, or an eye, and every one with a face hewn of rock; they numbered in the thousands. I thought of all the others, who had not come home, maimed or otherwise, but had fallen in some foreign soil, picked clean by foreign vultures; I guess the crowd felt it too, for though there were some hoarse ragged cheers, they soon fell silent, and one heard nothing but the uneven tramping and scuffling that marked their passage. I am no Roman, but I hate waste; these had marched forth and far from home in the bursting glory of their youth: for them it was no Triumph.

Nor was it surely for those that came after, the mercenaries of the conquered lands, though they stepped out bravely, and held their heads high, their pale or ruddy, non-Roman heads. The last of these legions was the famous one they called "The Lark," comprised of chieftains' sons of the savage tribes of Gaul, Germany, and Britain. The night I first met Caesar, wrapped close in my carpet, that had been the password: "The Lark"—for this legion had then just been formed, and was the favorite of Caesar. I looked for Cadwallader, my Briton friend, for he marched among them. But among so many redheads, and all dressed and armored alike, all huge as these northern tribes are, he passed me by unseen. The common folk clapped them on and shouted acclaim, for they were a handsome, showy sight in their fine polished brass and high-plumed helmets. Above the golden eagles of the legions, their special banner flew, a design of a myriad small black birds, cunningly painted against a storming sky.

Then came the worst sight of all, the captives; they, also, numbered in the thousands. Some hundreds of them carried on their backs the big crosses they would die on; these were mostly the big men, the enemy warriors, with no wounds except for the chafed places where their chains had bitten; they had been kept in some dungeon somewhere underground, for they all had the prison pallor, like old cheese. Their eyes, mostly light, glared fiercely from out their shaggy bearded faces; their ribs showed sharp in their half-naked bodies, still knotted with muscle. I caught the eye of one as he passed, not intending to; he spat viciously. Brutus whispered in my ear that these with the crosses were worse than beasts, untamed and showing no remorse; they would make a brave show in the slow cross death, for they were strong and rebellious and hard to kill; I stared at him in horror, but his blunt face was still kindly; he had no thought of what he had said, it was the Roman way!

Next came the poor creatures in wicker cages, too small for them to more than huddle in; these looked maimed and sickly, half-starved. Brutus said they would die the death of their own savage tribes, by burning, within these cages, as they had burnt those Roman soldiers who had fallen into their hands, a fitting revenge. I felt pity, and my stomach heaved, but I saw the Roman crowd felt nothing but hatred; they shouted curses, and pelted the cages with filth and clods of earth.

At the very last, surrounded by guards, came Vercingetorix, walking slowly in his chains. This was the great hero-warrior of all Gaul, emperor and general as well; he had fought a hard long war, unifying all the tribes under his banner, and very nearly won. I think he might indeed have come away with much victory, but he had reckoned the cost too dear. He saw how Caesar was butchering his people, in the millions, and made a bargain, giving himself as hostage for a peaceful settlement. He had been a prisoner now for six long years; though he was not old, his long yellow hair was streaked with gray, and deep lines were carven beside his mouth. His chains were very heavy, and his steps shortened by the length of chain between his ankles, but he did not stumble or bow his head; instead he paced his steps to suit the chain, walking slowly and with dignity, looking straight ahead, now and then blinking his eyes against the sun; he must have been kept in the dark for a long time.

He was not stripped naked, like his soldiers, or in armor either, but dressed in his king's garb; it was outlandish but still regal, a great bib of yellow gold lay on his breast and wide armbands encircled his lean arms, a thin crown of some metal, very old it looked, upon his brow. A great fur cloak hung from his shoulders, some thick red pelts worked round in layers and reaching to the ground; at his shoulders were huge gold ornamented clasps to hold it. The crowd, for once, held its breath as he passed; he was too royal to be mocked, though one little boy let fly a clod of horse dung, his mother slapping him afterwards. He had the name of hero, even here in Rome, did Vercingetorix. I had heard Caesar speak of him with respect and even awe; that night, by torchlight, he died with the rest of his countrymen, having refused clemency. The people did not get the straight of it, and many blamed Caesar, calling him cruel. But it was not Caesar's will, but the great king himself decided. These people still have the king-sacrifice that used to be in all religions; the king dies for the good of his people, and goes to his death consenting. Vercingetorix had meant this all along; it is a pity that it was misunderstood. But, perhaps, among his own, the sacrifice is remembered. I know that Caesar wept.

I did not watch the executions, though most of Rome did. The next morning eyes were red and swollen from lack of sleep, and some folk looked to be still drunk. This morning the parade began with animals from Egypt, strange to the Romans; giraffes, their long necks poking up through the bars of their cages and their huge eyes staring unafraid, while they chewed as peacefully as any cow; pretty little striped zebras led through the streets on a fine ribbon of silk; wonderfully colored talking birds from the jungle, squawking out curses in Latin; sad-faced monkeys that gibbered frantically at the crowd from their cages and hung from their tails; a great gorilla, that hairy creature so like a man, and so unlike, and, of course, the somnolent crocodile with its scales and its wicked eye; slaves flung buckets of water over it constantly, for it would have died otherwise. This creature does not live long in captivity, and it is a sacred animal to the ancient folk of my country; I hoped Casesar would remember my warning, to put it into a water tank before the day was over.

This was, of course, the day devoted to what he called "the Egyptian Triumph"; I let it go for now. Mostly the wonders of my country were displayed; models of Pharos lighthouse, all the museums, the Alexandrian palace, each of the temples, and even a long, serpentine representation of the Nile, with its sands and palms; at the last Caesar had included what is the most interesting and curious of all, at my insistence, models of the great Pyramids and that mysterious, long-ruined colossus, The Sphinx. The people cried out in wonder, though of course they had no idea of the vastness of these structures. There were some of the army of Alexandria, some of the priests, doctors, and teachers, all in the robes of their orders; and there were some works of ancient art, paintings and sculptures, borrowed from the tombs of the richest of the Pharaohs of the Upper Nile.

Last came the ugly, massive statues of Pothinus and the rest of our dead enemies, exaggeratedly ugly and fearsome, almost comical; the people of Rome jeered, and for once I did not mind the temper of this barbarian crowd. Then that woeful sight, my sister Arsinoëe and her paramour Ganymede, walking in chains; she was never fond of me, and I truly might number her among my enemies, but my heart was sick to see the house of Ptolemy so degraded. True, she was dressed in silk, and her chains were of light gold and set far apart for ease; she looked very small and defenseless as she trudged along behind her lover. She did not walk proudly, but with her eyes downcast; I thought I saw a thin red in her cheeks that was not painted. I could not bear it and stood up, lifting my arm, and giving the signal that meant mercy at the Games, or so I had been told. Caesar sat beside me; he did not ride today, out of deference to me; I heard him give a little sound of exasperation before he pulled me to my seat. "Sit!" he commanded. "Do you think I would condemn your sister?" He had been swift, but still my movement had drawn curious eyes; some of the common folk cheered me, for I suppose they pitied the poor girl, and approved my sisterly feelings; I had not known that I had them!

Caesar halted the procession, signing to a centurion;

when it was still, a horn was blown, and the centurion, at a private word from Caesar, led Arsinoëe, still in her chains, to the place where we sat; she looked bewildered.

Caesar stood, raising his hand for quiet. He spoke; I remembered he was known for his oratory. His voice carried well, and the crowd kept silent. He pronounced that, due to the pleas of the great and merciful queen of Egypt, her traitorous sister would be granted mercy; I cannot remember all his words, but they were well chosen, for a speech that was unprepared; the crowd was moved to tears—and to cheers.

He then, shooting a sly glance at me, his mouth in a pleased line, personally struck off her chains and, leading her to a place beside me, gave her the kiss of peace. I had to follow suit; it was the first contact we two sisters had had since early childhood. My lips, touching her cheek, felt salt; she was slippery with the sweat of fear. I felt pity, and embraced her.

A place was made for her to sit beside me, under the canopy, and I sent a slave to fetch a cool drink. Caesar clapped his hands; the course of the Triumph continued.

I stole a glance at Arsinoëe; she sipped the watered wine. I saw that her cheeks were flushed and her eyes overbright. She whispered low, "What of Ganymede . . . ?"

"He will die," I said. The ready tears poured down her face, but she made no sound. What did she expect? Someone must pay for it.

The third day dealt with Caesar's conquest of Pontus; I did not stay throughout, for the displays were dull, and bore no relation to me or mine. The only interesting thing was the huge banner with the words, *"Veni, vidi, vici,"* which was carried before Caesar. He was said to have uttered those arrogant, alliterative words, after the Pontus victory; of course I did not hear them. It sounded like Caesar, though; he had a common streak, like all Romans. And, like all Romans, he loved his upstart language. Well, it lends itself to such play well enough; it is otherwise when it comes to poetry or anything of subtlety; there one must have the Greek.

The fourth and last day was the celebration of the victories in northern Africa. Some offense was felt, and some of the Roman people shook their fists and shouted in anger, for images of conquered Romans were carried through the streets, as well as captured Roman arms. I was not consulted, of course, but I could have told him such a display would be a tactical error.

In fact, when the image of Pompey was seen before them, there was such a surge from the populace that the procession had to be stopped, and the image draped. The great dead Cato's statue was brought, after that, but by then Caesar had learned a lesson, for it was crowned in a laurel wreath of gold, hurriedly stuck on the marble head; by the time it got to where I sat, it was slightly askew, so that the great man looked drunk. But no one else seemed to notice.

There was a parade of other lesser enemies, some dozen or so; Gneus Pompey, my Neo, was among them. My heart gave a little jump when that image was carried past; the sculptor had got him to the life.

I did not watch the last of the executions either, where Ganymede met his death. I never derived any joy from such sights, and indeed, I prevailed upon Caesar to commute his sentence to a mere beheading, for Arsinoëe's sake; he insisted that she be made to witness it, as an example; I did not think she could bear to watch a crucifixion. Even as it was, she was hysterical, and I gave her a secret small dose of poppy juice to dull her wits.

I refused to have her in my custody, though; her claws had been cut, but still I did not trust her; I knew my sister too well. She was a problem, in truth, for she could not be locked up like a common felon; it would not look good. It took the two of us, Julio and me, a whole evening of planning to fathom what to do with her.

"I shall send her to Cornelia, Pompey's widow, at Alba," he said, finally, with an air of having found the perfect answer. "That lady is kind and will be merciful—but she will remember that Egyptians killed her husband . . ."

"Not Arsinoëe," I said, shaking my head. "She had nothing to do with Pompey's death . . ."

"No matter," he said, airily. "It will do."

He stared at me a moment, and snapped his fingers. "I had almost forgotten," he said. "We can have an exchange of hostages . . . there is another princess there . . . in Pompey's Alban villa. A girl who has lived in that house for years. I sent her there with my Julia when she married long ago—" His voice broke, as always when he thought of his dead daughter; I remembered Julia had once been Pompey's wife, and waited.

He went on. "That girl—Charmion, she was called—had been raised with Julia, after I took her from the royal house of Cyprus . . ."

"My cousin?" I asked. "My cousin of Cyprus?"

This was, truly, the Charmion I had given up for dead, daughter of that uncle I remembered for his kindness and, as well, for his nobility of mind. He had taken his own life, rather than be subject to Rome, when his country fell. "I remember her, dimly," I said. "We met once, I think, when we were children."

"Julia was fond of her," he said. "And now I shall give her to you for a lady in waiting . . ."

I curbed the answer that rose hotly to my lips; a Roman giving away a royal princess of Egypt! Well, but for the smiling gods, I should be in her place. I smiled at him, and thanked him prettily. "I will like that, Julio," I said.

And so Charmion came to me. We were long years together; in time she was my dearest friend, after Iras. A faithful girl, and a royal soul. It is difficult, now, to imagine life without her.

5

IF THE TRIUMPH WAS NOT WHOLLY A TRIUMPH, the dedication of the Temple of Venus was even less so, although the disapproval came from a different source. The common folk of Rome, as I had guessed before I ever knew their temper, sought, always, a figure to adore; which is why they would not have their old idols, Cato, Pompey, and the rest, pulled down. It is also the reason why they accepted, and even welcomed my deification as Venus-Isis, in the new temple. Not so the aristocrats; they had watched, unmoved, while the heavily caricatured images of the former great Romans moved ponderously through the streets, but they were too urbane and too knowing to grant immortality to a mortal—even a queen. A week before the formal opening of the Temple, paid scribes had copied out lengthy treatises against the whole ceremony and these were circulated heavily throughout the city. Oddly enough, they did not criticize me, the goddess object, but their own hero, Caesar, for the instigation of what they called "a blasphemy." I read these pieces myself; they were worded well, designed to rouse up all those nobles who had civic ambition or pride. I took one to Caesar, trying to dissuade him from the ceremony or at least to delay until the climate was more favorable. He would not hear of it; like his epilepsy, his fits of arrogance were becoming more frequent. "Caesar can do no wrong!" he said.

The morning of the ceremony, Rome's greatest orator, a man called Cicero, spoke against it in the open Forum; I did not attend the speechmaking, but Apollodorus did, and pronounced it both sensible and effective. Again I tried to sway Caesar and failed; the ceremony went on as planned.

It was nothing more than opening the Temple to the public, a few prayers, a sacrifice, and the unveiling of the statue, but the press of people was so great that we were hard put to it to get through to our reserved places. And this without free food or wine! Of course, there were no cheers, for we were within a holy place, but the simple folk bowed before me, their foreheads touching the floor at my feet as I passed through. I knew this adulation was for me; indeed, from their whispered words, it was quite obvious; Caesar, however, took it to himself, and inclined his head gravely, wearing the mien of an Olympic. Not that I felt usurped, but I had grown up with this goddess-worship, and wore the look from habit; it did not sit so well on him; he needed practice. But I did not dare tell him so.

There were some of the higher orders in the Temple as well, though I saw no woman among them. Brutus was there, and Antonius, to whom I nodded graciously; the others I knew only by sight. Cicero himself was there; he was pointed out to me, a short old man with a heavy face and very large nose, even for a Roman. One could not read his face.

When the statue was unveiled, nature showed she was on our side; the Temple was alight with rushes and candles, for the interior was dim, unlike our Greek temples; one of the heavy great doors was ajar, just a slit, but it sent a ray of light that struck the gemmed eyes of the image, making them appear to flash in living flesh. The common folk sank, with a soft sighing, to their knees. Then someone near the door, an aristocrat I suppose, shut it, and it was marble once again. Still, it was an effective moment; luck was always with me in Rome—at least in those first days.

Caesar gave a reception at his villa the evening of the

Temple's opening; it was to formally introduce me to Roman society. It was not such a small group or too exclusive, Roman society; I saw a number of the equestrian class, but Iras whispered that perhaps they had bribed the doorkeeper. I told her if she did not hold her tongue, I would see that she was barred the door. I spoke fondly, but still I feared that one of her sallies, fortunately timed, might set me to laugh aloud in some stern senatorial face. The gods know it was difficult enough to keep countenance among all that outmoded purple; I had almost persuaded Caesar to leave it off, though he still wore a narrow band at the edge of his evening tunic.

Brutus presented me to his wife; it should have been the other way around, but I let it go. She was a pleasant little woman with a pretty face, though somewhat dumpy of figure. I noticed that all these Roman ladies, close to, were dark-complected and dark-eyed, though most of them had bleached or hennaed hair or wore fair-colored wigs. There were two notable exceptions, Antonius' wife, Fulvia, a vivacious, quicksilver creature with a petulant mouth, and the gloriously beautiful, notorious Clodia; both wore their own luxuriant black ringlets, elaborately dressed. Clodia was famous—or infamous—throughout the world; she was the "Lesbia" of the late Catullus' poems; since his death a few years ago she had become more profligate than ever. I stared at her curiously; it had left no mark, her lascivious life, if indeed it were even true; her face was unlined, her eyes sparkled, and she wore no paint. I have never been able to share Roman enthusiasm for this poet's work; he is said to be the most "Greek" of all, but I found his poems offensively erotic; that has never been the Greek way! His translations from Sappho—yes, those are quite perfect, both in cadence and thought. But then it is difficult to cheapen Sappho; the words say all.

The orator Cicero was a surprise; I had thought I would sense disapproval, but his face and voice gave no sign of his feelings. He even admired my dalmatica! We spoke Greek; he had a Thessalian accent, but of course I did not say so; he was proud of his grammar. One thing I will give him; he is more cultivated of mind than his fellows here; he can speak, besides the Greek, most of the dialects of Italy, and is reasonably fluent in the Arabic. We discussed the origin of languages; he is interested in learning Hebrew; I promised to send to Alexandria for some books in that language.

"I can give you the alphabet, at least," I said. "But I have not tested myself as a teacher; it is an art in itself." If he took my meaning—which is that all the best teachers, in any subject, are Greeks—he did not show it. I cannot resist making remarks of that sort here in Rome, though no one gets the point, and I cannot, in courtesy, hammer it home.

It was an amiable gathering, and went off well, except that Marcus Antonius drank too much. Perhaps it was because his wife left early with an equestrian. I had seen his eyes flash moodily at her earlier; I did not think it a purely political marriage.

6

I DID NOT SEE much of Caesar in the daytime, for he was busy with his Senate duties; he had been made dictator again, and there was talk of making him dictator for ten years, though there was muttering against it too; I have my spies.

Time did not lie too heavily with me, though; after the reception I had many callers, the women arriving in pairs in the morning, each with a small house gift and a large fund of gossip, the men arriving in the afternoon alone, and being turned away at the door. Could it be they thought to trick me thus? We Greeks are long masters of such intrigues; no one could ever get a stick to beat me with—no, not all the time I was in Rome, nearly three years.

I never got used to the Roman customs; to my Greek mind they were always barbarians, pure and simple. They, to a man, loved all things Greek; unfortunately, they took from us only the bad (for even Greeks have some bad habits). The Greek love of festivals became, with the Romans, an excuse for the vilest orgy; the love of good food, well prepared, that the Greeks had learned from their Eastern neighbors, became a habit of day-long feasting, with every kind of food and sauce going into the stomach indiscriminately, and usually coming up again! Homosexual love, accepted in the Hellene world and even there abused, with the Romans became a vicious and even criminal practice. Their wine flowed unwatered, adultery was almost the rule; religious cults blazed up and died down like brush fires within the year; murder went unpunished; politics were a snarled mess, impossible to untangle. To name a few only. Long, long ago—before the great days of Hellas—Solon of Athens said wisely, "Nothing in excess." It became the cornerstone of Greek living. I do not think the Romans ever heard the saying!

The true barbarians, the Gauls, and Germans, and those northern tribes such as the one Cadwallader belonged to, practiced no such excesses; they lived by a rough, raw code of ethics, but it was a code. The Romans, as I see it now, were a young race, grown old too quickly, which passed all moderation at a gallop.

I have as yet said nothing of the Roman Games, which were held with regularity in the huge amphitheater, and paid for by any wealthy Roman who wished to court the plebes. The first of such games that I saw was organized by Marcus Antonius, and the cost was put on to Caesar's account, for Antonius was the solid mainstay of the Caesarian party. It occurred shortly after the dedication of the Temple of Venus and was partly done to call attention to that event. Caesar commanded that I go, with all my household. Although I knew what to expect, the reality was worse than the report.

"Games," they were called, after the old Olympic contests. But these were a corruption; there was no contest, really. Instead of champions striving for the victor's crown and the pride of being accounted the best, here the contestants were slaves, and the prize was life, for a little while anyway. The contestants were called gladiators and were bought up for that occupation from all over the conquered Roman world, and trained intensively, sometimes for many months, and at great expense to the state. And all to die in the arena.

For they did all die, eventually. I was told that the life of a gladiator was three months after he first entered the arena; the longest anyone had lasted was a year! And these were the trained men; sometimes, at the end, or the beginning, a great mock battle would be fought, by untrained men with simple weapons, a battle to the death, without a victor; it was slaughter, pure and simple. Spartacus, the great slave rebel, had been a gladiator, I remembered; no wonder that he rebelled!

We were in a group, all my household; Iras and my new-found cousin Charmion sat in the box next to me, with

Apollodorus and Cadwallader just behind, for Caesar sat in the donor's place, a little way apart. Charmion had tried to beg off, for she had gone before, having been reared in a Roman house; I would have allowed it, but Caesar said it would not look well, that all those close to me must make an appearance. I had grown fond of her already, Charmion; she was not pretty, like Iras, nor witty, either, but she had a wonderful queenly presence; she was royal, after all, on both sides, like me. She was big-boned, like a Roman woman, and inclined to put on weight; she picked at her food to keep thin, and drank no wine or beer. Caesar thought her overstern, but she made a good balance in our household; I knew, of course, that her sternness was defensive; she had lived among her conquerors so long! It stood her in good stead at these so-called Games, too. She was able to keep her countenance at the cruelest sights; Iras hid her face and even I had to close my eyes at times.

The noise was deafening; the smell of blood was rank.

After each event, the arena slaves dragged off the dead, the hacked-up carcasses, no longer human, and strewed fresh sawdust. Still the smell of blood prevailed; one might hold a scented cloth to one's nose, or sprinkle perfumes all about, it did not help. After an hour, in the heat and under the sun, one *felt* the blood, sticky on the hands, clogging the throat. I sat throughout the day without taking food, and drank barley water in sips; wine was a blood-color, after all.

There were a variety of weapons used; swords, spears, clubs, axes; one event, much applauded, was between two men armed with nets and tridents, the idea being to fling the net about the opponent and spear him, helpless, like a great fish. That particular Games day, my first, I think, if I recall correctly, closed with a lion hunt; the beasts had been starved to make them attack, for they do not like human flesh. It was, perhaps, the worst; it is hard to judge. The crowd liked it best; they are all Romans.

As I said, I was accompanied by all my nearest people; they felt as I did, but, except for Iras, showed no emotion. I sensed the temper of my Gauls, behind me, and of Cadwallader, too. They might all, each one, so easily have been in those gladiators' armor! Caesar and I had had our first near-quarrel about this day; he had ordered that Caesarion be present, for the look of it, and to advertise his parentage.

I could not countenance this, even for the gratification that his recognition might give me. A child, unknowing, to see such sights, and to become immune to them! And, bear in mind, I did not know how bad those sights were, truly! I was right in this, as was happening often now; at first Caesar was more prudent than I in all things; I had grown up fast at Rome.

Even in those first months of Roman living, I saw that Caesar, though immensely popular, needed to tread with care; the party of Pompey was still alive, in spite of its great defeats. It seemed to me, though of course I could not say so, that Caesar, to overcome the sympathy for this dead Roman, did all the wrong things. He spent enormous sums to curry the favor of the crowd, which was with him anyway, and, on the other hand, did nothing at all to win over those aristocrats and influential, monied merchants who had been adherents of Pompey. All the displays that he ordered and spent vastly on, were in the worst possible taste; there was a certain austerity in the minds of those finer Romans which was offended by all Caesar's actions at this time and after. Though there was no feeling like mine against the Games, for their barbarity (this was an accepted fact of life), Caesar's particular Games days were felt to be far too ostentatious. Feeling still ran high against the Triumph, because of his treatment of his fallen Roman foes; the upper classes never accepted my image as Venus in the Temple, and, in a subtler way, resisted Caesar's own image of himself; it could have been managed, all of it, if he had gone more slowly. Looking back on it now, I think Caesar felt his time was running out.

Besides the Games, Caesar gave huge banquets for the plebes; once he closed off several streets and wined and dined twenty-two thousand! He also staged a sea battle upon an artificial lake, with a hundred triremes and four thousand slaves; they were all destroyed, ships, arms, slaves, to the glory of Caesar, a dreadful waste; even the lake was never used again and had to be drained, for the water was polluted. This put him in great debt; I refused to help him out. I was not in Rome by his side to squander my country's monies! He wheedled like a spoiled child, that great man, and, in the end, threatened to go back to Calpurnia. I shrugged, though I truly cared a great deal, and wished him joy of her. He called me hard; I did not see him for a week. He came back penitent and bearing gifts, and no more mention of his debts; perhaps she paid them, I never asked.

For my part, I lived quietly, marking time. I loved Caesar, though I saw his faults clearly. Even with them, he was the greatest man alive, and the most charming. I knew that he would marry me, when the time was right for it; we must go slowly, for both our sakes, and Caesarion's. Calpurnia presented no problem; in Rome a wife is put away on no excuse at all; in her case, she was childless. She had not a leg to stand on, unless he was truly in debt to her, and in writing. I knew he was too clever for that; she had been a stick to beat me with, that is all. I resolved it should not happen again, and, from then on, never mentioned her.

I lived in his villa, but I thought it wise to pay rent, and to take over all expenses; it made for more freedom. Also, when it got about, as I made sure that it would, I was admired for it. I was admired for a great deal in Rome, not only by the common people, but by those higher placed. As I have said, all things Greek were beloved in this new land, and I was pure Greek. I played it up, wearing Greek robes and hairstyles, attending the theater when the playwright was Greek, and being seen in the Greek temples. My looks were in my favor in this; with a little help, I could resemble the Grecian sculptures of the finest period, particularly the Aphrodites.

My learning stood me in good stead as well; even Cicero attended my "Greek afternoons." I read from the classic poets, knowing my accent was flawless; everyone said I was better than the actors. The women were enthralled; I began to give Greek lessons once a week; all the best people came to me, with the eagerness of children. It was amusing to hear those aristocratic lips stumble over the words and butcher the cadence; Fulvia's face was clouded with temper, and poor little Portia was reduced to tears, but still they came; it was the fashion.

In later years it was said that I was not liked in Rome; this was far from true. The men hung on my every word, and paid me compliments, though I showed favor to no one; the women copied my dress. As for the crowd, they adored me, as if I were truly a goddess. I was, for that too-short time, very happy; happier than I had ever been, happier than I was ever to be.

7

"AN ARMY! YOU HAD an *army?*" The Honorable Fulvia's eyes went from long to round; she stared at me. Halted in her incessant prowling, the Honorable Clodia stared too. (Or perhaps she was not the Honorable; I think she was between husbands at the time.) "My dear, how utterly enchanting!" Fulvia, who had just been on the point of leaving, let her shawl slip once more from her shoulders. She sat down again. "Tell all," she demanded. Oh, dear, I thought, what a bore they are!

"Well, there is nothing much to tell," I said aloud. "It was simply a necessity . . ."

"But an *army* . . . ! And you wore armor—and rode astride . . ."

"And slept in tents . . ." put in Clodia, with a wicked little smile.

I disregarded her; one had to. "Well . . . we rode astride . . . it is not very pleasant, I may say. Armor—no. We did not wear armor."

"Who is 'we'?" asked Fulvia, lifting her eyebrows.

"Iras . . . Iras was with me," I answered, looking towards Iras and smiling.

"Oh, Iras." Fulvia's look flickered over her like a whiplash; Roman women are great snobs. She looked back at me, expectant.

I spread my hands. "That is all. I had an army. I fled from Alexandria into Syria. I waited for news from my spies. Caesar won the war and sent for me. I went to him. That is all." I shrugged.

The Honorable Fulvia looked disappointed. Clodia whirled around. "Is it true what Caesar says . . . that you were smuggled in to him in a carpet? Naked?"

"Oh, no, not naked!" I flushed, angry. "Is that what he says?"

"Calm down, dear," said Fulvia, lazily, showing little pointed teeth. "Caesar has never passed the time of day with Clodia . . . she probably heard it from a slave. Besides, why so prim? You are not wearing much more now . . ." It is true, of course; the fashion that fall was for diaphanous tunics, slit from neck to hem; even in the damp, all Rome dressed this way. Still, there was a difference.

"I do not like such gossip," I said, frowning. "Who has said this, Clodia?"

She shrugged, in her turn. "Oh, no one. I made it up."

Fulvia laughed. "It is what she would have done in your place."

Clodia shrugged again. "But of course," she murmured. "Why waste time?" I could not help but laugh; Clodia was so completely without guile. It was all she had to recommend her, except her beauty. It was enough; I think she had no enemies at all. Quite a feat, in Rome!

I felt warm toward her suddenly, and tolerant even of Fulvia. I told them both the whole story; my version, watered down. Still, they were charmed. I knew they would tell it, all over town, by next day. I had allowed for embellishments, and had even put back my age a little, just in case. I knew they would never have swallowed a tale of a twenty-one-year-old virgin!

"Well, my dear," drawled Fulvia, rising to leave, finally, "you have won all our hearts . . . my husband, for instance, is in *love* with you!"

"Marcus Antonius?" I shook my head. "You are so wrong . . . he does not even admire me!"

"Yes, he does indeed . . . and more! The things he mutters in his sleep . . . !" And she rolled her eyes up to heaven, smiling.

"Fulvia," I said, sternly. "Stop this joke . . . I will not have such things get around . . ."

"M-m-m-m," hummed Clodia. "What would Caesar say . . . ?"

I was on the point of stamping my foot in rage, when Fulvia said, "Well, never mind . . . it *is* a joke. No one would believe it, anyway . . . all Rome knows we do not sleep together . . ."

Clodia broke in. "Oh, but *I* have heard him . . . just last week. Oh, what a dream it was!" She grinned like a street boy, and came close to me, plucking at my sleeve. "What will you give me not to tell, sweet Cleopatra?"

"Nothing, sweet Clodia," I said, smiling as at a child, "for no one would believe you . . ."

"But you are so rich . . ." she said, pouting. She flashed me a look which would have melted a man in his prime. "And so *mean!* Ah, well, let's go, Fulvia—" She crossed to the open doorway, looking out on to the river. "For, lo, my dears—here comes the gentleman. . . . Speak of Pluto . . . ?"

It was true. Marcus Antonius was just then beaching his little painted boat. I looked sharply at the two of them, those silly women. Had they set it up?

No, Fulvia looked quite as surprised as I felt. She tossed her head. "I shall leave by the back door," she said. "I do not want an encounter. Come, Clodia."

Clodia went, biddably enough, but not without craning her neck for a last look at the man at the water's edge. "We can see ourselves out," said Fulvia, dragging at Clodia's sleeve. "Come—hurry!"

I looked after them, puzzled, then put it out of my mind; I should never, if I lived to be a hundred, understand these Roman girls!

I watched, still standing, as Antonius advanced; even from a distance I could see he frowned; I wondered if he had seen them, after all.

But all such thoughts went right out of my mind as he came near. He took my hands in his and held them firmly, without greeting. "You must come quickly, Lady."

"Caesar?"

"Yes. He has had a bad attack. Right on the Senate floor . . ."

"Oh, gods!" I exclaimed softly. "I will fetch Dioscorides . . ."

"No, Lady, there is not time . . . there are other doctors there . . . they have given him a draught . . . but he does not look well at all . . . you must come!"

I flung over my dress the first cloak that came to hand, and followed him. The way, all by river, seemed so long; I twisted my hands nervously. "Collect yourself, Lady—we will soon be there . . . it is just up this street . . ." And he handed me up out of the boat.

They had taken him to Cicero's house; it was the closest, a small neat structure made of rosy brick, one of the few such in the city.

I caught my breath as we entered; an acrid smell hung in the rooms, something strong, a medicine, that the doctors had been burning; I saw the black smoke of it still curling up from the wide dish. I thought with impatience; it will do no good, there is no cure.

As I looked about abstractedly, Cicero himself came out

from an inner room, putting his finger to his lips. He looked frightened; I supposed it was the first time he had seen such a fit.

"He is awake," he said, "and asking for you . . ."

Awake! O gods, I thought, that is not the pattern! But I said nothing, and went with him into an inner chamber. There Caesar lay, his face almost blue, his breathing labored; he opened his eyes; they seemed to have sunk deep in his head. He stretched out his hand, slowly. "What happened? I feel as though an axe had opened my skull . . ." And he gave a little mirthless laugh, terrible to hear, and clutched my hand hard.

I bent close to him. "It is nothing, my darling . . . a seizure from a god. A sign. It is past now . . ."

His eyes looked into mine, searching. "The old illness? Did you see . . . ?"

"I have just come . . . Marcus summoned me."

His eyes went past me to find Marcus. "Marcus—did you see? What was it?"

"That was it, Julius. You . . . it was the hand of a god, smiting . . ."

Caesar smiled. "I thought it was death . . ." And he closed his eyes. The word frightened me, and his stillness. I turned to look at Marcus and saw the same fright in his face. A doctor, robed in his dark saffron, plucked at the stuff of my cloak; I turned.

"He will sleep now," he said, bowing low. "The drug is working. Here—feel his heart." And he took my hand in his skinny dry fingers and brought it to Caesar's breast. I felt a slow steady thumping, under my fingers, getting stronger. I looked at his face where he lay against the pillow; the blue had faded, and there was a little spot of color high up on his cheekbones.

"He should not be moved," I said to Cicero; I had forgotten that I usurped the doctor's privilege, but I had seen it all before. "If you could keep him here . . ."

"Of course," he said, smoothly. "My house is small—but there is a chamber for you, as well . . ."

I felt divided; I had not slept away from Caesarion since he was born. Something must have shown in my face; Marcus said, kindly, "I can send word . . . or take it myself. I think, Lady, it is best you stay."

It was plain to see what he feared, what they all were

fearing. I heard myself say, amost in anger, "He will not die . . . he will not!"

And it was true; he recovered. But it was slow, so slow; this attack, the doctors said, was more than the epilepsy, very nearly a fatal stroke, and left him weak for months.

From all sides came advice which I could not easily follow, for Caesar must not feel our fear. While I was in his house, nearly a week, Cicero spoke often, urging me to persuade Caesar to make a will, and even offering to draw it up himself. "I cannot," I said. "Besides, I need nothing from Caesar . . . I have all Egypt's revenues . . ."

"It is not that," he said, waving his hand impatiently, "but you must insure the legitimacy of your son . . ."

I stared at him. "How can I? How can I—without marriage? And Caesar has a wife."

"He has a *Roman* wife," he said. "There are ways to get around that—even without divorce . . ."

I stared at him again, seeing that these Romans will bend all to suit them. Just now it was in my favor—but who knows if it would always be?

I shook my head. "You do not comprehend the problem," I said. "It is far more complex than that." I explained patiently and simply as one would do to a child. "The laws of my own country must be considered too, and the patterns of my dynasty. . . . The queen of Egypt cannot share a husband!" I could not explain, and was not ready to, that I wanted the throne of the world for my son, and nothing less. I let him think my royalty was offended; for the time it was best. This Cicero was not a man to put complete trust in; he looked as straight as one of the Roman cypresses, but those cypresses, sturdy as they are, bend with the wind; one has only to see a stand of them, slanted against a hill, stiff, but leaning where their protection is.

To Marcus, however, I spoke some of the truth. This man, that my childish self had hated, seemed to me now to be Caesar's only true friend, here in Rome. And he had changed greatly; what had been gross in the younger Marcus was easy and genial now, or perhaps I was the one who had changed. At any rate, I found myself turning toward this man, in Caesar's extremity, and afterwards as well.

He nodded as I talked; we were in a private place, away from Caesar's sickroom. After I had finished, he said, "Yes . . . I see. It will not be long now . . . and they will offer him the crown. I can see it coming. Already there is talk—and more than idle—of making him dictator for life . . ." He wrinkled his forehead. "Of course—it may take another war or two—"

"Oh, no!" I cried, softly. "Caesar is sick!"

He smiled. "Try to tell him that! He is already drawing campaign plans upon the bedclothes . . . he has his eye on Parthia. And India, too."

I was silent. I knew it to be Caesar's way. He had waved me out when last I looked into his chamber, happy to see him sitting up; I had supposed he was writing a letter.

"Listen," Marcus said. "Caesar *has* a will. I witnessed it—oh, two years or so ago. It is in favor of his nephew . . ."

I looked up quickly. "I had not known of his nephew . . ."

"Name of Octavian," he said. "A sickly youth . . . nothing much to fear there. But Caesar is very strong on family—and it was before he sired your boy." He rubbed his chin, thinking. "Let me see . . . the will leaves half his estate to the Roman people and half to Octavian and his sisters—and names Octavian as his heir." He thought hard for a moment; I waited. "He must sign another—a provisional one—for after he is crowned. *That* will be the one to name Caesarion heir. For he has—now—in effect, nothing to leave Caesarion. What can he give to a boy who is hereditary Pharaoh of Egypt, after all?" He laughed a little, and reached out to pat my arm. "Never worry, Lady. I myself will talk to Caesar. And he will listen. The will shall be drawn up—and you yourself shall have the keeping of it—until such time as it will come in handy . . ."

I looked at him and smiled. "I will leave it to you, then."

The look he returned me startled me; there was a glow along his face, a kind of open secret; one felt he thought I shared it.

I was uneasy, and dropped my eyes; why did I think of Fulvia?

8

EVEN AFTER HE RECOVERED, Caesar continued to make new plans for conquest; I had thought his enforced idleness had turned his mind in that direction. He would not brook opposition from me; for one thing, I was a woman, and even Caesar would not admit that I had any practical sense; for another, it was a touchy business, trying to convince him that his illness was severe and lasting; his manhood and his age were offended. So there was no way, really, that I could hinder his plans. I refused to lend him any money, as usual, but he shrugged, and borrowed elsewhere; there are many wealthy opportunists in Rome, who are happy to have others fight their battles.

Of these plans of Caesar's, it is obvious that they had been on his mind for some time; I had been so taken up with my dreams of our son, and sleepy with my pregnancy, that I had not realized what his full intention was, when he journeyed with me up the Nile; he was not simply sightseeing! By his relationship with me, he had access to the sea-lanes which led to the fabulous wealth of India; the only country which lay in his path by land was the small ill-defended land of Parthia. It was, naturally, the goal of Caesar, already a world conqueror, to destroy this obstruction, and secure both routes to the Indian land beyond. He had seen, while he was in Egypt, the wonderful stream of precious stones, silks, spices, and scents that poured into my land from the Indian trade; being a Roman, he saw no reason to pay for what he might have for himself by force.

He did not speak frankly of this to me, of course; perhaps he did not admit these predatory reasons even to himself. Instead, he spoke of wanting to follow in the footsteps of my ancestor, Alexander, who had decimated Parthia and much of India; as though world conquest were some sort of game!

This was not the only game he played; Caesar was a very sly politician; he was not one to leave his affairs at home undirected. More and more dinner parties were given with me as the hostess; he took shameless advantage of my popularity to ingratiate himself with the powerful Roman families. I did not mind this, really; though some of my guests were dull, most were not. I took care to invite, along with his fellow senators, the top orators, actors, poets, and playwrights; it made for lively conversation, and opened up Roman society as well. It had not been the custom to mingle with these folk, unless they happened, like Cicero, to be of a highly placed family. It was an innovation, a bit shocking at first, but copied everywhere afterwards; in those days I could do no wrong.

It was at Cicero's house, however, that I first met Caesar's heir, his great-nephew Octavian; I wondered, fleetingly, why Caesar himself had not brought this young man to the house we shared; perhaps it was that this family lived in the country. Certain it was they had country manners, all four of them, though I was told they were the foremost aristocracy of Rome (the Julians pride themselves not only on descent from Venus but boast among their forbears the legendary Aeneas).

Atia, Caesar's niece, was still a young woman; her coronet braid of black hair had a dusty look, but no gray showed in it, and her face was smooth. She was the first of her type that I had seen, the truly virtuous Roman matron, though all Romans would have you believe that such women are as common as swallows. Atia was short, with a square look, but stood as straight as a soldier; her face was stern, her mouth almost lipless, though she had fine eyes, like all the Julians. She looked at me with a kind of loathing, or at least I felt it so; Fulvia insisted that Atia always looked like that—"my dear, as though she smelled garlic, or worse!"

The boy and his sister, unfortunately, inherited the look, or perhaps they imitated it; they lacked Atia's presence, though, and would never have shown up in a crowd. The daughter, called Octavia, was a young woman of about twenty years, who towered above her brother, and had a habit, understandable, of stooping. It gave her an awkward air and spoiled her looks; she had a nice, neat-featured face, without distinction, but pleasant. The nephew-heir to Caesar, Octavian, was not even pleasant; I stared at him, attempting to see what Caesar saw.

Octavian was small, like Caesar himself, but he had none of the great man's sinewy strength; where Caesar was wiry, Octavian was weedy. He had the Julian face, good lines, but unfortunately his was full of pimples, an unattractive look. He would grow out of it; he was barely seventeen, and had been in poor health all his life as well. I found him quite repulsive and was more than cordial to make up for it, but he gave me a cold and fishy eye; it was difficult to like him.

The husband, a stepfather, was a man one did not notice at all, dry and scholarly with an apologetic look; I learned later that Atia had married beneath her. Poor man, I did not envy him; he was a great crony of Cicero, however; perhaps that made up for it!

Caesar without doubt felt some pride in this great-nephew of his; I understood that Octavian was an unusually fine scholar, especially of those writers, like Xenophon, who dealt in war tactics. He had no Greek to speak of, for I tried him; to my mind, there is no scholarship that does not make use of this product of our old civilizations. However, perhaps he had no gift of tongues; he must have been learned in Greek letters, or he could not have read the Xenophon.

There was something old-fashioned and stiff about them, this country branch of the Julians; very out of place they were in this company, which glittered with gems, paint, and wit. Indeed, I felt sorry for them, though I am sure Atia would not have thanked me for it; one could not help thinking of them as poor relations. I told myself that, indeed, this must be so, for I saw no other excuse for Caesar's will.

I thought of that other, provisional will that I carried about with me, folded small and enclosed in a gold pendant about my neck; true to his word, Marcus Antonius had drawn it up and persuaded Caesar to sign it. Not much had been said of it, though Caesar once asked me, his eyes unreadable, if I kept it safe, and nodded when I answered yes. In truth, I could not see the need for all these precautions; the will in Caesarion's favor was only valid if I was Caesar's wife. Marcus, though, shook his head and said it would serve as an earnest of his paternity. As if anyone could doubt that Caesar fathered him! For truly the boy grew more like him every day.

He had been brought along this night to meet his kin; the whole company smiled to see the sturdy child, feet planted far apart, chest out, and hands clasped behind his back—Caesar to the life. He looked up, measuring, at the slight, pale youth. He stood so a long moment, looking; then, unclasping his baby hands, he extended one for Octavian to kiss!

Octavian's fish eye never blinked; he took the hand and pressed it, in the old Roman way, placing his own hand afterwards upon his heart and bowing, his face still grave. I saw Caesarion's scowl and moved close to him, saying, "Caesarion—this is your kinsman, not a subject. In Rome, all are equal."

"That is not true, Mama—" he began, hotly.

"We will discuss it another time," I said, quietly. "For now, you will greet your cousin . . ."

Caesarion turned back to Octavian. "Greeting, country cousin," he said. There were soft cooing chuckles from all sides; Caesarion, baby that he was, turned round innocent eyes upon them; he had caught their temper. "Why, Mama—is he not from the country?"

He should have been spanked, of course, but it was impossible, before all the company; he was Caesar's son, and the Pharaoh of Egypt. I contented myself with saying, "Perhaps, if you are a good boy, you will be invited to visit your cousins in the suburbs . . . I hear their estates are very beautiful." He was not yet three years old, but he knew he had been naughty, and to save the day, was naughtier still. "You may invite me, Octavian," he said, in his little pipe; to my annoyance, even Caesar laughed. It was the girl, Octavia, who put me at ease; she was cleverer than she looked, and just as kind. She stooped down and put her head near the boy's.

"*I* will invite you, Caesarion," she said. "We have a mare that has just foaled . . . if you give her a bit of bread smeared with honey she will let you play with her baby. Have you ever seen a little horse?"

He was charmed. "Can I ride it?"

"Oh, no," she said, "it is too weak . . . its legs will not carry you. You are a big boy, you know . . ."

"Am I?" he asked, looking up at her with all Caesar's charm. "Do you like big boys?" She nodded.

"Very well," said the little king, "I will come." He looked at her again, and smiled. "You are very pretty," he said.

Someone laughed behind me. "He has a good eye, like his father . . ." I looked around; it was Marcus. He saw me and said, "Prettiest girl in Rome, that . . . don't you agree?"

I felt middle-aged, as once I had felt too young. I said, a little primly, "She is a bit over-tall . . ."

"Well," he said, looking down at me and shrugging, "That depends on the man, doesn't it?" And he squared his tall frame. I felt my cheeks go hot, and hoped they did not show red.

He shook his head, not looking at me but at Octavia, and laughing. "Well, they are marrying her off next week, anyway . . ."

I could not help myself. I said, sharply, "And you are married as well."

He looked at me, surprised. "Fulvia is a bitch," he said. "You called me that, once."

I could have bitten off my tongue; he stared, and I moved away, going up to Caesarion where he stood with the girl. "Come," I said, as roughly as I had ever spoken, "Come—it is time for you to be taken home. It is past your bedtime . . ."

Afterwards, Caesar spoke to me, chiding. "What has come over you, girl? The boy was getting to know his cousins, as I wished."

I looked at him coolly. "Caesarion is spoiled. Did you see the mother's face? And your heir! He was black, beneath his pimples. I should not like to have him for an enemy . . ." And I walked away, leaving Caesar to stare.

9

IN THE WINTER following, Caesar was made dictator for life, as had been expected. The other event was not expected, though it occurred within the week. My young brother, the titulary Pharaoh, whom we called Mouse II in private, died, and I became sole ruler of Egypt.

I had been terrified that this might happen, for this Mouse was even sicklier than the first; from the time he set foot in Rome I hovered over him like a mother, and assigned a doctor to him for his well-being each hour of the day. He had been pulled through innumerable colds and fevers, a broken ankle, and a split head, but no doctor could cure that sickness called in Rome, "the Egyptian disease." This was an illness known to ancient Egypt thousands of years ago; many of the old Pharaohs had succumbed to it, all in the flower of youth; it attacked those not yet ripe in manhood, and seemed to pass over women; there was no cure. It started with a runny nose, a cough, and a fever, so that one took it for a common ailment. The pain in the back of the neck, which came later, was the thing which told of doom; from that point, all went downhill, and we were powerless; he died within the week. He was twelve years old.

I had not been truly fond of him, sad to say; like all my family, he was a poor thing. Still, I felt sorrow at the cutting off of a life so young. And then, too, a monarch must tread carefully in such matters, particularly in Rome, where poisoning is the rule, rather than the exception; how many Romans have come to heirdom by this means is not clear, but there is no doubt that, to the Roman mind, it is the easiest way.

By now, Caesar was refusing to look upon events in a prudent fashion; he rejoiced in this death, and openly, for it assured our son of his succession to the Egyptian throne. I was appalled at this attitude, for I abhor the taint of murder, so often a cloud upon my family. I set events in motion which I hoped would quell these rumors, in some part. Marcus was helpful, for he understood my feelings, as Caesar might once have done. At his suggestion, I kept the small body here in Rome on view, after sending for the skilled embalmers of my country; this was a twofold precaution, for Romans could see the unmarked corpse, and the Egyptian emissaries as well. It was recorded in both countries that the boy died of spinal disease, like so many of his predecessors. Even so, there was talk; one cannot stop it all. Often, in the days that followed, I felt, deep within, chagrin that I had raised my hand in mercy for Arsinoëe; she had loved this little Mouse, and she accused me where she could. Though she was always watched, I did not keep her under any true restraint, and she managed to reach some few ears. Marcus chided me, calling her a viper who should have been put to death like one; I guess he had forgotten how she had caught his eye, long ago. Still, I let her live; the damage had been done already, and Mouse was her brother, after all, of the same mother.

Now Caesarion, barely three, was my co-regent; as I grew older, my consorts grew younger! I longed for the day when I could, in fact, make this custom of twin rule count, when great Caesar would ascend my Alexandrian throne beside me. I did not want it, of course, without Rome for myself; at any rate, it would be worthless, for Rome would wrest Egypt from us, unless we *were* Rome.

I felt we had little time, in view of Caesar's health, though of course I could not voice it. Caesar, however, thought he must conquer Parthia first, and secure the India trade; I searched for arguments to strengthen my own stand.

There is an old Etruscan prophecy, nearly forgotten; everything Etruscan is forgotten by Rome, as far as it is possible, for Rome belonged first to these people, and that first conquest was shameful. It said that Parthia would not be subdued until a *king* of Rome subdued it.

This did not really help; Caesar is a stubborn man. Now, as I look back, that may not have been all of it; I think perhaps that great Caesar, with age and the threat of illness upon him, had lost some of his old daring. He would no longer risk all; he would not play for the highest stakes. He would put his life on the front battle-line; he was used to it. He would not hazard the people's love, for to him it was dearer. And so he continued to plan, raise troops, and prepare for another war.

He took his time about it, instead of getting it over with; one could not push him either, for the sharp, decisive, pouncing Caesar was gone forever, buried with his health and vigor. I could do no more than listen attentively to all his strategies and approve his shrewdness, while day by day I nudged him toward his own royalty.

He took to this nudging only too well; in a Greek it would have been excessive, but most of Rome accepted it all, even the golden throne! But do not call him king—oh, no!

Caesar was now called *Imperator,* a Latin word for Commander-in-Chief. Not only had he himself proposed this title, but he had somehow managed to have it made hereditary; a first step toward monarchy it was, in fact, and I approved. Some of the other changes I might have ruled out, but I was not asked; it was a strange thing that now, when I was a wiser woman, with the judgment of my full womanhood within me, Caesar behaved as though I were a flighty girl, smiling at me and spoiling me, disregarding all my utterances. Once, when I did not deserve it, he had listened; now all Rome blamed me for his imprudence.

In the Capitol here there were seven statues, royal figures of the old kings of four hundred years ago; now there are eight, for Caesar put one of himself beside them. Moreover, he began to dress in the embroidered robes of those ancient monarchs, when he appeared in public, drawing them on over his official toga, like a child when it is dressing up for play; he carried a scepter of ivory and wore always a chaplet of gold in the shape of a laurel wreath. Sometimes, as he walked from street to Senate floor, the folk crowding near would fall to their knees and bow at his feet, hailing him as king. Always, then, he would turn gravely to them, fixing them with his sleepwalker's eye, and say, "Not King am I, but Caesar." It was a pride in reverse, and I understood it, but there were some, like Cicero, who frowned; they were spoilsports, for the people loved him, even to his excesses.

He had a royal chariot, too, modeled on mine of Egypt, and a golden throne to sit upon in his tribunal. He was given a kind of royal bodyguard of youthful senators also; I urged him to avail himself of them at all times, for I feared the sickness striking him, but he would only use them on official business. He was a man of contradictions, as I have said, and not always sensible, in those days of his waning health.

Daily, it seemed, he grew more haggard; sometimes, when he had been all day at the Senate, and arrived late at his house on the Tiber, I would see him, staring, as at a stranger, until he smiled. And once, when I had journeyed to Alexandria for some state festival, and was away for two weeks, I truly did not recognize him as he welcomed me back. He never knew, of course; I pretended the sun was in my eyes.

Marcus shared my concern; "Julius drives himself," he said, shaking his head. "But he always has . . . and no one can stop him—not even you." He cocked one dark eyebrow at me; it was a trick he had. "And it is no use prettying up his food either . . . it is all one to him."

We were standing in the little storeroom off the big kitchen; he had been bid to supper, for Caesar liked his company. Caesar was having a bath before his meal, and I, queen of Egypt and thirty years his junior, was playing the village mother and preparing his salad with my own hands; Marcus had followed me into the larder.

"Roman food is so rich," I said, deprecating myself with a smile. "There is a subtle dressing our Alexandrian cook invented, with pounded coriander and the oil from Lydian olives. The cresses are fresh today and—"

He grinned. "It is wasted on Julius. He will eat anything." He took the oil flask from my hand and set it down. "Look, Cleopatra—I'll take a wager on it . . ." He looked down on me, smiling very broad, and a wild reckless light in his eyes; I had seen Caesarion look so when he planned some little mischief.

"I'll stake ten denarii on it—he will not know . . . Make your salad—with the oil that we use to grease the chariot wheels . . ."

I gasped. "It will make him sick!"

"Not he," said Marcus. "His stomach is not his head . . . his stomach is a piece of iron. Come—take the bet . . ."

Something inside me began to giggle; I had been sedate so long. I raised the bet to twenty, and shook hands on it; there was no harm in the axle grease, it was only nasty.

Caesar's dish of greens was set before him, garnished with hard-cooked eggs and in a red clay bowl from Crete; it was the first course; I had insisted he take it on a fresh palate, for fairness.

He looked across the table at me, and smiled. "Something you have made, my dear?" For he was always polite. He took a big leaf, glistening with oil, and put it in his mouth. "Oh, delicious! You have surpassed yourself!" And he reached for another. I watched, horrified, as he ate the whole bowlful, wiping up the last of the dressing with a crust of bread. I did not bother my head about the twenty denarii; I was rich enough. But it was the last of my fooling about in the kitchens; there are queenlier tasks.

10

Caesar's preparations for the Parthian war dragged on, week after dreary week; he often went to bed as tired as if he waged that campaign already! For of course Caesar never was content with one project at a time; besides these war plans, he was busy deciding how to divert the Tiber from its course, how to cut a canal through the Island of Corinth, the best roadbed over the Apennines, and the likeliest site for a port at Ostia. To name a few.

Others had noticed his haggard looks; his physicians clucked their tongues at him, and his closer friends sighed; Calpurnia sent me three frantic letters, begging me to use my influence to temper Caesar's activities. She could not know, poor lady, that no woman could sway Caesar. I suppose she thought I possessed some magic, because he preferred my company. I was surprised at the letters, though; I suppose she loved him still.

I spoke of his closer friends; I was thinking of his niece, Atia, and her daughter, Octavia, for many of those professed friends had slipped away. It had all happened gradually; it was not until I sent out invitations for a supper party, meant to be intimate, that I realized the state of things. Except for Marcus, I had nothing but refusals, all with proper excuses, but unsettling all the same; in the end I had to make do with actors and orators and those equestrians, always available, who seek to better themselves. I was alarmed that Caesar would grow angry, but he hardly seemed to notice who was there. Marcus and I, putting our heads together, guessed the reason; we had not far to look.

A man like Caesar will always have enemies, especially when he is rising ever higher and higher; one expects that. And Caesar had grown quite arrogant in all his attitudes, even excusing the throne and diadem and all the rest. He had taken to keeping high-placed persons waiting hours for audience, and not rising to greet them, even his equals in blood; on the other hand, he grew quite angry when all did not rise from their seats when he passed. When his authority was questioned he swore great army oaths, even in the hearing of aristocratic women; there was much ill feeling. Cicero had written a number of treatises complaining of these slights, and Cicero was a much respected citizen. Marcus was able to laugh about all of it, for he is that kind of person; I was not, and could only hope Caesar would get off to his war and give people something else to think about; Marcus laughed about that, too. "Caesar is a law in himself," he said.

I shook my head. "No man is that," I said. "Not even a king—and Caesar is not that yet . . . and may never be, if he does not tread carefully.

"You worry too much," said Marcus, laughing down at me, for he was tall. "You are beginning to get a line between your brows."

"I have much at stake," I said. But I took to rubbing lotion on my forehead every night; I was too young for wrinkles.

In truth, I was even more disturbed than I admitted. The young man Brutus, Caesar's natural son, had been a constant visitor at the villa, and had offered himself as escort for me when Caesar was busy, but for some months now he had not shown his face; I had not missed him much, for I had Marcus. Once, though, as I rode to the theater, I caught sight of Brutus; I could swear he pretended not to have seen me; it was an uneasy feeling for a queen to harbor. I thought that perhaps the company he kept embarrassed him; the two men who companioned him had an unsavory look. But no, Marcus said they were nobles and tribunes, name of Cassius and Casca. *They* saw me, no mistake, for they followed me with their eyes; Cassius, except that he was thinner, might have been Pothinus' ghost; it made me shudder.

I dared not mention this encounter to Caesar; he abhorred womanish fancies, and would never hear a whisper against that son of his, as I had found to my sorrow. I had merely mentioned, as if idly, that Brutus had not honored us with his company of late; he looked up from his maps, his eyes pouncing on mine. "He is full of affairs, that boy," he said. "He does not have time for us old folk . . ." I lacked a year of Brutus' age! I checked my hot reply; if Caesar's wits were failing him, I could not afford to think about it; he was all I had.

I began, indeed, to think that, if Caesar would not stake his fortunes upon a throw, I had better make the throw for him. I had a plan which I had mulled over since the previous year; I let it go then, thinking the time not yet ripe. This year I felt it was now or never, and it must be tried. I needed help, and Marcus was the perfect partner; one never needed to persuade him to anything, if it was rash enough. This wildness was in his nature, as it is in the heart of a blooded stallion, however broken to the reins.

On the fifteenth day of the second month of the year, there is a Roman feast day, very popular, called the Lupercalia. No one at all seems to know its origin, but, oddly, it has much in common with an antique festival of Egypt. (I have often wondered if, in some dim reaches of time, all gods were not the same, when men and women were fewer and their languages no more complicated than grunts.) In old Egypt there is a god called Min-Amon, who makes all things fecund; barren women fight each other for his favor on his special day. Here, in Rome, the god is named Lupercus; otherwise they are much the same. Min-Amon, in his statues, holds a whip in his hand; upon looking closely, one sees that this whip is made from three jackal skins plaited together. A blow from this jackal whip will make a woman fertile, or so it is fervently believed still, up the Nile.

I have never seen the Egyptian ceremony, for in Alexandria our gods are Greek; so far as I can understand, the ritual is the same as the Roman.

In Rome two men, reasonably young and virile, are selected from the College of the Luperci, and these two, on the god's day, sacrifice a goat and a dog, which they proceed to flay and cut into strips, which they plait into whips. They then laugh loudly (this is ritual, too) and proceed to run about the city, thwacking every woman they see. Naturally, as in Egypt, barren women get in the way of this whip, which is called the Februa. Over the whole day the god Lupercus presides, in the person of a high-placed noble. Formerly he had been chosen by lot, but this year Caesar preempted the honor, for I had his ear. It was not difficult to persuade him that the Egyptians worshiped him as Amon, having made their queen fruitful; what more correct than that he should be the Lupercus of Rome, as well? Never mind that it was a bit mixed up in the telling (for Amon is not Min-Amon); Caesar no longer listened very carefully, especially when a god was mentioned; poor mortal, his ears rang happily at the sound.

He went a step farther, Caesar; he founded an order that he called The Luperci Julii, and decreed that the whip wielders must be chosen from this one alone. Even without this innovation, it would have been simple to see to it that Marcus was chosen, once the idea had been put into Caesar's head. Chosen he was, of course; the measure of Caesar's self-preoccupation was seen in the other choice, Dolabella. This was Fulvia's current lover, and all Rome knew it. Except for Caesar, who took no notice of the gasps, causing a few more; I have thought since that perhaps he *did* know, he had a sly humor.

I could not keep him from wearing purple on the day; beneath it his face was yellow as his golden crown. He sat on his throne in the Forum and watched the whole thing, the bloody sacrifice, the silly laughter, and the obscene mutilations; at home we do these old-fashioned antics with some decency, behind the temple doors.

It was a bright day, but freezing cold; we huddled in our furs, but Caesar's arms were bare; he stared straight ahead, as calm as the god he mimicked. Sick, and old before his time, still, the heart swelled to see him; he was more than man. All of Rome watched, or so it seemed; there was a vast crowd, stretching across the Forum and spilling out into all the narrow streets beyond. Those aristocrats who had used to grace our household were in the front ranks, seated for comfort and attended by slaves; most of them I had not laid eyes on for months; looking about me, I fancied I saw nothing but sour faces. It was a pleasure to turn to Marcus and his partner, the young Dolabella; an odd thing, they were much alike; except for their ages, they might have been brothers. Marcus Antonius had lost his full looks now, along with some excess of weight, and Dolabella's face still wore the clean lines of youth; they were both handsome men. Tall and broad-shouldered, with clustering black curls, they had, each, large wet-looking eyes and full lips; each of them, also, was marred by something womanish about the dimpled chin. Of course, I was used to Caesar's spare bones.

I gritted my teeth through the slaughtering and flaying; a queen cannot be squeamish. They were a bit slow about it, too; I had seen Caesar dispatch a victim in the flash of a knife. They had words to say, old Etruscan, dating from a millennium back or thereabouts; no one could understand them. A good thing, I suspected, for I saw by the light in Marcus' eye that they had not learned their speeches very carefully; I caught a good many repetitions, but then I am quick; no one of the others seemed to notice. When they had finished, and the carcasses had been hauled away, slaves sluicing down the stones, they laughed, as bidden, long and loud; neither was an actor, and the laughter rang so falsely that it made even those dour aristocrats in the audience smirk behind their hands. I saw that Caesar's lips twitched in a wintry smile, before he clapped his hands for attention and made his own speech. Obviously it was instructions; "Go out among the barren women." Or some such thing, for they left, running lightly, and cracking their makeshift whips; many fine gowns would be ruined this day, for the whips still oozed blood, and droplets flew through the air with each flourish.

We had to sit there most of the day, turning blue, for it never warmed up; there were a great many tedious ceremonies and speeches and some even more tedious entertainment, in the Roman style, bear baitings and some very vulgar clowning. Still, I was used to it by now, and kept a serene face.

A fine sleet, needle-sharp, was falling before the two chosen Lupercii returned; I had lost track of time, having grown numb with cold and boredom, but it must have been late afternoon. The two whip men were breathing hard and sweating like battle steeds; it had been a long day, and they were obliged by custom to run the whole way, into every quarter of the city. A huge crowd followed them, jostling and pushing; it looked like a riot, and sounded worse.

The blood had dried now on the whips, and the strips of skin looked shrunken and curled at the edges, drooping in those exhausted hands; I saw that Marcus carried something in his free hand, wrapped about with his mantle. My heart quickened its beat; I had not been sure he could manage to get the royal diadem. Caesar's statue had been wearing it, inside the Temple of Venus; I guessed that the priests had been distracted by the crowd; they are always afraid of looting on these feast days.

Most of the noblewomen shrank from them, uttering pretty little squeals, for the whips waved still; Brutus' wife, Portia, though, stepped forward in Dolabella's path, her eyes modestly down. He looked surprised, but shrugged and flicked her lightly. There was a kind of little silence then, for Calpurnia stepped into Marcus' path; his eyes narrowed. After a moment, he turned away, and, stretching out with his whip hand, touched me lightly. The shock was almost a shout, though no voice was raised; it might have been a scene in stone.

Suddenly a voice from the pack of plebes cried out; hoarse from the damp and in the roughest street accents, still it was understood by the daintiest ears. "The little queen needs somewhat else . . . the little queen don't quicken with such a limp rod . . . !" There were wild hoots of laughter, and a ragged cheer or two. As the noise died away, another voice, a woman's, called out, "How about trying it yourself, Marcus—you're a big one!" And then another, alive with laughter, "Try it over here, Marcus. . . . I'm ready!" Catcalls and "Shush yourself, old girl . . . behave, the god's not got all night!"

Marcus, thinking quick, turned and cried, just as coarsely, "You can take bets on it . . . he does not! There he sits . . . waiting. Waiting for your silence!" And he bowed low before Caesar, who, truth to tell, was beginning to look as though he had a thunderbolt at his dagger belt. The crowd was easy-going, like all Roman crowds, and loved Marcus' blunt tongue. They cheered loud and long. He rose and faced them, holding the royal diadem high. "Hail Caesar! Hail the god!"

There was a great cheer from all the people, and a kind of surge forward. Marcus held out his hand, as if to halt them. Again he held up the diadem; more cheering. He turned to Caesar and went down on one knee, holding out the ancient crown. "Great Caesar, you have been hailed as god-on-earth . . . take this, and take the kingship of Rome! Hail Caesar! Hail the King of Rome!"

There was a cry of "Hail" from Dolabella, and two or three more from the corner down in front where we had placed them; they sounded very weak in the sighing silence. I listened hard; nothing. They were not ready.

Caesar rose. He pushed aside the crown that Marcus held; his eyes looked sad and very old. "I cannot accept it," he said, shaking his head. "I am Caesar . . . and no king." There was a savage roar, wild cheering and stamping of feet. Caps were hurled in the air, and voices raised. "Caesar . . . Caesar! No king! No king!"

Caesar smiled and raised his hands for silence. "Marcus Antonius," he said, in his parade voice. "Marcus Antonius, my friend, and the people's friend . . . take back the crown! Take it into the Capitol and place it beneath the Jupiter. Inscribe that on this day of the Lupercalia the crown of Rome was offered to Caesar. Inscribe that Caesar refused it."

Cheers broke out again, the loudest of all. Under the cover of them Caesar sat, heavily, pulling his purple cloak, sodden as his dignity, about his arms; he beckoned and I went to him, holding my head high.

11

". . . . AND SO, MY DEAR, you had better go home, for I expect to be gone for three years at the very least." Caesar spoke calmly; it was as though he had forgotten the incident of the afternoon. I smarted with it still, for the offering of the crown had been my idea; it was the first time I had been in such error of judgment. I told myself that I did not understand Roman crowds, but still I was shaken; by this hour, twilight it was, I had thought I would be queen of all Rome! It was no use discussing it with Caesar; it was his way, to ignore failure. Lordly, and laudable too, perhaps, but not really very practical.

I stared at him, unwilling to accept what he said. He went on. "Of course, you are welcome to stay here—as long as you like. . . . It is just that I do not want you to be bored." And he shot me a keen glance, faintly tinged with a remote humor. "Rome does bore you, does it not? Romans are unmannerly, their entertainments are vulgar, the city is an overgrown village . . ." And I had thought I showed nothing of what I felt!

"I might go with you—" It was tentative; I did not really expect agreement. And he shook his head. "No, I will have no women in the camp—it sets a bad example."

"Well, I am a queen, it is somewhat different. I can bring you fighting men in the hundreds . . ."

He raised his eyebrows. "But, my dear, I have been counting on it, at any rate! But army life is no life for a woman—in any case, I expect to be on the march most of the time."

I was silent for a moment, thoughts scurrying like mice in my head. "Julio," I said, finally, "Wait for a bit. I think we can pull it off next time . . . Marcus—"

"Marcus! That is the trouble! He does not have the rectitude, the seemliness, for such a proposal. You should have consulted me . . ." He shook his head again, looking annoyed. "No, the people do not respect him—"

"Oh, Julio—they love Marcus! He is second only to you!"

He wagged his finger at me like an old nurse. "No, the man to offer the crown is Brutus. Brutus they look up to. Brutus they will respect and follow . . ."

I was aghast; how was it that Caesar, that worldly man, could not see what danced in front of his nose? By now all Rome knew that Brutus had left the Caesarian faction, but how to say it without offense?

"Julio," I began, "I think that Brutus is opposed to the very idea of monarch rule . . . often I have heard him say it . . ."

He waved his hand impatiently. "The hot words of youth! They mean nothing! Why, all his ideas come from me! Brutus' love of the Republic—his patriotism, his high principles—all come from me. Why, often in past years we have talked the night through . . . Brutus thinks as I think."

"Not in this matter," I said, firmly. "He opposed your dictatorship, even that . . ."

Caesar looked at me, rubbing his chin, a fatuous smile playing at his thin mouth. "Ah, well—I must have a talk with Brutus. Tomorrow perhaps. Yes, tomorrow. Will you—uh—see to it, my dear? Invite him for supper?"

I took my courage in both hands and said, "Julio—I have invited Brutus to my last dozen supper parties—he has refused all dozen times."

His eyes looked vague. "Oh, well, my dear, I think he dislikes crowds. Invite him alone. Yes, that will do it. Invite him alone."

I thought for a moment. "Perhaps . . . Portia as well? He is the kind of man who does not like to attend social gatherings without his wife . . . and also, we women can withdraw and leave you to your intimate talk . . ." It was my only hope, truly. I would send Portia a length of Lydian silk and some of the smaller British pearls. Short of rudeness, she could not refuse me, and the unwilling Brutus would have to tag along.

I took other precautions as well; I left the invitation open, saying that any night of the week would be acceptable; they could not be busy every evening! Word came from Portia, thanking me for the gifts and accepting the invitation for supper. She asked permission to bring her brother, who was staying with them; it would make an odd man, but what could I do?

I spoke to Caesar. "The party is growing," I said, and explained. "Well, it cannot be helped," he said, crossly. "But it is a man I do not trust . . . something about his eyes. Cassius has strange eyes."

So it was the man I had glimpsed once in Brutus' company in the street! I fully agreed; I did not trust him either, he was known to be anti-Caesar. Still, what could he do at a private party?

"I shall invite Clodia," I said, snapping my fingers at the idea.

Caesar twinkled; it was the first time in a long while. "It will do no good," he said. "He is proof against her charms."

"No man is," I said, believing it.

But I was wrong. That Cassius might have been a gelding, like Pothinus, as well as having Pothinus' look; he never budged from Brutus' side, though I had briefed the luscious Clodia, and she was plying all the seduction she was capable of, no mean accomplishment. He never glanced at her; in fact he was rather rude.

"You should have hired a pretty boy," said Clodia, pouting, when we three women were alone.

Portia stiffened; the man was her brother, after all. "Cassius is no boy lover," she said, haughtily. "He loves his wife. And his mistress is Rome."

Clodia giggled. "A smelly paramour," she said, her eyes dancing. "They forgot to collect the garbage again today . . ."

Portia opened her mouth, and shut it again, looking affronted.

Clodia put out her hand, impulsively. "Dear Portia—no offense. I love Rome as much as anybody. But, oh, dear, the city needs a firm hand . . . all those senators! They can never get together—and in consequence, nothing is ever attended to. The plebes hawk and spit in the theater, there are pigs in the street—quite wild, too—and then the Tiber had melon rinds floating in it, a disgusting sight. No," she said, tossing her curls, "What Rome needs is a king—"

"Not so," said Portia. "Rome must return to her Republican virtues. There is too much modern laxity . . . too much Eastern opulence . . ."

She would be accusing me next of all Rome's troubles! I clapped my hands, calling for music. I refused to be drawn into a political discussion with those two ninnies, and turned the conversation to pearls, British and Mediterranean.

"Of course, Cleopatra, I do thank you so much for those samples you sent me," said Portia. "But, you know, I don't think that, in the main, the British pearls can compare with our own . . ."

"Now, there, you are wrong—" began Clodia. It was a happy little argument and very safe; I left them to it, signing to a slave to take up the tray of honey-comfits and go before me.

The three men still sat where we had left them, around the supper table, which had not been cleared. I never saw a gloomier group; they did not recline but sat stiffly, like adversaries, which in effect they were. There was thick silence, but sharp words hung in the air like yesterday's sleet.

"Please don't rise," I said; no one had moved a muscle! "Do please have a honey bit," I said, gesturing to the tray. "It is my own recipe." I took up an amphora and poured some wine. "Wine of Lesbos," I said, "and very old."

Brutus took the cup from me. "Pompey's favorite," he said, his voice breaking.

"And Cato's," added Cassius, looking hard at him from under his heavy brows. So that was the bait with which they had caught this fish! Brutus had fought with Pompey, long ago, though Caesar had forgiven this youthful indiscretion; Cato had been an ancestor, on his mother's side, of course. The anti-Caesar party had him both ways, with a little care taken. And they had taken more than a little, it was clear.

Brutus drained his cup and held it out for more. He looked unhappy, and I felt a small pang of sympathy, for I knew he loved Caesar well. But I hardened my heart; he was a fence sitter, like Cicero; such men are dangerous.

I had formed a new plan, and was eager to have the company gone and place it before Caesar. I walked down to the landing place with them, for courtesy, slaves lighting the way, but did not wait to see them safely upon the farther shore, returning to the house with their soft farewell still ringing in my ears. Caesar was gone from his place!

A hand touched my shoulder in the half-light; I turned. The Briton, Cadwallader, looked down at me, smiling gently. "Caesar begs to be excused, Lady," he said, in a whisper. "He has work . . . and will rest in the anteroom, upon the couch there." This anteroom was fitted up like an army tent; I knew that Caesar had often slept there, before my time. He was a man who liked small places and austere surroundings. But this was the first night he had not shared my bed, here in Rome.

I looked at Cadwallader, a long look and keen. "Did Caesar send you? Are those Caesar's words?"

He did not speak for a moment; then he said, again very gently, "No, Lady . . . there was no word from Caesar. But the door is barred . . ."

"I see," and I nodded slowly. "Well, I am tired, as well. . . . Will you have all this cleared away, friend?" And I gestured to the supper leavings. "It is late . . ."

Well, my plan would wait till tomorrow, though my spirits fell. As for the rest, I would not miss it. Caesar, since the first onslaught of his illness, had been a sorry love partner. Often I heard his snores even while I was being attired and combed for the night; sometimes he turned from me and feigned sleep. Both of these actions, though, were preferable to those other nights, the nights when he drank the bitter wine of Cyprus, said to be an aphrodisiac, for then he strove till dawn, in vain, and muttering curses. I had bruises to show for it, and love bites, and a terrible sick compassion, which I could not show.

At first he was angry at himself and at the gods, and begged me tearfully to forgive him; it was more unmanning than the impotence, and made me weep in the dark.

Of late he had blamed me, saying my perfume was rank or my legs unshaven; once he called me a bag of bones, and advised me to eat my own cooking! I had borne it all, though I am proud, for love of him; I would be glad of the rest this night.

I tiptoed past the barred door, lighting my own way to my chamber, and dismissing my body slave; I would not need her eastern arts tonight!

12

CAESAR SELPT LATE in the morning, and so did I; we were both the better for our lonely rest. He looked fresher than he had looked in weeks, and there was a youthful bounce in his walk. He kissed me tenderly, and fed me little morsels from his plate; I saw that he had eaten a huge breakfast. "Help me with this toga, darling . . . I can never manage it."

"Must you wear it?" I said. "The wine stains never bleached out—and it is nearly threadbare . . ."

"It is my favorite," he said, sternly, and handed me the end of it to drape. The Roman toga is a frustrating piece of clothing, old-fashioned and awkward, but it is required dress for the Senate, no matter what weather.

"Good," I said. "You have your flannel vest beneath . . . it is still chilly."

"Well," said Caesar, "March is on the way . . ."

"It would be warm by now—in Alexandria . . . I can never get used to this dreadful climate of yours . . . there—"

I tucked the end of the toga through the loop at the waist. "If you keep it that way—so—the wine stain will not show."

"It is too tight," he said, frowning, and pulling the loop out; well, he was Caesar, after all; Rome would just have to put up with him, wine stain and all! I looked at him, merry. "Marcus said you were a law in yourself . . ."

"Did he indeed?" said Caesar, pleased. "Good fellow, Marcus . . . have him to supper." He kissed me again and left, walking down to the landing place, springy as a boy. From a distance he looked like a boy, small and spare, and standing erect in the boat, even as they shoved off from shore. It was a trick he had; I had tried it myself when I first came to Rome; it looked easy, but I narrowly missed a good wetting.

I waited just till Caesar's boat touched shore on the other bank, then I called Cadwallader to me. "Go and fetch Marcus Antonius," I said. "He will be at home . . . it is still early. Tell him it is very urgent." For I must brief him before he spoke with Julio.

He was not at all put out at being summoned so peremptorily; in fact I had never seen him irritated or annoyed; I could not understand why Fulvia did not thank all the gods for him. Well, each heart is made of different stuff; perhaps he was not so accommodating either, with a wife.

He had come hastily, as I asked, and was still chewing on a rusk of bread. "Have a bite," he said, grinning up at me; I had gone down to the Tiber shore to await him.

I pushed away the bread, impatiently. "I have eaten," I said. "Well, are you not getting out of the boat, then?"

"I thought perhaps we might go rowing," he said. But looking closely at me, his face sobered, and he clambered out of the boat, dipping it dangerously in the water; he was no lightweight!

We walked beneath the tamarind trees, their fronds brushing low at our faces, for I did not want to be overheard. I told him my plan; it was not that, really—only an idea, but a good one.

"Caesar to be offered the crown of all possessions outside Rome—king of all the Roman dominions . . . yes, that might work. Yes . . . the legions will like it, at any rate." He walked on for a bit, his face dark in thought. "How much time should we give it? We must put forward the idea . . . among the nobles, the equestrians . . . and we must pick the right time to propose it . . ."

"I thought—perhaps the Calends of March? Not really a holiday—but the start of spring . . . what do you think?"

"Yes . . . not bad. Caesar will sacrifice in the open Forum . . . he will be at hand . . ."

"He spoke of sacrificing at the Ides—" I began.

"Oh, no—he would not do that!" He stared at me. "It is unlucky. No one plans anything for the Ides . . . of course, you wouldn't know, not being a Roman." He shrugged, and laughed a little. "The gods know, at this point, what is unlucky about it . . . or maybe Cicero knows. Some old prophecy or warning, some such thing, out of the mists . . . but no—don't suggest it."

"The Calends then."

"Yes," he said. "We must see that the Gallic legions are present, and the new one, The Lark . . . they will sway the crowd . . . shall I offer the crown? Perhaps I am unlucky . . ."

"Oh, yes, Marcus! Who else? There is no other of consequence who would agree . . ." I told of the preceding evening, and Brutus, and Caesar's disappointment.

He nodded slowly. "There is some kind of plot, I think . . . to unseat Caesar, rob him of his powers . . . I am not sure. But I know Cassius is at the bottom of it. They have not many followers, though—or so I think. But I have seen writings—scribbling on the public buildings, calling for action against the dictator—an end to Caesarian tyranny—that sort of thing . . ."

I was aghast. "But that is terrible!"

"Oh, it always goes on . . . in Rome. It is just that it is a little more so just now . . . a definite faction is behind it this time." He laughed. "Brutus' house and the wall of his courtyard are covered with scrawls. . . . 'Wake up, Brutus'—'Join, Brutus'—'Oh, that Brutus were awake!' Last time I went past, Portia had a whole army of slaves out rubbing at it and scrubbing . . . but I'll wager it is all back again."

"Why Brutus?" I asked.

"Oh, he lends honor to it all, you see. He is very respectable."

"From last night, I would say they had his ear . . ."

"Yes, and more. I think he is in it very deep—whatever it is."

"What can they do?" I asked.

He shrugged. "Nothing, really. It is a campaign of slander, that is all. . . . Of course, Caesar cannot afford it . . . he has too many enemies."

"Enemies can do nothing, cannot matter—once he is crowned," I said.

"Well, I think you are right. And the Calends it shall be . . ."

We put it to Caesar that evening at supper, for of course Marcus came; he was always amenable. It seemed to give Caesar new life; there was color in his cheeks for a change, and the spring continued in his legs; we were all very happy, and drank a lot of wine. And that night Julio and I were lovers once again, almost as it had been long ago in Alexandria.

However, during the early hours, close to dawn, Caesar dreamed; for a sensible man, he is surprisingly gullible toward such things. Though I have noticed he takes no stock of the dreams of others, and only of his own. Soothsayers and bad omens mean nothing to him; he avers that Caesar is above them, but let him dream of squint-eyes, and he will send spies out searching for the man who owns them!

His dream was most curious; wolves in the sky, framed by the new moon; there was much more, but this feature struck him. He insisted it meant the propitious time to offer the crown would be on the Ides, or the appearance of the full moon, since the wolves were the symbol of Rome. I said that wolves were also associated with the full moon, at least in my country, for they are believed to change into men, or the other way around, at that time. That is why, as I pointed out, the Ides are considered unlucky, from long years past. "As a matter of fact, wolves and jackals, dogs even, howl at the moon at full—and men run and . . . murders and suicides, lovers' quarrels all happen in the full moon."

"Such things are not for Caesar," he said, waving his hand contemptuously. "No, I must receive the crown on the Ides . . ."

I had thought myself quite clever to have named the Calends, for the new moon is, naturally, associated with beginnings; however, it was never any use pitting oneself against Caesar when his mind was made up.

Marcus shook his head doubtfully when I told him, but agreed that at least it would give us more time. "Yes," I said, "I had better have the seamstresses make up the gold cloth . . ."

He laughed loud. "That is the first sign of vanity I have seen in you, little Greek!"

I drew myself up tall. "Not vanity," I said. "It is only seemly to be richly attired . . . my coronation will follow his." I thought a moment. "I shall insist that enough be left over for a kilt for Caesarion." He laughed again; I saw nothing funny.

It seemed that Caesar was right; on the Calends, at the feast of the New Moon, he sacrificed a goat; neither he nor the temple priests could find the victim's heart afterwards, considered the worst of omens. Our Egyptian doctor, Dioscorides, smiled sourly and said that the Romans fattened their sacrifices so that the heart was surrounded by gobbets of yellow; he was probably correct, for what creature can live without a heart?

Caesar was happily adapting his campaign plans to the new circumstances; he meant now to leave Rome a few days after accepting the Crown of the Dominions and join his legions; I would accompany him and we would establish a temporary seat of monarchy in the Troad lands, on the very site of Troy itself. It was a good choice, for the place has mystery and legend surrounding it, and the old city of Sigeum still stands, in a fashion. There we would be both married and crowned; I remarked, not without gravity, that it was about time.

Marcus, too, had been busy; he said that the new plan found favor with all those senators and nobles he had sounded out; we would be supported. I had no doubt, that, when Rome grew used to the idea of kingship, we could accomplish a Roman empire as well. My gold robe, and Caesarion's, was ready ahead of time, though Caesarion could not be fitted. I could not risk a child's babble, giving everything away. All my boxes and effects were packed for the trip, even dishes and furniture; we would need a few luxuries in Sigeum; it was a ruin. Caesar, of course, could have carried all on his backpack; "Soldiers travel light, my dear!"

My heart was as light as his pack, and I hummed as I went about the house. Even the news that Octavian would be joining us on our journey could not dampen my joy; perhaps he had improved!

Marcus was to stay behind in Rome as Caesar's deputy, along with another tribune named Lepidus, who had just returned from a governorship in Gaul.

This Lepidus was bid to supper on the eve of the Ides of March; he had official legion business, papers to sign and such things, and Caesar's time was very full; I complained that the house was not fit to entertain in, but Julio laughed. "Lepidus has been three years in a tent—when he was lucky. He will think it a palace!"

So we sat on camp stools and cushions and supped off the floor, picnic-style. The only other guest was Marcus, and Caesarion was allowed to stay up, and have a sip of watered wine; why not—tomorrow he would be heir to the whole world, or very nearly! He was on his best behavior, wiping his mouth after each bite and not talking to much; he did not even beg to stay up the whole evening, but made his farewells in a manly fashion and let the nurse lead him off to his bed.

Lepidus looked after him, waving good-bye as fatuously as the rest of us. "Smart boy, that," he said, "and could pass for five years old any day . . ." And he winked at Caesar, saying, "Easy to see where he gets it, too . . . his mother wasn't fooling around . . . begging your pardon, Lady!"

I took no offense; I was only too glad his son resembled Caesar. The man Lepidus was very likeable anyway, never mind his army manners; one could trust him at a glance; he had no guile. He was big, open, and friendly as a hound, and only a little awkward.

I cannot remember how the conversation turned upon death; strange, how some things flee the mind! I remember only that someone of us asked what manner of death we would, each, prefer; perhaps it was the wine talking, we had had a lot of it.

Marcus shook his head and laughed. "I never think about it!"

I said that Alexander, at such a question, had answered, "Glory over length of days . . ."

Caesar smiled, raised his cup, and said, "What death? A quick one!"

I thought of that afterwards, over and over. For that is what my Julio got. A quick death, in the Forum, the next day. For he was set upon by many assassins and stabbed with many death-dealing blows.

I only hoped that his death came quickly enough. I hoped that he had not seen the face, among his murderers, of his son, Brutus.

BOOK III
Actium

1

I NEVER THOUGHT that I could be homesick for Rome.

But I was; sick and wretched and low in spirits, in that year of Julio's death. Alexandria, too, was sick, and all the land of Egypt. For there was famine again, the worst of many decades. The Nile had not risen, the ground was parched, the crops failed, and the people died like flies. And this time there was no cure for it in the Old Religion. The sacred bull that I had played Mother to long ago still lived, among his heifers and calves; he was still washed and combed and fed precious grain, though no flowers could be found to deck his bull-brow.

The priests laid the blame to Caesar's assassins, weeping for the death of the Lord Amon, in the wounded flesh of our great Roman. I wept, too, in secret, for it seemed that all my hopes were buried with him.

In Rome, as well, the people mourned the passing of a god; there were prodigious signs; a comet blazed in the sky, through seven days and nights, and a haze hung over the sun. The day before I took ship for Alexandria I saw his image, in his temple, crowned with a star that blazed with gems, a gift from the plebes, who loved him.

Caesarion cried all the way home, for some fool had told him his father was dead. I despaired, fearing he would make himself sick; to calm him I said his father had gone away, to be a god among the others on Mount Olympos. "But he is not *here!*" he wailed.

The Briton, Cadwallader, who was his nutritius now, reached out and took him in his arms. "Look you, little Caesar," he said, in his lilt that never went away for all the years among us. "Look you—" And he held out a little mirror. "There he is, your father. Look well, little one. He is with us still . . ."

I do not think that Caesarion heard the words, true as they were. But he stopped crying, and took the mirror, turning it about in his fat baby hands. "Tin!" he whispered, in a voice full of wonder. "Is it tin?"

"Yes," said Cadwallader. "From my own country. I had it when I was a little prince, like you. I remember when my own father, the king, gave it to me, on my birthday . . ." And he was off, on his story, and Caesarion was quiet; one could usually count on him. But I smiled a little to think of the child's wonder at the thing. He had mirrors of silver and gold, electrum even, and set with ivory and jewels, all shapes and sizes, by master craftsmen. Of course, tin is very rare, for all that it is ugly and dents easily; this piece looked to be old enough to have been mined by Titans, or whatever passes for them in the Misty Isles. Indeed, some such story was the one Cadwallader was telling and I heard it with half an ear, but gratefully, for Caesarion was distracted from his grief. He would get over it anyway in time; children always do. But I would never let him forget.

I heard it all, the death of Caesar, from Marcus, who was there; he saw it from a distance, helpless, with the crown he was to have offered Julio still in his hand.

It is useless to go back and say, "If one did such and so, thus and thus would not have happened." I have tortured myself too often in that way, thinking if only Caesar had been delayed that morning, even by a fit! Or if he had only heeded Calpurnia's warning! For she had sent a note, frantic, telling of a conspiracy; he had read it, frowning, and crumpled it in his hand, tapping his head as if to say she was crazed. We heard afterwards that she had got wind of it all from Portia, Brutus' wife, so it was authentic. But then Caesar would never have believed any evil from that source, alas!

No, it does no good to look back, or regret. We are as we are, and events happen as they happen; we cannot change them, any more than we can choose the day we are born.

The senseless murder happened in the Senate house, just under the statue of Pompey. Caesar was accompanied by Marcus, but, at the entrance, a certain Trenonius detained Marcus; afterwards, he could not remember what the man said. The place was very crowded, as for a special occasion; Marcus had made sure of that, and so had the murderers. The mob was mainly made up of petitioners, seeking the ear of the dictator. A man named Tullius Cimber, whose brother was in exile, approached Caesar, who was seated in readiness; Marcus said that Caesar smiled at the man and made the sign of pardon for his brother. All at once confusion reigned, and the crowd moved in close; Caesar sprang to his feet. Tullius Cimber caught hold of his toga and pulled it from him, leaving Caesar only his thin short tunic. Another man moved in, Casca, and stabbed him in the shoulder. In a loud voice Caesar cried, "You villain, Casca! What are you doing?" Then, like a pack of wild dogs, they were upon him, Cassius, Bucolianus, Decimus Brutus, and his own fair son, Marcus Brutus. Caesar had no weapon, but pulled his writing stylus from his belt and fought back as best he could. Even after he fell to the ground, dying, they stabbed at him; even after there was no more life, they struck at him, slashing and stabbing, slipping in the great pool of his blood.

The din was like a battlefield, for the crowd took fright and shrieked and trampled one another to get away from the place. Brutus, covered with blood, took from his toga a long sheet of paper; he had prepared a speech! With shaking hands he unrolled the scroll, in an unnatural, breathing silence; there was no one to read it to, for all had fled or were fleeing. Only Marcus stood at the entrance; he said he felt as one feels in a dream, tied hand and foot. It was not till some of the conspirators started for him with their daggers, still wet and red, upraised, that he turned and ran.

He wept and wept, at my feet, and could not stop, calling himself coward; I had to piece the dreadful story together myself, for he was nearly mad with the horror of it. I could not take it in properly, even after I had heard it; I found myself repeating words of comfort, and patting his shoulder over and over. In the end I was infected too, and began to sob and shake, falling to my knees along with him and weeping, but still not knowing why I wept.

After a bit, I saw the crown, still in his hand; I quieted and stared at it. And then I knew. It came to me in waves, the knowledge, little by little, until my heart was flooded with it, icy, black, and full of terror. Caesar was gone.

When I say the murder was senseless, it is true; the conspirators had not even a political plan! Covered in blood, like butchers, they reeled about on the Senate floor, waving their knives and shouting catchwords about liberty and the Republic; they must have looked like drunkards or madmen, for there were no people to hear them, except for the few city guards that stuck to their posts; one of them was from Caesar's household, a manumitted slave, and we got the story from him. How the murderers, frightened by the emptiness and the silence, barricaded themselves behind the locked doors of the Capitol; how they ventured out, miraculously cleaned up, to the open Forum; how the people listened there, quiet but sullen, to the speech that Brutus read them, only growling a little when Caesar's name was mentioned. But, when a man named Cinna took over and began to revile Caesar and make ugly accusations, they moved forward in a roaring body and chased the conspirators back to the Capitol, where they spent the night.

For several days and nights, all Rome was in chaos; even on our side of the Tiber we could hear the noise, a kind of battle din; all that was missing was the clash of sword and shield. The sky was red with flames, for mobs went about setting fire to all sorts of places; grimly, afterwards, in Alexandria, I remembered the grain houses that burned to a blackened shell, and the cook shops, and the market stalls, and shuddered at the waste; Rome has never had a famine!

There is no justice in mob rule; the conspirators went untouched, not a hair of their heads was harmed, but scores of innocent folk died, in the crush and the fury. A poor little poet, harmless, named Cinna, like the conspirator—I remember him reading his work at an afternoon concert—was caught as he emptied his chamberpot, his slaves all having run after the wild mob. He was hurled from hand to hand, being mistaken for the other Cinna, and beaten and trampled to death.

Nothing was done to restore order; the senators, like the conspirators, huddled behind locked doors; the city guard reverted and joined the people, running in packs, burning and looting. The legions patrolled the provincial borders, many of them far away; even Caesar's own Gaulish regiments had been sent on before him; Rome had no defense against herself!

In the end, what order was established came from Marcus; he gave the funeral ovation and called the gods to witness the body of Caesar consumed by fire; when it was all ashes, pure and white, they buried them in an alabaster urn, and raised a great memorial stone.

The next day, Marcus read out to the people the contents of Caesar's will, the one which named Octavian as his heir. The common folk were silent, and no cheers were raised; they did not know this country-bred nephew; would they accept him, if and when he came? Marcus had his hopes, but I was inclined to think they would, once the idea took root; Caesar had set his seal to it, after all. There were huge huzzahs when Caesarion's name was read as the only legitimate son of Caesar, and cries of his name and "Little Caesar," and even "Cleopatra." It was something that warmed my heart, when the word was brought to me, but I knew there was no use counting on anything coming from it; Caesarion was a mere baby, after all, and I was an alien queen.

One can imagine the noise of the crowd when it was learned that Caesar had bequeathed to every Roman citizen 300 sesterces each; some of them would not have seen such a sum in a lifetime! He also left his estates across the Tiber, to be used as a public park; luckily, Marcus had alerted me about this, for of course this was the very villa where I had been making my Roman home! I had authorized him to announce that, as rent for this mourning month, I would add another hundred sesterces to each bequest; it was expensive, but it saved me from a very real danger, for I could not, with the city in such turmoil, get away from Rome.

As it was, I saw torches that night upon the river, and presently a good-sized boat touched shore on my side. I held back my guards, for I had a feeling that I knew who went there. I asked them to come forward without fear. They did so, stumbling in the dark and with the funeral wine, some eight of the plebes, their rough tunics stained and worn, and their legs bare and filthy in the torchlight. I saw they were very frightened, for the wine was wearing off.

"Come, friends," I said. "Have no fear—you will not come to harm. You are my fellow mourners, and dear to me, for Caesar loved you. . . . Have you come to look over your property? I promise you I will stay out the month only. . . . Come—bring your torches, and examine the grounds . . . Are they not beautiful, Caesar's gift?"

I led them even into the house, and let them peep into all the chambers, while my body servants scowled disapproval. Poor mangy creatures! They had never seen such a house . . . like a house on the moon it must have looked to them! They shuffled in embarrassment and pulled at their forelocks. I spoke kindly to them and let the tears come; it was not difficult; several plebes were sobbing too. At the end I gave them, each, a silk purse full of small coins, and a piece of gold plate from Caesar's table; it was a small price to pay, for their love.

Marcus, who had seen it all, chuckled when they left. "You have the common touch, my dear . . ."

"A queen must," I said, giving him a cool look. He laughed louder.

"I should be glad of it," he said. "For otherwise you would not like me."

"Do I?" I questioned, raising my eyebrows.

"Do you not?" he countered, a little smile playing on his full mouth.

I stared at him, appalled. What were we two playing at . . . Caesar was dead! His face fell, for he felt it too.

"In truth," I said, "I like you more than a little, friend. For I am so very grateful to you . . ." I looked at him very steadily. "I have had no other visitor, you know. Not one."

"And will not," he said, just as grave. "They are all waiting to see which way the cat will jump."

"Meaning Octavian?" I queried.

"Meaning Rome."

"I see," I said. And I did; I understood their feelings. "Perhaps, Marcus, you are foolhardy."

"I think not," he said, smiling. "I have always known which horse to back . . ."

I shot him a glance. "Another woman would take offense at the comparison."

"But you," he said, "are a queen."

"Yes—" I said. "And have the common touch." He threw back his head and laughed, and I with him, loud and long.

Afterwards, I looked at him, shrugging gently. "It is better than weeping," I said. "Will you take some wine, friend?" For he was a great comfort to me, Marcus.

It was no laughing matter, though; I must go back to Alexandria and wait, perhaps years, for another chance—chance for what? World mastery? The dominion of Rome? A bigger throne? Sadly I thought on the reality; my Alexandria, my Egypt, indeed, was at stake. Rome had swallowed larger prey. All hung, truthfully, on that sickly boy, Octavian. And on the strength of the weapons that could be used against him.

I had no choice but to leave the fate of Egypt in Marcus' hands; I told him so. He smiled broadly, looking down at me. "Oh, Octavian has bigger fish to fry than Alexandria

. . . for a while." His face fell into hard lines. "But he needs watching."

"If he comes at all," I said, remembering his weedy looks.

"Oh, he will come," said Marcus. "Caesar had a good eye, and he was Caesar's choice. He will come. He is on his way . . . with all the Gaulish legions at his back."

"I must go," I said. But there was a question in my eyes.

"Yes," he said. "Better so . . . We will meet again."

2

THERE WERE MUTTERINGS against me in the ranks of the Roman legions; I heard them, low and ominous, when I walked abroad, and even in the halls of my own palace. Every time I passed a knot of soldiers casting dice, or mending harness, I felt it between my shoulderblades—the point of the flung dagger or the thrust of the lance; I had to force my head up and my back straight. For Roman soldiers are not used to going hungry.

I had passed an edict that, while my people starved, all, even in the palace itself, must go on short rations. We had some surplus still in the private storerooms; each morning I watched while the pitifully small portions were handed out; there are always some who will take advantage of misfortunes. My heart wept bitterly for those little brown people of the upper lands; they suffered more than any others, for there was no way to insure that the grain could be got to them (horses must be fed, and even camels, to say nothing of the men who supervised). As it was, there was not enough. The people of the foreign quarters got nothing, the Phoenicians, the Assyrians, and the Jews; the citizens of Alexandria came first. My citizenry got very thin, but they stayed whole, at least at first. It was in the foreign quarters that the pestilence first broke out.

At early word of the dead and dying among those alien peoples, it was thought that they starved, and to this day it is called "the famine sickness." But when the doctor saw the bodies, they could not put a name to it; it was a new disease, and uglier than any yet seen.

The faces of the victims were suffused with blackish

blood, and in armpit and groin huge black boils appeared, large as a pomegranate. Sometimes, if the boils burst, the victim recovered, but most often death was quick and horrible. Whole families were wiped out, with none to bury the dead, so that in some streets, corpses lay in piles, stinking. Dioscorides ordered that they must be buried, at any cost, for he feared the infection was spread by the dead; it was not safe, he said, to breathe the pestilential air.

Whatever the cause, this disease raged, moving out of the foreign quarters and into street after street; even the Palace was struck; we had to close the kitchens, for several died while tending the fires or scrubbing. Even the house cats lay dead, huge, stiff, and bloated; Dioscorides decreed that they not be touched, except with a shovel. He said, after much thought, and poring over old books, that he believed rats carried the pestilence. "But I have seen live rats—" I cried, "all through the Palace, where they have not dared go before!"

"They are carriers," he said. "They do not suffer from the disease . . ."

I set the Roman legions, grumbling anew, to looking out for these rats, and spitting them on lance or spear. After a day or two, the Palace halls were piled with these vermin, bigger than any I had ever seen. Slaves were put to shoveling them outside and burying them.

We ate little but fruit, and drank unwatered wine, for Dioscorides feared the wells might have poison in them. "If a rat got in—" he said, shaking his head. I shuddered at the thought of a rat in the drinking water—even a healthy rat!

I sent an army of slaves outside the Palace walls, to bury the dead there; the legions refused to go, though it left us short-handed.

Even though the dead were buried quickly, still there was a strange, sick-sweet smell in the air; one had to shut the doors against it, and go about with nose and mouth swathed in veils. Perhaps that saved us; for a wonder, no one caught it among the Palace people, except for those first few scullery slaves. We were lightheaded from lack of food, and a little drunk from so much wine, but otherwise we did not suffer, neither the court nobles nor the soldiers; even the Palace slaves thrived.

Each night they reported fewer dead, and, all in one day, it seemed, the plague was over, though the rats were not dead and ran boldly through the city; it was a mystery. Dioscorides noticed that the cats had stopped dying as well, even those who stalked beside rat corpses; he said, shrugging, that perhaps the disease had simply run its course. "Some day," he said, "we will understand it, and how to stop the spread or cure the illness . . . but for now—" And he shook his head sadly.

When a census was taken, it was discovered that more than three-quarters of the people had died, all in a space of a few short weeks. It sounds a dreadful thing to say, but it went a long way toward solving the problem of the famine; there were less mouths to feed, to put it simply. I was able to get grain to the folk of the Upper Nile; many were saved. And, as always happens, supplies, long promised and long-awaited, began to pour in from all the trade routes. We learned, too, from the merchant trains, that our land of Egypt was not the only plague-ridden place; this sickness had swept through all the lands of the eastern world; Rome, only, had been spared. Grimly I got the news that Octavian, who was now calling himself "Caesar," was taking credit, and had proclaimed a week of thanksgiving. As for us, in Egypt, our week was a week of mourning.

But slowly, very slowly, the land recovered, and the next spring, the Nile flooded again, the highest water in many years; we were saved.

3

THE NEWS FROM ROME was not good. I had had no time to spare for it during the year of famine and pestilence, but afterwards, with leisure to think, I was appalled at the chaos which still reigned there. Of course, from my point of view, chaos was better than order; at least Egypt was not due for invasion for a while!

Not long after I left the city, Octavian arrived in triumph, with legions at his back, to take up his inheritance. He called himself "Caesar," offending many; I smiled to hear Marcus' words, repeated all over the world; "Little boy with a big name!"

Those two were natural enemies; aside from political rivalry, one could look far without finding two more unlike creatures; Antonius, large, open, powerful, friendly, and Octavian, thin and secretive, cold as a reptile. Upon their first public meeting, it was said, they embraced, as is the custom, each taking the opportunity to feel about the other's person for hidden weapons. The story of these two is not clear, and what went on far too long and involved to puzzle out; the open hostility could not last, for it would destroy one or the other, or both.

In the end, Octavian, with help from Cicero, gained the confidence of the Senate, and a grudging approval from the plebes, and for a time Marcus was listed as an enemy of Rome, and had to flee the city. I chewed my nails for weeks, for my fate, and Caesarion's, hung on this man; he was, in truth, my only friend in Rome (for well-wishers without power are useless).

Suddenly news came that a new triumvirate had been formed, an alliance between Antonius, Octavian, and Lepidus, with full approval of the Senate, and powers to match. I was much surprised, but there was nothing for it; I had to trust Antonius, whatever game he played. I pondered long over it; somehow he had made his peace with Octavian, a wise move, for the moment. Lepidus, whom I met once, was an easy man, and close to Marcus, surely; nothing to fear there; I called it two to one and nodded my head in approval.

The Triumvirate was called publicly, "an alliance for the reorganization of the Roman State," and given unlimited powers for five years, with the provinces falling under their separate rules. In effect, they governed Rome and all Roman possessions. Octavian was given Spain, and Lepidus North Africa; Antonius got the lion's share, as the desert people say; he had jurisdiction over all of the East, and Gaul as well. I breathed a sigh of relief; Egypt was still an independent kingdom, but it was eastern, certainly; I did not think Marcus would invade!

There are always troubles, in any kingdom, as there are, to be sure, in families. In my case, they were one and the same. I had no family left, except for my sister, Arsinoëe, long a prisoner; why was it that I, normally so wary, was always fooled by this girl? During the famine, and the great sickness, I took pity on her, and gave her her liberty; she made herself useful, and stood, like a true sister, beside me through all the hardship and want; I believed, truly, that she had reformed. That is to say, that I felt that now, in her maturity, she would behave as a royal person should, with some circumspection, and take her place below me without complaint. I was wrong, as it turned out, on both counts.

I had no worldly advisers, only my own inner voice; it must have spoken, though, in some deep silent manner, for I did not name her my successor, after Caesarion, though it was customary to do this on the day of Amon's Feast. Instead, remembering that Caesar long ago had given her, along with our little dead Mouse II, the throne of Cyprus, I named her queen of that place. "You will have no difficulty with that kingdom, sister," I said. "Serapion is my viceroy there, and has been for all our stay in Rome . . . he is a good administrator, and knows all the country's needs." I had forgotten that Serapion was also a man, young, unmarried, and ambitious!

Serapion was that rare thing, an Egyptian Greek; these races do not as a rule intermarry, at least in the upper classes. He had been born on Cyprus, his father viceroy before him; he had been to Alexandria only once, when he took office on his father's death; I remembered him as a beardless youth with clever eyes and a head for figures. No sooner had Arsinoëe set foot on the island than he became her Ganymede!

I thought little of it; she was a woman grown and must take her pleasure somewhere; indeed, I would have approved their wedding, for he was noble enough, and very capable, but she did not petition me. Perhaps she was too used to a clandestine embrace, or perhaps she had set her eyes higher than a mere viceroy; perhaps, in some secret way, she looked to Rome, as I did. I could never read her, Arsinoëe; to be on the safe side, I sent spies into Cyprus, special spies, for her alone.

The two leaders of the conspirators emerged as Brutus and Cassius; they had been exiled. Incredibly, the Senate, which I was beginning to think composed of doddering fools, gave the provinces of Syria and Macedonia to these confessed murderers, as though to award them. In truth, they were not free places; Caesar had presented Antonius with Macedonia and given Dolabella Syria, months before his death; these two forgot their war over Fulvia's favors and joined heads to think how to wrest their possessions away from the exiled conspirators. They began to gather troops and ships, and Dolabella sailed into the Mediterranean to confront the exiles.

The new Triumvirate, in the meantime, was busy getting rid of its enemies. Over a hundred senators, and some thousand rich and influential Romans perished in this manner. Their deaths were called "executions," but in truth they were butcheries; when my envoy began to tell the ghastly tale of Cicero's dismembered body, I stopped him, for my stomach heaved; I had known the man! I wondered by whose order the deed had been done, and hoped it was Octavian's; I could lay all manner of evil at his door, for I disliked him. Unbidden, though, came the thought of the millions that had died in my lover's wars, Caesar's dead; had I lain then in their blood, guilty after the fact? I thrust the thought away; I would ponder it later, much later, when I was old.

At about this time there came two envoys, each of them with an identical request; that is, one was couched in respectful terms, and begged a favor; the other ordered me, in the name of the Republic of Rome, to comply. I stared at the man, a perfumed Syrian with all the airs of a sultan. "To whom do I owe this honor?" I asked, my lip twitching. The irony, though heavy, was wasted on him; he replied, with a comic haughtiness, that he spoke for that noble Roman, Cassius.

"I am a woman," I said, "and soft-hearted. You are fortunate. You will get back to your ship and return from wherever you came. Tell Caesar's murderer that his next envoy shall be returned headless."

It would not have mattered, truly, what Cassius wanted, or indeed how he asked for it; my answer would have been the same. The other envoy was a Macedonian Greek, cleverly chosen, a messenger from Dolabella. He asked for the loan of the legions left in Alexandria by Caesar. "My country is in peril, Lady . . . for Brutus rules there. The Consul Dolabella promises to liberate us, but he needs soldiers and ships . . . he is vastly outnumbered."

"Is there haste?" I asked. "I will send them and gladly . . ."

"The sooner the better," he replied.

"They shall be ready when you are."

He left with my legions and a hundred good ships; in a month they were back, bearing a tale of woe. Dolabella had been engaged at sea by Cassius, and defeated with great losses, though he himself had escaped.

"That felon Cassius was too quick for us, Lady," said the Greek. "And he had Egyptian ships . . ."

"But you heard me refuse!" I was aghast.

"Yes, Lady. They came from Cyprus . . . and arrived before us."

Arsinoëe and her Serapion! Once more my sister! My insides seethed, but I was older now, and had learned to control it; I said merely, "Thank you, my friend. I shall see to it. . . . Convey my condolences to the good Dolabella, and take the ships and troops once more. Next time they may be of more use."

I pondered what action to take, what reprisals to make. I could not waste ships and men on a war against my own possession; it would have to wait. I doubled the spies, and sent them into Cyprus. And I sent word to Arsinoëe that I had need of two hundred Cyprian vessels and two thousand men. She sent back answer that she could not spare them, as that number had met with a storm and all had been sunk! She must have thought my kindness to her was a sign of failing wits; it was just another count against her, when my reckoning day should come. The time for mercy was long past; for now I let it go, and contented myself with demanding all the ships in Cyprus' harbor; she could not refuse, for I sent a large force to take them, leaving just as many vessels as could defend the island. I recalled Serapion as well, sending a replacement, one of the last eunuchs left at my court; she would count that suffering indeed! I put her ultimate punishment out of my mind, for I am squeamish.

4

We are not late, in Alexandria, getting the news; still it filtered in to us bit by bit. I rejoiced in the deaths of Caesar's murderers, Brutus and Cassius; I rejoiced too in that they met their defeat by Antonius' hands. They were beaten roundly at the battle of Philippi, with Marcus commanding; he did not have to share the glory with Octavian either, for the boy who called himself Caesar was ill. Cassius was killed outright, and Brutus took his own life; the world was rid of them, the leaders of the conspiracy.

Though there were many enemy deaths at Philippi, more were taken prisoner; it was told that all these prisoners, among them illustrious and wealthy Romans, bowed low before Marcus, calling him "Great Victor," and begged to be taken into the ranks of his army. On the other hand, they cursed Octavian, calling him upstart. It cannot have been true, one realizes; still, some such temper must have existed, however secret; Octavian was very unpopular. As far as I know, he had done nothing to deserve this disrespect; it is my opinion that he showed up badly against Marcus, and even Lepidus. He was a boy still, and a sickly, cold one; both the others of the Triumvirate were seasoned warriors, healthy, oversized, and open-handed, and Marcus, in his rough way, was as handsome as a god.

It was decided that, of the Triumvirate, Octavian should set himself to restore order in Italy, Lepidus should take care of Africa and its revenues, and Marcus should travel through the East, the richest of all the provinces, to collect money and to assert the authority of the Roman rule once more.

We heard that Marcus was journeying through the Greek mainland in a progress as leisurely and ostentatious as a Triumph; his train was huge, legion after legion, chariots, wagons, and a whole court on the move. All the great potentates came to greet him, bowing, bearing gifts, and worshiping him as if he were divine. With all the gifts and the tribute, his way was slow, and it took him the greater part of a year to traverse countries that could be walked across in a month.

I wondered if he would come here; there must be no signs of the famine, no look of deprivation; Egypt must be Rome's ally, not her trophy. I sent double the usual supplies up the Nile, dipping into the royal treasury, for it was worth it. My legions trained every day; all Romans liked a trim fighting man. All year thousands of craftsmen slaves worked on the Palace and the public buildings; Alexandria, always the most beautiful of cities, was newly glorious. And still he did not come.

"I think he has forgotten you," said Iras, sweetly sly; she had the license of a sister-playmate, always, and besides, she had never liked Marcus.

"Who?" I asked, though of course I knew.

"The Coin Face. The Hairy Legs. Marcus."

"He is thinner now . . . and I think he shaves, as well,"

I said, with a little smile. "But no matter . . ." Her first words came back to me, making me sit up. "Of course he has not forgotten me. He was Caesar's friend."

She shrugged. "And now he is Octavian's."

I nodded, slowly. "Yes . . . he plays a clever game, for all his open looks. One thing . . . of the Triumvirate, he has the greatest powers. And the victory at Philippi was his. In all but name, he is dictator of Rome."

She looked at me straight. "But he is not Caesar. Remember that."

"Caesar is dead," I said. "But Caesarion lives. And he must have a champion. Who else is there?"

"Well, you are right, of course." But she looked very grave. "However, I do not trust Marcus. He is all for himself."

"Who is not?" I answered, spreading my hands in a trader's gesture. "He still needs allies. And I must see to it that I—that Egypt—is his greatest. If he feels he can make use of me—well, then, it follows that I can best make use of him."

She took a sip of wine; perhaps it made her bold. "Yes," she said slowly. "You, also, are clever. Cleverer than he. The two of you—together—might add up to a Caesar." There was a small edge of scorn in her voice.

I laughed. "Fulvia would call that a bitch-bite. . . . Did you mean to wound me, sister? It is true . . . together we might. If we are *really* clever."

She sighed. "I am sorry." She was silent for a moment. "It is just that I wonder—do you dream, like Alexander, of conquering the world?"

I was not so much stung as affronted. "Of course I dream! For myself. For Egypt. For Caesarion. But—even if I did not—I cannot let Rome swallow my country! Greece is Roman—Gaul is Roman—and Spain, and all the rest! And you—" I cried. "Can you sit by and let it happen . . . even you?"

"I think I could," she said. "I am not a queen . . . only a waiting woman."

"You are my sister," I cried. "And a daughter of Egypt!"

She shook her head. "I am the daughter of the king you scorned . . . got lightly on a barbarian slave." She laughed softly. "Oh, I will help if I can. I will do what I can. But if I could truly choose—I would rather have my own barbarian . . ."

"Cadwallader?"

"You knew?"

I nodded. "It stands out all over you. Well, that is all right. He was a king's son. I will order him to wed you."

"Oh, no!" she cried, half-laughing. "You cannot order love! Just let it be, sister. If it happens, it will happen. *That* destiny at least I will master myself!"

I said no more, but resolved to push them together; Cadwallader was too much of a priest already. And she should have her wish, Iras. She was my sister, after all.

Charmion was made of stronger stuff. "Marcus will come," she said. "He needs Egypt. And besides," she said, looking as cool as Pallas Athene, "He desires you . . . I have seen his eyes."

"Oh, no!" I cried, too quickly, and getting as red as a maiden. "Oh, nothing like that!"

"Why not?" she asked, just as cool as before. "You are a woman. It is your greatest weapon. . . . You knew it with Caesar."

"I never thought about it," I said. But I lied.

And about Marcus I lied, too. I lied, even to myself, right up until the day he summoned me.

5

WHEN WORD CAME, finally, from Marcus, it was as flamboyant as the man himself. For he sent a troupe of actors as his envoys. Brilliant they were to look at, gaudy bright creatures, belonging to no nation, though their names and faces were Greek.

I had heard that he loved the company of these people, and had them about him always, disregarding class. Of course, in truth, they have no class, and reside outside society, in their own small, self-contained world.

I had seen the ship, Roman and very lordly, touch down, and came out on the Palace steps to greet the travelers. I saw them, the actors, though I did not know what manner of people they were, stream over the rails like sailors, disdaining the helping hands and the gangplank; even the woman of them was as lively as a monkey. One could hear them from afar as well; laughing, humming, their bright chatter spilling onto the air as easily as birdsong.

I shaded my eyes, for it was noon, and watched them as they climbed the shallow steps toward me. They did not even walk like other folk, with purpose or intent; they ambled, one stooping to pick a flowering weed from a cranny in the stone, tucking it behind his ear with a toss of his head, and another taking his companion's arm and turning about to point out to sea. The woman, tiny like a toy, saw me watching and ran the last few steps, as a child might do.

She ran lightly up to me, her face alight with a kind of mischief, and prostrated herself, like a Persian, on the stones at my feet.

I was startled and stepped back a pace; then I put out my hand, thinking to raise her up. I got a quick glimpse of a merry eye, and she sprang to her feet.

"We are a gift, Lady . . . a gift from Dionysos . . ." And she clapped her hands and began to skip about, chanting. "We are a gift . . . to act—and spy . . . act and spy . . . act and spy . . ." They all caught up with her then, some dozen, and, taking hands, danced round me in a circle, chanting along, "Act and spy . . ." I was bewildered, and felt, as most folk do when confronted by madness, a little foolish myself.

It was obvious, for they carried no weapons, that there was nothing to fear from these people, but as yet I did not know anything about them; their chanted words had not quite penetrated my understanding. I must have shown my astonishment on my face, contrary to my custom, for one of them, the tallest, stepped forward, bowing low.

"Allow me to introduce myself, Lady. . . . I am Sergius, of Athens." I stared still; then it hit me, like a blow. This was the tragedian, the protagonist, who had won the crown six times running; it was the first year such a thing had ever happened at the Dionysia. Last year a rival had taken it to court, but the decision held; I was honored indeed, and said so, holding out my hand in greeting.

"I have never seen you unmasked," I said. "But I have seen your Agamemnon twice . . . a beautiful performance." I examined his face, for I was curious. It was like a mask in truth, the lines strong and somehow larger than life, the head leonine; he was not young, far from it; in fact, the whole group, close to, seemed to be in the middle years. Or perhaps their calling marked them; it was hard to say. I saw that even the woman, dainty and agile as she was, was no dewy girl; her face was marked with fine lines about the eyes and a subtle look of strain, under the liveliness. He called her "Cytheris," and said she was daughter to the other man, who stood next to him, called "Hippias." Of course I knew him, should have recognized him at once, for comedians do not play in masks, and I had seen him often in Rome.

"I like your work, sir," I said, "but I could wish you to make a better choice of play . . . your last one was a disgrace. Even the plebes booed."

He grinned, not at all daunted. "Well, Lady, the purse was large . . . though no more will be forthcoming from that quarter . . ." And he rolled his eyes, pulling his face into long mourning lines; I looked my question. "Surely you knew it was Cicero's . . . ? And the money too . . ." I was profoundly shocked; I had not known Cicero to be such an enemy. The play, which did not deserve the name, was no more than a tasteless diatribe against Caesar; Sergius had got him to the life, epilepsy and all. I wondered, fleetingly, how he had done the physical aspect; he had a great mane of black hair; I suppose he had shaved it. A thought struck me, and I whirled to examine the woman.

She smiled. "I beg your gracious pardon, Lady. The money was too good." And she pulled herself up, haughty, me to the life, but dreadful. She held it a moment, then dissolved into laughter; such was her charm that I laughed too.

"I promise you, Lady, it is my last comic role."

"That is the truth," said Hippias. "And there is a great part for her in our current repertory—the Sappho. She will not play." And he shook his head, looking toward her reproachfully. I saw that, indeed, she was made for the Sappho part, small, dark, and vivid, as we are told the poetess was in life.

Her brows went down, in a look of pure fury; I was to find that every move of these folk was overdone, and emotions drawn out of all proportion; one got used to it after a while, but at first they seemed quite mad. She cried hotly. "It is a disgrace, that play! The Sappho is a figure of fun . . ."

Her father shrugged. "Well, it is comedy, after all. At

least you would not have to go naked . . ." He looked at me. "She hates that . . ."

I remembered the women's parts in the comedies; lewd and licentious; I had assumed, of course, that the actresses were all harlots as well. She must have read my thoughts, for she said, "Lady, I was born in a costume box, and cradled on soft wigs . . . it is my calling—what else? But—" And she gave me a sly look. "I have changed that . . . I am in masks now, with my husband." And she took the tragedian's hand, giving him a loving smile. He was too old for her, by a decade or two; but then so had Caesar been, for me, I remembered. Perhaps she loved him well, as I had loved.

"Shall I tell you a secret?" she asked, bubbling over with it, so that I smiled. She did not wait for an answer, but let the words tumble out. "You have seen me in a better part . . . parts. . . . Think! The Euripides—when Sergius was Agamemnon . . ."

"The House of Atreus . . . ?" I said, tentative. Women do not play in the tragedies, it is not done. Still, she was implying just that. I examined her closely. "You were the Electra . . . ?"

She nodded, her eyes like little hard black jewels. "And the Cassandra. And the bit in the beginning—Helen."

"But you were astounding!" I cried. "So real, so girlish . . ." And I heard myself, suddenly, and burst out laughing, as I would do with Iras, when I had said something foolish. She laughed with me, delighted.

"I thought it must be a very young boy, perhaps gelded, for the high voice tones . . ." And I began to laugh again.

"We do not geld actors," said the tragedian, as haughty as I myself. It was another thing I was to learn; these folk are prouder than any royalty, and take offense as easily as they put on their masks.

They were, in truth, as I came to know them, a fascinating puzzle in behavior, and like no others. Though they often quarreled violently among themselves, it was soon over, like a summer storm, and they were closer, all, than any family. As indeed they often were, for within their own troupe they married and begot babes, almost like Egyptian Pharaohs, so that one could find common traits in each one. Even rival companies resembled each other; there was the unmistakable mobile face, the voice pitched to the farthest reach of the amphitheater, the graceful fluid limbs, the ready laughter, and that strange air, common to them all, of self-sufficiency. I often thought to myself—if I were not born a queen, this calling would be my next choice, though I had no talent for it, except for my well-modulated voice, almost as full of color as one of theirs. But all of these folk, even the oldest and most dignified, could dance and sing, play instruments, beat drums, tumble, and improvise verse. I found much to admire, and more to enjoy; they turned my Palace into a market fair; we were never dull while they were with us.

As to the spying, why, of course, it was very clever of Marcus to use them so. They were constantly on the move, going from city to city and court to court, performing on all the feast days; in those days, also, they were above suspicion, for they were not given credit for so much acumen. Things changed later, and they were carefully searched at every new place for hidden missives. It did not help much, for their insides could not be searched, and their prodigious memories went unprobed. As Cytheris said, in her careless way—it came in handy, in a hard season, a second calling. None of them had any political sense, and would be happy in any form of government, however brutal, so long as they had a stage to walk on, a corner to lie in, and a couple of crusts of bread.

In the case at present, I learned that they were unofficial messengers from Marcus, ostensibly sent to entertain, all payment having been defrayed by our mutual friend, which made me smile; I could have bought twenty such troupes! The official envoy was a Roman officer named Dellius; Cytheris whispered, with a wicked smile, that he was an Octavian spy. "As opposed to us, my dear lady, who are Antonian spies. There is a fine distinction . . ."

This Dellius proved to be a rather terrifyingly effeminate young man with black lovelocks falling onto his shoulders and lips rouged into a pout; Iras giggled, and he shot her a look like a swordflash; he was not what he seemed. In a bored sort of way he relayed an order from Octavian, that I should meet with the Honorable Marcus Antonius at a port called Tarsus, not later than three weeks hence. Hot words rose to my lips, but I repressed them and heard him out, extending my hand civilly, and saying I would think over the matter. "There will be no 'thinking over,' Lady," he said, his voice in his nose. "It is an order from Caesar."

"Oh," I said, raising my eyebrows, "from the grave?"

He was not stung. "Augustus Caesar," he replied. So that was what he called himself! I smiled inside to think of the puny Augustus issuing commands, but inclined my head as if in submission; after all, Marcus was party to this "order"; it was best to see what was meant.

Sergius, in private, spoke to me. "Marcus urges you to conform, even against the grain, Lady . . . as he has done. For now—you both need Octavian—well," and he looked about to see if anyone could hear. "I carry a letter, most secret . . ." and he produced it, with an air of an eastern magician taking flowers from empty air. I thanked him and excused myself to read it. It said, in effect, that he had prevailed upon his fellow triumvirs to bypass Egypt and not treat it as part of the Triumphal procession, as planned (I bit my lip at this!). It was a missive full of courtesy, and veiled in obscurities, but it ended with the words, "Trust me, my sweet little Greek. As for me, I am longing to see you. Bring Caesarion . . . your Marcus."

The words were simple, surely; why did my heart pound? I turned away, having thanked the actor, and held the parchment to a candle flame; I saw nothing seditious in it, but it is always better to be on the safe side.

I could not still my heart, or stop the tingling in my veins, either. One cannot call a plague and a famine routine events, even for a queen, but somehow I had been feeling out of it, here in Alexandria; I am a woman who welcomes challenge, and I had been bored, odd as it may sound. There was excitement ahead, and I craved it; if I had not had a queen's prudence, I would have set out for Tarsus the next day.

As it was, I went about, feverish, from time to time putting hands to my hot face, and smiling secretly. Once, hurrying through the halls on some aimless errand best left to slaves, I caught my little Caesarion looking at me, crinkling his Julian dark eyes.

"What is it?" I said, tilting up his head with my hand. "Why do you stare, sweeting?"

"You look like your statue, Mama . . . the one in the temple back in Rome."

I snatched up the tin mirror, which he now wore like a precious medallion around his neck, and looked in it. My cheeks were a vulgar Roman red, bright as flame, and my eyes like the gaudy emeralds I despised.

"Pretty Mama," he said. I could have slapped him; he sounded like his father, mocking me.

6

THE ENVOY DELLIUS STOOD before my throne, two steps below. I had always scorned such obvious small tricks, preferring to rely upon my own considerable dignity and the true royalty which I was heir to. It was the comedian, Hippias, who persuaded me to this posture. "Lady," he said, "one must take men at their own values . . . this Dellius is a fellow of little subtlety, and much impressed by a show of power. As indeed are many others . . ." And he shot me an odd flick of a glance which I could not read. "It does not do to be familiar—shall we say accessible?—with such men." And he rubbed his chin in a way he had on stage, thinking out a piece of actor's business. "He is tall . . . be taller. He is haughty . . . keep him waiting."

I must confess I rather enjoyed it. I took the actor's advice on other things as well, for I saw the wisdom of it. I refused—oh, ever so courteously—to meet the time limit at Tarsus. "I cannot possibly arrange it," I said. "There are the next court hearings, where I must preside and make my judgments. It is a custom." Egyptian custom was a thing I used again and again; it was the custom to dine by moonlight, whether a Roman stomach growled or no; it was the custom to open all the windows to the rain, though the Roman sneezed; it was the custom, thus and so, and so forth. In the end, it was Dellius who begged leave to return to his master; I wondered which one, Antonius or Octavian, for I had been warned that this man served two at once, but always, as is the case with such persons, mostly himself. I, too, was glad to see him go, though I was uneasy that I might offend Marcus by my delay. "Strategy," said Hippias, putting his finger to the side of his nose and winking, "strategy." And he sighed. "It is splendid to be a part of it, even vicariously . . . actors must always be on time. And alas, they are subject to the whims of all—even of hetaerae and freemen—for they are all the audience." And he sighed again, looking pensive. But I saw he enjoyed it, his profession, and the sighs were all for show.

These actors had become very close to me and to my intimate court, as such folk always do, when they are given flattering notice. The license they take is outrageous, but they take it and welcome, for they give much pleasure. They are shrewd, too, and clever, seeing much that escapes other eyes. I took pride that I could drape a chiton three ways, and each one attractive and graceful; Cytheris, though, could drape a dozen, and in less time, and create a hairdress with a twist of the comb. The men, too, even to the least of them, were adept at all women's arts, sewing a fine, quick seam, or tossing a salad better than my own. "Ah, Lady—" said Sergius, rolling his great tragic eyes, "We are not always so fortunate . . . there are not always Palace cooks!" And I nodded, for I had listened through a night to Cytheris' tales of hardships suffered gaily, and cruelties laughed away; tales as light as the foam on the sea, but with the drowning dark beneath, unspoken.

She it was who shook her dark head and narrowed her bright eyes, saying, "You cannot mean to take so few as three hundred ships!" I had thought it a brave display!

"Listen, Lady, my dear," she said. "You have not seen Antonius since he came to power. No emir, no sultan, no Pharaoh, even, has his love of excess, his lavish hand. . . . In the East, throughout the Greek lands, he is worshiped as a god, as Dionysos come to life. And how he suits the part! One cannot help admiring him! Even long ago—" And she broke off, looking at me sidewise.

"Yes—long ago—go on," I commanded.

"I knew him . . . long ago," she finished, quietly.

"You are not so old as all that," I said, laughing softly.

"Lady, I am!" But then she laughed as well, and said, "True, I was not yet a woman, in those days . . . but I played the women's parts, off as well as on . . ."

She brooded for a moment; these people have a wonderful sense of catching life's moods, sometimes real, sometimes feigned. I let her take the pause, then said softly, "What was he like—Marcus?"

"He was worse than any actor," she said. "For he had nothing for excuse, nothing but whim. . . . He was wild and reckless and loved to shock the sober citizens of Rome. I remember once he took me driving—paid me, he did, of course—in a chariot drawn by two huge lions . . . I was afraid, but not he."

"What happened?" I asked, enthralled.

"Well, one of the lions gnawed through the reins and got loose—mauled a couple of freedmen . . . Antonius was suspended from the Senate for six months. Me they let go with a fine . . ."

"I hope he paid it," I said.

"His mother did." I looked sharply at her, but her face was grave.

"You knew his mother?"

"Yes," she said. "That was part of the shock campaign. . . . He took me to a family supper, a very serious event, to commemorate the dead, or something. I was embarrassed, but not he . . . or his mother. He behaved disgracefully, got drunk and vomited all over the tablecloth. I cried from nerves and fright . . . his mother sent me home in her own litter."

"A remarkable woman," I said.

"She was. . . . Underneath, he has some of her noble qualities."

I nodded. "Yes, I have seen nobility in him."

She went on to tell me other of Marcus' exploits, youthful follies. Such as painting mustaches and beards on the Forum statues, even the Jupiter; dressing up in the clothes of a flute girl; banging loud on the windows of honest sleeping citizens and running away when they woke, irate. He had played innumerable practical jokes on Fulvia, too; I thought the actress told those particular tales with a touch more relish.

"And you know Fulvia?" I asked.

"Not I," she said, looking a little shocked. "I have seen her, of course, for she loves the theater . . . she is an ambitious woman. . . ."

"I would not have described her so," I said. "To me she seemed quite frivolous."

"Oh, then you do not know . . . she has taken up with Marcus' brother, Lucius, and has raised an army . . . they harry Octavian's troops. As yet he has done no more than shrug them off, as one might an ant which annoys, but—"

"It could be an embarrassment to Marcus," I said, slowly.

"She is already . . . and the brother as well. But he can

do nothing. She has her own will, Fulvia. And her own money, too."

"I have never understood Roman women," I said. "They have no loyalty . . ."

"Oh, Fulvia would have it that she does it for Marcus—to further his cause."

"To sleep with his brother?"

"Perhaps." She shrugged, laughing. "One must realize—these aristocrats have indulged all their appetites from childhood on . . . the men as well. And all marriages are political in Rome."

"So are they everywhere . . . in high places," I said.

"Yes . . . that is where we are lucky, we landless players. No one cares how we dispose our lives . . ." She grinned. "It is odd—mostly we marry once only, and take no lovers, except in a true passion."

I looked at her, shaking my head. "Still—even you have married for advantage . . . you married a tragedian, and so get the parts you crave . . ."

She put her finger to her lips. "Sh—h-h-h, Lady. That is a thought I do not let have a voice. . . . And yet—I love him, Sergius."

"So did I love Caesar . . ."

"When heart and mind conjoin . . . ah, that is fortunate!" She smiled. "We are both lucky women."

"I *was*," I said, sadly.

"Perhaps you will be again."

I shook my head. "There will never be another Caesar."

"There will never be another Sergius either. Yet, if he died, I would cast my eyes around among the tragedians . . . I will not go back to comedy!"

I was astounded, for it seemed all one to me, and comedy and tragedy much the same—all make-believe. But I have said these people have their own world, not understood by the rest of us. And I saw she spoke from deep inside, and respected her for it. I could not be—nor let my country be—Roman, either. We were much alike; a queen, too, has her own world.

Cytheris said, suddenly, "Marcus Antonius cannot make up his mind—" And she trilled a high note of laughter, like a bird's song; I suspected her of practicing on me. "He does not know whether to be Dionysos or Hercules. Both parts suit him. One day he wears a leopard skin, and the next, vine leaves . . ." Her eyes looked wicked. "It is more often vine leaves, though . . . especially after a long day's marching."

I felt the bubble of laughter but did not smile. "You are irreverent."

"Well," she said, "he is not really a god . . ."

Alas, no, I thought, and wondered how often he got drunk, and remembered my father.

"He does not vomit anymore," she said, as though I had spoken aloud.

This time I laughed, and she with me. She reached out her hand and took mine (these people are very familiar). "Never fear, Lady . . . he is not yet a drunkard . . ."

I let my face go grim, for once. "Let us pray to the immortals he will never be. For so much hangs on him . . ."

"Your fate, Lady," she said softly, squeezing my hand.

We put our heads together then, for I saw she understood, and more than I had realized. Why should not these folk's talents be used? They were masters at the arts of illusion, after all. I set them to managing the stage, as it were, to choosing the costumes, and directing the action for the fateful meeting at Tarsus. It was no illusion, to be sure, that I was perhaps the wealthiest monarch in the world, even after a severe famine, but how to suggest, subtly, that I had no need of Rome—but that, on the contrary, Rome had much need of me and mine. That was the problem. They took to it with great enthusiasm, staying up half the nights, and I along with them, as eager as a child with a toy. The toy, of course, was power, and I must contrive to keep it in the air between Marcus and myself, much as a juggler does a ball, and him all unsuspecting.

Sergius said, his noble voice resonant with emotion, "Six hundred ships, I think, Lady, and six thousand mercenaries, all in purple . . ."

"Not purple," I said. "It is out of fashion, even on the stage."

"Red," he boomed. "The color of flame!"

"And all the ladies of the court—sea nymphs in pale green . . ." Hippias' finger was at the side of his nose; he was thinking. "And you, Lady, as Thetis . . ."

"Oh, no," cried Cytheris, jumping to her feet. "She must be Aphrodite, of course! She *is* Aphrodite—or Isis or whatever—yes, Aphrodite on a great fluted shell, in gauzy robes like foam—"

"And all the royal jewels," said Hippias, "to give the wavesparkle—"

"Not all—" I began, but no one listened. They were poring over a sheet of parchment, sketching in quick plans. I looked over Sergius' shoulder, but could make nothing of it, a puzzle it was, but they all understood, talking all at once like jackdaws. I left them to it, and went in search of iced water, to cool my brow, for I felt feverish.

As I closed the chamber door behind me, I heard Cytheris say, "Caesarion must go as Eros . . ."

I smiled to myself, wondering if I should have to drug him. He was close on to a decade old now, and thought himself a man.

7

TARSUS LIES ON THE BANKS of the river Cydnus in Cilicia; behind the city are high, wooded mountains, sloping across the sky like the shadows of Titans. Where the city proper is built, the river widens into a large bay; not large enough for my six hundred vessels, to be sure, but wide enough for half that number, though the sides of the ships touched softly, riding at anchor. The rest of my fleet stretched on behind, out into the open sea; from shore it must have looked to go on forever, a flock of unlikely sea birds, wings striped in red and gold.

I signaled an escort of ships to go on before, and kept my own vessel, the largest, in the bay's mouth, for I did not want to be seen till I was ready. The shore was lined with watchers, ten deep or more, and from this distance black as flies; Tarsus was larger than I had thought; the temples and dwellings spread in a great semicircle close to the curve of the river; I saw the rooftops had an eastern look, like so many Greek cities nowadays, with onion-shaped domes and stone fretwork along the walls. It was hot, and rather breathless; we had had to come in with rowers. I resolved to rest, under awnings, until the sun went down; besides, a waiting game was part of my strategy. And, of course, I thought wryly, it does not do for Aphrodite to sweat!

I lay back, sinking to my chin in a bath of almond milk and rose water; the surface curdled slightly and I fancied it had gone sour in the heat; still, it was a time-honored recipe, and the expense was nothing, to what I was spending on the rest of it. In the little canvas tent that covered me, I felt suspended in time and space; from far away I heard the thin wail of pipes, a phrase played over and over, irritating. Cytheris was rehearsing the musicians, or perhaps it was Hippias. Somewhere beneath me, in the cargo-place, an animal roared, a leopard, a lion? Another restless creature, like me.

There was a little scratching sound on the canvas, near the opening, then a voice; Iras. "It's all right," I said. "Come inside."

She was clutching a square of silk cloth together at her bosom; her eyelids looked swollen. She must have been wakened from a nap, her voice was hoarse and cloudy. "There is a messenger—from Marcus." She giggled. "It had to come through a hundred or so ships . . . he is awaiting you in the public tribunal . . . they say he has been sitting there for an hour!"

"In this heat?" I began to giggle too, stuffing the washcloth into my mouth to stop it. I looked up at her, still smiling. "Send word back that the queen is in her bath."

"That's all?" she asked, startled.

I nodded.

"It will take another hour to get back to him, your message."

"All the better," I said, closing my eyes.

"Gods!" she cried softly, "He will get sunstroke!"

"If he does not have the wit to get himself under shade—then none of this is to much purpose, is it?" She shrugged and left. I spoke more bravely than I felt; for all I knew he might abandon me forever; it was a gamble. I had Cytheris' word that such tactics worked with Marcus, the man. Up to now I had known only Marcus, Caesar's friend.

I stepped out of the tub, not calling for a body slave, but letting the air dry me; it felt cool, a surprise; I would take a little wine, and perhaps sleep. Nerves or not, the voyage had been wearying.

I did doze, actually; I counted it a good sign. And a better sign yet; another message from Marcus. This time it was a letter, in his own hand, quite courteous, considering everything. He said that he had many Roman envoys and town aristocrats in his company, and would be obliged if I would dine with him in the consulate, his headquarters. I sent back word that he must do me the honor of dining here on board my own ship; I added he might bring all his honored guests. "I shall sail right in to the quay," I wrote. "You will suffer no inconvenience." For it had all been planned, and rehearsed at home on the Nile: the long slow sail, past all the jostling crowds, the panoply, the music, the awesome display . . . and myself, the mistress of it all.

All things in the doing are different from the plan. I knew from the gasps that rose and the awestruck faces that lined the dockside that the spectacle we presented was a sight of wonder and beauty; still, the fluted great shell on which I lay, languorous, cut into my flesh in the tenderest places, and the incense, which had cost a king's ransom, stuffed up my nose, while my ears rang unpleasantly with the thin pipe music, too close. I could not help but look beautiful; a whole afternoon had been spent on painting and powdering; not an inch of my body was untouched by the magic of the actors' cosmetics. Even now, though, I felt a little slippery snake of hair slip down on my nape, from its elaborate Greek knot, bound with gold thread. There had been an hour's debate, no less, as to whether I should wear a wig; perhaps it would have been wise, in the heat, and my hair being what it is, so fine and straight. Cytheris, dressed as a demigoddess, bent close, shielding me with her bright ostrich-feathered fan, to tuck it up and pin it firmly. The pin dug into my scalp, but no matter; I saw, slewing my eyes round to shore, that the crowd was parting. It was Marcus, of course, though I could not look yet, in my Aphrodite role. Behind me, Iras giggled, unchecked; I wondered why.

I had been well coached; I was not to lie immobile, like a statue, but present an Aphrodite all unaware, secure in the power of her seductive charms, to the beholders' eyes, unapproachable, yet intimate. I was permitted to move a little, in a graceful, measured way, raising a languid hand to smooth an eyebrow or stifle a delicate yawn. Or I might shift upon my shell, ever so daintily, to show the rosy flesh, alive beneath the transparent gauze that swathed me. But, like a true player, I must not see my audience; I fixed my unpracticed eyes ahead, for I had not the art. In my broad vision, at the sides, I could see the hand-picked maidens, slim and graceful, golden-haired, my nymphs; straight ahead Caesarion stood, stiff-backed, clad in light armor. I remembered his alarming behavior when he was asked to dress up as the little boy-god of love, Eros; he had fallen onto the floor of my chamber in a fit, beating his fists and banging his head. I wondered, fleetingly and frightened, if he took after his father in this, too, till I saw his eyes, squeezed shut, open in a quick spy's glance, keen and cold. But for that, it was too good an imitation, and I knew, shuddering, that he must have once seen Caesar so. He would not be Eros, or even Hermes, only the war god, Ares; it would have been funny, were it not so exasperating, for of course Ares is no stripling, but a powerful, well-muscled man. But he got his way, as always; I sighed, as always, for he is dreadfully spoiled. Underneath, though, I saw his bad temper would serve us well, at least this time, for the armor and the arms pointed up all the more his great resemblance to Caesar. He had not seen Marcus for a long time, as a child counts time; would he remember him? Would he behave? I had time to say a little prayer to the real Aphrodite, before I felt the boat stop. We were there!

I heard the creak of the winch, the running feet, the scrape of the boat against the quay; we were moored. The music changed; horns now, loud and blaring, a paean to great Antonius. The boat dipped a little as he stepped aboard with his retinue. I raised my eyes and held out my hand.

8

I KNEW AT ONCE why Iras had giggled. Marcus, on this occasion, had not been able to make up his mind which god to be. His hair, curling by nature, had been crimped into the traditional flat ringlets of Dionysos, and there were vine leaves, wilting a little in the heat, scattered in it, and his full lips had been reddened as with the grape; however, he wore a cloak of leopard skin, Hercules' symbol, and the brooch which fastened it was formed by twin serpent heads. Still, he looked magnificent, quite like a god, any god; I had seen him only in the most casual dress in the past, and thought him rather careless of appearance.

He took my hand and kissed it, dropping to one knee; I was somewhat startled, for it was not the Roman custom; of course, he had been traveling in the East.

"You look so different," he said. "Beautiful." How had I looked before? I said nothing.

"You might be Aphrodite herself," he went on. I felt as though I should pat him on the head for mastering the third letter of the alphabet!

I lowered my eyes, and fluttered my lashes, beaded in black wax to look long. Cytheris had taught me the trick; I had not expected it would work. But Marcus Antonius turned a dark red, and I felt his hand tremble where it still held mine; so it was that easy! Caesar, of course, would have laughed. I withdrew my hand, gently, before it began to sweat.

"May I return the compliment?" I said. "You, too, have a god look . . . except"—I could not resist it—"except that I cannot tell what god . . ."

"I know," he said, with a comic little grin. "I cannot decide which. Some say Dionysos, and some Hercules . . . I compromised."

All my cloudy doubts disappeared then; I laughed aloud, throwing my head back, and he with me.

"I don't mind telling you, Cleopatra . . . I would welcome changing costumes with you. This thing—" And he ran his finger round the neck edge of the leopard cloak, shaking his head. "This thing is warm . . ."

"An understatement, I am sure." I smiled, forgetting to make dimples. "Please feel free to remove it." I flicked my eyes over him. "Besides—I think I prefer Dionysos. And there is well-chilled wine to help the god guise; old Cretan it is."

"My favorite," he said, unfastening the cloak gratefully, and handing it to a slave.

I rose from my shell, and gracefully, for I had practiced long. "Shall we go below?" I said. "Until the sun sets, it is cooler." I put my hand on his arm and looked up into his eyes. "You are so tall," I said. "Surely—taller than I remembered."

Little points of light danced in his eyes. "An actor's secret," he said. "My sandals." I looked down; he wore the platformed sole of the tragedian, a half-foot thick. "You would not think it," he said, "but one can learn a lot from these theater folk."

I looked up quickly, fearing that he mocked me. But no, his face was grave; he had not seen, then, the thespian touch that flowered all around him.

I kept my face very straight and raised round eyes. "How very clever of you, Marcus."

Downstairs, truly, was a sight more magnificent than any in my Alexandrian Palace, at least if one did not look too closely; a ship, after all, can only carry so much. To my own mind, everything was far too ostentatious, but I had a sneaking hint, and had had it all along, that my actor friends were right, and it would not prove so for Marcus. He had been entertained by all the potentates of easternized Greece, most of whom are not Greek at all, and have no moderation and live for show; at least my taste was impeccable, and all my luxuries exquisite. I heard him gasp beside me at the first sight, and let out my own breath in relief.

"You like it, Sire?" I asked.

"Like it? . . . why, you must have beggared Egypt!"

I showed round eyes again. "It is only my old earthenware—second best . . . and a few mended tapestries, good enough for a boat."

The dining salon was huge, the ceiling inlaid with ivory and with god-figures sculpted in gold; the floor with eastern mosaics in a tiny intricate pattern. The walls were hung with priceless embroideries, depicting the greatest scenes from Greece's glorious past, the whole blazing with color, lit by ten thousand candles, perfumed. There were twelve triple couches (I had been brought word long before of the number of guests), ebony and gold, with silk cushions from the Far East where only our Egyptian traders go. Before each couch was a table set with my "earthenware," golden dishes thick with emeralds and rubies; never mind that earthenware is the more practical! The tableknives were of obsidian and alabaster, with set-in blades of the precious tin, sharpened like razors; I hoped, fleetingly, that no one would get drunk and quarrelsome!

"I swear, Cleopatra," cried Marcus, "I have never seen such splendor . . . talk it down as you will!"

I could not make my eyes go rounder; I simply shrugged and said, "My dear, if it pleases you—have it!"

It was his turn to go round-eyed. "You cannot mean it!"

"But of course I do! I insist! Let us dine first, of course. Then, when all has been polished and put straight, I will have it taken to your quarters. Have your slaves take an inventory—if you like . . ."

"Oh, that won't be necessary," he said, with an abstracted look. I think he was adding it up; I had just given away some ten thousand pounds, counting in silver coins! I turned aside, and with my finger quickly brushed away a fine line of moisture from my upper lip; I was going to have to get used to it; I reminded myself the stakes were high.

The dinner went well, better than I expected; I always suffer a little unease when there are Romans at a feast. But none of these were drunkards, gluttons, or braggarts—or perhaps they were only awestruck. Though they were feasted royally, there was no one present of any real importance; I had decided to ask the comedian Hippias to share the regal couch with Marcus and me. It was a clever stroke, for he was a very old friend, delighting Marcus, who was probably bored with the provincial dignitaries as well as with the overfamiliar faces of his Roman companions.

Caesarion, to my relief, was manly and courteous, and remembered Marcus perfectly; I reminded myself that at his age I would have been the same; so often, when we are grown, we forget our child selves, so much less childish than our elders see us. He was grave, quiet, and perfectly poised, even when he defied Marcus to guess the god he mimicked.

Marcus, straight-faced, replied, "Ares, of course . . . any fool could see it. What other god should your father's son be?"

Caesarion flashed me a look that said "I told you so," and then smiled Caesar's thin, winter smile. He asked a few eager questions about the battle at Philippi; he was a boy, after all, like any other. But then he remembered to thank Marcus for avenging his father, and one saw, all at once, the prince. He stayed for the first toast, and wet his lips with the wine, then excused himself, and left; it was almost too good to be true.

"Where is he going?" asked Marcus.

"Oh—" laughed Hippias, that irreverent. "He has to eat with the help!"

I smiled. "He likes it better."

"So did I—when I was a boy," said Marcus. He looked thoughtful for a moment, a rare look on him, and said, slowly, "I have a son about his age . . ."

I was startled, for I had heard nothing of this boy. "He is with his mother . . . ?"

He laughed. "Fulvia? No—Fulvia is too busy . . . she has always been too busy. He lives with my mother in Verona."

"But that is Gaul!" I exclaimed.

He smiled. "It's very Roman now. A family place . . . we hardly keep a garrison anymore." He reached out for his wineglass. "I have not seen him for more than a year—Antyllus."

"Antyllus . . . a pretty name. Perhaps—one day—he can visit Caesarion."

"I would like that," he said, looking at me over the rim of his glass; I saw his eyes were not brown, as I had thought, but a deep amber, pleated with gold, lion's eyes. Had I then, never really looked at him before?

I spoke no more of families and homes, for I thought it made him sad; I changed the subject, clapping my hands softly for the music to begin. "I have no flutes, you see—" I looked at him, crinkling my eyes and waiting.

For a second his face was blank, then he said, "I thought you had forgotten our first meeting . . . long ago, in Alexandria."

"I have forgotten nothing," I said.

His look rested on me briefly, the amber empty as glass; I thought he was wondering how much to say. Then he looked down, clearing his throat, and said, "Well . . . Auletes was a fine flautist, I'll give him that."

"It was his one accomplishment," I said. I was always cruel about my father; a sad failing, and sadly human.

"Well," he said, "he did not choose his life, remember. And not all rulers are born with a talent for it. . . . Not all people are like you, Cleopatra."

I felt my triumph rise in my throat, like laughter, at his words; it should have been enough for now, but I was greedy and wanted more, like any silly woman.

I said, a little sharply, "I hope your opinion of me has changed since those days."

He looked surprised. "I always thought you lovely," he said. "You were lovely . . . so little and young . . ."

"You said I was skinny and cold."

"I never did! What do you take me for? I was a guest, after all!"

"You did not know I understood . . . you spoke barracks-talk. I was furious."

"I shouldn't wonder—if I said it. But I didn't."

I shrugged. "Well, no matter," I said. "Let us forget it." I think he would have been well content to do just that, but, womanlike, I did not let him. "You preferred my sister," I said suddenly.

He did not answer, but his eyes narrowed. "Speaking of your sister—" he began, and stopped, looking at me hard. "It has come to my ears . . . look, Cleopatra," he said, setting down his wine, "were you in this with her? Honestly—tell me honestly. I do not want a woman's answer . . . or a queen's."

I saw he was far more decisive than I had thought; I saw the general in the field now, for the first time; I was glad of it and nodded my head.

"You mean that business of Cyprus . . . ? No. I give you my word. No. It was Arsinoëe, and Serapion."

"Who is Serapion?" His question was sharp, a knife point held to my throat. I liked it; since Caesar, I had had to do all the weapon-carrying myself.

"Serapion is from my court. Harmless—till he met her."

"He will have to die, as well."

I felt my face go stiff, but said only, "I know."

"We will say no more about it," he said, after a bit. "I trust you. But the word in Rome—and in the legions—is that you sent ships and men to succor Cassius."

"Caesar's murderer? You must know I would never do that!"

"I thought not. In fact, I have taken steps already to squelch that rumor for good and all. They will be seized and brought here—to Tarsus. But you must give the order for the execution. I shall not take it on myself again—as I did before, with Berenice." He stared at me, then smiled. "You have a troublesome family, Cleopatra."

I did not speak for a moment. "I know . . . it is my task. I know. But I cannot help but think—if I had been in Arsinoëe's place, I would have done the same."

"You cannot afford such thoughts. You are a queen."

The dinner went well, and Hippias was at the top of his comedian's form, making Marcus laugh. All the food was excellent, subtly flavored and perfectly cooked, served at its peak of flavor.

But I could not eat, thinking of Arsinoëe. I simply pushed the meats from one side of my plate to another, and crumbled my bread.

And against my better judgment, I drank an extra glass of wine.

When we came on deck again, the long meal finished, the stars were out, and larger stars hung closer; my designers had done their work well. From a forest of interlaced branches hung a thousand candles, all alight, a dazzling spectacle to catch the breath.

As we sank upon cushions to watch the entertainment, Marcus beside me, he slipped his hand beneath my thin chiton, through the slit at the side. It was as hot as a brand against my night-cooled skin, but I did not move away. Perhaps it was the extra wine.

9

"NO ONE EXCEPT YOU, Cleopatra, ever calls me 'Marcus,' " he said, sprawling on one elbow in the Roman way. "You would not know, being a Greek, but in Rome every other boy has Marcus for a first name. It is like calling the dog . . ."

It was my third night of feasting, and this time we were in his quarters in the Tarsian consulate; it was so noisy I had to lean close to catch his words. He went on. "Cicero was a Marcus, and Brutus, too. Lepidus carries the name, as well, and the gods know how many Gauls and Spaniards have taken it for their own."

"Are you displeased then?" I asked, fluttering my lashes again. "To me it is yours alone . . ."

He smiled. "No. I like it. Mother used to call me Marco . . . when I was young."

"No longer?"

"I don't remember. I see her so seldom."

"How is that?" I asked.

He shrugged, but his face brooded. "Oh . . . a soldier's life. And then—Mother never got on with Fulvia. Or with the other two either, for that matter."

"I had not known you had so many," I said, though of course I had made it my business to find out.

"Oh, I hardly remember them, I was so young then. Political alliances, really. The first was a widow, twice my age. Ugly, and a witch . . ."

"There are no witches," I said, smiling.

"She thought she was. She dabbled in magic—eastern stuff, levitation and all that, cults and blood baths . . . it was how I got the divorce, and the dowry."

I said nothing, but I was aghast. Roman law!

"I never liked her much, anyway," he said. "She used to laugh at me. It was hard . . . at fourteen."

I looked down at him, thinking how young he looked, even now, well into his thirties; the full, pouting lips, with a look of discontent, the suggestion of roundness about the chin, the clustering damp curls at his forehead. I spoke again, softly. "And the other one?"

"A cousin. Young . . . and sweet. She died." He sat up, straightening his toga; I saw his face had a closed look on it. He took up the wine and poured a glass for me, holding it out.

"It is dry work," he said, "listening to the story of my life . . ."

"Not at all," I answered, taking the glass. "It brings us closer."

"Now it is your turn."

"Mine is an open scroll—with one name. Caesar."

"Truly?"

"I swear it."

He reached for my hand, suddenly, making me spill the wine.

"Oh, I am sorry," he said. "I have spoiled your dress."

"No matter," I said, dabbing at the stain with a napkin. "No one is looking, anyway . . ."

I spoke truth; most of the guests had fallen asleep, those with the weaker heads, and the rest were wine-blind. I had never seen such prodigious drinking, even in my father's time. The room looked as though a hurricane had swept through it; broken crockery littered the floor; hounds nosed among the split foodstuffs, looking for scraps; the slaves, clearing away, slipped in pools of wine and vomit; the candles, in their golden sconces, guttered, fouling the air, for it was late, almost dawn.

Marcus must have seen it suddenly with my eyes, for he shook his head a little, and said, sadly, "I tried to match your magnificence, Cleopatra. But I do not have the touch . . ."

"It is a—Dionysian banquet," I said, trying to keep my mouth in a straight line.

He burst into laughter, loud, and slapped me on the back, soldier-fashion, so that I nearly choked. "You're a good sport, Cleopatra," he said. "Most women would be angry."

"Well, I am not most women . . . and besides, it was a new experience."

It had been, indeed. I remembered Fulvia's eyes, rolled to heaven as she spoke of one of my Antonius' nights," and heard again Clodia's lascivious giggle; thinking of these things, I was sure I had missed something.

"What are you smiling at?" demanded Marcus.

"Oh . . . nothing," I replied.

I had not wanted to be entertained, in this or any other fashion; I had planned evening after impressive evening, on my handsome ship, each surpassing the one before. But Marcus had wanted, in his turn, to impress; well, it was only one night's delay. Besides, it would give my people a chance to breathe; they had been working at this trip for weeks.

Last night, our second in Tarsus, had been so lavish an entertainment that the first had seemed a niggardly display. Each guest, as well, had gone home with the couch upon which he had lain, the dishes and goblets with which he had been served, litters and slaves, and horses with gold harnesses, presents all. The poor creatures were as dumb as their horses, from awe. Perhaps that was why they were in this state tonight; they were unaccustomed to refinement, being mostly Romans. Well, I thought, let them sleep it off tonight; tomorrow evening they must have good manners again.

I had not, even I, known exactly what my actor-managers planned; actually, it cost less, but what an effect! Every guest would feel himself a god! The floor of the ship's dining salon was covered with roses, to the depth of two feet; somehow the flowers were held solid; looking close, I saw that a fine net had been laid upon them, holding them in place. It was like walking on perfumed air, truly.

"They are real!" cried Marcus, stooping to pull a blossom from its net. I saw it in his hand, dark red, the petals still tight-curled, but ready to open. "There is even dew upon it!" he said in wonder, like a child. It was not dew, of course, but water sprinkled for freshness, but I said nothing, and took credit for the magic.

"So many thousands . . . millions! There are not so many roses in all of Tarsus!" said Marcus.

"They are from Samos," I said, airily, wondering myself if that island of roses was barren now.

I looked at him and laughed, for he was walking as if he walked on eggshells, a bear on tiptoe. "Think nothing of it, my friend," I said. "The gods walk where they will, and trample more than roses." It was a banal remark, not worthy of me, but Marcus smiled and straightened his broad back. "So much gold!" he said, shaking his head admiringly. Cytheris had known him well; this sort of thing was the way to his heart.

"It is little enough, friend," I said, my lashes fluttering again, "for the master of the world."

"Not so fast, little Greek," he said. "That takes a bit of doing yet."

But his smile was the smile of a palace cat that has been at the cream; I almost expected him to clean his whiskers! However, I reminded myself, it was not funny, but a life-and-death matter, so I did not smile, but said, placing my hand on his arm, "Do not think of it now . . . there is time to plan these things. . . . Come, here, is our couch, a couch for two tonight."

The couch was mother-of-pearl, cushioned, like the floor, in netted roses, but yellow ones, a rarer breed; they matched my chiton; coolly I seated myself, holding out my hand to him. He sank down beside me, murmuring, "How clever you are . . ." And then, shaking his head again, "But such an expense . . ."

"Let me tell you a secret," I said, coming close. "These roses . . . all of them . . . they cost far less, even with the cost of shipping, and the fastest oarsmen . . . far less than the fittings of the other nights. But I am pleased with you, Marcus . . . for only a god appreciates the use of nature's beauty so."

"What have you planned for tomorrow night?" he said. "You cannot hope to surpass this . . ."

"Oh, wait!" I said, laughing. "Just wait!"

I had remembered an old book, dusty with time, that I had read as a child, when I had had little to do but explore our Alexandrian library. What was in it might be called a recipe, though an odd one; I never thought I would have occasion to use it.

I had in my coffers two British pearls from Caesar, perfect, matched, and, according to him, the largest in the world; certainly they were as big as birds' eggs, perhaps bigger. I had never worn them, though Caesar had had them set for my ears; I had thought them far too gaudy. The next night, when I held a mirror to see them, I still thought so, but for once I would wear them; with the simplest of creamy wool robes, they would pass. I wore no other ornament, not even my serpent crown; my arms and neck were bare and powdered with pearl dust; I had the candles placed at a distance to catch the gleam.

It was all wasted on Marcus, though; he looked around the salon and said, "I see nothing out of the way . . . more gold dishes, but—and surely the light is dim?"

"It will suffice," I said, reaching out my pearly arm in a wordless signal.

"So white," he said, lifting my wrist. "So fragile . . ." He was very easy to fool.

A slave brought a golden goblet; I took it. "Something special?" asked Marcus.

"Just vinegar," I said. "Want some?" And I thrust it under his nose.

He made a face. "No, thanks. I had enough of that on the march. It's the legionnaires' drink, you know. Great thirst quencher, mixed with water. We call it hyssop."

"Well," said I, reaching up to my right ear, "I shall sweeten the hyssop." And I dropped one of the great pearls into it.

Truth to tell, I had not known for sure if it would work, but, as we looked into the goblet, the pearl disappeared; in a moment there was nothing but a milky fluid. The pearl, of course, was priceless; even Marcus knew that. I raised the goblet and drank. The taste was just vinegar, that was all, no worse than a bad medicine, but it made my eyes water.

As for Marcus' eyes, I thought they would fall out of his head. "Why did you do that?" he asked, almost in pain.

"To show you how rich I am," I said. "And how little I care for gold. I have just drunk seventy-five thousand pounds of it!"

"Great Zeus," he whispered. He looked quite comical; I did not laugh, but raised the goblet for the slave to refill. "And now for its mate," I said, loosening the other pearl from my ear.

"No—oh, no!" he cried, catching my hand. "I believe

you! I see how wealthy Egypt is . . . you have made your point—I concede it! No more!"

"Oh, let's not be niggardly, my friend," I said, handing the goblet to him. "You drink this one!"

"Oh, no-no-no—never! I could never!" he protested, shaking his head and pushing away the goblet. He was laughing, but I think truly he was a little shocked. "It is enough! One pearl is enough!"

"Well—" I pondered, weighing the huge jewel in my hand, "Perhaps you are right. I always thought them far too large . . . I shall have them cut in half. Amusing, don't you think . . . to wear half moons in one's ears?"

He was looking at me strangely. He said, slowly, "I hope, Cleopatra—that you never have need of that gold that went so easily down your pretty throat."

"Oh, I never shall," I said. "There is always enough gold in Egypt." I spoke more coolly than I felt, but no matter. I could see I had made the effect I wished. "I agree with you, Marcus . . . gold could be used better. It could be used—for instance—against an enemy. Even an *august* enemy . . ." I almost grimaced as I said it, but there was no one to hear my bad pun, except Marcus. And he did not count, as such things go; he hardly knew a pun from a sonnet.

If he could not name the word play, though, he took its meaning. He grinned. "It could . . . if its owner wished to march under Antonius' banner."

"Not *under*," I said. "*Beside*. We are equals. Or we are nothing. Agreed?"

"Agreed," he said. "It is agreed, little warrior." He looked down at me, smiling, and looking like a god again. "Let us drink to it."

10

"I DON'T NEED all this gold! What shall I do with it?" One would have thought I had offered Cytheris a useless gift, like an elephant for a pet; her player's face was a study in woe; I had to smile.

"I thought only to reward you, darling girl . . . what would you rather have? Jewels? A villa? Land?"

She spread her hands helplessly. "Nothing . . . I want nothing. Except to act . . ."

"Take it, take it, girl—" said her father, Hippias; he had already pocketed his share and cheerfully.

"Gold can buy anything, my darling," said her husband. "A theater, even. A company of our own. We cannot always be sure of a patron . . ."

"We have Cleopatra," said Cytheris. "And Antonius too—"

I saw she was amazingly unworldly, for all her clever ways. "Put the gold away, my dear," I said. "You need not spend it now; there is always a tomorrow . . ." "Save it for a rainy day—" said Sergius and Hippias together, bursting into laughter afterwards. I was to learn it was an ancient saying among these folk, for whom tomorrow is always uncertain.

"You keep it, Sergius," she said. "You know me . . . I would only lose it."

"You cannot lose a chestful of coins!" said he, laughing again.

She pouted like a little child, though I knew she was older than I, and tossed her head; then, lightning-swift, another look came upon her face, moon-struck, with a soft priestess smile. I saw it was all some kind of little private show, and they indulged her in it.

To me she looked quite like an idiot, and made me impatient; then I brushed the thought away, remembering her value to me. After all, it was her face, not mine; we all show images to the world; who was I to judge? My face of power and pride might be, to her, a bird of prey.

And *that* thought made me smile. This morning I felt like no bird—unless it be a sick chicken. My mouth was dry as the desert, my tongue grew fur, my head felt axed, and my stomach heaved like the sea in a storm. Last night had been my seventh night of feasting; I had no hope that it would be the last.

I came back from my third visit to the private closet below, feeling weak and empty. The three actors were lolling on cushions, eating and laughing, served by slaves; the table before them was piled high with food. Hippias, as I watched, held up a salted herring by its tail, and opened his mouth; something moved sluggishly inside me; I turned my eyes away. Cytheris laid down her honeyed rusk and swallowed, wiping her mouth. She peered at me, her lively face as sunny as the day, the pouting child discarded.

"You have the wine-sickness, dear lady," she said, nodding wisely. "A piece of dry bread . . ." And she held it out to me.

I shook my head. "Oh, no, I couldn't!"

"You must," she insisted. "It is the only thing. If it comes up—well, at least there's something to work on . . ." I took the rusk from her and chewed it cautiously. It stayed down. I took another bite.

"I'm thirsty," I said. "So thirsty . . ."

"Barley water," she said, pouring some. "But mind you sip it . . ."

After a bit, I felt, not better, but less bad. I looked at them, trying to smile. "What shall I do?" I said. "Shall I lose all—because I cannot hold my wine?"

"Lady—" said Sergius, shaking his head. "You are not alone. No one can expect to drink along with Antonius. He is a bottomless well."

"But he wants me to!" I cried. "He gets angry and calls me a poor sport . . . for now—I cannot afford to cross him . . . I tried pouring it into a plant pot, but he caught me at it. It really is not funny," I said, seeing Hippias' smile.

"Forgive me, Lady. I only laugh because the answer is easy."

I curbed the sharp words that rose to my lips; I had learned that I needed these folk. I said merely, "Please tell me."

"Look, Lady . . . in the theater, when there is wine to be drunk, a libation . . . or, if you will pardon the expression, an orgy of sorts . . . we drink this." And he indicated the barley water. "With a few drops of coloring, it passes for Samian or Chain. . . . You must be sly, of course. Say you have a preference for your own vintage, something made in the Palace or by your own vintner, or call it Caesar's favorite . . . you will know what to say. And have a bottle of it by you always . . . and drink nothing else. He will understand that. Drinkers always do."

"What if he asks to taste it?"

"I doubt if he will . . . but cross that bridge when you come to it." And he waved his hand airily.

I had some doubts, but the first time I tried it, it worked. I have abided by it all my life. How often I have smiled at the strange rumors that have come to my ears. It has been said, and by respectable sages, that I had been given a special doctor's potion that rendered me immune to drunkenness. Others, less sage, have attributed my level head to witchcraft!

I had solved the wine problem, but there was another, and one I could not bear to face. Like all of us, I hoped against hope that, if I put off facing it, it would go away. "Let the gods wait for their due," I thought. "They have all eternity." Of course, they never wait.

There was another week and a day of feasting, and Marcus beside me easy and light of mood. Then one night his face was dark with some hidden anger; his brows drew down, he did not smile, and his eyes rested on me, brooding. I thought at first it was a wine-mood; Father had looked so now and then, and all the Palace went in fear until it passed. But this was not the case; in fact, Marcus took no wine at all, ate little, and dismissed the dancers before the end of their dance, though they were the best Phrygians.

I felt his eyes on me. "Well," he said, heavily, "what have you done with her? No lies . . . I shall know. Where is she?"

My mouth went dry, though I was guilty of nothing; my voice came out in a little croak. "Who?" I asked.

"You know very well. Your sister. Arsinoëe. She has flown Cyprus—and Serapion with her."

Hope flared in me, but I shook my head, showing nothing. "I know nothing," I said. "Perhaps she has sailed back to Alexandria . . . ?"

"My soldiers had orders to proceed there. No, she has vanished." He turned to me, as stern as Caesar at his worst. "You must know something . . ." And he actually shook me! If he had been another man, I would have had him seized and flogged. But this one I needed, and it was not the way to handle him; I burst into tears, sobbing loud and throwing myself into his arms. Even through the noise I made I could hear the stunned silence; the whole room was holding its breath; Romans love a scene.

I could feel the fury go out of him; he patted my shoulder awkwardly, looking embarrassed; few men know what to do with a weeping woman. I heard him making low, gruff sounds above me, and raised tear-stained eyes to look at him; I hoped the black stuff had not run.

"Cleopatra—" he whispered, "is there somewhere we can be private—we must talk . . ."

I waited till my sobs died down; it was half-real, from anxiety and sudden relief; also it was my time of monthly pain when all is on edge. "Outside," I whispered. "On deck—my private tent . . ."

As we sat alone I spoke low, so that he had to lean close, and my voice had a little tremble, learned from Cytheris, "You do not trust me," I said. "We are allies . . . you swore it. And you do not trust me . . ."

"I am sorry, Cleopatra . . ." But he took my shoulders firmly in his hands. "There is no question of trust. But do not think to disarm me . . . you cannot save Arsinoëe, so the whole thing might as well stop. We will find her, anyway, in time, whether you help us or not . . . I will take the blame, but remember—it is you, more than I, who will profit by her death . . . so let us have some honesty . . ."

"She is of my blood," I said. "The royal blood of Egypt. Would you have me less than human? Even Caesar wept for Pompey."

"Yet Caesar gained a lot from that death . . . he got Egypt. And you."

I did not speak for a little, then I said, "I hoped to do no murder in my time as queen . . . my house has been so marked with it always. But , . . it may be that I know where Arsinoëe has fled."

"It is not murder, but a just death. She has been a traitor always . . . you do not even love her."

"It would be easier if I did," I said sadly. I saw, though, that he did not understand; it was a fine point, after all, too fine for a Roman heart. "She will have taken sanctuary . . . with Artemis. It is our titulary deity . . . no priest could deny it to her."

"Where?"

"Either Miletus or Ephesus. Probably Ephesus."

"I will send to both places," he said, squaring his shoulders as if he might do it then and there, in the middle of the night.

"You need not hurry," I said, bitterly. "People grow old and die in sanctuary."

He shook his head. "Not this one," he said.

They dragged her from the altar, and speared her like a fish; Serapion they crucified, poor loyal lover.

The High Priest who had sheltered her they brought to

me in chains, an old man, nearly blind. I pardoned him. It was the least that I could do.

The scandal of the sanctuary death did not die with its victims; it haunted me for years. Well, if one uses a blunt sword, one can expect a wound or two.

11

No sooner had our fleet reached Alexandria, and home, than another emissary from Marcus arrived; he must have been dispatched while I was still in Tarsus. It puzzled me, for there was I, his guest and at hand; I had not thought Marcus to be so subtle; it pleased me, for it added a dimension.

This time it was no actor, nor a captain over hundreds, but Herod, the king of Judea. He did not come by sea, but marched up boldly to the city walls, with an armed escort of some two thousand men. I sent orders that the arms be left at the gate, with my own legion guards, and his men and horses quartered in the Outer Camp, and I prepared to welcome him. True, Judea was a petty kingdom, but this man was reputed to be wealthy, clever, and worth the cultivation; besides, his wife was half-Greek.

The court was in the Little Hall, used for private festivities; he strode in alone, the crowd of merrymakers parting before him, and stopped before the platform where I stood. I held out my hand, saying, "You have interrupted a wedding, friend." And I smiled the smile of courtesy.

I caught a white gleam of eyes, bold, in a desert face, before he bent over my hand, brushing it with his lips and dropping briefly to one knee. It was a form of greeting new to me; graceful, but faintly insolent, like the man himself. I caught his eye with mine, and did not smile, but waited for him to speak.

I have been called a cold woman; perhaps it is true. Certainly I am no Roman matron, to eye up a muscled slave, or to exchange love sighs with a friend's husband. I am a queen, answerable to my subjects and the world. Or so I have always told myself. "Looking inward," at Apollodorus' gentle command, I have perceived the truth. Of all the men who had crossed my path, only four have set my heart to racing; those two great Romans that I took for my destiny; Neo Pompey, long ago, that I loved on sight; and this proud swordblade of a Jew that I hated, as instantly.

Julio and Marcus were as near opposites as one can come to; Neo and Herod, though I never came to know either of them well, seem to have followed that same pattern. For Neo was golden, sunny, a Bringer of Light, like Apollo, and the king of Judea was shadowed and subtle, a dark deity. Yes, there was some nobility there, and arrogance, and a splendid restive beauty; he put me in mind of an Arab stallion, wild and fleet and finely bred, but not a horse to trust. I was drawn to the man, against my will, and hated myself for it, and hated him, too, all in the time it takes to draw a breath. Because of this, and its unreason, I behaved to him with exaggerated courtesy, cool as mountain snow; I think he guessed the cause.

He was not much above my height, fine-boned and slender; his face was narrow and aquiline, burnt dark by the sun. He wore Roman dress, but the fabrics of his tunic and cloak were some heavy eastern silk, and his strapped sandals were gilt; his Greek was flawless.

The tale of his errand was distasteful; I had had enough of bloodshed, but I had to hear him out, for the deed was done by Marcus' order. It seems that, in Phoenicia, an army had been got up with the purpose of ousting me from the Egyptian throne, and placing another upon it. It had been brewing for months, but secretly; Marcus had only just heard of it in time. They marched behind a pretender who claimed to be my brother, that poor Mouse, drowned in another battle long ago. I had never seen the body; they recognized it by the heavy ceremonial corselet that he always wore. The corpse was kept in an open box and shown to the people before its burial, that all might see that neither Caesar nor I had any hand in his death.

Marcus had sent Herod, for he counted him a friend and ally, to deal with the situation and put down the rebellion; he had done so with comparative ease, for the followers of the pretender were not many, nor skilled at war. The leaders of the rebel band were killed, along with the pretender, who had been formally executed.

My scalp crawled, and I had to swallow hard before I could speak.

"How did he die—the boy?"

"He was not a boy, Lady," said Herod, with a thin, curling smile, "and I gave him hemlock to drink."

I let my breath out softly; I had been holding it. "You were kind," I said. "I thank you."

"Lady—he was only a poor babbling madman. And put your mind at rest, he could never have been your brother. He was much too old, stooped and wrinkled. Someone had made him a wig, the color of your brother's hair. He fell into a fit when he was captured, and the wig came unstuck. The man was entirely bald."

There was silence between us; he had the kind of eyes that seem to bore holes where they look; I held my own steady, but it was an effort.

"Well, Herod," I said. "You have done well. I thank you. And now, if you will join us . . . ? For, as I said, you have interrupted a wedding feast. Or perhaps you wish to retire to your quarters?" I glanced at him as I signaled a servant; he was straight-backed and showed no signs of saddle weariness; indeed, his tunic was spotless.

"It will be my pleasure," he said, with a bow. "If I may be excused for one moment—to wash away the dust."

I nodded my permission, and turned to face my guests. The bride, my sister—for it was, of course, Iras, who had successfully captured her Briton—gave me a wan smile. The ritual paint stood out in blotches on her white face; of course she had heard, they all had.

I embraced her, saying softly, "Don't think about it, Iras, darling . . . it could not have been Mouse. He died long ago; they buried him. This was a poor deluded creature, used by my enemies . . ." And now I fell silent, feeling cold, suddenly. "Only . . . I did not know I had so many—"

The Briton, Cadwallader, looked at me sadly. "It is the way of the world, Lady. My father—he was the third brother to rule over our tribe. The others had been killed by treachery. And yours is the highest of all thrones . . . a prize indeed."

"Yes, I know," I said. "It was a womanish thought . . . and now it is gone." I smiled, and took up a cup of wine; it was my dear sister's happy day, after all.

The cymbals began to sound again, softly, and the flutes. For Iras had requested flute music; she honored our father's memory, as I did not. But then I am not musical either, and if it pleased her—

A voice at my elbow cut into my thoughts. "Forgive the intrusion, Lady. At such a time matters of state, cruel matters, strike hard on the heart." It was the Jew, Herod, attired now in fresh white linen; how had he done it, so quickly? He went on, looking about him. "I trust the bride was too full of her own happiness to attend our words."

"I'm afraid not," I said. "She is my half-sister. Egypt's welfare is close to her heart . . ." I looked at him and smiled. "But she will forget. We all will, thanks to you."

"And to Marcus Antonius," he said. "I could not have acted without his orders . . . the orders of Rome." I thought his last words had a bitter sound, and looked at him sharply, but his face told me nothing. We watched the dancers, weaving in and out between long garlands of blossoms, a Greek custom.

"A beautiful sight," he said, after a bit. "I should have liked it well—at my own wedding . . ." He laughed a little. "But we Jews are very solemn."

"I had heard your wife was half a Greek," I said.

"So she is. But her heart is all Hebrew. She is a Maccabee."

I did not understand and raised questioning brows. "The Maccabees are the proudest of our noble families . . . they are descended from heroes. And it is said, also, that the Messiah will come from that line . . ."

"What is the Messiah?" I asked.

"The savior. He who will lead the Jews back to the ancient glory they once knew."

I raised my eyes, surprised. "I had not known of these days of glory—"

He smiled; I thought there was a glint in his eye—mockery?

"So the old books would have it . . . I suspect all peoples have memories of lost greatness."

"Well," I said, "in most cases there is evidence. Athens still stands—and flourishes . . . even Troy and Mycaenea have their fallen roofs and pillars. As for my country—Egypt's temples are magnificent beyond any other—to this day."

"I know," he said, smiling whitely, and still with that odd light in his eye. "Perhaps our Jerusalem was made all of mud, and did not last. We are a desert folk, you know, wanderers, tent dwellers. Saul was at war, mostly, mad as well. And David had to fight to keep his throne. It was Solomon only—or so we are told—who built a palace."

"Those are the great kings?" I asked. "One has never heard of them. Curious."

"Not curious, Lady. We Hebrews are a subject people . . . for a hundred years and more we were slaves here—in Egypt."

"In the long years of Egypt's supremacy, every race had its slaves here . . . one time or another." I shrugged. "It is the fortune of conquest. Egypt was the ancient Rome . . ."

He nodded, looking at me hard. "And you, Lady—you would bring back those days. You have a dream . . ."

"You think it is a dream only?"

He spoke slowly, each word very clear. "I think that you cannot do it alone."

"No one can," I said. "Do you take me for a fool?"

"Never that," he said, his mouth curving. "One has only to observe you with a little care, Cleopatra."

It was the first time he had addressed me by name; I stiffened, but let it pass.

He went on, his eyes very still, on mine. "I think, as well, that the game you play is high but hazardous . . . and that it is not the only game there is."

I stared at him, wary; I did not trust the man. I signed to a servant to fill his cup, and offer him a tray of sweets; I needed time to think. He waved the tray away, and sipped the wine, still watching me.

I said, "Would you care to explain yourself, King Herod?"

He set the cup down. "It is this. The Triumvir Antonius is a great Roman, very high in his city, and in the East as well, and he has his soldiers' hearts with him. The Triumvir Lepidus can be discounted. But the other—Caesar's heir—he may come to be higher still."

"Octavian is a stop-gap heir," I said, quickly. "My son is the true heir, the heir of Caesar's body."

"True," he said. "But he is a boy still, and needs a champion for his cause."

"You think then, Herod, that I may not have chosen the right champion?"

"No. Antonius is the man. It is obvious he means to cast his lot with you . . . and Caesarion. But Rome plays strange games . . . there are tangles in her politics that only the gods—or demons—can unsnarl. If fortune is with you . . ." And he shrugged; it was eloquent, and I felt a little shiver go through me. I never permitted myself to think of failure.

"You spoke of another way, Herod. Do you plan to tell me of it—or must I guess?"

He laughed; it was the first unsubtle sound from him. "You have a lion's heart, Cleopatra. . . . No—I will tell you my meaning."

I waited. Still, he did not speak straight, though. He said, "Why not come against Rome . . . without a Roman?"

"Explain."

"With force of arms—and openly."

I smiled. "I may have a lion's heart, Herod. But I am a woman, not a warrior. Nor is Egypt so strong. An open fight for power—it would be madness."

"Not alone," he said. "You cannot do it alone. No, come against Rome with allies. There are all the small kingdoms of Asia . . . there is not one that would not wish to cast off the yoke that threatens them. Phoenicia, Syria, Macedon—my own Judea—to name a few only . . ."

"I think," I said, slowly, "that there would still not be enough strength to win over Rome . . ."

"There is another, with great strength and many numbers . . . there is Parthia . . ."

Parthia! That savage land that Caesar had ached to subdue. I shook my head. "The Parthians are wild—wild as beasts—or centaurs. They live on horseback and eat their meat raw . . . I cannot see an alliance with Parthia. You will be suggesting India next!"

"That too," he said. "It will take some doing . . . but it can be done. With time . . . with care and proper handling. These savage places do not want Roman rule either. If all band together . . ."

"Gaul tried that," I said. "The numbers of all the Gaulish tribes were countless. Still it did not work, and Gaul is all Roman now."

"They were too late at it in Gaul," he said. "A few years earlier—and there might have been another story to tell the Gaulish children."

"And who for general?" I asked coldly. "You?"

He was not stung. "Yes," he said. "Me—for one. There will be others. We have to find them."

We! The man was insolent, truly. I curbed my tongue

and answered him civilly. One never knew; perhaps one day I would need him.

"I thank you, Herod, for all your concern," I said, giving him my hand. "And what you say has merit. I will think it over."

"That is all I ask, Lady. And—" he pressed my fingers. "Secrecy . . . ?"

"I will not speak of it to Marcus, if that is what you mean."

"It is."

"I understand perfectly. One cannot have it both ways." I let my hand rest in his a moment before I withdrew it. "And now," I said, "we have had enough grave words. You must greet the bride . . ."

Herod had brought word also that Marcus was coming to Alexandria, perhaps within the month. It was a bit longer; I had quite a lot of time to ponder the strategy Herod offered. It had its pros and cons, as the Roman orators love to say; I would examine all that the plan offered, send spies inside those small kingdoms, sound out the rulers, weigh it all.

And when Marcus came, I would decide.

12

THE RAINY SEASON PASSED, month after month, damp and drear, and still no sign of Marcus, though each new ship brought a letter, each naming another arrival date, and each more intimate than the last.

When he came, finally, I lost all my queenliness and became a woman only.

For it was winter already, the windy winter of our seas; the harbor was filled with shipping, for no captain would venture his cargo or his crew in such chancy weather. All the old sailors nodded and looked grim; a "big one" was brewing, no question. The astronomers saw evidence in the skies, and old wounds throbbed, while dogs whimpered and birds took refuge under the temple roofs.

The great storm came, not as it usually does, swooping suddenly, but slowly. I awoke to the sound of flapping shutters; it was dawn, but gray, with no glow in the sky, and the wind increasing all day. All day, too, it grew darker instead of lighter, and folk hastened about their business and fastened doors against what was coming.

Even before true nightfall the beacon was lit on Pharos; its light threw a strange yellow path along the angry water. A keeper from the lighthouse came, his eyes scared, to tell us ships had been sighted, foundering; he said they were Roman. Some of us from the Palace braved the flattening winds to cross to Pharos tower and climb the winding stairs. One could feel the slender tower sway, sickeningly; I remembered that the architects had explained it was built that way, to conquer the stress.

In the little room at the top, all windows, one could see for many miles; I even recognized the Roman eagle and Marcus' Antonian colors; I had been sure the ships were his, but my heart lurched as I watched them, like toy boats, spinning, dipping, sometimes hidden behind a great wave. The lighthouse beacon made a path bright as day, and lightning illuminated the whole sea in wild flickering. Once we saw a ball of fire roll along the surface of the water from one side of the harbor to the other and then vanish without a trace, though another set a fire that spread through four of the anchored ships. The Roman fleet, too, burned in several spots; there was no way of knowing which ships or what captains were aboard; they sank, their masts still aflame, while others rode waves as high as mountains and suffered no harm.

I had sighted upwards of thirty ships when I reached the tower room; there had probably been more. When the long night was over and the storm played out, there were three, mastless, rowing slowly toward shore.

We ran down the stairs of Pharos and out upon the shore steps to the very edge; the harbor water was like glass and blue, reflecting the sky. It was a beautiful, still day, sunny but cool, a perfect Alexandrian morning; it might have been like this always, but for a few charred bits of wood that floated near the shore, and a smell, faint, like a bonfire far away.

The first ship pulled in to shore, the oars creaking and scraping against the dock stones. The first to step overside was Marcus. I did not think, but ran forward to throw myself into his arms; I trembled as with marsh fever and my face was wet all over with tears. There was no pretense between us and no courtesy; my eyes blurred and I could not see his face, but I knew he was alive and whole and filling my arms, solid and warm. I cared nothing for the crowds, curious, or the courtiers' faces, empty and smirking; I would have lain with him there, upon the marble, still-wet stairs of my Lochias palace, with the world and its kin watching. For I felt desire, strong, aching, primal, knotting my stomach and raining fire down my thighs; born of my long night of terror it was, a reasonless thing, mute and wild, and Marcus recognized it; perhaps he felt it too. He picked me up, and carried me, as one carries a little child, up the long flight of shallow steps and into the Palace. And so it was in that same chamber where I lay with Caesar that first night, a raw girl, that I took my other Roman. It was over soon; torn clothing lay on the floor between us, thrown down uncaring; fear and god-thanks drove our flesh together deep, so deep that blood ran, painless, from some virgin spot within. It was a union beyond pleasure, mystic, as though Titans strove there on my couch.

After, slippery with sweat, and the soft indoor air cold upon me, I said, shakily, "The queen of Egypt is an easy mark for Romans, it seems . . ." And he laughed as he pulled me to him. But I saw, searching his face, that a dream lay on it, and he said, softly, "A god has touched us, little Greek . . ."

13

MARCUS WAS IN HIS MIDDLE YEARS, and I was nearing thirty, but in that first sweet Alexandrian year we might have been two children, just old enough for love, at play on the slopes of Olympos. A fanciful thought, but it has come to me often, its edges blurred by regret. For such times cannot last; the world moves, and we move with it. But we had that year.

In those days, no one would have taken Marcus for a Roman; he was all Greek. He set aside his tunics and wore the chiton and the white Attic shoes; I remember a very funny sketch that Hippias put on at the comedy theater, very popular with the crowds it was, and he had to repeat it over and over. He wore a huge beak of a nose and a wild black wig and painted his cheeks dark red; he entered carrying a large wine jug and stumbling over huge white shoes as big as boats. It was a little cruel, as such things always are, but Marcus laughed as loud as anyone. "So my feet are big—what of it? That is not all—" And he leered at me, and jabbed me in the ribs; his humor was very coarse; in another man I would have found it disgusting. But the eye of love cannot be trusted; it sees what it wants to see.

In any case, Marcus, big feet and all, was beloved of all Alexandria; when he went abroad by my side, in a chariot or on horseback, the streets were lined with cheering people, and he bore himself like a god, even when drunk.

There were a few sour faces of course, and a few bitter complaints; some sobersides muttered that the Roman barbarian was corrupting their queen. But that was to be expected; such mutterings were no doubt being heard in Rome, against me.

It is true, I suppose, that we conducted ourselves, upon occasion, without dignity; looking back, I think that on my part it was the child in me coming out, that child which had never been allowed to show its face. And then, I did as Marcus wished, for I was intoxicated with love. And Marcus was a child always; he loved to play the fool, sometimes even on state occasions. I have known him, when receiving envoys from Rome, and deep in grave concerns, to spring up from his chair to join me as I passed by the window in my litter. Or he would make silly faces at me while I held council, or contrive to tickle me so that I lost composure. I never had the heart to reprove him.

He was a very gregarious man, too; he formed a club and called it "The Lovers of Life." It was composed mainly of actors, poets, musicians, and the like, and their task in life was to feast, drink, tell tall stories, and play practical jokes. They used to dress up in odd garments, sometimes like peasants, sometimes mountebanks, and run through the streets of Alexandria after midnight, ringing bells, knocking on doors, waking honest citizens, and then vanishing. I have to confess, to my shame, I sometimes joined them! But Marcus would never esteem a stiff-backed woman. Besides, there was no real harm in any of it, and, to my knowledge, I was never recognized.

Marcus was good for Caesarion, too. Caesarion, like his father, was born old; he never had a childish quality and was inclined to take himself and his royalty too seriously.

And then he had been so much in the company of women, which spoils a boy.

He learned things from Marcus that no tutor could teach; dicing, games, and tying knots like a sailor. Best of all, Marcus sent for his son, Antyllus; the two boys became inseparable. Caesarion's stern little face wore a softer look; for the first time in his life, he, like his mother, was having fun.

The banquets were magnificent entertainments, lasting for many hours and through dozens of courses, a different wine for each food; as well as tumbling, dancing, singing, acting, there were wrestlers from mainland Greece and even gladiators from Rome. I never knew when Marcus wanted to actually eat, for the preliminary drinking was something he enjoyed greatly; often I must order as many as eight oxen or boars, all roasting in succession, so that one or the other would be done to a turn at the desired time. Did I pamper the man? Of course; no one else ever had, neither his mother, who was not wealthy, nor any of his wives, who never thought of it. It gave him pleasure and made him feel as important at home as he indeed was abroad in the world. And my Alexandrians understood; they were great luxury lovers themselves.

Besides, Marcus learned some things from me as well; he had never really taken the time to read or study, except when compelled to his lessons as a boy. Often I found him deep in some dusty scroll, ruining his eyes in a dim, dark corner of my vast library; when I scolded him he laughed and said that his eyes would last as long as he would. I hated to hear him say such things, I do not like the mention of death; it is, I think, my one superstition. But he would stare at me and laugh again. "Darling girl," he would say, "soldiers face death every day . . . it is just another hazard. So do we all, for that matter. It is the human condition." And he would shrug and raise a black eyebrow. "But let us be gods for now, anyway, little Greek . . ." And he would pull me down beside him in the thin dust and kiss me quiet, while I crossed my fingers like an ignorant peasant.

Sometimes he would sketch in one of the museums, copying some great old wall painting, then shake his head and tear it up. And he sought out the famous scholars of Alexandria, men who had not left their lairs of learning for years and had to blink at the raw light of day. He was quick at everything, all manner of knowledge, once he started on it, as quick as I myself; I was proud of him. "But," said he, "I will never catch up . . . I am too old."

Oh, they were lovely days, the days of our first loving. He taught me to ride a horse, a proper Roman horse, bred to the saddle, and we rode together down long lanes lined with flowering bushes that nearly met over our heads, cool and vernal, and galloped wild as Parthians across wide meadows, the horses' hooves trampling my young crops and I not caring. I taught him, in turn, to swim, remembering it from my childhood, when all of us children from the Palace went in and out of the deep harbor waters at the foot of the Lochias steps, knowing no fear, as though we had been born to it; I suppose we had been taught once, perhaps by the sailors, but I could not remember; only the skill came back, as easily as walking. And darkly a thought crossed my mind; how had Mouse drowned? For I saw him as if it were yesterday, a tiny mite, climbing onto the shore step, his hair plastered to his little head and his skinny brown nakedness all glittering in the sun. It was a thought I had to push away, lest it take hold of me in the night.

We fished, too, from boats, on the Marcotic Lake, putting me in mind of Neo, and again of Mouse, till I said fretfully that the fish were better in the Nile. It was not true, of course, and Marcus looked from me to the great string of his Marcotic catch, his eyes questioning; he shrugged, though, and gave in, with a smile; he was always amenable, in those days.

Once, as we fished in the deep harbor waters (for, as I had known, the Nile was no good; hot and with muddy waters), I saw fit to play a trick on Marcus. He had played many on me, of all sorts; he thought I was not on to his latest, setting a slave to dive under and attach great prize fishes to his empty line, and then bragging of his prowess. This time I did the same, but my servant hooked on a well-salted herring from our basement barrel. There were smirks on every face, but Marcus took it well, throwing back his head and laughing loud, and then eating it on the spot, with every sign of relish. He turned to me though, and said sadly, "I do not have much luck with your Alexandrian fish . . . it seems they will not bite for Romans." And he gave me a keen look. "Do you think it portends ill, my sweet? Maybe the gods laugh at our alliance . . ."

"Never!" I cried. "But I know what it means. It means the great Antonius should leave fishing to lesser men . . . the sport of Antonius is kingdoms and cities, thrones and crowns . . . not fish and rods and lines . . ."

He bent close, for my ear alone, and his face was grave. "Yes, darling . . . we have played too long. It cannot last."

Indeed, in more ways than one our carefree pleasures could not last; that very night, seated at the royal couch in the sight of all, I was seized with the most dreadful nausea; I could not even contain it till I reached a private place, but vomited up my food, like a Roman drunkard. Marcus held my hand, and, when it was over, carried me from the hall. "Say the queen is ill," he said, "and make our excuses." I do not know the person he spoke to, Sergius, perhaps, or a soldier-companion; I felt very ill indeed.

He put me down on my bed, as carefully as though I might break; I opened my eyes and saw, through my dizziness, his face, black with anger; I heard him give orders, furious, that all the Palace cooks be brought to him in chains.

"No, no—" I said, weakly. "It is not poison . . . do not send." And I raised my hand to countermand the order. "Come close, Marcus. And send my women away . . . I am with child, that is all. I thought to tell you soon—perhaps tomorrow, for I have been almost certain for weeks . . ."

He was wild with joy, his face clearing; the gods and the fates were smiling on our union. There would be another heir for Egypt—and, with luck, for Rome! I was not exactly sad, myself—only sick.

I could not toast our unborn child; in fact, I had to hold my nose against the wine fumes from Marcus' glass. "Go back to the company," I said, "and send Iras to me. I would not keep you from your celebration."

He kissed me tenderly, and long, but I saw he was mad to be off and feasting. "Go now," I said. "I do not want you—this is women's business . . ."

He stood looking down at me and smiling. "If all wives were like you, Cleopatra . . ." And he shook his head as he left me.

I shook mine too, even in my sickness. For I was not wife yet.

Nor was I like to be—for a while at least, though we

planned a ceremony here in Alexandria. It came to nothing, as it turned out. For bad news struck in two places, taking Marcus away.

Word came from Rome that Marcus' true wife, Fulvia, and his brother, Lucius, to whom she had been truer, had been met in battle and badly beaten by Octavian; it was all very vague, but it was believed that they had fled Italy.

The other news, the news from Syria, was very bad indeed. Some of the Syrian princes, deposed by Marcus earlier, had banded with the Parthians and were marching down from the northeast against Decimus Saxa, the governor of Syria. The Roman forces there were few, and the bulk of Marcus' legions were in Gaul and Macedon; Syria might quite easily be overrun and lost. Marcus could not be in two places at once, obviously.

"I have no real choice," he said. "Syria must be dealt with first. Fulvia's defeat is a defeat, after all. What can I do? I cannot fight the battle over again . . ."

He would not take any substantial aid from me, only some ships to get him out of harbor. "For I have all those other sources on the way," he said. "Let us save our Egyptians till they are truly needed. Lie low, my darling, in a manner of speaking . . ." And he smiled broadly, for his double meaning had given him much pleasure.

It was strange; he drank so very much, more than I have ever seen in another. Yet, no sooner had this news come, calling for quick action, than he set all wine aside, and drank only water. Food, too, he lost interest in, and, like Caesar before him, gnawed on a crust of bread while he pored over maps and plans. He was slim as a boy by the time he sailed away.

I watched the sails of the ships till they were gone from sight. Then I turned away, back into the Palace, saying sadly to myself, "Oh, yes, Marcus my love—your waist will grow thinner and thinner, while mine—" For just that morning I had had to let out my favorite chiton.

14

I HAD HOPED AGAINST HOPE that Marcus would put down the rebellion quickly and easily, and send for me to join him somewhere soft and peaceful; I even hoped he could return to Alexandria and be with me when I gave birth. For I was fretful and uncomfortable, even in the cool freshening of spring. It was not like the first time, when I carried Caesarion; perhaps I was too old, a frightening thought. Dioscorides said it was a foolish thought, and that no one could call me anything but young and healthy.

Astrologers came to court from all over Egypt, each with scrolls and charts and mappings of the stars. Egyptians set great store by this science, though in Greece it is discredited now; Dioscorides even laughed. "Magic!" he cried, with scorn; doctors think that nothing in the world is of worth except medicine. As for me, I had little to do, and with Iras and Charmion, I spread out the charts on my tables and listened to the astrologers, though they made little sense, really. They saw this star and that meeting at the conception, or this star and that missing each other at the birth, and many conflicting opinions as to what it all meant, and much jealousy running between these learned souls. They all saw glory and riches, beauty, too. But of course my child would be royal and rich, and Marcus and I were not ill-favored. I was beginning to cast my lot with Dioscorides, it was all a little silly. One old, old man, though, a priest of Thebes, blind, and with that eerie dignity that the unsighted own, said more. He said that the queen would bear twins, a boy and a girl. In old Egypt, centuries before, that would have been rejoicing news, for legend has it that the first god-born Pharaohs were just such twin boy-girl rulers; Dioscorides said the ancient predicted thus to please me, and perhaps get a little extra for his own temple. I could not think so, for he was strangely impressive, but I gave him some gold anyway, for I revered him and pitied his own condition. "In truth," I said bitterly to Iras, "I can well believe it; I am already as big as a sow, and it is only five months of carrying . . ."

The months wore on, into the hot season, and still Marcus did not return and did not send for me; it would be too late now anyway, for I was grown too big for traveling. News filtered in, but it was always depressing. Practically all of Syria had fallen to the Parthians and Marcus had no hope of recovering ground with the few troops at his disposal there; he had bypassed it and gone on to Ephesus in Greece, where he heard details of Fulvia's troubles. This last news was brought by Sergius, who had sailed off with Marcus as our courier. He said that all Marcus' family and friends had fled Italy to escape Octavian's wrath; Fulvia was to join him in Athens. I was beside myself with jealous rage; it was unlike me and unfair, for I knew Marcus did not love her; it must have been my condition.

I held myself in control, though, and kept my voice low and gentle as I commanded Sergius to go back to Marcus and see how events were shaping. "Lady—" he protested. "I have just arrived! I thought to see my own child born . . ."

"Oh, don't be foolish, my good man! Cytheris is still as slim as a boy!"

"Nevertheless, she is due—any day now. And she has had three stillbirths . . ."

I let him stay, of course; I am not such a monster as that. When it was another stillborn baby, I cried as though she had been my sister. The poor girl had to comfort me! "Hush, Lady," whispered Cytheris. "Hush, Cleopatra—you will make yourself sick . . . and I am used to it. I am the wrong shape," she ended, sadly. But Dioscorides said, no, it was not that; she had pulled something inside by her tumbling and contortions, the tools of her trade. "All the more reason for you to be calm now, Lady . . . we cannot have our queen in the same case . . . and I am well, Sergius can go back now." Truly, I am fortunate in my women. Even this low-born little actress was ever faithful and kind.

Sergius was soon back, with more sad news. Fulvia had never even got to Athens; she had fallen ill at a place called Sicyon, sixty miles away, and died there. And again, like some wild creature, I behaved in a demented fashion; I was overcome by a passion of grieving, and wept bitterly for hours, tearing at my hair and wailing aloud, as though she had been my kinswoman or my dear friend. Perhaps none of us are made all in one piece; for surely, if I were, I would rejoice at this obstacle gone from my destiny. I have thought in later times that remorse sent me this grieving, for surely, deep within, I had wished Fulvia dead. But mortals cannot look too deeply; this is for the gods.

At any rate, Marcus had no such feelings; no sooner had he heard of the death than he made his peace with Octavian, shifting all of the blame for the little war on his poor dead wife's shoulders! The two Roman triumvirs met at Brundisium; I was told they feasted and made merry; it was hard to imagine merriment from Octavian! But they concluded a treaty of peace, promising to keep it for five years. I had an uneasy feeling about this treaty, for Antonius lost nothing by it, keeping all those provinces which had been originally granted to him by the Senate; in short, he suffered no penalty. It was difficult to credit, and my mind was in a turmoil, darting about like a weasel, now fastening on this piece of information, now that. For the messenger who brought the news was none of mine, but a soldier sent by Marcus, one I had never seen before; I could not trust that he told me all.

I called Sergius to me again; poor man, the dust had only just been cleaned from his sandals, one might say; still, I asked him to set forth again, this time for Brundisium. "See what you can ferret out, my friend, I beg you. None of this smells right, to my mind . . . get Marcus alone . . . get him drunk, even, if you must. See what is going on between these two enemies . . . what is the game they play . . ."

He set off, Sergius, with a goodwill and a wink. "You can count on me, Lady. Never fear. And put your mind at rest."

"That is asking a lot, my friend," I answered. "But I will try. I trust you."

Soon after, though, all anxiety vanished from my mind; one might say, indeed, that my mind itself vanished. For I was taken with tormenting cramps, and could not walk; for a week I lay upon my bed, enduring these. I could take no food and grew very thin, except for my belly, huge as a mountain under the coverlet. It was early, according to my counting, and I feared a miscarriage or a stillbirth, but Dioscorides insisted all would be well, and ordered thin broths spooned into me, for strength.

At the end of that week, I woke at dawn to find the sheets beneath me wet and sopping; Cytheris, who came at my call, said, with frightened knowledge in her eyes, that the waters had broken, and ran to fetch the doctor.

"It will be a dry birth," said Dioscorides. But I scarcely heard him, for the true birth pains had started.

I can remember little of that long labor, for I was heavily dosed with poppy juice; it was a mercy, for I was told it lasted two nights and a day.

I awoke to a fresh breeze that smelled faintly of woodsmoke; the windows had been flung open; it was near to twilight, shadowy and cool; someone outside had been burning leaves, for it was autumn and the trees were already bare, their branches like black Persian writing against the rust-red sky. My eyes went down the bed, seeing a flatness that surprised me; my body looked as though it had caved in. I smiled, and heard an answering chuckle. At the side of the bed stood Iras, with a babe in her arms, and beyond her Charmion, with another. Slowly I said, still smiling, "So the blind Theban was right . . ."

I had borne twins, a boy and a girl; very red and wrinkled they were and small, and the boy bore the marks of Dioscorides' forcep tools upon his temples, but they were healthy and handsome. Looking long, one could see Marcus in our son's face; the girl was my image, in little.

I named them Cleopatra Selene and Alexander Helios, for the moon-goddess and the sun-god in the old Greek; I did not want to offend either Egyptian or Roman hearts. But it was Isis-Osiris, or Artemis-Apollo; the gods are the same, whatever they are called. All Alexandria rejoiced, with temple prayers and sacrifice, and the streets were fairplaces, with feasting and wine and no work for a week. And I sent Hippias after Sergius, to bring the news to Marcus, for my heart was very high.

15

THE BABIES WERE NEARLY A MONTH OLD before the two envoy-actors returned, for they had had to follow Marcus all the way to Rome.

They stood before me, Sergius and Hippias, but neither would be the first to speak. I had bade them come straight in to me, and their robes were travel-stained; dark stubble showed at chins and cheeks. I called for wine.

"Friends," I said gaily, "you shall rest and feast, bathe too—but take a cup of wine with your queen first, for my happiness."

It seemed they would not meet my eyes, shuffling and looking down at my feet. Finally Hippias looked at me straight, and cleared his throat. "Lady—we cannot drink, for it is shaming news we bring you . . ."

"You did not speak with Marcus? Is he a prisoner then? Or . . . ?" My hand went to my throat in fear.

"No, Lady, he is well—" And again Hippias paused.

It was Sergius who said it, finally. "Lady—he is married. In Rome. Not two weeks since. Oh, it was a fine wedding—" And his actor's voice grew bitter. "The streets ran with wine, and a few more tenements went up in flames . . ."

It seemed as though my heart stopped; I could not take it in, but stared stupidly. At last I whispered, "Who . . ."

"It is Octavia, sister of—"

"I know," I said, dully. "Sister of Octavian. I have met her . . . once."

"Lady," said Hippias, "There is a letter . . ." And he reached into his tunic and brought it out, a flattened scroll, tied carelessly and not even sealed.

I took it, between two fingers, as though it were dirty; indeed, this untidy missive affronted me, as though it, and not the unhappy news, bore all my pain.

"Was he drunk then?" I asked, loud and harsh, not opening the letter.

Hippias looked startled. "When he was wedded?"

"When he wrote this!" And I tore it across, unopened, the stiff parchment breaking a fingernail down to the quick. I welcomed the pain, for it made me take control of myself. I smiled. "Indeed, my friends, drunkenness would be the kindest excuse . . . for the entire mess. But I have been unkind and lacking in courtesy. . . . You are both weary to the bone. Please go to your chambers and refresh yourselves. I will have food and wine brought to you there. And tonight we will dine together—and perhaps talk . . . to more purpose."

Sergius bowed low. "Lady, we thank you. Another queen would have put us to death for such a message."

I smiled. "Like the ancient rulers in your tragedies? No,

my friends—those days are gone forever." I laughed a little then. "But truly, I regret it . . . it is a gesture more satisfying than tearing a parchment."

They smiled then, for the first time, knowing I was still sane, and Hippias made a comic face, rolling his eyes and sawing his hand across his throat.

"Go now, you faithful fool," I said. "You have made me laugh—but I cannot guarantee how long it will last . . ." And I pushed them out.

I cannot recall how I got through that day; I suppose it was no worse than many another in the next weeks and months; my pillow was always sodden with tears, and unchanged so as to hide it from my women.

I know I very nearly wore a path in my carpet, clear through to the marble beneath, where I paced back and forth, back and forth, from window to couch. But if I had not done this, I would have destroyed something in my rage and pain, as some poor caged beast will tear at a stick or a rag.

At any rate, I kept the news to myself all afternoon, and was calm enough at dinner, though I remember that I wore too many jewels and too much paint.

"How does she look, Octavia?" I asked. "For when I saw her, she was still a raw girl."

Sergius looked at me, a little at a loss, for once. "Well—she has grown very tall . . ."

I smiled. "I hope not," I said, with some malice. "She was already well above the normal . . ."

"She is as tall," said Hippias, "as her brother is short . . . nor do they resemble one another."

"Is she well favored?" I could not help but ask it.

Hippias shrugged. "She is not to my taste. A bland dish."

"Marcus called her once . . . the prettiest girl in Rome."

"Oh—she is pretty enough, I suppose. The eyes are large and soft, the nose is straight and small, the chin round, and the lips well cut . . ."

"She sounds a paragon," I said, drily.

Sergius spoke. "Lady—she is describable. Tall, a little too full of figure, the head a trifle small, darkish hair, a sweet expression. But the indescribable elements—of charm and aura—those are not there. As we would say in the theater, she has no spark . . ."

"And the legs of an elephant," put in Hippias, nastily.

"Of course she wears her dresses long; she has that much sense."

"One must be fair, though. She is courteous and kind. She asked after you, Lady . . . and I'll swear she looked anxious," said Sergius. "I'll wager this marriage was none of her doing. She was widowed only the week before, and still wore white for mourning. They say she loved that husband . . ."

"They also say," said Hippias, "that it was a good thing he died, for his life was over anyway, as soon as Octavian heard that Marcus was free."

"You think then," asked I, "that it was Octavian's idea entirely?"

"Oh, Lady—there is no doubt at all!" Hippias' voice rose. "All Roman aristocrats think alike in such matters. It is all politics. Think! Does Octavian stand to profit by a constant enmity with Antonius? The people do not love him, never have and never will. Marcus is the most popular man in Rome, with the plebes, with his soldiers—even with the aristocratic faction. Octavian is wise, if he is nothing else. This alliance is all to his favor; some of the popularity, he hopes, will rub off on him."

"I think," I said slowly, "that this alliance is to everyone's advantage . . . except mine."

"It will certainly open gates for Antonius. Gates that were closed by Fulvia," said Sergius. "The stuffier types love Octavia . . . she is esteemed as the perfect young Roman matron."

"Not by the plebes, though," said Hippias. "In the procession after the wedding, stones were thrown, and the crowd shouted, 'Cleopatra!' "

I felt a tide of blood rush up into my face, and a hard knot formed in my throat, so that I had to swallow before I could speak. "Is it true? Did they truly?"

"Lady," said Hippias, "I swear it. And many times. They had to put soldiers among them to keep order. And they called for Caesarion too . . . and there were some cries at Marcus—for traitor. And a woman called out, 'Shame!' So—you are remembered in Rome . . . and loved."

I smiled a little. "Marcus said I had the common touch."

"One can get nowhere without it," said Hippias, nodding sagely.

"My friend, I fear I am getting nowhere *with* it—at the moment."

"It is a bleak moment for you, Lady," said Sergius. "But it is only another Roman marriage, remember. They are easily made and as easily dissolved . . . and you have his children."

"May the gods smite me for a selfish woman!" I cried. "I have thought of nothing except my wounded pride. . . . What did Marcus say? How did he take it . . . two babes at once?" I was almost gay.

"He laughed," said Hippias. "And said he could trust you to get more out of anything than you put into it."

"I wonder what he meant by that?" I asked. "But forget it for now! He was pleased then? And what did he do? Did he like their names?"

Hippias held up his hand, laughing. "One at a time, Lady, please! He nodded at the names . . . approval I guess. And he got drunk . . ."

"Well—that is nothing new," I said, a little disappointed. "Though I am sorry to hear it. I thought he had given up wine."

"Well . . . it was his wedding night," said Sergius.

"And the bride was in mourning," said Hippias.

That was something, at least, I thought. But then I remembered it was weeks past; Romans do not mourn long.

"Next day," said Sergius, "he announced the birth in the Forum."

"What!" I cried. "He never did!"

He nodded. "Yes. Read it out from a written speech, names and all. Something like, '. . . the queen of Egypt has been delivered of twins, a boy and a girl, my children. For we are wedded in the Egyptian rite . . . and these are the heirs of Egypt, after Caesarion, the son of great Julius."

"We are not wedded at all, by any rite," said I, "but let it go . . . Marcus is clever; he has turned it to his advantage by the reminder of Caesar—the true one, not the one who calls himself August."

Hippias nodded. "*That* one's face was a thundercloud . . . you should have seen it. And again—the cheers were wild . . . Octavia sent her congratulations; I think she was even sincere."

Privately, I thought this could not be, but I said nothing. It was impossible to blame her for any of it, at any rate; she could have had no choice in the matter; I knew that much about Roman custom.

The worm of jealousy still gnawed at me; I could feel it

like a physical pain, against all reason. I envied Marcus his wine; it was not my way.

Later, when I came back to my chamber, I stumbled in the dim lamplight, treading on something. It was the letter from Marcus, torn in two, still lying where I had flung it in my first anger. With shaking fingers I picked it up, thanking the gods that I had admitted no cleaning slaves.

The tear was clean; it was not difficult to piece together. It was a letter that explained all, or tried to. He said that this marriage was the only step open to him, that he was in no position to wage war on Octavian, he must conciliate. ". . . my darling, you must trust me. You do not know the situation here at Rome, and the power that Octavian has taken to himself . . . he is very wily. (I will remind you to destroy this letter.) Remember also, my sweet, that it is a marriage in law only, and does not touch us. I long to see our babies. The gods keep them and you . . . Marcus."

It was a marriage in law only, so he said, but it bore fruit a short year later; the next autumn, Octavia gave birth to a daughter, named Antonia. And though Marcus longed to see little Cleopatra and Alexander, they were nearly four years of age before his eyes looked on them.

16

HOW TO PASS over four long years as though they did not happen? Life does not stop for a woman because she is apart from her lover, nor for a queen because her rule is quiet. Much happened in those years, in Alexandria and abroad.

The twins flourished; small at birth, they grew quickly and in perfect health. The boy walked first, but the girl was quicker to make a sentence; Dioscorides said that was the proper pattern. For me there could be only one Alexander, he who slept in fearful beauty below the Palace; we called the boy Alexo. The girl we always knew by her second goddess name, Selene; it seemed to suit her. They were beautiful children, though it is their mother who says it, beautiful and good as well. Not like Caesarion, who daily grew more autocratic and more troublesome. He had been a gentler boy with Antyllus, but Marcus sent for his son within the year; he explained that he wanted the boy to know his new sister! I sent him, of course, and with many gifts for the newborn; what was one more insult?

But the boy wept as though it was death he faced, instead of a parting. I saw, later, beneath the leather wrist-strap that Caesarion wore, the old scar of brotherhood, where the two friends had mingled their blood, in the ancient Greek tradition. They had been reading Plato together as well; a lock of dark hair lay between the pages as a marker; it had the look and texture of Antyllus' curls. I said nothing, but thought privately that perhaps the separation was not such a bad thing, after all. Such friendships can claim the heart forever, excluding all else. And Caesarion was born to rule.

Iras bore twin girls just months after me; twins have run always in the family of the Ptolemies. They were fair as pearls, and as delicate, for, alas, they died before they cut their first milk teeth. It was a fever they took, in the spring; the whole household was down with it, but we counted it a mild illness, just a running nose and a few aches and pains. It carried off my darling Apollodorus, too; he went as gently as the babes, in his sleep. I buried him, along with the little ones, in the royal mausoleum; I counted him among my heart's kindred, and mourned long.

The Nile flooded every year; there were no famines and the country prospered. In Alexandria all was peaceful; there was one small riot, in the Egyptian quarter, when a Roman soldier killed a cat. They are sacred animals in the old religion; never mind that this one had run mad. There was no loss of life, though, just a few broken heads and a bloody nose or two. It was not a bad record, for a city so large.

As for me, the days run into one another as I look back, for the most part. I washed my hair every day, and bathed in milk, spending much time with paints and perfumes. I kept the servants busy, polishing furniture and plate, and the cooks at new recipes. My legions I kept in good trim and training hard, and built many new ships. For all the while I hoped against hope that each dawning might show me the sails of Marcus' galley, rosy against the sky.

Once, in a fit of rage, I sent for Herod, the king of Judea, thinking to take him up on his offer of alliance; I never granted him audience, though; he cooled his brown heels for a week, and then went home. I suppose he put it down to the changeable nature of women; for all his Roman clothes, he is an oriental, after all. They count women somewhere below a favorite mare.

I still kept up, all the while, with the news of the world, Rome, and Marcus; sometimes I got it from my actors, sometimes from other spies, but it was reasonably up to date. Shortly after the birth of his daughter, Marcus took up quarters in Athens, and Octavia with him. It was said he feasted sumptuously, drank prodigiously, and wasted time and money. It was also said (perhaps for my ears only) that Octavia had turned into a shrew, scolding and reproaching. One day I pitied her, and the next exulted that she could not keep him by such behavior. Marcus, report had it, ruled like a despot there in Greece's heart, but a benevolent one, much loved.

By contrast, the tales of Octavian were dreadful, if indeed they could be credited. So many were tortured and crucified by him that he earned the nickname of "the Executioner." His manner was controlled and his mien imperturbable, whenever he was in the public eye, but in his private life he indulged in wild debauching among the lowest of companions. Many a Roman noble sent his wife and daughters to live in the country, for this unprepossessing nephew of Caesar preyed on virtuous women, even to the extent of taking them by force! It was said, indeed, that even courtesans, disdaining his gold, fled from him. I have said I hesitate to credit it all, but so the word went. I know he changed wives three times in this period, the last, Livia, being snatched forcibly from her husband in the eighth month of her pregnancy, and divorced and married in the space of a day. I know, as well, that many of his subjects hated the very sight of him; Rome had never had so many factions.

One of the most important of enemies was Pompey's second son, Sextus, dead Neo's brother. This man was a famous sailing master, and had come to be known as "the Sea Rover"; in truth, he was no more than a pirate, his fortunes having waned with his family's. But he was a popular hero; Rome loves an underdog. When he defeated Octavian at sea, a decisive victory, there were demonstrations in all the provinces, and rejoicing mobs in the streets of Rome itself.

At almost the same time, a commander called Ventidius, Marcus' man, and acting under his orders, won a great battle against the Parthians, securing Syria. The Senate decreed a Triumph for both Marcus and Ventidius; it took place in Rome, under Octavian's nose, immediately following Octavian's defeat. I was not so low as to rejoice; it was, however, a step forward for me, far away and out of it though I was. I began to haunt the harbor again, posting double watches on Pharos lighthouse. For I knew in my heart that Marcus would come.

It was a pity it did not happen that way; I would have forgiven everything, and asked no questions. I am of a contrary nature; I will calculate when I must, and throw calculation aside when I will. I am a Greek, and bred to a largeness of gesture; perhaps I was wrong to expect it of a Roman.

Three and a half years had passed since he sailed out of Alexandria's harbor. These years had brought him power in the East and victory at home; Parthia seemed likely to go down before him, and Octavian's image to be eclipsed. Yet, from this good fortune, he found nothing to offer to me except prudence.

For he sent to me a man I had never met or heard of, a man like Cicero, by the name of Fonteius Capito. He had that same fussy, prim, Vestal Virgin manner of Cicero, and the same cold, thin-lipped face, complete with big nose. I had liked Cicero well enough, but not to carry a message of love. And so it was with this one; he looked down his long nose at me and read off Marcus' words; dull as they were, I should rather have read them for myself!

The missive did not even mention our two children, much less salute them or inquire after their health. Nor was there mention of Caesarion. Indeed, there was not even a salutation to me; the entire scroll was simply a summons to a meeting in Syria; he was kind enough, or uncaring enough, to leave the time and the city up to me.

I bowed and thanked this Capito, and put him to the care of my courtiers for entertainment, promising him an answer in the morning. I had learned much patience during the last years, but it did not extend to what my actor-friends would call "a second-company senator"!

When I had dismissed him, I stood for a long while, thinking. At last I decided on my advisor in this matter; I could not trust myself to be fair. I called the Briton, Cadwallader, to me. He had made a good husband to Iras and a wise tutor to Caesarion; he was an unworldly man, like my dear Apollodorus before him, but often such minds look deeper, piercing through the veil of wit.

He had already begun to age, Cadwallader, though I think we had the same number of years. His hair was faded to a grayish yellow, with here and there a ruddy strand, like a rust streak, and his eyes had the wrinkled lids of kindness and humor; he was still straight and tall, with power in his shoulders.

He listened quietly to the end; there is no doubt that he had surmised most of the situation anyway, up to that point. "So, my friend—" I finished. "What shall I do?"

He looked at me for a long moment, smiling a little. "I think you know that yourself, Cleopatra, for you alone have access to your heart."

"I would have you know one thing, dear friend," I said. "Before all else . . . I would have you know that, against all reason, I love this man . . ."

He nodded. "Yes. And it is difficult to be firm when the heart yearns. Still . . . you must, for the sake of your children and your country. Let me put it into plain words . . ." And he was silent for a bit. "First, Antonius did, in fact, desert you, and for a good long while. For, to his mind, he needed Octavian more. Now, the position is reversed, and he no longer needs that brother and sister—"

I broke in. "Does he expect me to believe that his marriage and his long absence were simply political maneuverings? That he has never ceased to love me? That he never for a moment loved Octavia?"

"You will know that better than I, Cleopatra," said Cadwallader. "A man will always take what is to hand . . . only you can know how strong is the bond between you . . ."

I was quiet, thinking. In spite of all, I felt the bond he spoke of, pulsing across the seas. Could I trust this feeling? I laughed a little, and said, "Can I trust Marcus?"

"No," said Cadwallader. "For, like all Romans, he becomes involved in the means he uses to reach his goal. They are an intriguing race, and cannot walk a straight path—even the best of them. . . . No, you must bind him with more than love—and with more than honor. For, in spite of high words, Romans have little of it."

"Caesar was honorable—" I said.

"Yes. To you. And to me. But not to my father. Not to Gaul and its leaders. And not to the babes spitted upon his sword in the village across the Rhine . . ." He looked at me hard. "And—do not be angry—not to Calpurnia."

Oddly enough, because I was a woman, the mention of Calpurnia made it all clear to me. I nodded. "Yes. I see. I must stop giving. I must take. . . . The way I see it, after years of sleepless thought . . . I cannot fulfill my destiny alone. There is no way but through Marcus. No sure way—even of keeping my throne. I suppose I have always known it, somewhere within. . . . But this time I must have assurance of his good faith."

"More. You must have more. First, he must marry you. Second, he must stop his manipulations, so dear to him. He must become the open enemy of Octavian. Further, he must aim at complete conquest, with you, of the limitless East, and of the entire West. He must act in all things as the successor of Julius Caesar. He must aim at Caesarion's becoming heir to all your joint efforts. And, at this meeting, he must put it in writing, with witnesses—yours and his."

I smiled a little. "You think I can get him to do all that?"

"You must," he said, simply.

The next morning I called Marcus' envoy, Capito, to me, and stated my demands. I dressed myself in my robes of state, which I seldom wore; the serpent crown of Old Egypt was on my brow, and I held the scepter of Isis-Osiris; I even wore, clasping my upper arm, the ancient bronze arm ring of the Pharaohs, two twining asps. Though I dislike the thing; it was roughly crafted, the inside having two sharp points, which, though filed down again and again, always left raw angry marks on the tender inside of my arm. My eyes were lined with kohl, in the antique fashion; it gave me a remote goddess-look.

"I will meet the Triumvir Marcus Antonius on the first day of the winter solstice, sea winds permitting, in the city of Antioch, in Syria. Have him arrive in advance of me and arrange for shore accommodations. I will have a small train, some three hundred. The governor's palace will probably serve."

His jaw dropped; I almost smiled. "I shall want confirmation within two weeks," I said. "Therefore I suggest you do not delay. Another time I will offer you the hospitality of Alexandria."

"The Triumvir Marcus Antonius has asked for a brief

outline of the proposed terms," he said, faltering a little at my cold eye.

"My terms are for the Triumvir's ears alone. He will hear them in Syria, in good time. And now, Fonteius Capito, you must make haste."

I watched his retreating back, still stiff, like Cicero's, but looking somehow comic. As the slaves closed the heavy audience chamber doors upon him, I laughed aloud, startling my court. I composed myself, and dismissed them, proceeding in a stately manner to my chamber.

Iras stood ready to take the heavy ceremonial cloak from my shoulders; I saw, above her head, Charmion's questioning eyes.

"It is done," I said. "Let Marcus stew in that for a while!"

I pulled the heavy arm ring from my arm, and rubbed the sore place, wincing.

17

ANTIOCH IS AN ORIENTAL CITY, turreted and walled; the harbor, unlike our own, is alive with trade, like a market quarter. From shipside one can see the life that thrives there; sailors from all countries mingle with the merchants and harlots that go openly among them. Our six ships were hard put to find harbor space, so crowded was the shipping. And folk did not look seaward as we sailed in; they were too used to newcomers. That was all to the good, for it suited my plans.

We came in at sunset; some of the trading booths had been dismantled or were being covered over for the night, though the crowd was still not thinned out. Cytheris, who was beside me at the rail, said that all trade did not stop here when night fell, but went on still by lantern and torch. "This is a town that stays up most of the night," she said. "There is gambling and whoring, and there are shows at every corner—tumbling and dumb show, of course, and no masks—not the real thing, but still . . ." I thought, in spite of her scorning words, that I heard a wistful note in her voice; the "real thing," as she called it, the theater proper, is a thing for feast days and contests, and so the performances are sparse and much time goes between them.

I looked at her thoughtfully. "We ought to have a court theater," I said. "At the queen's command. But a good one, not just the usual slapdash thing . . . when all this is settled—this matter of Marcus—I give you my word . . ."

"You are good, Lady," she said, her little dark face lighting up like a flare.

"Now," I said, "Let us decide on the time for this . . . plan of ours." I stared at the throngs on the dock, that looked like so many colored anthills. "When, think you, that Marcus will retire?"

"Oh, Zeus—not till near dawn, in this place. Well, perhaps just before . . . just as the sky gets gray. He will have fallen asleep by then. . . ."

"At least we hope it," I said, smiling. "We want him snoring. . . ."

She flashed a smile back at me, and we went below to sup and to prepare.

I rested after an early dinner; I must look fresh and feel lively. The night was full black when she shook my shoulder gently. "Wake up, Lady . . . it is time. I have all laid ready . . ." I blinked and started up; Iras was lighting some candles one by one; they flickered in the corners. I sat up, rubbing my eyes; Cytheris brought watered wine and Charmion began to bind my hair loosely on top of my head; I saw that all of them were ready ahead of me.

"Oh, it is a wonderful look," I said. "Scythian horse boys . . . but you cannot wear the beard, Charmion, it does not work well . . ."

"No," said Cytheris. "We cannot pretend to any great age, we are all too small and slim. It will have to come off." And she reached out and whipped off the black property room hank of hair from Charmion's chin; she looked so disappointed we all laughed.

"And anyhow, cousin," I said, gaily, "if you look too fierce we shall not pass the guards."

"Hippias has seen to everything . . . all the sentries are bribed—those that are not in the know. He is waiting outside the gates of the palace where Marcus is staying. Sergius is ready and will set out with us, and Cadwallader as well." Cytheris spoke with authority; it was the sort of thing she was used to, this putting on of shows. I gave her hand a little squeeze and reached out for the leather drawers.

They were dyed a coral color, the softest doeskin, and fitted like skin. The other girls' had drawstrings at the waists and fell loosely, under a sort of tunic. It was the look of those Scythian riders that go fleet as the wind, without saddle or reins, and sometimes stand on a pair of horses and shoot their arrows at full speed; they are much in demand for exhibitions everywhere, even in Rome; a small people, so we girls would get away with the pretense well.

I stood still while Cytheris sewed me into my drawers; the leather had been pierced and thin thongs drawn through, and tied together at the waist in back, where I could not reach it myself. But it was part of the plan. When she had finished, she took a wet sponge and held it to the knotted thongs. "When it dries, it will be impossible to untie," she said, giggling. "And here is your dagger—so, at your belt. . . ."

I wore a leather tunic, saffron, shaped to the body, with knitted sleeves. None of the transparent dresses I had worn in Rome brought such blushes to my face; I might as well have gone naked. But, it looked good, and, after the first glance, not like a boy either. I tucked up all my hair under a Scythian warrior-cap; flaps came down over the ears and along the jawbone; it was an Amazon look, and becoming. The actress rubbed my face with a piece of chamois till it shone; I wore no paint; in the mirror I looked like a half-grown lad, but perhaps it was the soft light.

We came on deck, in the soft dark. The dock was deserted, and the silence was like an ache; the water that lapped the boat sides might have been from a far ocean. After a moment one grew used to it, picking out the small lights on dock, while the boat rocked gently under our feet. Sergius and Cadwallader came close, whispering; by the light of their one lantern I saw they were dressed as we girls were, but with helmets that covered the lower half of their faces; made of some thick hide they were, and rising stiffly to a point.

We went overside, using a rope ladder that swayed sickeningly; I heard Iras gasp, above me. "Steady," whispered Sergius. "It is only one more step . . ." And then we were all in the small boat putting out for shore. The water was shallow here; we had to wade through it up to our ankles, after the boat was tied up.

There were mounts for us there; I never knew the men who held them, Sergius had arranged all; maybe they were true Scythians. The horses were small, like ponies, with narrow backs; it was a good thing, for otherwise we might have fallen off, for there were no saddles or padding, just short reins. "Hug with your knees," cautioned Sergius. "And we will keep them to a walk."

"I can almost walk, myself," said Cadwallader, with a low laugh. "My legs hang down near to the ground."

It was not a far way we had to ride, and it was serious business ahead of us, though we went in disguise; still one or another of us women giggled, each hushing the other.

Sergius pointed out a black shape, large and low, to the side of the road. "That is the governor's palace, Lady, where you should be sleeping tonight. If Marcus had knowledge of your presence, that is." It did not seem all that grand, a walled structure like all the others we passed, though cressets burned at a heavy gate carved with lions' heads and barred with thick iron.

"We are here!" said Sergius, softly. "Quiet!"

We dismounted before another gate; two soldiers came to take the horses; I saw a grin on the face of the nearest one. So I knew these were confederates of Sergius and Hippias. I never knew how these folk managed such things; it was just another of their talents, and what they were paid for, after all. I thanked the gods again, silently, for these valuable servants that had come my way.

We were led through long, winding halls, dimly lighted, going on tiptoe past closed doors. "You are certain he is asleep?" I whispered to the soldier. He nodded. "Lady, I stumbled over an empty jug, a big one and clattering . . . he never moved. Out for an hour now, he's been—they've been feasting since yestermorn . . ."

Oh, oh—I thought a little grimly—I hope he is not *too* sound asleep. Well, one must hazard something, always. We came to a great door at the end of a hall. "This is it, Lady," said the soldier. "This is where the general sleeps."

"Lend me your sword," I said. It was almost too heavy; I had to use both hands to raise it and pound upon the door. I was not strong, but still it made quite a din; we heard nothing from behind the door.

Sergius took my arm. "Stop, Lady. You will wake the whole guard! Let us in," he said to the soldier.

Inside, the air was close and foul; the candles had guttered and the wax, burning, caught in the nostrils. And there must have been something left upon the cooking brazier, too, for there was a smell of charred meat and oily fat. I coughed. "Open a window, someone—"

Though I spoke low, this Marcus heard. I saw him start up from the couch where he lay; the wall torches had been left alight, and I could see the whites of his eyes, looking huge. We all began to stamp and screech, as rehearsed. I knew no Scythian, but neither did Marcus; we all shouted gibberish in an Arabic dialect, waving our arms about and circling the couch.

He looked thunderstruck, not moving where he half-crouched, staring at us as we danced about him. But then I saw him reach for his sword; of course, he had gone to bed fully dressed and armed! He rose suddenly, turning to face the largest of us, Cadwallader, and raising the sword over his head. He was no coward, Marcus!

Neither was Cadwallader, of course, unarmed though he was. He caught at Marcus' arm, and the two stood dead-locked; I ran behind Marcus and began beating on his back with my fists, still shouting in my Arabic. I felt, rather than saw, Marcus' effort, as he shook off Cadwallader and whirled to face me, the gnat at his back. He reached with his free hand and took me by the throat, holding me at arm's length and shaking me like a little dog, while the other hand held the great sword poised above my head.

The Phrygian cap loosened and fell off; my hair fell about my shoulders. His face was very comical, a clown's look, stupefied, but I could not laugh, for his fist was choking me. I felt his grip relax, slowly, and heard the sword clang on the stone floor.

"Marcus!" I cried, softly, and flung myself into his arms, bearing him backwards onto the couch. "Are we too late for the feasting?"

His face beneath me still wore its stupid look, though something was creeping into the eyes. "It is I, Cleopatra!" I cried.

"Yes . . . I see," he said slowly. "Yes, you wild woman . . . but who are the others? And—you are squashing me . . ." he said, struggling to rise.

"No swords?" said I. "You promise?"

He nodded, and I rose, pulling him to his feet; I watched as he looked around at the others, who had pulled off their headgear and part of their disguise, and stood facing him, waiting. It was a wonderful thing to watch, his face; like the shore when the tide comes in, it changed, slowly at first, then suddenly—a new land. He threw back his head and roared with laughter, so hard that tears streamed from his eyes. I cast down my own eyes and stood waiting, looking as shy as a maiden first come to court.

He wiped his face with the back of his hand and shook his head as if to wake himself. "Why do you wait, woman?" he cried suddenly. "Come here!" And he held out his arms.

I went into them, like coming home. "I thought perhaps . . . you might be angry . . ." I whispered, pressing close and hiding my face on his shoulder; we had rehearsed it so; uncanny how it worked, I had not believed it would be quite so easy.

"Angry!" He held my face between his hands. "Cleopatra, my darling . . . it is the first real laugh I've had in four years!"

"A long time . . ." I murmured. "Have I changed?"

"Only for the better . . . I had forgotten how lovely you are . . ."

And for a little moment or two, so it went, each to each, and the words between us, spoken low; lovers' words that have been spoken over and over since time began and do not grow dull with the repeating. His chest was hard as wood, and his hands were rough; his kisses hurt my mouth; four years, inviolate, had made me tender. I thought, fleetingly, I will show bruises, and blotches, too, tomorrow; and, wondering, I thought, too—is this what I have longed for, all this time, alone on my couch? But then the sly, slow fire crept over me, weakening my knees, and making me glad.

"Send out our friends," he whispered.

"Yes . . ." And I loosed myself and looked behind me. I saw they were all pretending not to see; I went close to Cytheris and spoke low.

"Stay just outside . . . for I will need you. Aphrodite give me strength!" And I giggled softly.

"You had better pray to Artemis," she said, "who protects maiden virtue . . ." She smiled and pressed my hand, signaling to the others.

I had always understood that much wine makes men slow in love, but it had never been so with Marcus, and it was not now. He smelled like a whole barrel of the stuff, even to his hair; it was as though he had bathed in it; moreover, he had just waked from a deep sleep. Still, no sooner was the room empty than he began to tear at my clothing; leather, of course, will not give so easily. He fumbled and sought, calling on the gods, and nearly pushing me through the couch to the floor. Stallion images, grotesque, went before my eyes, and my throat ached from holding laughter back; this was no time for it, surely. It was no time either for what I was going to do next, but do it I must, or lose all in the end.

I caught his hands, under me, where they struggled with the thongs of my leather drawers. "The struggle is vain, my friend," I whispered. "You must wait . . ."

I managed to get the parchment out from the breast of my tunic; it crackled in my hand, and the sound stopped him, in midair, as one might say. "There is a knife, hidden," I said. "It will cut through the leather easily . . . when you have signed this."

He moved to sit up, easing the pressure on my thighs. "What in Hades . . . ?" He took the paper from me; he was red in the face and sweating, poor love! "Is this another joke?" he demanded.

"You had better not think so," I said, deadly quiet. "Read it."

"Of all times!" He shook his head, gathering a little of his dignity around him as he smoothed the skirt of his tunic.

"It is the best of times," I said, calmly; my insides were not so calm, for this was a gamble.

I watched him as he read, bending close to the candle and squinting at the letters. On the second line he began to chuckle.

"Who but you, my love . . ." he said softly. He read it through and looked up. "Of course I will sign it," he said lightly, and shrugging. "I have no writing things, though . . . it must wait."

"It cannot," I said. "It has waited too long. Cadwallader has all that is needful, and I will call him in—and the others as well. This must be witnessed."

"Actors cannot witness," he said, "nor freedmen. Nor can women. So, there is no one . . ."

"My friend, there is," I said firmly. "Iras and Charmion are royal—daughters, both, of a Ptolemy. Even in Rome that is good enough and better. And Cadwallader is my chancellor." I had this moment created the position, but no matter; what Marcus did not know would stay forever silent. "And—for good measure, you will call in a true Roman . . . he that you sent to fetch me here. Fonteius Capito."

He stared at me for a long time; his eyes, always too large, bulged alarmingly. For a bit I was not sure he would not, like Caesar, fall down in a fit. Or hit me. But in the end he laughed again, and said, "You have won, Cleopatra. I will sign it, before witnesses—and wed you and all—but I still say it was a filthy trick you played."

I did not contradict him, for of course it was. I said, merely, "There will be other nights . . . many of them."

"Oh," he said, airily, "there is still a bit of this night left. It does not take long to put five signatures down." And he gripped my leg above the knee, hard, making me wince and hold back tears.

At breakfast, in full light, much later, in high good humor, he said, "I have a document, another one. Not drawn up yet . . . but I will do it now—while the mood is still on me."

And that was how I got Sinai, Arabia, part of the valley of the Jordan and the city of Jericho, a portion of Samaria and Galilee, the Phoenician coast, the Lebanon coast, part of Cilicia, most of Syria, all of Cyprus again, and a good piece of Crete.

18

In not much more than a year I was a mother again—but this time I was a wife as well, with documents, witnessed and signed, to prove it. It seems a paltry thing, for a queen, but one must bear in mind one's children and their inheritance. The new little one was a son, whom I called Ptolemy Philadelphus Antonius, and who popped from my womb as easily as a whelp from its mother hound.

Marcus and I had wintered in the city of Antioch, in Marcus' new house, which stood in a wealthy part of the town, known as Daphne. It was a beautiful spot, covered with thick groves of laurel and cypress that reached for miles; a thousand tiny streams ran down from the hills, filling the air all about with soft music. It was a little pocket of perpetual spring, always green; a light cloak would do, even at nightfall. My children I had by me there, and Marcus sent for Antyllus; for us all, it was a time of idyll, short and piercingly sweet. Like all such times, it could not last.

But it was there, in Daphne, that we celebrated our marriage; though it was quiet, for public people like ourselves, still it was legal, except in Rome. In Rome, Octavia resided still in Marcus' house; there had been no divorce or mention of it. First things first.

Marcus was busy, in a lazy sort of way, with plans for continuing his Parthian campaign. I could no more dissuade him of it than I could Caesar before him; Parthia seemed to be a Roman challenge. I thought of it as something always there, like death and the settlement of debts, a thing best postponed, but, though I could trick Marcus into many actions, he never took my advice, given straight. In my opinion, Rome and Octavian should be faced, then and there; we were not getting any younger. But Marcus planned for Parthian conquest; in March he set out for Zeugma, a town on the Armenian frontier, where he would muster his troops from the East.

I sent my children and my followers home to Egypt, and went with him; after all, a great deal of my own money was in this venture; I did not want to see it misused. Besides, I felt wonderfully young and vigorous, and, from long ago, I had loved the life of the campfires.

No sooner had we come to Zeugma, though, when my belly swelled again; I was glad, and unglad, too. There was nothing for it but that I go back to Alexandria and await this, my fourth child. I thought that Marcus' brow looked lighter as he bade me farewell.

"Never mind, my fair friend," I said, half-laughing, "I shall yet go to battle at your side . . ."

And he, in turn half-laughing, answered, "Campaigning is no life for a woman . . . even an unfruitful one. There is one place no woman is needed."

Poor Marcus. It was not very long before he had to eat those words. For, if he did not need me to go forth to meet the Parthian enemy, he needed me when he came limping back.

The limping was literal; Marcus got an arrow in the foot at the siege of Phraaspa, the Parthian stronghold; it was not a great wound, but on the long and dreadful retreat, it festered; he was lucky not to lose it.

He lost much else; twenty thousand foot and forty thousand horsemen. After twenty-seven terrible days, during which the Roman legions beat off the Parthians eighteen times, they crossed the Araxas and brought the eagles safely into Armenia. Their troubles, however, were by no means over, for the winter, cruel in those places, had to be faced; he wrote that there was sickness throughout the army, the men were in rags and half-starved. He begged me to come to his aid.

The word reached me the day I rose from childbirth; allowing time to gather supplies, ships, and men, I made all haste, for I felt great fear for my husband and ally. As for myself, I had never been in better health, strange as it sounded; the new baby must be put out to nurse, and all left in the care of my faithful women; I would not hesitate.

Marcus had brought the remnant of his force to a place known as the White Village, on the coast, between Sidon and Berytus. The shore was rocky there, and bleak; as we sailed in, we saw tents, filthy and torn, and a few men, busy upon the jagged slopes, but not one looked up from his labors to greet us. When we finally set foot on land, we saw heart-shaking sights, half-naked men, blue from the cold and skeletal, glared whitely at us out of faces black with ingrained dirt; scarcely human, they sat or lay upon the shore rocks, bitten by the icy wind, unable to crawl to shelter. Others, unmoving, lay stretched out stiffly, as though they had crept to the sea to die. Though the wind was gusting heavily, the smell was horrible, sweetish and rotten, like garbage. Dioscorides, who came with us, said it was the smell of death, even on the living. "Muffle your cloaks about your mouth and nose," he warned, "for it carries disease." Vultures, black against the sky, whirled overhead, low. At our approach, one or two rose, with beating wings, slowly, sated. I turned away my eyes, thankful I had eaten no breakfast.

As we came on, toward the tents, bending our bodies against the wind, some officers came to meet us, saluting me; they were in tatters, and their faces haggard with privation and strain, but I thought I saw a look of lightness pass over them as they eyed the baggage trains. All about were men, laboring, looking like hollow-eyed shades. I could see no purpose to their labors; they seemed to be moving large stones, reasonlessly, from one spot to another. All about the camp, men in large numbers were occupied thus, but in no sort of order. There were no labor gangs, no work songs, just these strange figures, listless, straining, muscles knotting in their emaciated arms, picking up a stone, carrying it, and putting it down.

One of the officers, a man I recognized beneath his gray locks, said, "Lady . . . they have run mad. No one can stop them from this, for they hear nothing. They will keep it up for an hour or so, and then they will die."

"Mad?" I said, horrified. "Mad . . . from hunger?"

"No, Lady. There is a root that grows here, just below the ground . . . as you see, nothing else grows. They have eaten of it—these that you see—though they have been told not to . . . it is some kind of poison. Some die immediately, turning black and spitting blood. They are the lucky ones. Others scream for hours. Some fight, killing one another. And these . . . these move stones, over and over, until they die."

Dioscorides stared at the scene, and turned to the officer. "Have you a specimen of this root?"

"We burned all we could find, sir . . . for safety to the rest . . ."

"Yes," said the doctor, "of course. But if you find one left over, keep it . . . it should be studied." He looked longer at the men, lugging rocks, his eyes thoughtful. "What did this root look like? Where does it grow, and how?"

The officer looked bewildered; he was young, beneath his hollow looks, and weary. "It is twisted, rather, and shapeless, blackish gray in color, and soft—for a root. It crumbles at a touch . . ."

Dioscorides nodded. "Yes . . . my guess is that it is not a root at all, but a kind of fungus, such as grows often beneath rocks in barren country. It is poisonous, taken in quantity—but a small amount produces pleasant dreams and a euphoria. These men are not mad—not truly. They search beneath the rocks for more of the drug."

"But they are not even looking under the rocks!" I cried.

"No, for the drug has hold of them . . . they are half-awake only. If they have eaten enough, they will die, being underfed already. If they have had only a little, they may recover . . ."

"Yes," said the officer. "One did recover. One only. But he is blind."

I saw the eager light of knowledge-hunger come into

the doctor's eyes. He said, musingly, "Ah, if I could have one plant . . ."

I thought it best not to answer him, but hurry him along. For surely he was sorely needed in the tents. I turned again to the officer.

"Marcus . . . does he know we are here?"

"Lady . . ." he looked ashamed, somehow. "Lady . . . every day he has rushed down to the shore to watch for your ships, even in the midst of a meal. Not that there is ever much of a meal," he said wryly. "Some grains of corn and some dried fish, portioned out . . . and wine . . ." At this he sent me a peculiar sort of glance, half-humorous, half-sorry. "Lady, I will take you to him."

Picking our way between the dead, the dying, and the poor mad ones, we came, with Dioscorides, to a purple tent, stained and watermarked, larger than the others. The officer held aside the flap of the entrance; I bowed my head and went through.

Inside was the same smell of death and corruption, but here it was nearly overcome by the fumes of wine. It was dark, all the candles having long burnt down, and the fire as well; the air was musty, rank, and very cold; I shivered. "Marcus is not here," I said.

The officer gave me another strange look, and gestured to the low campbed along one wall; I could just make out a long bundle upon it. Coming close, I saw it was Marcus, wrapped from head to foot in heavy ragged robes against the cold. He was sound asleep, or so I thought, and did not stir when I spoke his name. I leaned over and shook his shoulder, gently at first, then harder.

"He will not wake," said Dioscorides. "He is in coma."

"Oh, gods . . ." I cried. "What has happened?"

"Only wine," he said, shaking his head sadly. "He has had far too much on an empty stomach . . . he will be all right," he said, straightening up from where he had examined Marcus. "Lady, he must just be let to sleep it off. No harm is done . . . it has probably kept him alive. Grapes have some nourishment, after all."

"Yes, Lady," said the officer, eager to explain; Marcus' men always loved him well. "He has had some shame at this defeat . . . and such sorrow at his great losses . . . and then he would not eat when his men had no rations . . . oh, Lady, he needs you . . ."

And it was true, a sad truth. For the men who were

dying I could do nothing, but those who still had a remnant of health survived, once we had fed them and given them good shelter. Dioscorides took his doctors among all the ranks, and many were cured and saved. As soon as they could go safely on board ship, we took them back to Alexandria.

And Marcus recovered well, even from his lowness of heart. I waited long, a matter of some twelve hours, till he woke, busying myself at the cooking brazier, like some doting mother. When he was ready for it, I spooned good strong beef broth into him, and porridge later, sweetened with honey. He said it was the best food he had ever tasted.

And at night he lay in my arms, sometimes in love, sometimes too weary for it, till his spirit strengthened. I said no words of reproach, but wept with him for the fallen.

"You will come home now," I said. "Come home with me to Alexandria. Let us forget the world for a while. It will still be there. And you have another son . . ."

For just a tiny second he looked startled; I think he had actually forgotten! Poor Marcus, he, too, had nearly run mad. I swore to myself, silently, that such a defeat would never happen again, though I had to force my will upon him.

For men are rash, all, in some matters; I have known the two best in the world.

19

It seems odd to record a Triumph on the heels of the great Parthian defeat, and of course in truth it did not come quite so soon, but some two years after. But events are not remembered by the years between; the Roman ways of intrigue and complexity had seeped into our Egyptian life, which before I had kept simple by my sole rule.

In all these days and months I had urged, but subtly, a confrontation with the true enemy, Octavian; I had made little headway. It seemed, still, that Marcus preferred to step off the road and beat down jackals by the way, rather than continue straight to the end and conquer the lion that awaited. Three little wars he had fought and won, with Media, Armenia, and Syria; each one might have been subdued by policy and negotiation, and no blood spilled; perhaps it is the way of men, who love the clash of arms, I cannot say.

Still, much had been won, or won back; privately I thought it need never have been lost. We were the richer for it, never mind, and I saw it apportioned out; Marcus was content with the glory. At least I persuaded him to hold the Triumph here, in Alexandria; it was the first time ever that a Roman Triumph had been celebrated outside of Rome. In so doing I hoped to show the world that Alexandria was true rival to Rome, and to goad Octavian as well.

It was a beautiful spectacle, for our actors staged it well, and better than any yet seen, to my mind. The spoils of war, the captives, walked in the procession, but none wore chains, golden or otherwise, for I forbade it. Our three captive kings did willing obeisance, swearing fealty to the rulers of Egypt; in return they were promised protection and succor in time of need. It was a pleasant end to war and a good bargain for all; to the king of the Medes there was more; he had no heir, and his only daughter, Iotapa, was betrothed to our little Alexo. Thus our son would gain a kingdom, ready-made, for his own, and a wife still young as he when they came to be wedded. There were no caged animals, and no executions at the end; what animals walked in procession were trained to wonderful tricks and given, afterwards, to the circus, and full pardons were issued to all the captives, even the lowest. No wine ran in my streets, but all the wineshops for this day were free and the doors open, and the cookshops as well. So there was nothing to clean up, and no old scores to settle.

After the Triumph, another ceremony took place, one of vaster importance, to my mind. In the spacious grounds of the Gymnasium we had erected a large platform, covered with beaten silver, and six gold thrones were placed upon it; in the late, slanting sunlight, the whole spectacle glowed like some gorgeous great jewel. I had had some doubts of the wisdom of including a two-year-old, my little Ptolemy Philadelphus Antonius, but of course he had to be present; I made sure it was at the last moment, at least.

It was Marcus who had decided on all our costumes; he loved to dress up. By now the people thought of him as Dionysos, and it came as no surprise to see him so; I took the throne beside him in my flesh-tinted Venus robes and wore the royal diadem and the ancient bruising arm ring. Caesarion appeared in his father's wardress; it was the real thing, for he was tall enough already to fit into them, though in all else he was Julius to the life; I gasped when I saw him, and the cheers from the crowd were wild. He knelt before us, and Marcus proclaimed me sovereign of Egypt, and ruler of all those territories he had bestowed upon me in Antioch. He then proclaimed Caesarion co-regent, and gave him the title of "King of Kings," crowning him with a replica of my diadem, and giving him a golden scepter. He took the small throne next to mine with dignity, grave-eyed, but I saw him look about him, and whispered, "Antyllus is there—in the front row . . ." The boy Antyllus, flushed with wine, like his father before him, smiled and threw a garland; it landed at Caesarion's feet; he bent to pick it up, and to hide his own flush. The nearer folk laughed and applauded at this little byplay; all Alexandria had seen these two friends, arm-in-arm in the streets and at the Games. And Greeks, of course, love these boy romances.

Little Alexander Helios, our Alexo, was the next to enter our presence. He looked frightened, but full of importance; and no wonder, for his wedding was also to be celebrated this day! He was six years old, and his bride was five, but it was royal custom here in Egypt, and the two children were friends already, a happy thing. They advanced hand-in-hand, looking very solemn; all over the Gymnasium one could hear soft cooing murmurs, and indeed they were an engaging sight. They were dressed in the costume of the Median countries, the little girl veiled to the eyes and the eyes painted; Alexo wore a high, stiff tiara atop a turban, a flowing cloak, and the trousers, baggy and gathered in at the ankles, the Persian look. Marcus announced the marriage formally, and high priests of Egypt and Media muttered words over them; when they came to repeat their vows, little Iotapa grew tongue-tied, frightened of the unfamiliar Egyptian words; Alexo, putting his arms about her and whispering in her ear, finally got her to speak up, and he himself brought out his words all in a rush and very loud, drawing applause mixed with some laughter. Marcus laughed too, but I did not, for I saw Alexo's face, threatening storms. The couple stood while Marcus read out that Alexo would have the combined thrones of Media, Armenia, and Parthia. I gasped at the last, for Parthia was as yet unconquered; in fact, Alexo would not have Media either, till his father-in-law, the king, died! However, Marcus was always too casual about such niceties, and at any rate, it made good hearing for the crowd.

Alexo took his throne, with Iotapa at his feet, and his twin sister, Cleopatra Selene, came in alone, dressed as the moon goddess from whom she took her name. Iras and I had made her costume, of the finest Egyptian cotton, and she wore a crown made of tiny silver stars; Selene was a lovely child, tall for her age and slender as a dryad. She was fair, like me, but her hair was already beginning to darken, and it showed a curl, like her father's. Well, I thought, crimped hair is the fashion in Rome; she will be popular there, when we have conquered it. To her Marcus gave Cyrenaica, Libya, and those small countries of the African coast that he had won, naming her queen, and handing her to her throne as if she were a lady grown; I saw it pleased her. She was always her father's favorite.

We were ready now for my baby, Ptolemy Philadelphus Antonius; I said a little prayer, just in case; one never knows what a child so young will do. He could walk, but for this occasion Iras bore him in and gave him into his father's arms. Marcus threw him up into the air, making the baby crow with delight, and holding him up for the crowd to see. "Here is your new Ptolemy, the youngest of his line!" he cried loudly. "I am giving him this day the lands of Phoenicia, northern Syria, and Cilicia. I'll wager this is the smallest king in the world . . . what say you?"

There was much laughter and more cheers, and a voice called out from where the Phoenicians stood, "Long live Phoenicia's king!"

I saw the child was bewildered by the noise and the throngs of faces turned up at him; he began to struggle in his father's arms, wanting down. Marcus did not understand and continued to throw him above his head; it was a game he usually loved. I called to Marcus, keeping my voice low and under the cheers, "Put him down . . . he wants to walk . . ."

He looked no bigger than a mouse, truly, and the thought of my small brothers crossed my mind; I made a vow to myself that no one should ever call this Ptolemy by that nickname. "Come, Tonio—" I called; it was the first time I had used this name. He beamed all over, repeating the sound, and it stuck afterwards.

Little Tonio was dressed in Macedonian dress, boots and mantle and a round little cap encircled by a diadem. Beneath his short tunic he looked bowlegged; I was dismayed, but then I remembered—he was wearing three cloths wrapped round between his legs! He was quite forward for his age, and the training had taken well; still, one cannot rule out accidents. He toddled over to me and rested his little elbow on my lap, looking up at me and waiting for a kiss. I snatched him up, and caught him to me; he had still a milky smell, as small children do, fresh and sweet. "You must sit now on your own little throne, my king," I whispered. As I put him down again, my hand felt damp, in spite of the three thick swaddlings; I smiled a little to myself as Marcus led him to his place and helped him up into the seat.

It was a long afternoon for all the children; we had to sit, by custom, until the whole crowd had thinned out, and a bit after as well; Marcus had ordered bronzes of all the children, costumed, and the sculptor was making his first sketches. Meanwhile, Marcus busied himself writing, in his own hand, an account of the whole afternoon and its events, to be sent to the Senate at Rome, together with a report of his victories. In a separate letter he told his agents to obtain a formal ratification of the changes which he had made in the distribution of the thrones of his dominions.

Some weeks later, when the news from Rome reached us, we learned that all Italy was astonished at these eastern affairs, and there was, naturally, much disapproval in official circles; Rome has the name of Republic, where all matters of state policy must go through endless corridors of opinion. But they were his dominions, after all, some by grant or agreement, and some by conquest. As for me, I kept out of it; I was not even privy to his decisions. Though, of course, I was blamed for everything, as usual.

Marcus' agents at Rome, wisely enough, decided not to have these documents made public; however, Octavian insisted, and, after some time and a great deal of wrangling back and forth, they were read aloud in the Forum.

Immediately stories began to circulate in which Marcus loomed as a kind of oriental sultan, living at Alexandria in a life of voluptuous degeneracy. He was declared to be constantly drunken, which was not true, for he had a very strong head. They could not accuse me of such things, for I drank little wine; but the tale went that I had magical powers to keep a sober mien; it was said that I owned an amethyst ring which kept the fumes of wine from reaching the head! It is difficult to imagine how such nonsense starts; one must just disregard it.

In any case, war was not far away, war with Octavian, decisive war. Marcus was reluctant to confront him, but all his actions goaded Octavian to a point that truly must have been unbearable to that autocratic tyrant. For one thing, Marcus had severed all connection with his Roman wife, Octavia; he did not answer her letters, but even sent them back unopened. A plain divorce action would have been kinder, for the poor woman did not know where she stood; she bore his insults nobly, and truly I felt much sympathy for her. But it was always difficult for Marcus to come to a clean decision, about anything; he was not made that way. Even if he hankered to dismiss an unruly or sullen servant, he must bring himself to the point of senseless anger before he could do it, upsetting himself more than the creature who was the cause. For months I had watched him, brooding over Octavia, complaining of her dull housewifely ways, her submissiveness, her solicitude; never mind that in another he would have called them virtues!

Finally the long-suffering woman sent to him, asking that he meet her at Athens, or indeed, anywhere in Greece that he liked; she was bringing with her, as escort, a gift of some thousands of men and horse. He sent the messenger back with word that Octavia should go home and attend to her spinning! I was appalled, and said so. "I would have killed you, my fair friend!" I cried.

He was lolling upon the cushions of my couch, as was his habit in the afternoons, having a little appetizer before the night's long feasting. Setting down his wine cup, he lazily reached for a bunch of sweet grapes, holding them up and taking them one at a time into his mouth. He glanced at me from the side of his eye, his lips curling in a smile. "Would you, my dear?" he asked, in a languid manner.

The thought of the four years he had deserted me flashed through my mind; I had been patient, and forgiving too, I thought through policy. Was it from slavishness? I was silent, and felt my face grow stiff. I laughed then, though I forced it, and kissed him lightly.

"You are beloved, my dear . . . and well you know it.

Your present wives adore you." I kissed him again. "You are sticky from grapes," I said, making a little face. Then rising, and throwing the remark over my shoulder, as it were, I said, "But truly . . . you must choose between us."

"I have chosen, darling." And he shrugging, "Am I not here—with you?"

"It will have to be legal," I said. "Sooner or later you must divorce her."

"At the moment," said Marcus, heavily, getting up from the couch and stretching, "at the moment I am more concerned with her brother . . ."

I thought on what he said. The Triumvirate would come to an end soon; it seemed likely that Octavian would make a move then, if so be it Marcus would not; at any rate I was counting on it. As it was, Octavian had already attacked him with savage words, and violent threats in public session before the Senate, attempting to rouse up feeling against him. Vile letters, too obscene to quote, had been sent between the two; what can you expect—with Romans?

Marcus had written, afterwards, to say that Octavian had not returned some ships he had lent him in the fight against Sextus Pompeius; moreover, he had not divided the spoils of that battle. On top of all, Octavian had parceled out all the free land in Italy to his own soldiers, leaving none for Marcus' men. "And soldiers will not fight without reward!" He looked up from that letter then, hot with anger and getting hotter.

"Calm yourself, my dear," I soothed. "You have left out an important thing." I leaned over him, stroking his cheek as I explained. Lepidus, the third member of the Triumvirate, had retired during the last year; Octavian had seized his holdings, with no offer of sharing. "That is true," cried Marcus, his eyes bulging and getting red.

"No, now, my friend," I said, softly. "Temper your missive . . . it does not do for statesmen to behave like a couple of tomcats. . . ."

"Ha!" Marcus cried. "I have not shown you the letter where that little lecher abused me for living immorally with you!"

I felt the hot blood rush to my cheeks, and clamped my lips shut; I would not be baited by these Romans! "Perhaps," I said, silkily, "perhaps you should show it to me . . ."

"I have destroyed it," he said softly. "It was disgusting."

Gods, I thought, what must it have said, to disgust a Roman!

"I will show you my answer, though," said Marcus. "For it is here . . . in this first page." And he held it up to my sight.

It read, "What sort of accusation is this? There is nothing scandalous in my relations with the queen of Egypt. She has been my wife for many years, we have three royal children, and Caesar's heir is in our keeping . . ."

There was a hard knot in my throat; I clasped Marcus' head to my breast, cradling it; tears, rare for me, came to my eyes.

"My sweet Marcus," I whispered. "I love you well . . ."

And I said no more of divorce . . . then.

20

OCTAVIAN'S ANSWER CAME SWIFTLY, as if shot from a Parthian arrow; one could almost feel the poison at its tip. He replied that he would divide the spoils of the Pompeian war as soon as Marcus gave him a share in Armenia and Egypt. A share in Egypt! "It is not yours to share!" I cried, stung to anger for once. "My country is independent of Rome . . . let Rome look to us—and beware!" I was beside myself; if my ships had been lying ready at anchor, I have no doubt I would have sailed to battle then and there.

It was Marcus' turn to soothe me. "Quiet, my sweet," he said. "That phrase was to push you into hasty action—no more. He knows well—Octavian—that Egypt is in no one's gift . . ." He read on. "The rest is no matter," he said, tearing it across and dropping it on the coals. But I saw the flare of his nostrils, like a stallion's, smelling blood, and though I behaved in a mild and womanly manner, my heart inside me exulted. Somehow, in some manner, Octavian had gone too far; Marcus was ready to declare our cause.

Once roused, he lost no time; he sent messengers in all directions to summon his forces together. "You, also," he said, "you must prepare for war. Your ships must be overhauled, and repairs done where they are needed . . . and your own men must be mustered."

I forbore to answer that all my preparations had been long made, and that my troops trained every day; moreover, there was not a ship of mine that could be called unseaworthy. However, we sent word to those countries, all, that were now the possessions of my children and me. At Marcus' order, all were summoned to meet at Ephesus, a city he felt to be in perfect strategic position. By early winter we were there, and joined by many of our allies; my heart was very high.

Ephesus was situated near the mouth of the river. Caystrus in the shadow of the Messogia mountains, not far south of Smyrna, and overlooking the flowery isle of Samos. It looked directly across the sea to Athens; I felt it a good omen.

The whole aura of this city shimmered with omen for us, or at least for me and mine. It was from ancient times sacred to my own deity, here called Diana; a glorious temple to the goddess stood in its midst, white marble, cypress and cedarwood, with rich gleamings of gold everywhere. The famous statue was housed here, the many-breasted Diana; it was in the old tradition and ought to have been revered, but in modern times it had become a tourist spot where folk went to snigger, forgetting the symbolism. The priestesses, offended, kept the goddess covered now, like an obscenity; one had to pay two obols to see it unveiled. I paid, of course, for I had long been curious; it was disappointing, a crude thing molded in the archaic manner, without beauty. Still, I was glad the children had been left at home; to the untutored eye, the tortured mass of it, twisted and lifeless, could look erotic. In that same temple, though, was a beautiful and heart-catching portrait of my great ancestor, Alexander, covering the far wall. The colors were faded with time, but the face was the face of the tomb, the face I knew so well. I caught my breath and cried softly, "It is Alexander to the life!" I heard Marcus laugh beside me. He said, "How would you know, little goddess . . . were you alive then?" And I remembered that I had never led him belowstairs to gaze upon that face with me; I wondered why, but said nothing.

That ancient sacred city soon came to be the largest military and naval center in the world. I had brought with me from Egypt two hundred full-manned warships, and a host of sailors, soldiers, workmen, and slaves. From Syria, Armenia, and Pontus, vessels were arriving daily with further supplies, and Marcus' own ships, in the hundreds too, were rapidly mobilizing at the mouth of the river. All day and all night the roads thundered with the tread of armed men and the hills gave back the echoes of hoofbeats ringing against stones, as the rulers of the East marched their armies to the mustering. And each day Marcus made speeches to rally them, proclaiming the cause of Caesarion, the true heir of great Julius. We exulted at this, for it seemed Octavian was popular nowhere, but once Marcus turned on me, angry, and said, "We were fools not to bring Caesarion!" I kept my temper, but answered that never would I risk the boy in war. It had long been a point of contention between us, but I was convinced I was right. If Caesarion should die, we *had* no cause; Rome would never accept a woman's rule, however victorious, nor a plain republican Roman, either, however well loved . . . Caesarion *was* our cause, and Rome's future king.

The armies that marched daily were made up of almost every nation in the world. There were nineteen Roman legions; troops of Gauls and Germans; contingents of Moorish, Egyptian, Sudanese, Arab, and Bedouin warriors; the wild tribesmen from Media; hardy Armenians; black men with nose rings and huge plates in their lips, bearing deadly great spears; savage hill fighters from the Black Sea countries; Syrians, Greeks—even some Jews, though these people seldom fought for others; Herod must have told them that Caesarion was their long-awaited Messiah!"

The streets of Ephesus were packed with men in every kind of dress, bearing all manner of arms, and talking a hundred languages; even I could not follow the meaning of all the tongues! I think, truly, that never had so many far-ranging folk assembled at one place at one time—and all for my son and Caesar's. I wondered fleetingly if he had got my happy letters, or if, indeed, he cared. For all I knew he might be content to write poems to his darling, Antyllus, or talk philosophy with the weedy youths of Alexandria. When I thought of it, I grew uneasy; I had seen him take no exercise of late, even in the Games arena or at the hunt, except to walk up and down the grassy park paths, listening eagerly to some shabby Eclectic, or filthy Stoic. "Think nothing of it, my dear girl," said Marcus, airily. "It is a stage all boys go through . . . he will get over it."

As for me, so often I thought of the long-gone days when I lay, a young girl in Caesar's arms. Then I was queen, but barely, and queen of a country Rome might claim at any moment, but for his strong, gentle presence; now I ruled over dominions more extensive than any that the great Pharaohs of the past had owned! All Ephesus hailed me as queen of the world, and my vassal kings did homage to me every day; at night my dreams were of administering justice on the Capitol. Though of course I dared not tell these dreams to Marcus!

In the spring, some four hundred Roman senators arrived at Marcus' quarters. These men said that Octavian, after denouncing Marcus in the Senate, had advised, under pain of death, that all who were on the side of his enemy must leave Rome; hence they were here. Those senators who had remained in Rome, perhaps seven hundred—even those, they said, were not with Octavian's cause, but had simply not committed themselves, seeing that war had not yet been declared. "There will be many others, have no fear," said Publius Canidius. This was a man I had known in great Julius' day, one of the most respected men of Rome; we had read Greek together. When I reminded him, his eyes misted over and he said, "Dear lady, I would shame you in these last days . . . I cannot make a sentence anymore . . ." And he shook his head sadly.

"My friend," I answered, "we will have more Greek afternoons . . . it will come back to you."

But not all these men of Rome looked upon me with such fondness. There was one Ahenobarbus, of an ancient Republican family, stern-lipped as a very Zeus, who always turned his head from me when I spoke, and did not answer my counsel. When I heard that he had advised Marcus to return me to Alexandria, I was wounded to the quick, as well as outraged. "Who does he think he talks of," I stormed, "a housewife?"

"It is not I who said it," protested Marcus. "You must take the man himself to task . . ."

And so, in a grave and seemly manner, swallowing my ire, I confronted the old gentleman in his tent. "Dear sir," I said, "I cannot take your point as being made in earnest. The bulk of our war supplies are mine, and all of the monies. Should I not protect what is mine?"

"The battlefield is no place for a woman," he said, frostily. "You ought to step down in favor of your son."

"My son," I said, just as frostily, "is not yet sixteen years of age. Would you be led by an unformed youth, simply because he is male? I have been a sovereign since I was myself not much older. In what way is my judgment of over twenty years of ruling inferior to, well, let us say, a senator's?" If I had caught him out, he did not show it, but said, "Cleopatra, you must know that your presence here is causing your paramour embarrassment . . ." My paramour! I bit my tongue. He continued. "It gives a false impression and will jeopardize our Republican cause."

Now I was all ice. I drew myself up to my full height and looked him in the eye; like most Romans, he was low of stature. "Our cause is not Republican. And my title is 'Queen.' You will remember it."

However, he had sown a seed. There began to be murmurings among those senators; I saw it worried Marcus; he was no rock of strength at best, and it is never easy to be caught between two factions; no man can serve two masters, as the old saying goes, though Marcus had played that game more than once. It was his only failing, save for the wine; and one did not help the other. At length he came to me, looking beaten, and said, in a tentative way, "Cleopatra, I have been wondering—are you not longing for your children? Perhaps you should go back for a little . . . and then Egypt is without rule . . ."

"Marcus," I said, firmly, "My country is in good hands. Do you think I would leave it otherwise? My children, yes, I miss them. But this war is for them, in the long run. And I cannot leave the fighting of it to a few hundred dissenting senators who have never borne a shield."

He smiled, something sly in his eyes. "And you, my darling . . . have you borne a shield?"

"I have thousands of shields—and swords and spears, too—in my hire. Would you have it that I withdraw them?"

"No, of course not, my dear," he said softly. "For we need them . . . and I need you . . ." And he took me in his arms. I kissed him fiercely, and said no more.

But after, I was uneasy, for I saw he could be swayed. And my threats were empty, for what did it avail me to take my troops and all my effects out of the battle? It was my battle, truly, and not something to be settled in our bed, either. I must somehow persuade him, with no trickery, that I belonged there beside him, as much as any man.

I knew there was one Roman, at least, loyal to me; I

called him to me privately. "Publius Canidius," I said, "I count you as my friend. Am I wrong?"

"Lady," he said, and bowed with his hand over his heart in his aristocrat's way, "Lady, I am yours to command, always."

"You have heard that there are some who speak against me?"

"None speak against you as a queen or as a mother of kings . . . but there are some, old-fashioned, who chafe under the guidance of women. And then, too, there are Republicans here who seek to further their own cause. Many Romans do not want to see a monarchy in Rome."

"That was true in Caesar's day as well . . . and I know it," said I. "But, my friend, whether they want it or not, it is coming. If not with me and mine, then with some other. Your Rome is too huge to stay Republican. The Greeks' democracies worked because they were small and self-contained. Any slave-teacher will tell you that. But Rome—Rome is mistress now of half the world and more . . . its government is like a nest of vipers, biting at each other . . ."

"It is true," he said slowly. "I have long thought as much. And I supported Caesar while he lived."

I reached out and touched his arm. "Will you support his son?"

"An untried boy . . . ?"

"But with the best Roman of all as regent . . . with Marcus Antonius."

"And with the wisest queen . . ." he smiled, a gentle smile, old and understanding. "Yes. He has my fealty and my oath as a Roman."

"You are kind, my friend. I knew you faithful . . . will you help me—now? I need it badly."

"With my whole heart, Lady."

"Tell as much to Marcus. Speak it strongly . . . and in plain words. Plead my case . . ."

He smiled again, this time with a wry twist. "My Queen, one does not plead a case before your husband with plain words. One uses strategy." He seemed to think heavily, and when he spoke his words were measured. "I will tell Marcus that I have seen signs that your Egyptians will not willingly fight without your presence; in a way it is true. And I will say that it is unfair to take your money while discarding your counsel. Also I will ask him pointblank which of these hundreds of senators shows better wisdom than Cleopatra. 'After all, my boy,' I will say, 'the little queen has learned it all from you!' How does that sound?"

I clapped my hands together, smiling. "It is perfect—that last! Exactly right! That will do it."

"I hope so, Lady. I will try."

And indeed his "strategy" worked. Marcus came to me and said that he had thought it over, and please would I stay? "After all, my dear—to which of these senators are you inferior in wisdom? Seeing that you have learned in my presence the way to handle large affairs."

I nodded and said, "Of course you are right, my darling. I have had many advantages . . ."

21

"IT IS CLEAR TO ME," I said, "That these little moves are doing nothing to provoke Octavian . . . you must make up your mind to divorce his sister. It is the only way."

"So you say." Marcus looked, by now, like some moulting great bird; nothing seemed to fit; his tunics fell unevenly over the bulge of his stomach, and were not overclean; moreover, the folds fell lumpishly, for he, impatient, usually draped it himself. He shunned the barber and let his hair curl down upon his nape and his chin show blue. As I looked at him, I saw new lines in his face, graven deep, and his nose seemed to have got longer. It was the effects of feasting and wine, idleness, too; there was a pettish discontent in his eye, and purple pouches under; I was appalled.

He sighed, and spoke in a heavy way. "My dear, you urge me constantly to divorce . . . well, it is a woman's way, I suppose, to brook no rival. . . . But on all sides I am getting pressure to the opposite. It wearies me, I don't mind telling you."

"Naturally, from the peace party!" My voice rose sharply. "What are they doing here then, amidst the preparations for war? Have you thought on the expenses of this halting stay? Men must eat, and must draw wages—whether they fight or not. But they are fighting men! They have taken to quarreling amongst themselves . . . there was a riot only last week—how many did we lose . . . thirty . . . thirty-five? An appalling waste!"

I saw that he stared at me, as though he had not seen me for a long time. "My dear," he said mildly, "You do not look well. I can see your bones—right through your dress! And you are pale . . ."

"What do you expect?" I cried, my voice thin and ugly. "When *you* are beset by nerves, you eat and eat . . . and drink! It is otherwise with me . . ."

"Poor girl," he said. "You are showing your age . . ."

Something in me snapped apart then, looking at the fifty-year-old wreck that sat facing me. I began to laugh and laugh and could not stop, while hot tears rained down my face. I felt, too, my heart leaping painfully within my chest, and my breath coming in labored gasps, while the sweat stood out in beads upon my body. He moved quickly then, gathering me up in his arms and calling for Dioscorides; I could not speak. Truly I was sorry to distress him, but I was powerless. I had to be put to bed with hot stones at my feet and a sleeping draught.

When I wakened, feeling drained, Marcus still sat by me, gazing in a melancholy fashion upon me. I spoke, my voice sounding far away and weak. "My love," I said, "think nothing of it . . . forget our quarrel—do as you think best . . ."

"No . . . I will do it. I will move for divorce. You are right—I have delayed too long . . ."

"No, no—" I protested. "I felt ill, that is all . . . I am better now. You must not be hasty . . ."

He smiled; something of the old Marcus showed then, bright and bold. "My dear, let us not quarrel over the reverse now. You are my love and I am yours . . . I am a little drag-footed sometimes." He kissed me tenderly, and afterwards said, with another wide smile, "It is done—while you slept. We cannot take it back now. I have sent a messenger with the order to Octavia to leave my house, and consider herself divorced."

I stared. "Is that how it is done? So easily?"

"Yes," he said. "It is the Roman way."

"But—if a woman were to do the same . . . ?"

"Oh, that would not be legal."

"I see," I said slowly. "It is, truly, a man's world . . ."

He laughed. "With the notable exception of the little queen of Egypt . . ."

What he said had small truth, when I thought of all my effort, but no matter; everything, I suppose, is comparative.

"I have given the order, too, while you slept, to move on to Athens, with all our troops and ships. We will await Octavian's answer there."

"You have been busy, truly . . ." I murmured, and fell asleep again.

I could not expect, of course, that Marcus would do anything in a straightforward manner; on the way to Athens we stopped at Samos, for a wild round of celebration and entertainment. I kept my patience, but it was very unwise; such behavior leaves one open to much vile gossip; what were we celebrating? But I said nothing and bore with it all; I was still weak and could not brook more quarrels.

When at length we reached Athens, there was still no word of Octavian's reactions. But one by one, this senator and that began to desert to him; it was only to be expected, I suppose, after so many delays.

Still, there was damage done and exaggerated talebearing. Some of these men, privy to Marcus' plans and co-signers of his will, told Octavian its contents. He, upon learning that it was in the keeping of the Vestal Virgins, marched into their temple at Rome and seized it. There was nothing incriminating in it, of course, but he made much of the clause that asked that Marcus' body, in the event he should die elsewhere, should be brought to Alexandria and buried next to mine.

Octavian went so far as to announce publicly that I had gained ascendancy over Marcus by sorcery! Is it so strange that a man wishes to rest forever next to his wife? Ah, well, he hoped to discredit me with the people, who in Caesar's time had loved me. Who knows, perhaps it worked; there are ignorant folk everywhere.

For a momth he caused all manner of rubbishy tales to be told of me and of Marcus, too. Then I suppose he thought the time was ripe for war; he did not declare against Marcus, though, but solely against me.

"Rome is at war," he read out formally in the Forum. "Rome is at war with the queen of Egypt . . ."

Octavian's decree went on to deprive Marcus of his offices and his authority—because he had allowed a woman to exercise it in his place! He added that Marcus had evidently drunk potions from my hand which had deprived him of his senses. He said further that the generals against whom Rome would fight could be easily beaten, since they were simply eunuchs and hairdressing girls. The only eunuchs were a few old toothless creatures from my father's time, and the hairdressing girls were Iras and Charmion, royal daughters of Egypt!

22

WE WERE WAITING FOR OCTAVIAN to attack, a tedious business. I have often wondered if all Romans suffered from this same odd disease, this procrastination, for neither he nor Marcus made a move. If I had not insisted, our troops would never have even seen exercise. "Sweetheart," drawled Marcus, "you are more warlike than any general!"

"I know nothing of war," I retorted, with some crispness, "but one must have sense. Idleness surely has no place in an army . . . and all skills must be practiced." I tried, always, to keep our quarrels to a minimum, especially where others were present, but often it was difficult; I, too, suffered from idleness, boredom, and impatience. Besides, I missed my children. I dared not say so; Marcus would have welcomed the opportunity of packing me off home; the pressures on him had only increased after the declaration of war.

After the first month of waiting, I said that perhaps we should attack first. "Oh, no," said Marcus. "You do not understand our advantage . . ." And so he explained.

He felt confident in the ability of our great fleet (he called it his) to destroy the enemy before it landed in Greece; he believed that Octavian's forces would become mutinous even before they set sail, for the state of war would affect the economy disastrously in Italy, whereas in Greece and the East it would hardly make any difference in the price of provisions. Egypt alone could supply enough corn to feed the whole of our army, while Italy would soon starve. "Also, my dear, you will always see to it that our troops are paid," this with a sly smile, "and Octavian does not know where to turn for gold. In fact, I do not expect to have to fight a land battle at all. Look, my dear, I have left four legions in Cyrene, four in Egypt, three in Syria—as well as small garrisons throughout the coast. Our army here consists of some hundred thousand foot, and twelve thousand horse; Octavian cannot raise the half of that."

"Are you sure?" I asked. "My agent last week reported eighty thousand men and twelve thousand horse . . ."

"Well, it make no matter; we outnumber them, for sure. That was my point. One does not need to stick to nice numbers . . ." So did he always dismiss me; it was very galling. Yet I loved him well.

Winter approached, and we removed to winter quarters at Patrae. I saw no sense to this, for it made an expensive excursion, to my mind, and without advantage. But I was told that armies always went into winter quarters; well, I could see better ways of spending money. The fleet was sent to the Gulf of Ambracia, a bit farther north; this was a huge natural harbor with a narrow entrance, a protection from both storm and attack. I studied the map of this place; a thought struck cold at my heart. I turned to Marcus. "How wide is the mouth of this gulf?" I asked.

"Just wide enough to admit one ship at a time," he answered. "That is the beauty of it. Octavian's fleet cannot get in."

"But Marcus," I cried, "neither can our fleet get out! They could be bottled up there forever . . . like old wine!"

"Oh, nonsense," he said, waving his hand, "It will never happen. Octavian will never think of it . . ."

"Octavian is not liked," I said. "But no man has ever questioned his military ability. He will have learned his strategy at Julio's knee. You must withdraw the fleet!"

"My dearest," he said, smiling indulgently, "really, you try one's patience. Go . . . read your Greek somewhere . . ."

I suppose we quarreled then; I cannot really remember. The days began to run into one another as time stretched out. At any rate, though I was far from happy about it, I was proven right about the matter of withdrawing the fleet, and in a way that even I had not foreseen. The winter storms came, making the seas unsafe; the fleet's supplies began to run out, and privation and disease killed a third of the rowing slaves and sailors; they had to be replaced with untrained men, and worse; ploughboys, farmers, even the odd traveler or criminal. On top of this, our long lying at anchor rotted the timbers and rusted the iron. My spies reported great discontent on all the vessels; sailors are used to privation, but all men chafe at delay.

There was so much in this year—for so it turned out to be—of waiting that rubbed at places in me already raw. We were none so comfortable ourselves; the garrison at Patrae was no palace. Add to that my worry for my children and my country, and my anxiety over Marcus, a thing that was always present in these days. He drank so heavily that I was afraid he would fall ill from it; his looks suffered, and his stamina; though the common soldiers still adored him, he was losing the respect of his officers. Often I surprised looks of contempt or pity, or heard a laugh suddenly broken off. There was no one to punish; they were not my people.

Winter came and went, and still no move from the enemy. "Marcus," I said, one day when the first green showed upon the hills. "I should like to see how our fleet has fared there in the gulf. Can we not make a visit?" It was a tactful way of suggesting that this was his duty as commander. He hemmed and hawed, but some three or four days later, we set out, bearing fresh supplies.

As we neared the place where they lay at anchor, I was assailed by a sinking feeling; the coast was grim and gray, a few sea birds wheeling above, and foam dashing high against the rocks, desolate. We had to sound every few feet, for the depths there are treacherous; close up I saw ugly reptiles, of a variety unknown to me; Marcus said they were harmless, but their jaws held rows of teeth, like crocodiles. Snakes, too, I saw in plenty, slithering over the rocks; I shuddered at the rail.

"I am surprised at you, little goddess," jested Marcus. "Those asps are sacred to Isis . . . here—" And he made as if to catch hold of one. "That spotted one would make a fine pet."

"Oh, no!" I cried. "Besides, they are not asps . . ."

"You are familiar with asps, then?" He was laughing at me. I laughed, too, but reluctantly. I shook my head. "I have never seen one—except on my royal jewelry . . ."

We threaded the projecting bays, picking our way through the shallows; our boat was small and fast; I wondered how the huge warships could possibly do it. When we finally reached the fleet, we saw that the seasoned sailors were hard at work, repairing the winter's ravages; the hulls were all blistered, the paint peeling, and there were rotting beams in many places where the water had lapped month after month. The men seemed cheery enough, but I saw that their smiles lacked teeth; they had had no fresh food, but only hard biscuits and dried corn. They were ill-clad, too, for everything had had to be brought by land—land that had been in the grip of winter. I tried to take heart, knowing that spring was now upon us, but it was difficult; on all sides we saw the effects of hardship, discontent, and neglect. Marcus, looking more alert than he had for many weeks, questioned a man who sat on shore, mending a torn sail. The sailor looked up from his work; his face was crisscrossed with a hundred wrinkles and as brown as a cured hide, but his eyes were a pure light blue, as if they had soaked up the sea color. "Ah, well, General," he said. "It's to be expected. There's wear and tear, you know, on any vessel, be she solid as stone. We turn to and take care of it . . . those of us that are left, that is."

"Have you lost many friends, then, my man?" I asked. If he was surprised at being addressed by a woman, he did not show it; sailors, I have learned, are a law unto themselves. He answered, mildly. "Well, there's been a few . . . some not so friendly, too." And he gave a single dry cackle, mirthless. "That lot—" And he jerked his head toward the near ship; a knot of men stood idle at the rail, though one or two trailed lines in the water. "That lot . . . all they do is fish, seems like. Though they don't catch any that I can see. But of course, you can't expect much . . . them not being sailors and all." He drew the needle through, and snapped off the heavy twine. "Been a few fights, too, I won't deny it. Squabbles over the beer and such. Always happens when you lay up . . . even with your proper seamen, much less these . . ." And he spat with contempt. "Say, tell me, sir . . . is it true what some are saying . . . that this here Octavian's got old Iron Agrippa on his side?"

"Agrippa is his naval commander—yes," answered Marcus.

"Oh-oh," cried the man, softly, shaking his head. "That's an old sea dog, that is. He's the one cleared the seas of Pompey's son. Yes, sir, old Agrippa knows his business. We're in for it . . . begging your pardon, sir."

I felt a cold finger upon me at these words, for they had the ring of prophecy; it was true that we had no such commander as Agrippa on our side; he was thought to be the most skillful naval fighter of the world. Also, I was offended that Marcus had made no mention of him to me, though it was plain he had this knowledge all along.

Marcus, however, seemed to disregard the sailor's words, for, with a shrug and a smile, he said, "That's as may be, my good man . . . I think we will prevail, and easily. We far outnumber the enemy."

"Numbers . . . well—" And the seaman shrugged in turn, and spat again. I saw he was thinking of the kind of makeshift fighters that made up our fighting navy. Over half our "numbers" knew nothing at all of the sea, and had been pressed into unwilling service as well.

"Come, Cleopatra," said Marcus, cheerfully, "let's take a look at the biggest boat, our flagship."

He pointed out the name as we came alongside, *The Daughter of the Nile*. I was touched, and not a little proud, for truly this was a formidable vessel, rising high out of the water like a fortress, and looking just as solid. She was fitted out, along her upper decks, with giant catapults; the stones that fit were so heavy they had to be lifted by four sailors. "And she has thirty banks of oars," said Marcus. "They will have to take siege ladders to her," he went on. "So you see, my dear, we cannot lose. And there are two hundred more, almost as large."

I saw, though, that here, too, there were timbers that needed replacing, and tattered sails; the planks of the deck sagged and creaked under our feet in places. Another sailor said that worms had got into them. "But give us a month, General . . . we'll have her in shape."

A month! Another month of waiting! When we were back at camp, I said to Marcus, "When the month is up . . . then, my dear, you must make a move. Time is passing us by . . ."

"Oh, no, my dear," he said. "Octavian must make the first move." And he did. Or, rather, his Agrippa made it for him. He took a squadron of ships on a raid into Greece and captured the port of Methone. It was a small stroke, but brilliant, for it served two purposes. Stationed at Methone, his ships could forestall our cargo vessels coming up from Egypt; more grain lost! And it diverted Marcus' attention; while he readied his troops to march to the rescue, Octavian, with more ships, landed at the port of Toryne, directly above the gulf where all our fleet lay. It is true, he could not storm our fleet, for the entrance was narrow and well fortified; still, as I had foreseen, neither could our ships get out. And, plain to see, he was well able to cut off all our sea supplies; we were blockaded.

Marcus, now that action was called for, did the about-face I had seen before. He gave up feasting, and took little wine and ate plain food only; within the week his eyes struck sparks and the pouches beneath smoothed out; he tightened his swordbelt to fit his narrowing waist, and vigor, almost visibly, pulsed through his person like drum-beats. In no time at all, he had marched our huge force in orderly fashion towards the scene of conflict; we encamped on the southern peninsula, at a place called Actium. Octavian's army was on the northern side, but some miles inland. Marcus dispatched part of his forces to the tip of the northern peninsula, so that we now commanded nearly the whole coast, right up to the entrance of the gulf where our warships rode at anchor.

As I saw it, we had two options. One was to march around the gulf and engage Octavian in pitched battle; the other was to burst out of the blockade and defeat Octavian at sea. Though most of those Roman senators who traveled with us urged Marcus to fight a land battle, I feared that Octavian's army was too well fortified; also, such a move meant, virtually, the abandonment of our fleet. Night after night I urged sea action; night after night Marcus hesitated, harried by all the opposing factions. "If we lose our fleet," I said, "we will have lost, as well, all the gold and supplies we have brought with us."

Weeks went by, draggingly. Agrippa, who it seemed let nothing drag, took in a number of his ships, and, with amazing skill, deployed them to capture the towering lime-stone island of Levkas. This island, only separated from the western coast of Greece by a narrow channel, commands the whole area to the south of Actium; now not only was our fleet blockaded but our army! "Can you never, never look at a map?" I cried bitterly. It was an unfair thing for me to say, but my nerves were undone by Marcus' waiting game; besides, one always thinks one could do it better oneself.

On top of this clever move of the enemy, there came those awful portents that always occur in the wake of set-backs. From Athens came word that the famous statue of Dionysos, Marcus' identity, as it were, had been hurled to the ground in a violent thunderstorm; from nearer, from our Patrae stronghold, we heard the news that the temple of Hercules, Marcus' ancestor, so-called, had been struck by lightning. I am inclined, always, to attribute such things to mere coincidence, but even those staid senators in our company looked grave, and some of the common soldiers made the sign against the evil eye when they caught sight of Marcus. Poor Marcus! He had been so good; now in a trice, he was back on the wine again.

We heard that Octavian's camp held most of those senators who had not thrown in their lot with us; Octavian had promised them glory and a share of the booty. It was very astute of this nephew of Caesar, for thereby he kept it a war against a foreign enemy, Egypt, and not a civil war. One by one our own senatorial allies began to go over to him as well. I felt the situation was becoming desperate.

Summer came, and with it heat such as I had never felt, even up the Nile. For here it was low-lying ground, and marshy; mists hung in the air, so that one felt as though one walked through water; drops of moisture beaded our hair, and breaths came short. And soon there came also hordes of mosquitoes, rising in clouds from the swamps. In the royal tent we slept under netting, but the men of the army had no such protection. They went about swollen and red, scratching and miserable, and many were stricken with a sickness carried by the creatures. It turned men yellow of skin and eye, and sent fevers high; a few died, and hundreds were half-dead from weakness, and lay on their pallets from dawn to dusk, until the fever broke. Morale was very low. Two thousand Galatians and their command went over to Octavian's camp; Ahenobarbus, always a dissenter, deserted too, and a petty king from Paphlagonia, with his thousand men, went with him to swell the enemy ranks. With sickness, deaths, and desertions, we no longer had the advantage of greater numbers, though Marcus refused to count with me, behaving as though nothing had happened. The sickening truth was that, so far as could be conjectured, we had, on land and sea, less than fifty thousand men left, and some of those unfit for protracted battle. Though many of the Romans pressed, still, for a land war, we really had no choice; one segment or another must be abandoned. Experienced legions can always, at a pinch, live off the land, I had learned that from Caesar; sailors and cargo must sink with their ships. We must use our fleet, or give it up. At my insistence, Marcus finally called a conference; Publius Canidius, Marcus, and me.

It was decided, after a long night's planning, that Canidius would be left in full charge of our land forces, with what supplies we could spare. Our fleet would be divided into four squadrons, three under Marcus' command, and one, some sixty Alexandrian light vessels, under mine. These ships of mine were fast and light, and could outdistance most vessels on the sea, given a good wind. We planned that I should carry all our gold, supplies, and assets on these ships, take no battle action, and simply observe from the rear. If victory was in sight, we would make for the open sea and Rome; if it went otherwise, we must sail as fast as possible back to Egypt, saving thus much strength for another day. This was to be kept secret from the rest of the fleet; my ships had to be loaded under cover of darkness. I think Marcus believed that this could be accomplished; privately I was sure that most people caught on to it. For, even if all manner of cargo can be brought on board silently, it must have been apparent that my courtiers, household servants, and slaves had vanished from the garrison; one does not take such a retinue into battle!

By the end of summer we were ready. After discarding those really unserviceable vessels, we had, including my squadron, which was not to engage in battle, about three hundred ships, carelessly manned. Octavian had four hundred, with extra legions aboard. True, his ships were a great deal smaller, but that might be, in some cases, an advantage; I could not afford to let myself think about that; it must be as the gods willed.

Our ships were lined up in the proper formation, positioned inside the mouth of the gulf; it was just after dawn, and still cool. We waited the signal from the lead vessel, Marcus' *Daughter of the Nile.* I stood at the prow of my own light vessel, directly beneath the carved wood figure of helmeted Athene; her outstretched spear arm pointed due west, toward the mouth of the gulf. I felt a fresh wind, crisp, in my face, and smiled. Cytheris stood near me, among my women; I felt her eyes upon me and turned to face her, the breeze whipping my hair from its careless knot. "Ah, Lady," she sighed. "Do not smile yet . . . it is a westerly wind. I have known them to blow for a week." Of course she would know; these theater folk depend upon boats to take them from engagement to engagement. And it was true, the wind came from the west, through the mouth of the gulf, against us; we were becalmed as long as it blew.

"Look—" cried Cytheris, "The enemy is putting out to sea without sail . . . there must be hundreds of rowers!"

"They, too, have no choice," I said. "Their light ships would have been blown right in to us. Agrippa is taking no chances . . ."

"He has, no doubt, good knowledge of these west winds . . ." muttered Cytheris, looking grim.

It was four days before the wind blew itself out; it was a bright, hot summer day, calm and still in the early morning. Marcus, in a small rowing boat appeared below us; he had visited every ship, giving encouragement and sampling their casks of wine and beer. "Great Zeus," I cried, half-laughing, "where have you poured the stuff?" For I saw no sign of drunkenness, for once. His countenance was bold and bright, full of cheer; I had not seen him so in many a long month.

He pulled himself up the rope ladder and kissed me hard, the rail between us. "Remember what you have promised, my darling . . . no battle for you. And a quick retreat if the day goes against us . . ."

"But how shall I know?"

"You will know," he said, setting his mouth in a thin line. "But, cheer up. It will not happen. The word is that Octavian is seasick."

But not Agrippa, I thought. But I said nothing, only, "Take care, my husband . . . do not get in the way of anything . . ."

"You know what they say . . ." And he winked a great wink. "Drunkards never get hurt . . ." And I watched him row away, his back as straight as Caesar's had been, for once.

Beside me Cytheris murmured, shaking her head, "He should have been an actor . . ."

"What do you mean?" I demanded.

"Can't you see? Fear trembles within him . . . but he puts up a brave show."

I hoped she was wrong.

I watched as squadron after squadron took their places, under oar, in double lines, stretching all along the gulf to the mouth. Then I saw the left wing take the lead and move out cumbersomely through the mouth into open sea, the others following.

"Give the order to bring up the rear, Lady," said Cytheris, her eyes narrowed against the sun. "And lay on sail . . . the wind is drawing onshore."

"I cannot feel a wind," I said.

She pointed; sails were going up, billowing forward, all along the strung-out double line. "It is coming," she said. "We must be ready for it."

I took her advice, moving well out to the west of Levkas Island, some distance from the battlesite. We had a good view of all the sea for miles around. We watched as the vessels of Octavian, under Agrippa's command, moved in to meet Marcus; both sides were now maneuvering with rowers, for no sea battles can be fought under sail.

The enemy ships, from this distance, looked incredibly small, but there were a great many of them. Marcus' vessels were huge and ponderous; they had no capability of charging, but must wait for the attack, like a town under siege. Agrippa, with perfect strategy, sent in four or five ships to each one of ours. When the smoke and fire cleared for a moment, one could see that the scene resembled the hunt, a pack of hounds surrounding a huge boar. When the boar managed to sink his teeth in, he might toss the ruined hound off to die, but there was always another dog to take its place. Or so it seemed here; many of Agrippa's vessels caught fire, or were sunk by the great holes in their sides made by our catapults, but there always came another to hammer at our great ships' beams and hull.

We were far enough away that we saw no carnage; the men that toppled off the ladders into the sea looked like insects, tiny specks against the great blue void of sky. I did not see the bodies floating in red waters, or the severed limbs and mangled torsos; I simply imagined them. All watched as I did, helpless, terrified, dry-mouthed, with fingers numbed from gripping the rail.

Ship after ship of ours went down, like great fish, diving; it was so very quiet; we were too distant to hear cries or the crackle of the flames; somehow it did not seem real. I felt dazed and far away; I had lost track of time.

"Lady," and a hand plucked at my sleeve; Cytheris. "Lady," she said softly. "Give the order to sail south . . . the sun will set soon."

"It is so late . . . ?" I rubbed my eyes, sore from salt and strain.

"Yes," she said, still speaking low. "The battle goes agains us—near half our ships are gone . . ."

I saw she was right; I knew, as well, that I had known it myself, but *would* not. "Marcus . . . ?" I whispered in a small voice.

She pointed. "There . . . his flagship. The mast is broken but it is still afloat."

"I cannot leave him . . ."

"You must—and quickly. It was his order, and agreed upon. Don't think about it—just go. Think of your children, your country . . . think of Caesarion!"

I nodded the orders to my captain, and he signaled the rest of my squadron. "Yes, Lady," he answered. "Best thing, begging your pardon. And the wind comes full now. We'll turn tail and she'll push us south fast as the gull flies . . ."

I looked ever behind me as we skimmed away; after a little while all I could see was some dark smoke, and then that faded too.

I turned to Cytheris. "We can still win . . ."

"Oh, yes, dear lady," she said, "the battle can turn . . ."

But I did not believe her.

23

SOMETHING WENT OUT OF MARCUS forever, after the defeat at Actium—for of course it was a defeat, and almost inevitable, I see now. Perhaps what happened to Marcus was inevitable, too; the natural result of creeping age or eroding wine habit. It is difficult to put a name to the thing that was gone, though its absence was plain to see. It was not hope, or love of life, or joy—no, it was as though that essential thing that makes each person unique had vanished; Marcus was no longer Marcus. And whatever the cause, I noticed it first when he came on board our fleeing vessel, the battle was raging behind him.

We had not planned it that way, though when I had recovered from my surprise, I praised him for his good sense. "You are alive, there will be other battles," I said. He did not answer, but stared through me, as at something a thousand miles away. I saw it in his eyes then, the tenantless look, and a quiver of fear went through me. He never properly answered me, either, except to say, with an odd note in his voice that was almost pity, "Little queen, you will never understand . . . you have never betrayed anyone . . ."

For three days he spoke to no one, sitting alone on the forward deck; he took no food or water, and wore still his battle-stained clothes. At last, when we reached the harbor of Taenarum, he set aside this mood and went below to wash and refresh himself with supper. This was the first of such periods of dejection; they came oftener and oftener, and lasted longer each time.

It was there, at Taenarum, that our one surviving ship caught up with us, bringing the news that we had lost all; every ship had been captured or sunk, and the loss of life was incredibly heavy. The worst death of all, it seemed to me, was that of Dioscorides, my beloved friend and my doctor; I had not wanted to spare him to the battle, and Marcus had insisted. I turned to him, with a sharp word on my tongue, but never said it, for I saw again that empty look upon him. So often in these last months have I checked myself; one cannot belabor a creature who is absent!

Dioscorides' scrolls had been saved, though, and most of his medicines; a young colleague, who had trained with him, name of Olympos, survived, and brought all these things from the battle. He himself was badly burned, and feverish with it, but would not rest, for there were others, wounded, who needed his ministrations. We stayed nearly a week in harbor there, to tend the sick and water our vessels.

Worse news, if it was possible, came to us there; the land army had deserted, all, to Octavian, Canidius and the other officers escaping, none knew where. Octavian, it seems, had promised them the same treatment as his own soldiers, and reminded them that their great commander was a coward who had run away. Marcus heard this with great tears washing down his face. "My dear," I said, gently, "it is a tactic of war . . . do you expect him to praise you? Look what he has said of me!" For indeed, the report was that I, through my magic powers, had caused Marcus to take ship after me; no Roman was a true coward, and it was truly all my fault. "And now, my husband, we must go back to Alexandria with all speed and show ourselves free and unhurt, still masters of our destinies."

But he shook his head. "I cannot," he said.

"You must come with me," I said. "You must organize your affairs in the East, make sure of your allies . . . build more ships. Egypt is still wealthy."

He said nothing; I gave the order for our departure, feeling that action would sweep him along with it. But when the ships again put into harbor in the small garrison town of Paraetonium, he lifted his head and said, "I shall stay here."

It was a barren outpost; a tiny fort overlooked the headland where a narrow inlet of the sea ran between limestone cliffs. It is surrounded by desert and the heat is oppressive; hot winds from Africa blow there all afternoon like furnace blasts. "It is only another hundred and sixty miles to Alexandria, my dear," I said, still speaking gently, as to a child.

He shook his head again. "I cannot face it." And I could not budge him; no argument, no persuasion prevailed; in the end I had to leave him, for my children and my subjects needed me. Some of his faithful companions stayed with him; he did not even look up as we sailed.

My heart was heavy, for my dear love; I think he was close to madness. And then the news was always worse than one could have believed. All the cities of Greece went over to Octavian; we heard that the statues of Marcus were torn down and smashed to rubble, all the glory that had been heaped upon him not many months ago smashed too. For myself I did not care; I was Rome's foreign enemy, after all, and it was to be expected. But for Marcus, it was his world, toppled; I hoped only that the news would not reach him, there, in his lonely exile.

The defeat at Actium was on everyone's lips, everywhere; it could only be a matter of time before the eastern provinces and client states went over to Octavian. Still, Egypt was left. And Alexandria was still the greatest city in the world. There was no time to lose; I must salvage what I could.

I sent little Alexo and his bride to her father's court at Media; there they would be safe, at any rate. And with Media as an ally, I could set about building a new kingdom. I started with ship-building. There is an isthmus which divides the Red Sea from the Mediterranean; it is the boundary between Asia and Libya, and its narrowest part measures only three hundred furlongs. I planned to build ships there on the narrow strip, easily transported and launched into the Red Sea. Alas, like every plan now—just when the ship-building was going well—there came a massive raid, and my docks and ships were burned to the ground; it was the Arabs of Petra who did it, an old enemy I should have looked to. Too late we wiped out the nest of them at Petra, and routed the towns all about; the damage was done; the ships were gone. I had only those vessels, somewhat worn, with which I had fled Actium.

Marcus came back to Alexandria from his exile, only to exile himself again in another place. I could only accept it; when he gave himself up to despair, he did it as fully as he had given himself up, in times before, to the wine jug. This time he built a dwelling for himself near Pharos, upon a jutting peninsula; there he moped and brooded all along, calling himself the new Timon. It was all dreadful nonsense; this Timon had been a citizen of Athens, who, feeling himself abused and wronged, shunned all mankind. There was no parallel in fact, for many of Marcus' men died for him, and those who lived still were loyal and kind.

I could not allow Marcus to rot there; I sent his son Antyllus to him, and somehow, I never knew how, it worked. Antyllus brought him back to the Palace and Alexandria. But my first sight of my husband shocked me profoundly; he looked suddenly very old, his hair turned white and his face deeply lined. His clothing and his person were filthy and neglected, and many of his teeth had fallen out. He was weak and biddable; when I put him in the hands of the new court physician, Olympos, he did not protest as once he might have, but allowed himself to be put to bed and dosed with drugs.

For a month he lay quietly, sleeping long, reading, listening to music; he was forbidden wine, and took only a light ration of thin beer. This regimen worked wonders; it did not bring the old Marcus back, but he spoke no more of Timon or of pessimism, and his person took on a look of health. "I am grooming myself for my death," he said, with a kind of gaiety. His words struck cold, though I laughed with him as though it had been a merry quip; in my innermost parts I knew that our defeat could have but one end. Well, at least it should not take me unawares, my death. And no enemy should have the ordering of it. I put it out of my mind, for then; Caesarion was coming of age, an important ceremony.

To this event Marcus brought some of his old verve; his own boy, Antyllus, would put on the *toga virilis,* too. It was a solemn affair, done in full view of the whole populace, in the Gymnasium; though the words were all in Latin, which few of our subjects understood, the crowd cheered Caesarion, their young ruler who was this day officially a man. At the banquet later, Caesarion looked at me, the thin smile of his father's playing about his young mouth. "Well, Mother," he said, raising his wine cup as if to toast me, "This day you have signed my death warrant . . ."

The breath caught in my throat. "What do you mean?" I whispered.

"Do you think Octavian will let me live . . . another Caesar—and a man now?" He shrugged and put the wine cup to his lips, drinking it down all at once. "Never mind, Mother," and he patted my hand. "I don't mind. At least it will have the name of execution, not child murder."

"We shall have glory, like Alexander," said Antyllus, his cheeks flushing, "rather than length of days . . ."

"Don't be foolish, Antyllus," said Caesarion. "Octavian can have nothing against *you.*"

"We made a pact—remember?" Antyllus' voice trembled a little.

"We were young then," said Caesarion, smiling sadly. Gods, I thought, young! They are babies still, in spite of the manly togas and the lofty Roman words.

And I sat thinking, behind my easy banquet talk, of my other children, true babies. Was Alexo safe in Media? Surely his sister was no threat? And the little one—Ptolemy . . . was he in danger? It would be long years before he came to boyhood even. And would Octavian remember that he himself had no heir, only a daughter? If I renounced my throne, would Octavian spare my children? I drafted a letter in my head—there at supper—and wrote it out in the morning, putting it into a messenger's hand. Octavian was Caesar's nephew—surely he was human?

24

THE ANSWER CAME SWIFTLY; its messenger looked frightened, as though he knew what was in it. The letter from Octavian said nothing of my children or their fate; it was very brief. He said that I would receive "reasonable" treatment if I would be sensible and have Marcus Antonius put to death. I turned to the messenger, a man called Thyrsus, with a face of wrath; with an effort I smoothed it out, for it was not his fault. I replied calmly that he should have my answering letter in the morning. I never like to be overhasty when the impulse strikes me to be; one can say it all wrongly. Thyrsus came closer and said in a low voice, "Lady, I have another letter . . . a secret one . . ."

"From Octavian?"

"No, Lady. From the Honorable Octavia."

"A secret letter? Secret from whom?" I felt I must go warily; the woman was her brother's sister, after all.

"It is a sworn secret. For your eyes alone." No wonder he had looked frightened; tyrants do not brook secrets. He was no coward, though; he said, and it took some doing, to a queen, "I must have your word that you will honor it . . ."

"No one shall ever hear of its existence, I promise you, my friend."

I took the letter, and dismissed him, saying he would have my answer to both next day.

The letter from Octavia caught my heart—with gratitude, and then, after, with fear.

> To the Lady Cleopatra of Egypt:
>
> In admiration and pity I offer you what I can guarantee: safe sanctuary for your three small children. My brother has sworn to let them be, if so be it they live in private seclusion in my care. I promise you they shall want for nothing, and they will have good company. My own Antonia is near to the twins' age, and I have the care as well of my brother's little Julia. We shall be like a small school here in Rome, and in the heat of summer we will go to the country where the air will refresh them. We have good teachers,

Greek, and a fine nurse for the little one. I realize you may not want to part with them just now, but be assured that the offer stands, no matter what the circumstances.

There was a second sheet, blank. I turned the letter over; in small Greek characters I read, "Hold this to a flame's heat. Destroy both letters, I beg you." It was signed, "Julius Caesar's niece, Octavia."

My hands were shaking as I held the second missive to a candle. Words appeared, faint and brownish; she had written them in milk, a schoolroom trick, but I did not smile. "Get Caesarion away." That is all the writing that was there, but it sufficed to put me into true terror. I had to think of a safe place of refuge, and it must be as secret as this letter. Did she know Caesarion's peril from Octavian's words, or was she guessing? I suppose it did not matter; she had risked a great deal to warn me; the ties of blood are not so sacred to Romans as to protect her if her brother found out. I watched her message burn to black ash while my mind ran in circles.

The next morning I called the messenger, Thyrsus, to me and said, "There is no written answer—to either message. Convey my thanks and gratitude to the Lady Octavia . . . as for the other—tell Octavia Caesar that Marcus Antonius is my husband and the royal consort of the queen of this land. That is all."

"Lady," he said, "Octavius Caesar is marching into Asia Minor; I go to him there. I pray you—while there is yet good distance between you—arrange your affairs with discretion." I saw that even in the privacy of my chambers, he feared to be overheard. I nodded. "Yes, friend, I understand. Caesar's son shall be sent away to—"

"Do not say it, Lady, I beg you!" Poor man! He feared the knowledge could be tortured out of him. I said no more except farewell, and sent him from me with a royal gift.

"Mother," said Caesarion, when he heard my plans, "I will go—but it will do no good . . . no one can escape his fate." Those were sad words, too weary of purpose for his youth; I wondered what new philosopher had spoken them and when, but I said nothing; it was no time for wrangling.

"For me, Caesarion . . . do it for me. You will be safe there, I promise you . . ."

He shook his head and smiled a little. "Even you cannot

promise that, Mother, strong heart that you own . . . there is no room in our world for two Caesars."

My plan was to send him, in company with the three actors and his tutor Cadwallader, to Berenice, a far port on the Red Sea, and our principal trading center for Arabia and India. The actors were to choose a troupe in the city there, and rehearse a play, as though commissioned by me, with Caesarion as deputy; it was hoped that this would serve as excuse for Caesarion to stay there till I sent for him, without any suspicion that he was in hiding, and tempting no informers. If, by some last chance, luck went with us somehow, he could return to Alexandria; if not, he could make his way easily by sea into India and find refuge.

"Perhaps, Mother," said Caesarion, "they might give me a part to play . . . beneath the mask I would be truly safe."

I saw he mocked me, and my sick nerves snapped; tears started to my eyes, and I threw myself despairingly into his arms.

He patted me awkwardly, as big boys do when they are all at sea and burdened with strange adult passions. "Mother," he said, holding me at arm's length, "You are so little! I never knew . . ."

"You have grown tall, my son," I said, and managed a smile.

"But your bones are like a bird's . . . and there are dark shadows under your eyes . . . oh, Mother—" And for once I saw moisture mist his eye. "Oh, Mother, you were so beautiful once . . ."

Sad words, painful words. So much was gone forever. I wiped my eyes. "We all grow old, Caesarion . . . but, if I do not look too often in a mirror . . . why then, I can be brave, at least for a while." I held my head high, laughing. "And then—paint helps. I have forgotten it this morning . . . but never mind, Caesarion . . . remember me beautiful."

I kissed his cheek and tasted salt; I think he had not cried since he was toddling. He straightened; I saw him look at Antyllus.

"I wish you would let me come with you," cried the boy. Caesarion shook his head. "No, Antyllus, your father needs you . . ." He held out his hand. "Never forget me, friend . . ."

"Give over, boys," said Cytheris, briskly. "You will have us all weeping in a moment. Save it for the theater . . . now tell me, Sir Caesar, what shall we do?" And in her bright and brittle way she caught him up; he bent his head in easy conversation.

And so, when in the afternoon, they took ship on the Nile, Caesarion stood in good cheer at the rail, and waved and waved, till the ship turned round a bend. Antyllus looked at me and said, "He will be safe there, won't he?"

"Oh, yes, of a surety," I answered. But the words, so brave, rang hollow in my ears.

"Why didn't my father come?" asked Antyllus. "I thought he loved Caesarion . . ."

I could not answer; I had wondered too. After a bit I said, "Your father has not been able to get over the defeat—and look ahead." But even as I said it I knew that no one could. "And then he broods over the desertion of so many who were once friends . . ."

"They were never friends!" he cried. "Friends never betray . . ."

"Oh," I said quietly. "They do . . . even Canidius, and I thought him steady as a rock . . . and so many more. The news is bad, one way or another, each day."

He looked at me, alarmed. "Lady, never have I heard you speak so—we *will* win . . . in the end, won't we?"

"In the end—if our hearts are high—yes, in the end we will win." But I did not mean it as he did.

Another messenger awaited me in the great hall; I could tell at a quick look that the message was woeful, as usual. I turned to Antyllus. "See if you can find your father . . . and keep him where he is. Take him fishing or something . . ." For truly I never knew how much Marcus could bear; another blow on his mind might be the one that would break it.

Herod, king of Judea, had gone over to Octavian; his domain lay northward, in the tyrant's path; now the road to Egypt was open.

There were not a great many blows my mind could bear either. I hunted out Marcus myself, in a fury of recrimination. "How often have I begged you to take Judea and make it mine! You had it in your hand—once!"

Marcus shook his shaggy head, as if to clear it; the gesture reminded me of a winded horse. "Sweet, I thought that Herod loved me . . . I thought he was a man of honor . . ."

"I could have told you otherwise! He tried to sway me from you long ago . . ."

"But you hid it from me. So how could I act upon it?" And he shrugged. "Ah, do not scold, Cleopatra . . . you were always so kind . . ." And he caught at my hand.

I caught the hand up and kissed it. "I will be kind . . . it was adversity that spurred me. I am sorry." He held me in his arms and for a long moment we clung together in a sort of weary calm.

"We still have each other," he said. "I count that riches . . ."

"Yes," I whispered. "Octavian seeks to divide us . . ."

"I know," he said, with a strange little smile. "He suggested that I do away with you and so have back all my honors . . ."

I looked up quickly. "He said the same to me . . ." Our eyes held for a long moment, then suddenly we burst out laughing, together.

"What did you reply?" he asked, wiping his eyes.

"That Marcus Antonius was my husband and royal consort, and father of my children, guardian of Caesar's son. And you?"

"Oh, I wrote nothing. I simply had the messenger flogged."

"Oh, Marcus, it was not his fault!"

He shrugged again. "He got off lightly . . . he is alive."

And so once again Marcus weathered the storm, and I too. Still, each day worsened our position. Octavian marched into Syria where all the garrisons surrendered to him. His general, Gallus, seized the garrison town of Paraetonium, where Marcus had gone into wretched retreat after Actium; Egypt was about to be attacked from both sides.

Without consulting Marcus, I gathered up all the royal treasure, the ancient symbols of wealth and power—gold, silver, emeralds, pearls, ebony, and ivory; they were brought into that part of the Palace above the great mausoleum, where they gleamed like strange fires. I placed them on a covered bier, of sorts, and beneath put faggots of wood, ready for the torch; the treasure and glory of the Ptolemies should never fall to the Roman upstart!

On and on came the dread reports, inexorable as advancing time; Pelusium fell, without a struggle; the road to Alexandria lay before Octavian like a belt for his tunic. In three days one could see the yellow dust cloud of the advancing army, filling the horizon, spreading out on wings onto the fields that lined the road.

"One last stand, my friend," I cried. "The Roman troops will be weary and dusty, dry from their desert march. Take all our land forces, march to meet them. You have surprise on your side!"

Marcus, with something like his old spirit, buckled on his armor and rode forth; he returned a short two hours later, his cavalry troops singing forth a victory in voices hoarse and heavy. "We pursued them all the way back to their own camp," he said, his eyes alight. "Corpses line the road . . . they must take breath, mend their ranks. I have an idea—"

He did not consult me, but went about his business with a boy's excitement. He dispatched archers, who rode close to the Octavian camp, and discharged arrows, tipped with written messages, promising rewards to any who would defect; not one man answered. He sent also a private note to Octavian, challenging him to a single combat. Octavian, of course, was far too shrewd to be stung into this; even at his youthful prime, he was no match for Marcus in pure brute strength. No, Octavian replied that if Marcus wished to die there were plenty of ways open to him. "You cannot expect a hero's heart," I said, "in the mind and body of an accountant. Forget your Homeric songs, my husband, and prepare for siege. Alexandria can last a long one . . ."

But he set my advice aside and prepared for another strategy—a double attack. He manned what ships we had left and prepared to send them out at dawn to meet Octavian's navy, which had been sighted still some distance away; at the same time, our land troops were to advance again along the road and engage in battle. "A double victory!" he cried. But my skin pricked under my hair, for I saw his eyes, wild and rolling, with flickering lights like marsh fires in them.

"One last night, my love," he cried, "we shall have a great feast—before victory . . ."

In the great hall, banquet-spread, we could look from the windows and see, so close they were, the fires and flares of Octavian's camp, brightening the northern sky.

It was a solemn feast; tears flowed instead of wine. For Marcus addressed his friends and officers, saying if the morror went against him, he would not lead them on to their deaths, but fall instead upon his sword. "Fair friends,"

he said, in the breath-held silence. "It is the only way . . ."
There was the sound of a single sob, choked off; Marcus was still loved.

Later, in bed, and the city quiet, I dreamed, or thought I dreamed. It seems I heard sweet music and soft wild cries, like the Bacchic calls on Dionysos's day. They rose to a muted crescendo, and then faded to a ribbon of sound, and then to nothing; I woke, as I thought, to stillness, my cheeks wet. Marcus, beside me, was so still that I leaped to fright, as one will, half-awake; I shook him gently.

"I am awake, my darling," he said softly. "Did you hear it too?"

"I thought it was a dream," I said.

"No," he answered. "It was no dream. It was my god leaving me."

25

THE SHIPS OF EGYPT moved out slowly, under sail; they were a remnant only, but still it was a proud sight, brilliant against the pale dawn. The land breeze ruffled my hair, blowing it into my eyes; I pushed it away impatiently. I stood on the royal stairs, where so often I had watched ships come and go, where I had watched my Neo sail away, so long ago, where I had flown to meet Marcus, wild with a goddess passion; the wind freshened, and I held my cloak together at my throat; it was late summer, and would be a hot day; still I shivered.

Far away, lining the horizon, and almost fading into the colorless sky, were the sails of Octavian's fleet, blockading the harbor; white mist hung over all.

To the north, Marcus' legions were drawn up for the attack, the golden eagles blinding bright, the banners brave. Marcus, with his officers, stood on a little hillock, commanding a view of land and sea; I could just make out the purple of his horse's trappings. In the stillness, a horse neighed loudly, then another; the sound was like the tearing of cloth. I saw Iras, beside me, put her hands over her ears.

The ships moved slowly, so slowly, though we saw from

the silver wake that they were using oars as well; it was an unbearable thing to watch.

"Why don't they attack?" It was Antyllus, sounding fretful, like a small child.

"Well," I said, my voice sounding thin and strange in my ears, "they are not close enough yet—and they must take down their sails, too—"

"No, no, Lady . . . I mean the legions!" And he pointed toward the ranks of them. "Octavian's troops are on the move already!" He was right; the huge dust cloud was coming closer.

"Your father will know when . . . never fear." So often had I heard Marcus say that there is a time, not too soon or too late, that is perfect, and one must trust to instinct; I prayed it would not fail him now, that instinct. "Watch the ships, Antyllus . . . soon we will see them loose the fire baskets, for at last they are getting near enough . . ."

We looked, straining our eyes, but they were like pictures still, or toys. "What are they doing, Lady?" Panic rose in Antyllus' voice. "Look, they are shipping their oars!" His eyes were younger; the rest of us saw it a moment later, the bright wakes gone that had streamed behind, the sea unbroken, and there, as we watched, incredibly, our ships lining up with the enemy in an ordered pattern.

"Oh, Gods, we are lost!" cried Charmion softly. "They have joined forces—they will not do battle!" I held my breath till I thought my chest would burst; when I let it out, it was on a long whistling sigh. We stood helpless as the two fleets moved slowly together towards the eastern harbor.

From the north there came a far-off iron sound, a clang, a ring; I thought the troops were closing in at last, in the first charge, and turned to look. But, clear in the morning light, we saw that the sound was the sound of weapons dashed to earth, and the iron-shod horses galloping in even lines to meet the advancing Octavians.

"Lady, they have deserted! They are marching back together . . . Romans all!" It was Antyllus again; poor lad, he made an odd Cassandra.

It was true, though—only the legions, with Marcus at their head, held firm. But not for long. A spear went high, pointing towards the harbor, where the ships moved serenely eastward, nearly gone from sight. Even above the war clamor, coming close, I heard the high, keening cries, the harsh jangle of arms, the hoofs striking; suddenly the whole line of the legions broke and ran, scattering, into the city. I could not find Marcus among them; I supposed he had no choice, borne with them as he was; he would make for his quarters. On that entire hill where once stood a thousand men and horse, there was nothing now but some few flung standards, and here and there the gleam of a dropped spear; the ground, though, was as it is always under an army, trampled and torn, with deep ruts and the chaotic pattern of hoof marks upon it. The dust cloud that was the enemy was a cloud no longer, but banners and shields, plumed helmets and faces beneath; the first line had even now reached the barren hill; panic sang in my veins. I snatched at Antyllus' arm, gripping it. "Get to your father! He will be in his quarters I think . . . but find him! Tell him I shall bolt myself into the mausoleum and open to none but him . . . tell him I await him. Go!" And I pushed him forward.

"Charmion . . . Iras . . . the children! Find the children! Come!"

And we three women, like creatures driven by the Furies, ran into the Palace, throwing open every door, wild with terror. As, at the end of the corridor, the nursery door yielded under our hands, little Ptolemy looked up, surprised, from where he rode a wooden painted steed. "Come, my darling," I cried, and snatched him up, clutching him close. 'Mama, you hurt!" he protested, and squirmed in my arms.

"Hush, baby . . . hush, mama's darling! Where is your nurse? Where is your sister?" I frightened him; I could not help it. I made an effort and loosened my grip on him, though still I held him close. "Selene?"

He pointed to the window; she was leaning far out, her feet in their small flat slippers off the ground. "Selene!" I called.

She turned her head. "Mama! So many soldiers—and horses! Where are they going?" Her eyes were round with excitement and her cheeks flushed. "Never mind, sweetheart . . . go with Charmion!" The nurse was nowhere to be found; we could spare no time to search, but ran, each with a child, and Iras, with an armful of snatched-up toys and clothes, back down the hall.

The part of the palace above the mausoleum stood apart

from the rest, reached by a covered walkway. Between the columns that lined the passage we could see, to our right, the sea, empty. We rushed through the great door, panting, and flung it closed. I put little Ptolemy down; he began to cry. "Selene . . . comfort your brother," I said, as I turned to tug at the heavy bolt that barred the door. As we three women shot the bolt home, gratingly, I heard Selene. "Cry-baby!" I could not worry about her manners now, but beckoned to the others. We tried all the locks on doors and windows; they were secure. "We had best go upstairs," I said, "for double safety . . . at least there we can have a window open . . ."

The first of the Octavian soldiers had reached the palace walkways; as we watched from the upper window, we saw two officers, faceless behind their cruel helmets, come out onto the steps where moments ago we had stood. They were looking out to sea, empty sea now, as we had; one of them dragged off his helmet to see better. Then he gave a short harsh laugh and said something we could not hear, flinging an arm across his companion's shoulder. They strolled away then, past us to the east, as if they took their ease in a park; an insult. At the same time we heard hammering below, and the great doors ringing hollow under the spear-butt blows. Then creaking as it gave, and footsteps, steel-shod in the hallways. Fast on this sound came a pounding at the door below, where we were refuging. Iras' hand went to her mouth. "Oh, sister, they have found us!"

"Hush . . . do not answer!" I listened, my heart knocking hard.

"Lady . . . oh, Lady . . . !" It was Antyllus' voice; it broke, as it often did now, on the last word.

"Come—" I said to Charmion, taking her by the hand. "Watch the children, Iras!" And we crept down the stairs and close to the door, waiting. Antyllus' voice came again. "Lady? Are you there?"

"I dare not open," I said. "There are Octavians all through the Palace—and this bolt is rusty as well . . ."

"Oh, Lady . . ." And I thought he could not speak, a sob was there, under. "Lady, it is my father. He is wounded—I think he may be dying . . . His sword—" And he choked on the words, and then went on. "It is still in him, his sword. I think he fell upon it, to take his own life . . . his man Eros is already dead."

"Oh, Gods," I cried, and tugged at the bolt, uncaring.

Even as he slipped through, we saw soldiers in pairs, starting toward us from either end of the walkway. Antyllus was alone, his face all smeared with tears and dirt.

"Marcus—where is Marcus?" I wailed, shaking him. "Oh, Charmion—shut the door!"

"I could not lift him, Lady . . . and should I pull the sword out . . . ?"

"He is still in his rooms?" I asked. He nodded, and I shook him again. "You must not give way, now—you are his son. Listen . . . go and find Olympos the doctor . . . if you cannot, get help and make a litter . . . bring your father here. Where we stood this morning—if it is clear of Romans—the upstairs window gives onto that place. Bring him there . . . get ropes—we will haul him up. I cannot open the doors again . . . hurry!"

I thought that he would never come. I thought I must rush after him, and twice started to, and was stopped by Charmion. I paced the upstairs chamber, wringing my hands; the children, terrified by my behavior, sobbed softly in a corner; Iras watched by the window. I heard, through my own soft sobs, noises on the stairs below and ran to the window to look. Antyllus was beneath, with a secretary, Diomedes, and Olympos; between them they bore a litter, such as is used to bring wounded off the field. The form stretched on it looked so long, so flat; a sheet covered it, already bloodsoaked, and a red trail marked the path they had come. I could not see his face, but he did not move where he lay; the way down seemed very far. Charmion, she was ever a useful woman, had found some rope somewhere and was letting it down, snaking past the walls.

Olympos looked up. "Is he . . . ?" I could not finish. He nodded.

"He is dying, Lady . . . but there is still a little time left to him."

I cannot think how it was accomplished, for Marcus was a big man, and heavy with his death upon him, and we were three slight women, but we pulled him up somehow, and into the chamber. It is said that the gods send strength when it is sorely needed.

Dimly I recall that Antyllus had got a ladder from somewhere, and the men climbed up afterward. There was blood all over Marcus, even on his face; he must have tried to stem the flow with his hands and then wiped his face, my poor love. The color was gone from him; he was like a waxen candle, his face scored with deep lines beside the mouth and black marks below the eyes. Olympos had wound many thicknesses of cloth about his body, but the blood still welled from the place; already a pool was forming on the floor. I wondered dimly how so much blood could be in one man, and that surely he was a god.

They had laid him on a long table; I bent over him, and put my hand to his face; I did not dare take him in my arms, for fear I might hasten his end. His eyes opened; around his mouth there was a little tremor, the ghost of a smile. "I made a bad job of it, darling . . . wouldn't you know I'd miss the heart? The gut, that's where I got it, sweet . . . but at least—this way—we can say farewell . . ." He held so tight to my hand that its bones scraped together; I knew he suffered dreadfully.

"Oh, my darling," I whispered. "Why . . . ?"

One eyebrow raised, a parody of the old gay Marcus. "It was the only way," he said. "The August One would have made it harder—think you he would not? Crucifixion, maybe . . ." He closed his eyes; I knew it was a great effort for him to talk at all. He was trying to wet his lips with his tongue, over and over. I turned and asked for water.

He opened his eyes. "Not water—wine . . ." And he nearly managed a true smile. "Not what you think, poor girl . . . but it will help, truly . . ."

I looked at Olympos. He nodded and said, softly. "It will finish him . . ." I put my hand to my mouth, but still a cry escaped.

"Let him have it, Lady . . . he is in great pain." And he took the cup that Charmion had brought.

Marcus shook his head, a small and weary movement. "You—sweet—I want you to give it to me . . ."

I took the cup, willing my hand not to shake, and with the other hand raised his head gently to meet the cup; he tried to sip it, but the wine all ran down his chin. He raised his eyes to mine. "Weak I am . . . so weak. Well, we die as we are born . . . I could not drink from a cup then either." And I thought I saw a fleeting slyness in those eyes, the beginning of a jest, incredibly. Oh, my Marcus—there is no other like you . . . I held the cup again; this time he drained it, and fell back against the litter. "There was salt in it, my dear . . . no good for a queen . . . no good." He shook his head from side to side. "Do not weep, my own . . . I die a Roman death . . . be happy for our happiness, for it was great . . ." And then his eyes glazed over, staring past me; Antyllus came forward, but he was already gone.

"He did not say good-bye . . ."

I looked at him; what did he have left, poor boy? I took his hand and drew him close, for I was still calm, as though frozen. "Listen, Antyllus . . . he said good-bye—and that you must be brave, and a good Roman. It is that he could not speak loud enough . . ."

"Oh, Lady!" And he put his head down upon my shoulder and wept.

I held him till he had finished, and turned away. I kneeled still where he had left me, beside my husband. A little breeze blew upon me from the open window; it would be a hot wind, this time of year, but I shivered. I looked down, seeing that the whole front of my robe was soaked with blood, and my hands looked as though they had been dipped in it; my face, too, was wet with tears I did not know I had shed. From the far corner came a whimpering, like puppies hurt; oh, gods—it was my babies, poor innocents. And at the thought, the ice broke in me somewhere, and I wept aloud, and could not stop.

26

IT IS NOT SO EASY TO DIE of grief, though the old songs sing of it; there is too much of the world that we cling to, in spite of ourselves. For me there were my children, my poor broken country, and my pride; in the end, only pride was left.

The days that followed Marcus' death are all jumbled together; I was very ill, in mind as well as body. It must have been almost immediately that the soldiers came, swarming up the ladder that we had forgotten. I snatched up a table knife; it was dull and would not cut butter, but they disarmed me of it anyway; they took away even the pins from my hair!

I did not know where they took my people, even my children; I was confined alone, with not even a woman slave to serve me, and without a change of clothes.

Through a daze I saw the soldiers carry out all my royal trappings, the plate and jewels of the Ptolemies; I had meant to destroy it, rather than that it should fall into Roman hands. Somewhere in my chambers lay the chest with the ancient symbols of power—diadem, scepter, and heavy serpent arm ring, wrapped in silk against the next wearing; I wondered if Octavian had found them.

They had removed all the furniture, too, and brought in a low bed, narrow, such as is used on army campaign; the doors were all locked and wooden bars were nailed across the window; it was a prison I lay in. I think that for many days I knew nothing; I was sick and fevered and did not eat. Dimly I remember that I followed Marcus' body belowstairs to his last resting place among the Ptolemies, and I must have wept wildly again, for I had somehow hurt myself; my arms and breasts were all bruised and aching; perhaps I had beaten them with my fists, though I have no memory of it.

The fever left me one morning at dawn; I awakened in a pool of sweat, but my mind was clear; I was alone. I looked down at my body where I lay; my ankles were not much more than bones, and hardly bigger than my wrist, and I was dreadfully weak. The door opened, gratingly, and two soldiers came in, bearing a tray with food; steam rose from a bowl, soup or a broth, the smell making me feel faint. How long since I had eaten? They set down the tray on a little table beside my pallet, and stood looking down at me

"What a skeleton!" said one, laughing harshly. They spoke the barracks Latin that I understood from a child. I think they were not legionnaires, but common soldiers, for they had the stunted Roman street look that the tenements breed; they did not look unkind, only stupid.

The second soldier laughed too. "Still—" he said, his thin grin showing missing teeth, "Still, she's none so bad a dish, even now! A man could get an armful, light as it would be . . ."

"Better stow that kind of talk," said the other. "Old pock-face has her marked for himself."

"Ah, no such thing! The emperor'd never take Antonian leavings! All he wants is to fatten her up for the Triumph . . . by Hades—I'd rather have the food than her! Pheasant broth and wheat bread . . . good beef, too! And all a waste! For that one'll never eat it. She means to starve herself—what else?"

The other looked down at me; I saw curiosity in his eye, and perhaps some pity. "Here, she's too weak to spoon it up . . . want I should feed you, Queen?" I stared at him. "What eyes! I could swear she understood!"

"Well, she's a witch, they say . . . don't touch her!"

But the other picked up the bowl. "Look, little lady . . . I'll just hold it for you . . . mayhap you're not strong enough . . . ?"

I shook my head and tried to smile. "You are kind," I said, in their own rough speech. "But no . . . if you would pour a little wine . . . ?"

Their eyes bulged as if a bird had spoken; the kind one poured the wine from shaking hands, so that most of it spilled, the other tugging at his arm all the while.

"Come away," he said, fear in his voice. "Come away . . . I told you she was a witch. Do you want to get hung on a cross?" They backed out, like courtiers, rough men that they were, fright and awe in all their posture. "Thank you, friend," I said. The great door clanged shut.

I managed to raise the wine cup to my lips without losing much of it; it made me dizzy for a moment, but afterwards I felt a little strength seep into my bones. I drank a mouthful of the broth and ate a little bread; it was good. I fell asleep again.

When next I woke, it was to a slanting light; late afternoon. I wondered if I had been drugged; the wine, the broth? I turned upon my bed, and saw a face close to mine; crisp curling black hair, large eyes that bulged a trifle and full womanish lips; for a heartbeat I thought I looked at Marcus. The man, from where he sat close to me on a low stool, spoke, smiling. "Do you remember me, Cleopatra?"

I shook my head to clear it; the curls were still unmarred by gray, and there were no pouches beneath the eyes; not Marcus, but I knew the face. "Dolabella—is it?" I asked, uncertainly. "I have forgotten your first name . . ."

His smile stretched a little. "There is a string of them—no matter. I am mostly called Doley."

"Long ago—" I said. "In Rome . . . the Feast of Lupercal . . . I remember."

"Other times too—but you have forgotten them—I was younger and not very important. But, I was Caesar's friend."

"And now?"

"Now, I am in the other Caesar's employ."

"Octavian? He sent you?"

He nodded. I caught at his arm. "My children . . . where are my children? What has he done with them?"

"They are safe—for now. He has announced it to the legions . . . that he means to bring them up with his own." I thought of Octavia's letter. Perhaps the bond between brother and sister was stronger than I thought. "But—" he went on, "I am sent to warn you. The emperor says that if you continue to starve yourself, you will suffer for it."

I reached out and caught his arm. "What?" I asked wildly. "What will he do?"

Dolabella shrugged; his face was grim. "He is a cold man. And he wants you strong and fit—for his Triumph."

"Sir," I said, "I have not meant to starve . . . I remember nothing—not even how long I have been confined here . . ."

"It is nearly two weeks," he said.

I was appalled. "But who has cared for me?"

"Your doctor . . . has been permitted to see you—under escort. You have been very ill."

"And my women—my sisters?"

He frowned, puzzled. "I thought—your sister was dead . . ."

"My waiting women . . . they are royal daughters of Egypt. Iras is my half-sister and Charmion my cousin . . . are they . . . ?"

"They are well, confined apart. The emperor does not trust them. They fought like lions, as you did yourself." He looked about him, uncertain.

"Speak Greek," he said, doing so himself. "Here the walls have ears, as they say. Cleopatra—for the sake of Caesar, our old friend, I am turned traitor . . . I have smuggled in the children's Egyptian nurse."

"But they have no Egyptian nurse!"

He put his finger to his lips. "Wait." And he went softly to the door which gave on to the stairs, opening it. A figure, small, bent, and cloaked heavily, scuttled through.

She came toward me, looking like an old Egyptian slave, brown and work-worn, but, close to, she threw back her hood. I cried out softly, and held out my hands. Under the brown stain and the crone look, it was the actress, Cytheris. I held her close, not speaking. Then I looked into her eyes; reluctantly, for I read the answer there, I asked, "Caesarion?"

"Dead," she said. "They are all dead. The Briton . . . and the others. Octavian's soldiers were there already—waiting for us." She spoke in a dry, old voice, like rustling dead leaves. "He has good spies, Octavian."

I had no tears left; from my tight, painful chest I croaked out one word only. "How . . . ?"

"They fought," she said. "They fought well. At least they were spared the Triumph—and the cross." She gave a harsh little laugh. "Me they took for Caesarion's whore . . . they did not kill me. When they finished, I got away. The tale is long—and dull." She smiled crookedly. "I was able to pass into the Palace . . . said I was the Palace nurse."

"My children—"

"They are well. Octavian visits them every day—they're fond of him, call him "uncle." They think you have gone to Rome . . . and that they are going too—an adventure . . ."

"Oh, watch over them, my friend!"

"With my life, Lady." She laid down a bundle, knotted and tied. "I have brought you some soaps and oil . . . paint and combs, too . . . and a clean shift." She rummaged inside it, taking out toilet articles. I felt something being pushed into my hand, a vial; my fingers closed on it. I saw her face, small and shut. She came close, whispering. "Hemlock. Enough for a regiment. Hide it."

It was my death, and welcome; I smiled. "Thank you," I said, very low.

There was a scratching at the door; Dolabella came forward. "Come, my girl, it is time for the changing of the watch . . . we'll slip you through. Say your farewells."

"Can I trust him?" I asked, in her ear.

"I think so. Fortune attend you, Lady. Farewell." And she was gone.

Dolabella stood looking down at me; his face was kind. "I am sorry. I wanted her to tell you."

"You know her, then?"

"From long ago. . . . But I will not give her away." He took my hand. "Poor little queen—you do not have many friends left . . ."

I looked my question. He shook his head gravely. "There have been beheadings each day since the city fell. All those officers who were not quick enough to draw swords themselves . . . all your cabinet—most of your court. Your secretary. I think all that remain to you are your doctor—and your women . . ."

Again I knew before I spoke. "Antyllus?"

"He had fled to the Temple of Venus. They dragged him out . . ."

"A child . . . why?"

"Who can tell? Revenge, perhaps—for having been cheated of the father . . ."

"He is a monster, then, Octavian . . ."

"He is a puzzle—like all great men. For he *is* great . . . our emperor."

I felt my lip twist a little. So Rome would have an emperor after all! "When is the—Triumph?"

"He means to take you to Rome very soon now . . . you have perhaps three days—to prepare."

I looked at him—a long look. Did he guess what I planned?

"Among other things, the emperor likes to surprise people. I am reasonably sure he will visit you—unannounced. Perhaps tonight."

"Then leave me, friend, for I am filthy with two weeks' dirt—" I smiled and held out my hand. "Will I see you again?"

It was his turn to look long at me. "I am to bear your golden chains, in the Triumph."

"I see." I raised my chin, the weakness leaving me. "No farewells, then . . ."

"No farewells." And he kissed my hand and left.

I tucked the little vial into my undergirdle, next to my skin, and reached for the soap and basin.

27

OCTAVIAN DID NOT COME that night, nor for two days after, though I hurried to make myself presentable, fumbling the soap and tearing my tangled hair with the comb; I have never been used to serving myself, and my weakness made me unhandy.

I might have swallowed the vial's contents then and

there, but I told myself I *would not* go to the gods as a sick beggarwoman and alone, I, the royal child of Egypt and Alexander's kin. And then I suppose some tiny part of me, deep within, hoped still, against my mind's will.

I was alone, except for the soldiers, bringing food; it was never the same ones; Octavian was taking no chances. Those who came set down the trays silently, with averted faces, and left as silently; they did not want themselves bewitched.

I ate a little, growing stronger, and I slept; I did not dare to think, beyond those first bitter thoughts. When Octavian came, he wakened me from a half-remembered dream; I heard Gaulish voices, barking commands, and thought my Julio walked there. I started up from my bed, a dream-joy written on my face, my arms held out. It must have disarmed the conqueror, for he embraced me in a cousinly fashion, kissing my brow; I smelt the smell of him, musty and old, though I knew he was younger than I. "Royal Cleopatra—" so he addressed me! "Be seated, I beg of you . . ." And his soldiers set down two chairs in that empty room; dimly I knew them for Palace chairs, ivory and gilt, from my own chambers.

He came with a guard of twelve, Gauls or Britons, huge fair brutes with rock faces. He snapped his fingers for distance and they ranged themselves behind him, covering the doors, spears in hand.

Octavian looked as though his mother still made his clothes, in the country; they were awkwardly draped and frayed at the hem, gray from poor washing. He was small-built, as I remembered him from long ago, almost to the point of delicacy; his skin was yellow against the drab of his robe; I remembered that Marcus had said he was prone to seasickness. But for that, and his ill-kept person, he would have been a handsome man, even with his thick-pocked face that looked like a statue pitted by age. He wore his smallness well, standing very straight; his every move was crisp and measured; his eyes were cold as gems.

He wagged his finger at me, his thin smile a mockery of great Caesar's and of Caesarion's, slashing at my heart. "You have been a bad girl, Cleopatra . . ."

For a moment I could give no answer; this jocularity sat ill upon him.

"Why have you spoiled your looks? Your Caesar is displeased . . ." And he reached out to cup my chin, placing his mouth on mine. His lips were cool and hard, but his tongue, wet and gagging, filled my mouth; I nearly spat.

I cast down my eyes, masking them, and ordered my shrinking flesh to sit quietly. "I have been ill, sir . . . and unaware."

"You may call me Octavian," he said, inclining his head.

"It is good," I said, my eyes still downcast, "for I think of you as Caesar's beloved nephew."

"I am Caesar now," he said.

"Yes, Octavian."

He cleared his throat. "I have a list here," he said, snapping his fingers, and taking it from the soldier who held it, "a list of the royal assets—plate, coins, gold bars, electrum, silver, jewels . . ." He ran his eye quickly down the scroll. Again he wagged his finger at me. "You have not been honest, my dear . . . there are several items here—got from your steward before, got from him earlier this week—which cannot be found. . . . You should know better than that, my dear," he said, shaking his head sadly. "Rome will have her due . . ."

"I was not consulted," I said, with a small show of spirit. "I have told you I have been ill. I have been entirely alone—with no servants—nothing!"

"Well, we will remedy that. Caesar is magnanimous . . ." He scanned the list. "Now here are the items—a diadem, gold, with entwining serpents, a scepter—serpents again—various gold and ruby rings, two gold anklets, a bronze arm ring in the form of a serpent . . . what is this preoccupation with serpents?"

"It is the Egyptian Isis symbol," I said. "From the time of the ancient Pharaohs . . . they are sacred objects in the old religion."

"I see," he said, rubbing his chin thoughtfully. "Important symbols, are they?"

"They signify Egypt," I said, simply. "I thought—now—they would make fair gifts for your wife and sister—that they may look kindly on me when I come to Rome. They are all I have." I tried to sound humble, though my tongue was thick on the words.

"These things—" and he pointed to them on the scroll, "they are still worn sometimes?"

"Oh, always," I said. "The queen is no queen without them."

"Well, my dear, queen you shall be—for one last time.

Rome will see Egypt in all her lost splendor. I thought golden chains—but perhaps electrum . . . ?" I think he had forgotten me for the moment; when he looked at my face, something must have shown there, for he leaned forward swiftly and took my hand. "Oh, my dear, you will not *wear* chains, of course! There will be the highest officers of Rome to carry them for you. You will ride in a flowery chariot on a throne—the throne, too, bound in chains. Symbolic, you might say . . . ah, yes—that's it! You must wear them all—all the royal jewels. I will give them into your keeping—we will fetch them straightaway—where are they?"

"They are in a chest in my chambers. My waiting women have the charge of them . . ."

"They shall fetch them. And they shall stay with you . . . and attend you in the Triumph as well."

"I should not like to be their death," I said, sadly, but with honey upon my lips.

"My dear," he said, waving his hand royally, "they shall not die—no more than you! There are plenty of stout Roman nobles who will give chamber room to such foreign beauties. And Caesar, of course"—and here he actually smirked—"Caesar will have his own . . . like his uncle before him."

I was learning deceit now. I cast down my eyes again, and said, softly, "You do me too much honor, oh, August One . . . I am old . . ."

"You will do," he said, "when we have put a little meat back on you. I have always—I don't mind telling you—always I have had my eye on you. I have never had a royal concubine . . ."

I swallowed my distaste and murmured, "I fear I shall disappoint you, Octavian."

"My dear," he said slyly, wetting his lips, "how can that be? You—the greatest courtesan of the world!"

I stared at him; he believed his own lies!

"I will try, then," I said, all humility. "And I may have my women—truly? For I have need of much care . . . I would be beautiful—for the Triumph . . ."

"You shall have them," he said. "What else do you desire? Just ask . . . Caesar is in a giving mood." And he smiled and reached out, grasping my leg above the knee.

"A little freedom only . . . here all is barred."

"Well, I cannot unbar the doors . . . it would not look

well. I have my Roman peers to think of—my allies. You have been very naughty, you know! Well . . . you may have the run of this building—upstairs and down. And slaves for your service . . ."

"Clothes?" I asked. "I am barely covered . . ."

He smiled again, looking to where my breasts showed through the thin stuff of my shift. "It becomes you. But no matter—you shall have what clothes you like . . . I trust your taste . . . as Caesar did before me."

"Thank you. I shall consult my women . . . when they have come to me."

I grew very tired then, from dissembling, and from relief that I had got through it; I begged leave to rest.

"Yes, we must give you an opportunity to mend," he said; it was his country manners coming out; I saw again the shy awkward boy with a blotched face, Caesar's nephew.

"I will send you all that you asked. You have a day and a night. We sail for Rome day after tomorrow." He bent and kissed me again, squeezing a breast so that I nearly cried out. But I smiled and said, "Until the Triumph, then."

The day passed, and the night as well; my last day has come.

This morning I went again to the tomb of Alexander, belowstairs. Though this time it is not my birthday. Or perhaps it is; the old folk of Egypt thought so; I am following their example. I shall go forth royally, to meet . . . what do we meet? Whom?

I am not afraid. Iras and Charmion, my royal sisters, my dear friends, are going with me; I shall not be alone.

It is my Triumph.

Author's Note

CLEOPATRA DIED IN 30 B.C. Her body was discovered, along with those of her waiting women, in the mausoleum wing of the great palace. She was dressed in her royal Greek robes and the serpent crown of Egypt. The means of her death remain a mystery, though the Romans seem to have accepted her physician's, Olympos', diagnosis of snake venom. This explanation seems unlikely, as no snake was found, though two faint marks under her heavy arm ring were cited as evidence of its fangs. It seems more plausible that all three women died of the same poison, somehow smuggled in past the guards. The physician's story may have been an invention to divert suspicion from himself.

Octavian's Triumph was celebrated in Rome in 29 B.C. All the wealth of Egypt was displayed, and a life-size statue of Cleopatra, dressed as she appeared at her death, was borne through the streets. Her three children by Antony, too young to walk in chains, were carried in golden cages.

The following year Octavian became the first Roman emperor, under the title of Augustus Caesar. He was also named heir to all the Roman possessions, including the latest and richest, Egypt. He died in A.D. 14, and was succeeded by his stepson Tiberius.

We do not know what happened to Cleopatra's sons, Alexander Helios and Ptolemy Philadelphus; after childhood they are unmentioned in history. Her daughter, Cleopatra Selene, was married to Juba, king of Numidia, and later of Mauretania. Their son, another Ptolemy, was murdered by the emperor Caligula. He was the last Ptolemy to bear the name.

Of the many portraits and statues of Cleopatra, none survives today. It is supposed that they were destroyed early in Octavian's reign, for political purposes. Writers of antiquity describe her much as I have, a fair Macedonian Greek.

As the enemy of Rome, slander and calumny were heaped upon her, in her lifetime and after. In the cold light of history, none of it has stuck. The only crime that can be proved against her is ambition.

Selected List of Source Material

Ancient Literature

Julius Caesar, Cicero, Dio Cassius, Lucan, Strabo, Suetonius, and, most importantly, Plutarch.

Modern Literature

Bradford, Ernle. *Cleopatra* (New York: Harcourt Brace Jovanovich, 1971).
Duggan, Alfred. *Julius Caesar* (New York: Alfred A. Knopf, 1955).
Forster, E. M. *Alexandria* (New York: Peter Smith, 1951).
Hadas, Moses. *A History of Rome* (New York: Doubleday/Anchor, 1956).
Hadas, Moses. *Imperial Rome* (New York: Time-Life, 1965).
Kinross, Lord. *Portrait of Egypt* (New York: William Morrow Co., Inc., 1966).
Komroff, Manuel. *Julius Caesar* (New York: Julian Messner, Inc., 1955).
Lindsay, Jack. *Men and Gods on the Roman Nile* (New York: G. P. Putnam's Sons, 1966).
Toynbee, Arnold J. *Hellenism* (London: Oxford University Press, 1959).
Volkmann, Hans. *Cleopatra, a Study in Politics and Propaganda* (London: Elek Books Ltd., 1958).
Weigall, Arthur. *The Life and Times of Cleopatra* (London: G. P. Putnam's Sons, 1936).
Wertheimer, Oskar von. *Cleopatra* (London, 1931).